His face hovered mere inches from hers. Her heart thumped and heat built in the pit of her stomach. Did he mean to kiss her?

For the first time in her life she wanted to yield, to know what a man's lips on hers felt like. A muscle above his jaw ticked and drew her gaze to the scars.

He may have murdered his wife.

She inhaled deeply.

She had to resist. She had not spent the last few months starving and cold, borrowing and begging, searching for respectable employment, only to now become the fallen woman they said she was.

Pungent silence hung in the air. Pendar stared at Velvet, his eyes sharp as daggers. She stared back, refusing to cower, refusing to let him think her submissive and wanting . . . wanting him to take the choice from her, yet terrified he would.

Romances by Katy Madison

TAINTED BY TEMPTATION

Tainted
by
Temptation

KATY MADISON

AVON

An Imprint of HarperCollinsPublishers

This is a work of fiction. Names, characters, places, and incidents are products of the author's imagination or are used fictitiously and are not to be construed as real. Any resemblance to actual events, locales, organizations, or persons, living or dead, is entirely coincidental.

AVON BOOKS
An Imprint of HarperCollins*Publishers*
10 East 53rd Street
New York, New York 10022-5299

First Avon Books paperback printing: February 2011

Avon Trademark Reg. U.S. Pat. Off. and in Other Countries, Marca Registrada, Hecho en U.S.A.
HarperCollins® is a registered trademark of HarperCollins Publishers.

Printed in the U.S.A.

10 9 8 7 6 5 4 3 2 1

Acknowledgments

I want to acknowledge the people who were vital to me in getting this book written: Keri Smith, Heather Snow, and Elisabeth Burke, my wonderful critique partners. Esi Sogah, my fantastic editor, who was able to see what I was trying to do and helped me make it better. Maureen Walters, my agent, who deserves a medal for hanging in there with me. And last but not least, the amazing Carla Cassidy, who gets me and likes me anyway. I don't know what I would do without her.

Tainted
by
Temptation

Chapter 1

"That's where Mr. Pendar threw his wife off the cliff," the housemaid pointed out to her traveling companion in the mail coach. "See, there's his house."

Threw his wife off a cliff? Shock jolted through Velvet Campbell.

Her fellow occupants crowded against Velvet to see the jutting spike of land. An imposing square-built hall of dark gray stone perched on the outcropping like a demonic gryphon. Below the sinister house, a rocky cliff dropped down and down to jagged teethlike boulders. Waves gnawed hungrily against the rocks waiting for any scraps the gryphon might drop—or to devour the beast itself, should he fall.

That house contained her new living quarters. Mr. Pendar had employed her. What kind of man threw his wife over a cliff? A wave of dizziness assaulted Velvet.

"They found her broken, bloody body on those rocks," added the maid. "Not three years gone."

Velvet's stomach roiled. She wished she could plug her ears or cover the mouth of the young woman spewing the local lore. He'd written that his wife had passed, but hadn't spoken of the violence of her death.

Velvet shook her head. Gossip was often exaggerated, or just plain wrong, but a shiver slithered down her spine and moisture beaded her upper lip.

"That must be a hundred-foot drop," murmured a rotund cleric. "May God have mercy."

The idea of falling so revolted her, she retched. She swallowed repeatedly, fighting against the bile rising in her throat. She fumbled in her reticule for her handkerchief. Her fingers brushed the letter from her employer, and her heart thumped erratically. With the limp lawn, she dabbed at the perspiration and wished for an end to this journey.

Velvet wanted to look away, but the sight of her future home mesmerized her, though the darkness of it repelled her. It was as if the house had been built to defy God and nature.

The thin young man who had tried for the last twenty miles to engage Velvet in conversation pressed closer. "Beautiful view, is it not?"

Beautiful was not the word she would have chosen. Daunting. Menacing. Those were the words that jumped to mind. "Quite," she answered dryly.

"Can't say I like that house there disrupting the vista." He pushed his thigh against hers. She turned away, lest her refusal to look out the window give him encouragement.

Velvet forced her gaze beyond the crashing waves pummeling the jagged rocks. Under the threatening skies, the ocean eased into whitecapped swells that did not look as hungry, but dark and murky and every bit as dangerous. But if she had her druthers, death by drowning was a thousand times more preferable than death by falling.

She leaned back in her seat wishing she could think of anything other than the plummet and Mrs. Pendar's violent death. She closed her eyes reminiscing about the easy green roll of the hills and dales of Dorset where she'd grown up. But instead her mind's eye recalled the last sight she'd had of her brother: his face twisted in terror. Her eyes jerked open.

"'Tis said her ghost wanders the cliffs at night," whispered the girl. Not that a whisper was effective in the cramped coach.

"What happened to *him?*" asked the friend.

"Nothing."

"Nothing?" repeated the girl with the appropriate amount of horror and fascination.

The girls' conversation interested Velvet more than she wanted to let on. He wasn't in prison. Surely that meant he hadn't murdered his wife.

"He had scratches on his face, but *he* said she fell."

"And they believed him?"

"No one saw him do it." The storyteller shrugged, her expression smug. "At the inquest his servants gave testimony that he hadn't left the house."

"Then he couldn't have done it."

The former housemaid gave her companion a look that suggested the girl was far too naive. "A lot of them heard her screaming at him. I was to start work there a fortnight later, but no decent woman will work for him now."

"Oh my," said the country girl.

Velvet pressed her lips together. She had been called much worse than "less than decent."

"Fitting house for Lucifer."

The name Lucian formed on Velvet's lips. His name was *Lucian* Pendar, not Lucifer, but she resisted the urge to blurt it out. The young man pressed his leg harder against hers.

She rearranged her skirts, piling as much of the excess material between the encroaching young man and her limbs as she could.

The road finally began to curl away from the cliffs, moving farther inland. Velvet unclenched her fist.

"His fortune comes from smuggling, you know," said the informed maid. "My grandda told me the Pendars smuggled French brandy when good Englishmen were dying fighting the French."

Another quarter hour of swaying and mumbled conversation about brutal deaths and how there were those who misused their authority dragged by. Velvet resisted the urge to voice her opinion. In her experience, men in power could get away with anything—or at least they believed they could. But as her father had always said, God would be the final judge.

The coach drew to a halt. Velvet clutched her reticule to her bosom and made her way to the door.

The storyteller stared. Her smugness was gone. "You aren't getting out here."

"Yes, I believe this is my stop." Velvet lifted her chin.

An hour away from the inn where they stopped for lunch, the coachman had said. She no longer had her father's watch to check the time, but it felt like a year since she'd paced the yard while the others ate.

You'll see the house afore we reach it, the coachman had told her. Then he'd given her a look. *Iffen you'd don't want let out there, it'll be the inn at Lands End.*

Of course, I shall get out there, she'd answered. She had no choice. She was expected, and her new employer had paid her fare. If she didn't arrive, she could add theft to the accusations leveled against her.

The coachman opened the door. "Here you go, miss."

Relieved to be free of the close confines and the five

other passengers, Velvet descended the stairs. "It was good to meet you," she said generally. Even better to take her leave of them and the gossip making her dread her new position.

The young housemaid paled. She reached her hand out as if to call Velvet back. The coachman shut the door. Velvet turned toward the house.

Two wheel tracks broke the thin and scrubby grass, but no transportation met her. The glowering house waited at the top of the headland.

The coachman folded up the step. "Just a few minutes walk up the lane, miss."

"Thank you," Velvet answered.

The coachman climbed back on his box and stared straight ahead. "The mail runs every Tuesday. Shilling sixpence will get you to Plymouth."

The wind whipped up from the shoreline and threatened to shred the remaining tatters of the ribbons holding her hat. Her thin relief at being out of the coach blew away. Velvet clamped a hand down on her head as she stared up at the man. Did he expect her to stay to be so short? She wouldn't be leaving anytime soon—she couldn't. Without two pennies to rub together let alone shilling sixpence, her destiny lay here.

Her legs shook, and she told herself firmly it was the lack of food, the hours of motion in the cramped coach, the layers of clothing she wore, not the proximity to a hundred-foot plunge to the sea. It wasn't as if the ocean would reach up and snatch her down into the murky waters. Nor would she be frolicking on the edge of the cliff anytime soon.

There was no need to be frightened of the whims of nature when there were humans about.

Her portmanteau thudded on the ground and the

coach rumbled off. Apparently a governess did not rate a ride up the lengthy drive. It was good to know one's place, and it always went better for her when she wasn't given much thought. With any luck, she might not see her employer for weeks on end.

She picked up her portmanteau, filled with the last of her father's books wrapped in petticoats and a spare dress. The two-stone weight of the bag, the maximum allowed for an inside passenger, tore at her shoulder. The extra clothing she wore tangled around her legs as she stumbled in the rut that with its twin marked the way. She felt as if she was traveling to the end of the earth. No, just the end of England. They'd warned her Cornwall was different.

She promised herself ten steps and she could rest. Of course, she didn't rest. The steel skies and the ripping wind threatened rain. The dark house in the distance might look forbidding, but inside was shelter and food. Perhaps the maddening tilt of the world would right itself if she ate.

She struggled up the long track, the wind thrusting her skirts between her legs and clawing through the layers of clothing. She walked for what seemed like forever. Her heart thumped erratically and sweat built beneath her arms, yet she shivered. She hoped she would not soak through the three layers of shifts, two dresses, and extra petticoats she wore.

The skies broke and icy rain poured down on Velvet. She squelched toward the distant house. The more she walked, the farther away it seemed. What she thought was a short squat house loomed large, with four stories and pointed arched windows with obsidian panes. In spite of the wide stone staircase, the house was the most unwelcoming she'd ever seen.

Water seeped through the cracks in her half boots, while her fingers and toes ached with cold.

She slid and dropped to a knee. Struggling to her feet, she attempted to brush the mud from her dark skirt, but only succeeded in muddying her glove. Water dripped from the straw brim of her hat. She trudged on, determined to conquer this last leg of her journey. There was nowhere to go but forward. Her life in London had degraded to the place where she'd nearly become what they said she was. And then she finally had been offered this position.

She'd always understood she deserved punishment, but did God intend to strand her in this wild place so far from any home she'd ever known?

Finally she reached the massive house and the wide stone staircase leading up to the first floor. The steps rose above her like an Egyptian pyramid she needed to scale. Her legs felt like wooden stumps and her fingers refused to curl around the balustrade. Above her, water spouted out of gargoyles' mouths. One broken creature missing half his face allowed a stream of water to spill over the stairs. The water cascaded over her toes as she tried to gather the strength to climb. She lifted a foot to the first stair.

Velvet's legs shook and she couldn't even say if it was the cold, fear, or that she hadn't had a decent meal in months. Black dots danced in front of her eyes. She had to pause and heave in deep breaths, although they didn't clear the blackness closing in from the sides. She was so close, yet the massive doors seemed so far away. Her bag thudded down and she didn't remember releasing it. Then there was nothing.

She'd died, she was sure of it. Velvet rested on a cloud. The weight of a dry coverlet kept her from float-

ing away. A nearby fire snapped and crackled with
newly added firewood, warming her face. An angel
leaned over her. A very male angel with a strong jaw
and deep-set black eyes evenly spaced on either side
of a classical nose. A dark lock slipped over his forehead. Thickly lashed eyes searched her face. Only an
angel could have such beautiful lashes softening the
masculine angles of his face.

"Have Mrs. Bigsby bring tea." He rubbed Velvet's
bare hand between his.

Heaven. Hot tea would be heaven. She hadn't been
sure she would rate entrance through the pearly gates.
But the cups of hot water she'd drunk in the last few
months were nothing compared to a real cup of tea.

The angel turned to look over his shoulder to the
man he'd addressed, and revealed three shiny pink
scars trailing down his left cheek. Velvet reached out
and touched the defects in this perfect creature's face.

He jerked back, his chin rising high enough that she
could see a tiny slice of whiskers missed by a razor's
blade under his chin. He dropped her hand and stood.
"Miss Campbell, I presume."

The edge to his voice jarred her. This wasn't heaven
at all. "I'm sorry," she whispered.

Her hands began to sting and she realized she was
reclining on a red and gold chaise longue shoved near a
massive fireplace in a formal drawing room. Her cloak
lay heaped in a pile on the floor, but her muddy boots
encasing her wooden toes must be making horrid stains.
She struggled to sit and realized her dresses had been
unfastened and her stays loosened.

After dropping a load of firewood by the fire, an older
man brushed off his gnarled hands and cast her a dis-
paraging look.

The dark-eyed man pushed her shoulders back and held her pinned. "Be still. You fainted."

His words didn't reassure her. Panic clawed at her throat, as she didn't see a female present. Only this man who had the face of a fallen angel and hands that had turned brutal as he pressed her back into the plush upholstery.

Who had unfastened her dress and loosened her corset? Had he? A flush rolled through her.

"My stays weren't too tight," she said.

She had no need to lace her corset tight. Actually, she'd lost so much weight she might need to have it refitted. But her protest was too late and only served to call attention to her loosened garments.

"Then you are ill, Miss Campbell," said the man who must be her employer.

"I'm not ill," she protested. She'd just been too long without eating. She'd been light-headed and weak from the days of travel and lack of nourishment.

"Don't need no illness in the house," said the servant shuffling toward the door.

"That's enough, Bigsby." Mr. Pendar straightened and turned so he was once again in profile, the firelight illuminating the unmarred side of his face.

Velvet felt powerless lying on the chaise, her dress unfastened. She drew the coverlet up around her shoulders. But she just couldn't feel comfortable reclining in this man's presence. He was just too male and her reputation too tattered.

A steady drip echoed in the room, while outside the pounding of a torrential downpour added its steady drone to the hiss and crackle of the fire. At least he had removed his hands and she could breathe, albeit in pants that did not seem to fill her lungs with enough air.

The silence stretched out, until she poked at it, "Are you Mr. Pendar, then?"

He gave a curt nod. "Bigsby was to meet you at the road, but he mistook the day," Mr. Pendar said brusquely.

If he meant it by way of apology, he did not sound at all contrite. He sounded angry. Perhaps he was disappointed that such a miserable excuse for a governess showed up on his doorstep.

He paced away from her with a caged energy in his steps. He'd gone from angel to demon in the space of seconds. She wanted to escape, yet she couldn't tear her eyes away from him.

He circled around to the fire and leaned down to light a spill. He carried it to a lamp, removed the chimney and lit the wick.

Velvet pushed up to a half-reclined position on the fainting couch. The exertion tired her when it shouldn't have. She hoped she wasn't sick. She wasn't feverish, just weak. "It was not a great distance. I fear I am not a good traveler. If I might be shown to my room to wash up, I'll be right in a trice."

"You should take a few days to get well."

Under no circumstances would she give him the ammunition to dismiss her for dereliction of duty. "I'm anxious to meet my charge and begin our lessons."

He snorted.

She jerked back. His derision was the last response she expected. Surely he wanted his daughter to begin lessons soon. According to his letter she had been without supervision for months.

Velvet swung her feet to the floor. The room tilted and she leaned forward. Her dress slipped from her shoulder and she grabbed at it. Her chest heaved as she tried to fill her lungs.

"Miss Campbell, lie down."

"I'm fine." She hoped she sounded more determined than she felt.

Reaching for the crumpled wet heap of her cloak, she realized the outer of her two dresses was part of the pile. He pushed her back against the curved rest. Her heart jumped into her throat.

"Lie back. That's an order, Miss Campbell," he said on a low note. "I have no idea how long you were lying outside in the rain." He caught her legs at the knee and forced them back on the chaise longue.

Startled by the physicality of his move, she offered no resistance.

He lowered her legs gently and shifted his hands back to her shoulders. Her heart thumped erratically and she stared up at him. His eyes narrowed while his fingers closed around the curve of her upper arms. His thumbs moved in the indentation between her collarbone and neck. Her breath stole out of her.

His face hovered mere inches from hers. Her heart thumped and heat built in the pit of her stomach. Did he mean to kiss her?

For the first time in her life she wanted to yield, to know what a man's lips on hers felt like. A muscle above his jaw ticked and drew her gaze to the scars.

He may have murdered his wife.

She inhaled deeply.

She had to resist. She had not spent the last few months starving and cold, borrowing and begging, searching for respectable employment, only to now become the fallen woman they said she was.

Pungent silence hung in the air. Pendar stared at Velvet, his dark eyes sharp as daggers. She stared back, refusing to cower, refusing to let him think her submissive and wanting . . . wanting him to take the choice from her, yet terrified he would.

Her gaze lowered to his mouth and her dry lips parted, while she waited for the kisses to be pressed against her cheek when she turned her head. And waited for the groping hands, the assault she would fight. Only she wasn't sure she would turn away. Her breath quickened. Her body felt loose, no longer in her control.

His upper lip lifted in a sneer and suddenly his mouth seemed cruel.

Her heart pounded and her mouth felt dry. Had he seen her struggle with temptation? She was so tired of resisting, only to have her situation turn worse. She was so tired of being cold and hungry. Would it be so horrible to submit to this man with the face of an angel?

The air sizzled with energy.

The door opened and Mr. Pendar jerked away from her.

The breath she'd been holding blew past her lips. Like a spell had been snapped, shame flooded through her. Oh God, she *was* ill, if she even considered—

"Set the cart by the fire, Mrs. Bigsby," he said in a rough voice as he walked to the window, then yanked the drapes closed against the premature gloom. "Assist Miss Campbell with the tea and inform her of the household hours."

He strode across the room and opened the door. "I will see you at dinner, Miss Campbell."

With that he was gone. Velvet wasn't at all sure what had happened, but in that moment before Mrs. Bigsby arrived with the tea tray, something had happened. A flash of energy traveled between them and put the heat of the fire to shame. And she didn't know if she feared him or the turn her life was about to take.

Chapter 2

Mrs. Bigsby lumbered across the room, her footfalls heavy against the floor. Her gray hair was scraped back into a wiry knot at the nape of her neck and her homespun apron was not the bright white starched affair that Velvet was used to seeing on domestic help. She looked more like an aging barmaid in a slovenly tavern than an upper servant.

Velvet pushed herself to a sitting position and reached around her neck to fasten the top button of her gown. At least that way it would not fall off. She arranged the coverlet as a shawl, as much to cover the disarray of her dress and corset as anything.

Mrs. Bigsby took it all in, and Velvet knew that things didn't look good. She hadn't been in the house more than a few minutes and already she'd been caught in compromising circumstances.

Fighting the dizziness that kept assailing her, she swung her feet to the floor again. As she feared, her half boots left a swipe of brown on the upholstery. Mrs. Bigsby's lips flattened as she pushed the cart into place.

"How do you take it?" The woman's voice contained an accusation.

Velvet straightened her spine and assessed the contents of the trolley. "A spot of cream would be heavenly, although I am accustomed to drinking tea without such indulgences. Won't you join . . . me . . . ?"

Only one cup and saucer were on the tray. A single scone set on a plate. Apparently a governess in this household could be served tea in the drawing room, but other servants were not allowed. Or perhaps it was only a concession for an ill governess.

The cup once filled was shoved in her direction, and a bit slopped into the saucer. Velvet took it with a murmured thanks. "Are you the housekeeper, Mrs. Bigsby?"

The woman gave one short nod.

"I must apologize for the mark on the couch. I would not have put my dirty boots upon it."

Mrs. Bigsby gave a sniff as she wiped her hands in her apron as if they had become soiled serving tea. "No matter. I'm sure Mr. Pendar would prefer to be rid of it."

The red tapestry fainting couch was the only stylish piece in a room full of blocky functional sofas and chairs. The navy and green upholstery on the other furniture was faded with bits of stuffing showing through on the corners. Why would he want to be rid of the most modern piece?

Velvet lowered her eyes to the muddy swirl of her tea. She hadn't been handed a spoon and she didn't see one on the trolley. She took a sip, wanting to be done. The scalding liquid stopped her from drinking quickly as Mrs. Bigsby stood by, her hands folded under her apron bib.

"We keep country hours, miss. The master dines at five." Mrs. Bigsby shifted impatiently.

"And does Miss Pendar dine with her father?"

"No. She has her supper in the nursery and then is required to come down to the drawing room from six to seven. Then you will need to put her to bed."

"She does not have a nursemaid?"

"My daughter, Nellie, but she has other duties in the evenings." Mrs. Bigby sniffed. "If you need anything after five, you'll need to fetch it yourself. Most of the staff leaves then."

"Are there any other members of the household?"

Mrs. Bigsby shook her head.

So she would be dining alone with Mr. Pendar. A shiver coursed down her entire body.

Velvet reached for the scone, but Mrs. Bigsby's sharp gaze on her made the pastry turn to grit in her mouth. Her stomach protested and she swallowed more tea to force the bite down. She needed to eat in order to regain her strength, but she didn't feel hungry. She'd stopped feeling hungry a long time ago.

Finishing the tea as quickly as she could, she left the remainder of the scone on the plate. "If you would show me to my room, Mrs. Bigsby, I'd like to get settled."

"To be sure. This way, Miss Campbell." Mrs. Bigsby crossed the room, her hands firmly planted under her apron's bib. She walked past the heap of soggy material on the floor.

Velvet scooped up her soaking cloak and her muddy dress. Her portmanteau was by the door. Closing her eyes, she picked up her bag too. Grateful Mrs. Bigsby was at least holding the door, Velvet breathed in deeply. She still felt shaky and weak, but the tea warmed her belly as she entered the dark passageway.

She couldn't keep up with Mrs. Bigsby's march up the staircase. The housekeeper scarcely seemed to notice as she rattled off the members of the staff and the hours of service.

Velvet's legs quivered in protest as she took each step. Her cloak dragged behind, and she feared that, like a slimy sea creature, she left a damp trail in her wake.

The housekeeper huffed out an impatient breath as Velvet paused at the landing. "It is another flight."

Velvet didn't bother answering. She was breathing too hard to form the words. Only the fear that someone would come upon them while the back of her dress was open kept her moving.

Spots danced in front of her eyes as she entered the barren room assigned to every governess. Bare wood floors stretched out before her to a wrought-iron bed positioned near a window overlooking the ocean.

"Got a nice view," Mrs. Bigsby said. "When the weather is better, you can see all the way down to where the surf breaks on the shore."

Velvet couldn't think of anything she wanted to see less. Her chest and lungs spasmed from restrained coughs.

"The schoolroom is through that door, and on the other side is Miss Iris's room."

"Where is Miss Iris?" When would she meet her charge?

Mrs. Bigsby shrugged. "She's about here somewheres."

Now that Velvet had finally made it to the relative sanctuary of her bedroom, she stepped to the side of the doorway and said, "Thank you, Mrs. Bigsby."

The housekeeper turned and glared as if she did not relish the idea of being dismissed by a mere governess.

Velvet just wanted to collapse and regroup, but she stood with her back to the wall, holding her cloak, dress, and valise.

"This is a godly household, Miss Campbell," said the housekeeper.

Her hackles rising, Velvet looked directly at the older woman. "Then I shall feel quite at home here, won't I? My father was a reverend."

Had her reputation preceded her? Or was the older woman assuming too much because she found the new governess with her dress unfastened alone with the master within minutes of reaching the house? With Mr. Pendar leaning over her as she reclined on a decadently soft chaise longue, it had to have looked bad.

Mrs. Bigsby brushed past her with a sniff. The door clicked behind her with a distinctive air of disapproval.

Velvet let her portmanteau fall to the floor. Her arm suddenly felt light enough to float.

She sighed. The room had a moldy unused smell to it, but it was nearly thrice the size of the room she had rented in a squalid London neighborhood. She shivered as she crossed the floor to drape her wet cloak and dress over the solitary hard chair.

Averting her eyes from the view, she crossed to the washstand with its pitcher and bowl. Her reflection in the cloudy mirror made her start. She looked like a wild creature, her hair half pinned, half hanging down. Her eyes appeared huge in her ghostly white face.

She needed to put herself to rights before supper. She removed her remaining dress. The loosened corset fell to the floor and she stepped out of it, while removing the extra shifts and petticoats she wore. Stripped to her drawers and chemise, she shivered in the chilly room.

The door banged open and Velvet whirled around, grabbing her discarded shift to her chest. Her gaze caught the chair across the room where her dress and cloak were draped. She should have shoved the chair under the door handle.

Iris Pendar lifted the cloth covering a ball of dough on the wooden kitchen table.

"You leave that alone, miss. It needs to rest now."

Cook stirred a pot of fish soup on the stove.

Iris plunked down on a stool. Sometimes Cook let her kneed the dough or would give her beans to snap, but it was too close to dinnertime for Cook to welcome her in the kitchen. But Iris had seen her new governess weaving up the lane, and if she didn't share the information, she might explode. "My governess arrived."

"Yes she did," Cook said, taking away Iris's joy at breaking the news. "You should run along now and wash up. I'll be sending your supper tray up soon."

"I'm to eat here in the kitchen."

Cook swiped at her sweating brow with the corner of her apron. "Where's Nellie?"

"She had to fetch coal because Meg left early. Meg said she didn't *relish* the idea of walking home in the rain." Iris stressed the unfamiliar word. "What does relish mean?"

"I reckon you can ask your new governess that," Cook muttered as she slapped a fish on a cutting board, then sliced a knife down the belly.

"I don't know. She might be as bad as Miss Grimes."

Cook paused with her fingers full of bloody fish guts and looked across the wooden table. When she smiled, her eyes would practically disappear behind the fleshy mounds of her cheeks, like raisins in a hot cross bun, but she wasn't smiling now.

Iris rushed to fill the void. She dreaded lessons with the new governess, but if she was like Miss Grimes and slept through the hours in the schoolroom, she might be better than the next woman her father managed to hire. Or he might carry through on his threat to send her off to school. "She's very pretty, though. She has hair the color of that pot." Iris pointed to a shiny copper kettle hanging on the rack.

"How very fanciful you are, Miss Iris." Cook resumed gutting and deboning the fish.

Feeling disloyal, Iris added, "She's not as pretty as Mama was, though."

"Mmm," answered Cook.

Her mama had been a true beauty. Everyone said so. Miss Grimes hadn't been pretty at all. Three teeth on the one side of her mouth were missing, and all her front teeth had shifted over so her mouth looked crooked. Even so, she still had a hard time closing her lips. Her mousy hair had always been slipping down in lank strands.

Miss Campbell's hair had been falling down but was as shiny and sparkly as if fire fairies liked to play in it.

Iris reached under the cloth, pinched off a bit of the dough and slipped it in her mouth while Cook tossed the fish guts and bones in a slop pail.

As Iris let the yeasty dough melt in her mouth, she looked around at the extra serving dishes lined up on the table. Cook was preparing a company dinner.

"Meg shouldn't have left early on a day when new help arrives," muttered the cook.

Iris had told Meg the storm clouds gathering on the horizon looked bad. She'd only had to shake her head and add that the governess's room hadn't been thoroughly cleaned in a long time before Meg started fretting about walking home in the rain.

Iris had asked Nellie every day if it was the day her new governess was to arrive, so they'd both known the day, even if it seemed no one else paid it any mind. She had spent the morning watching the road for the mail coach. When it finally rounded the bend near the cliffs, she had run to the entry hall where she could look out on the drive.

She'd seen the new governess stumbling, in much the same way as Miss Grimes would stumble after she finished the bottles she walked to town to buy. Then Miss Grimes hadn't had enough money and started pinching this and that to pay for her bottles.

After the new governess drew close, Iris had waited and waited on the stairs, staring at the front door. Finally, she peeked outside to see Miss Campbell lying at the foot of the stairs. Miss Grimes had fallen asleep in strange places, but never in the pouring rain.

Iris had dared to run to her father's office to tell him. For once he hadn't given her that look that said she shouldn't have interrupted him. But then he hadn't looked at her long at all before he ran to the front door.

Pinching off another piece of dough, Iris speculated, "Maybe she'll teach me to play the harp like Mama did."

"I think your papa would prefer you learn your schoolwork," said Cook.

Iris curled her nose. Mama had told her she only needed to learn to sew and play the pianoforte and know how to make a comfortable home for a future husband. Being pretty would be enough to attract suitors. "She might not last anyway. She might be sick. Papa had to carry her inside. He carried her all the way up the stairs to the drawing room."

"So I heard," said Cook.

"He had me help unfasten her dress."

Cook gave her a sharp look.

Not quite understanding why, she added, "He said her corset was too tight. 'That makes foolish vain women faint.'" He'd also said he didn't need another woman dying on him.

Iris had been thrilled to be asked to help her father,

but she'd quickly been sent to fetch Mrs. Bigsby. She found Mr. Bigsby first and sent him.

"I don't think she'll stay long. She's too pretty," said Iris. The governess before Miss Grimes had only stayed two weeks, and the one before that only a few months. Miss Grimes had made it near a year. Miss Grimes would rap her on the knuckles with a stick every now and then upon discovering mistakes or missing assignments. But though Grimes was harsh at times, the torture of the schoolroom had been sparse. Perhaps Iris could persuade her new governess to avoid lessons. If she set her mind to it, she could avoid lots of things.

A woman lugging a coal pail entered the room. Velvet put her hand over her fluttering heart. She had half expected to find Mr. Pendar at the door.

Instead the woman was a more angular, younger version of Mrs. Bigsby. Without saying a word, she lugged the coal to the fireplace.

"You must be Nellie," said Velvet. Was she to be ostracized before the staff even got to know her?

The woman grunted. Velvet turned to pour water from the pitcher into the bowl but found a layer of dust on both of them. "May I have some water?"

The woman turned and stared through her with vacant eyes. "There is a water closet on the floor below."

So there was running water in the house. Velvet hadn't been sure there would be, as the house was so far removed from any city. She lifted the thick pitcher from the bowl and carried it across the floor to where the maid knelt in front of the fireplace. "Would you be so kind as to fill this for me?"

"I'm lighting the fire."

Velvet paused, uncertain. Holding the pitcher out

made her arm shake. She lowered it. In her present state, could she carry a full pitcher up a flight of stairs? She would have to dress first and then undress again to wash.

She set the pitcher on the floor and sank down on top of her wet clothing on the chair. The room was cold and she wanted a fire. She laid her head on her arm, trying to breathe deeply enough to chase the dancing spots from her eyes.

She just had to get through this evening, and surely the meal would help restore her strength, but the thought of food left her nauseous. Somehow she managed to stand and retrieve her clean gray dress and shift from her portmanteau.

While Nellie worked at starting the fire, Velvet shimmied into the clean shift.

"You ain't nothing but skin and bones," said Nellie.

Velvet found the comment offensive, but she wasn't about to bypass an opening to be chatty. A governess's lot, caught between the upstairs and downstairs, could be miserable enough without cordial relationships with the staff. "Yes, well I haven't been eating too well lately."

"Why's that?" asked Nellie.

Velvet hadn't wanted to be that friendly. "Living in London can be expensive, and I went a few months between positions."

She'd been dismissed from her last position without her pay. She was tossed out in the street in her bare feet and torn nightgown. Her bags were packed and tossed out to her, but her savings had not been included. One of the servants might have taken her money, or a member of the family had. The pittance she received for selling her father's watch had been gone before a month was out.

"That explains it," said Nellie cryptically.

Velvet picked up her corset to put it back on and realized the strings hadn't just been loosened. They'd been cut. She couldn't dress without it, or she'd look like the floozy she was reported to be. "Explains what?"

Nellie brushed off her hands and moved to the door, leaving the coal bucket and the water pitcher on the floor. "No one who has a choice comes to work here, not since the mistress died anyway."

Velvet closed her eyes.

"Can't keep help. You have to fetch your own coal and water. You're allowed one bucket o'coal a day." Nellie left the room and closed the door.

Velvet was left alone with her destroyed corset strings and the patter of rain on the windows.

Velvet was late for dinner. Using her shoelaces to string her corset had eaten up precious time. She didn't know which room was the dining room. Her heart fluttering, she scurried along the ground floor and peeked behind closed doors. If there were footmen about, they made no move to direct her.

The house was empty and dark. The wind howled, and every now and then a draft scuttled down the corridors. Each unfamiliar creak of the floor made her heart flutter. She wasn't a timid woman, but the house left her feeling small and defenseless.

She opened another door. In the dimness she made out a round table and a large sideboard, but the room was dark. The breakfast room perhaps. She had to be close to the dining room.

The next room had a double door. Velvet rolled her eyes. She knew enough about the layout of country houses that she should have looked for double doors. She paused, trying to collect her emotions and failing.

She hated being late, especially if anyone was waiting on her.

She opened the door and slipped inside. Mr. Pendar stood in front of the fire at the far end, his back to the entrance. She saw only him. He was not burly, by any means, but his sloped shoulders veed down to narrow hips, leaving no doubt about his masculinity. Just his presence filled the elongated room.

His gaze seemed fixed on the flames licking the blackened bricks of the fireplace. She clicked the door shut.

He swiveled, giving the impression of a wild animal startled out of solitary contemplation. Tightly controlled energy radiated from him.

She hesitated. The apology she'd rehearsed in her head evaporated before the words could pass her lips. Why this man turned her into a quivering ninny, she didn't know. She stepped forward, encountering the long expanse of a dining table. Two places were set at the far end, near the fire.

Velvet resisted the urge to back away. Her father's admonition to meet his eyes echoed in her head. Looking down or away was tantamount to admitting guilt, according to him. In fact, she always met a man's gaze squarely, rarely did she feel like turning away. But Mr. Pendar's gaze cut through her as if he could see all the way to her damned-to-hell soul.

He drew out the chair on his right hand side. "Miss Campbell."

His voice vibrated through her. She wanted to turn and leave. She forced her feet forward. Her steps felt wobbly, as her boots were missing laces. She'd done her best to secure them with the remnants of her corset strings.

He watched her as she moved past chair after rosewood chair. The table would easily seat twenty on each side. Her heart pounded and she was breathless by the time she reached the chair he held for her. She lowered herself to sit, all too aware of his proximity, his dark eyes on her, and the very maleness of his essence. He eased her seat in underneath her.

She thanked him and was dismayed to hear her voice all breathy and high. She despised weak females and feared she had become one.

Her employer gave a yank on the bellpull and seated himself at the head of the table. The slashing scar was away from her view.

"I trust you are feeling better," he said.

Velvet paused in the middle of pulling her mended napkin onto her lap. "Yes, thank you." She tried not to breathe too hard, for fear she would snap the worn shoelaces in her corset. Even though it wasn't laced tight, her shoestrings had seen better days.

Mrs. Bigsby entered carrying a large tureen. She clunked it down on the table and ladled soup into their bowls. Her movements were brusque. Soup splashed on the rim of the bowl and onto Velvet's last clean dress. Discreetly dabbing at the spill with her napkin, she waited until her employer picked up his spoon.

Too nervous to risk a silent prayer when he didn't offer one, Velvet mimicked him. The rich chowder settled in her stomach like lead.

"Have you taught a girl before?" asked Mr. Pendar.

Her stomach too unsettled, Velvet put down her spoon. "A long time ago."

He watched her as he continued to raise his soup spoon to his lips. His mouth fascinated her. His lips were angular, not quite thin, but a long way from sensual, poised on the edge of cruel.

She clasped her hands in her lap. "I assisted my father in the parish school. We taught girls as well as boys."

"I am told you can teach Iris to play the pianoforte and feminine skills."

His agent in London had asked her these questions. "I can teach her rudimentary pianoforte, watercolors, and needlework skills. But my true strengths are in the classroom."

He gave a slight snort. "You'll have a hard time getting her in the schoolroom. She's like her mother."

"Her mother didn't value education?" asked Velvet.

His mouth twisted in a slightly cruel way. "Not for women."

All Velvet's positions had been with families with boys. Boys she'd taught Latin and mathematics, readying them for Oxford and Cambridge. "Do you share that view?"

He met her gaze, and a shiver raced down her spine. "Iris should know how to read and write and enough math to manage pin money."

Mrs. Bigsby entered and slapped a platter of fish and potatoes on the table. Velvet jumped. Mr. Bigsby followed with rolls, wine, and a bowl of peas. The housekeeper scowled as she removed Velvet's barely touched bowl of soup.

Mr. Bigsby splashed red wine in her glass.

"Will you be needing anything else?" asked Mrs. Bigsby.

"Thank you, that will be all," said Mr. Pendar. He served himself from the nearest dishes.

The Bigsbys left the room.

"Anything beyond rudimentary skills isn't necessary. If you can get Iris ready for marriage in a half-dozen years, I'll count myself lucky."

Velvet's heart plummeted. Her love of academics would be wasted in this household. But then she was grateful to have a job at all. In six or seven years perhaps her reputation would be forgotten or she would be too old to be considered a threat. She'd have thought most would have considered her well past her prime now.

"I'll do my best," she said, then took a sip of the rich wine.

"Iris will be in your care from nine in the morning until she goes to bed at eight." He placed a portion of the flaky white fish on her plate. "I'll leave it to your discretion whether she takes dinner with us or not. I suppose she is getting too old to exclude."

Velvet breathed a sigh of relief. Surely having her charge dine with them would be better than dining so intimately with her employer. Or perhaps he had insisted they dine together to discuss her duties. "Very well, sir."

"You may have Saturday afternoon and Sunday to yourself."

She nodded. An afternoon and an entire day off was generous.

"As you know, keeping a governess for Iris has been difficult." His eyebrows tightened as he dished peas on his plate and passed them to her. "You will not receive your wages for twelve months."

To be paid twice a year was not unusual, but without access to any of her wages for a year was a long time. She would be virtually trapped here. "What if I need to make some incidental purchases?"

"Give a list to Mrs. Bigsby, and I will review and authorize each purchase on your behalf."

So much for the shilling sixpence she'd need to get to Plymouth. Besides she needed new strings for her corset. Even though he was responsible for cutting the strings, she wasn't sure she wanted him reviewing her need for them.

"I see," she said dryly. She bit back her objections. She couldn't go back to London or she would become the fallen woman they said she was. What was left except trolling the streets, or submitting to an employer's advances?

"If I have to dismiss you for cause in the interim, you will be paid only half wages. Is that clear, Miss Campbell?"

"Clear as a bell," she answered, refusing to be cowed. "I will not give you cause."

He nodded. "Fair enough."

She studied Mr. Pendar's profile. His face was angular, with long flat cheeks, an aristocratic forehead, and a sharp nose perhaps too thin to be classically handsome, but there was something compelling about his looks. As if aware of her scrutiny, he turned his dark eyes in her direction.

Velvet reached for a roll and buttered it with shaking hands. If her father hadn't taken ill, she might have been married a dozen years ago. She had expected, fervently desired, to be a wife and mother by now, but her penance must not be complete. A governess's lot was to be isolated on the nursery floor or occupied with minding her charges the few times she was out of the house in church or family trips. Meeting a suitable man was impossible.

She tried not to think of such things often, but Mr. Pendar was probably only her senior by two or three years. He'd been married and had a nine-year-old child. An unbidden curiosity about what he did to satisfy his manly needs popped into her head.

"Occasionally after Iris is abed, you'll have extra duties." He took a bite of his fish.

As a handsome young widower, he surely didn't need to harass a live-in governess for *those* needs. Her fork clattered to her plate. She waited for the revulsion and outrage. Her stomach fluttered wildly. That he would broach the subject so boldly instead of just cornering her in a corridor or groping her in her room when the household was asleep shocked her.

Her thoughts scrambled through her limited options. Could she find work or would it just be better to stop trying to preserve her virtue?

He was not too old or too young. But the rumors about him . . . the scars on the cheek he kept averted from her could have come from a woman's nails as she tried to keep from being tossed off a cliff.

That thought scared her bad enough that her stomach roiled. She pressed the back of her hand against her lips, hoping she was not about to disgrace herself as beads of moisture appeared on her upper lip. "I'm sorry. Please excuse me."

She pushed her chair back and fled to the door.

Chapter 3

The dark corridor closed in on Velvet. Running from the dinner table was childish. She was ashamed of her actions, ashamed of her thoughts. His broaching the idea of her becoming his mistress at the dinner table was laughable. She had added two and two and come up with fourteen. Usually her math skills were better. Heaving in deep breaths, she leaned against a side table.

Her rebellious stomach settled.

Mr. Pendar gripped her elbow.

She started.

"Miss Campbell, you are still ill."

The sound of rain had covered his silent approach. He slid his arm around her waist and guided her back toward the open doors of the dining room. "Sit down. I will have Mrs. Bigsby or Nellie help you to your room."

She desperately needed to eat, not go to her room without supper. "I'm fine."

"Clearly you are not," said Mr. Pendar. His grip under her elbow was supportive, not suggestive, but his touch burned through her as he guided her back into the dining room.

Perhaps she would be safe if he thought her sick. Perhaps she would be safe if she were locked in her room. Perhaps she would be safe if she didn't want to collapse into his arms.

Oh, God, what was wrong with her?

"Let me ring for Mrs. Bigsby." He pulled out the nearest chair, and she sat.

She grabbed his arm. "Please don't."

He froze.

Her fingers had closed around his brick hard forearm. She snatched her hand back aware that she had overstepped her bounds. Governesses didn't grab the master of the house. She *never* wanted to give the impression that she condoned physical contact. "I'm sorry. Please don't summon the Bigsbys."

"They're just at their supper." He touched his arm where she'd laid her hand. "They are not far."

Velvet searched for an explanation. "No servant likes a governess requiring special treatment. I should hate to get off on the wrong foot with them."

He paced away from her, and she feared he would call for the housekeeper anyway. He pivoted and stalked back. "Miss Campbell, you are ill."

"I'm not. I just need to eat." Fascinated by the caged energy in his smooth stride, Velvet stared too long. She ducked her head, mentally berating herself.

He crouched in front of her and looked at her with a furrowed brow.

"I am keeping you from your dinner," she protested.

His head tilted. "Did the sturgeon put you off? I'm sure Mrs. Bigsby could coddle an egg for you."

"No, the fish is fine." She pushed the chair back and stood. His eyes burned holes in her as she walked the interminable length of the dining room. She slid back into her seat, returned her napkin to her lap and deliberately ate a bite of the cold fish.

The doors clicked shut.

He took his time returning to his chair at the head of the table. His expression was contemplative as his dark eyes raked over her.

Her heart pounded. The fish turned to chalk in her mouth. She swallowed hard.

"You think eating will improve your health?"

"I'm certain of it," she answered.

He folded his arms and leaned back in his chair. Velvet tried to ignore his scrutiny as she cut her fish. Risking only a nibble, she waited for him to resume eating. Her chewing seemed overly loud.

Her heart thumped unsteadily. His study of her made gooseflesh rise on her arms. Trying to sound nonchalant, she asked. "What additional nightly duties would you expect me to perform?"

The question seemed fraught with innuendos, and she hadn't meant it to be. Staring at her plate, she dreaded the answer.

He uncrossed his arms, leaned one elbow on the armrest and planted his opposite hand on the other. His position lessened the distance between them. The air crackled with a charged energy.

Fisting her napkin in her lap, she turned toward him waiting for his answer.

He'd turned toward her, exposing the pink scars. His eyes narrowed slightly, he said, "I need a hostess when I entertain."

Velvet nearly sagged with relief.

"Mostly my guests are business associates. I am expecting to conclude a major deal soon and will have several guests. I'll need you to guide the service." He reached for his wineglass and scowled at the ruby liquid. "Your last position was in the undersecretary of state's household. Surely you could help the staff to serve the correct wine with a meal." He raised his gaze to her face.

Her relief dissolved at the mention of her last situation. "Certainly, I could manage that, but that would usually be the butler's purview, wouldn't it?"

"Bigsby is loyal, but choosing wine is above his calling." He twisted as if uncomfortable. "Good help is hard to get here."

She could easily take his words as an insult. Not that she could afford to be affronted. She needed this job.

"Present company excepted."

He drank his wine and set the empty glass on the table. His eyes never left her face, and she was unable to break away from his scrutiny.

Only she was a governess most people wouldn't touch with a ten-foot pole. Not after the maelstrom of humiliation in which she'd been embroiled. She tensed waiting for his question about why her name had been dragged through the scandal sheets and finally through the mainstream papers. Cartoons depicting her in a diaphanous nightgown beckoning to a line of paunchy MPs and spotty boys sold like meat pies at a fair.

"Do eat, Miss Campbell." He picked up his silverware and cut his fish. "Are you feeling better?"

She nodded. "Most assuredly." It wasn't exactly true, but she suspected with regular meals recovery would only take her a few days. She took a bite of her potatoes. Her stomach rebelled at the cold congealed food, but she forced it down anyway.

They ate in silence for a few minutes. "Do you have anything you'd like to tell me about your . . . condition?"

Trying to read his narrow-eyed expression, she blinked. "N-No."

He wiped his mouth and set his napkin beside his plate with deliberation. "Perhaps I should send for the doctor."

"There's no need." She didn't need a physician to tell her she was malnourished.

He stood and stalked to the sideboard. With his back to her, she heard the clink of glass, then pouring. He turned with a snifter of an amber liquid. He swirled the brandy, releasing the fumes.

"Perhaps an examination would relieve my mind that you are not carrying contagion into my house." Leaning against the sideboard, he took a slow drink. "You have fainted and grown nauseous in the space of a few hours."

She looked down. Must she humiliate herself by exposing how near she was to starvation? "I assure you, what ails me is not infectious."

He leaned forward as if to see into her face. "How do you know you are not contagious, Miss Campbell?"

"I know." She chose to ignore his request for specifics. "It is time for me to fetch Miss Pendar, is it not?"

"She's probably already waiting in the drawing room." He swirled his glass again. "Do finish eating."

Velvet shook her head and pushed back from the table. "I'm anxious to meet my student."

"She's already met you. She helped me remove your wet dress." He swallowed the last of his brandy.

Velvet shuddered with the reminder that he had half undressed her and cut the laces of her corset.

He set the glass down on the table with a discordant clang. The chime reverberated through her like a bell ringing a death knell. The hint of restrained violence alarmed her. Was he irritated with her already?

* * *

Lucian led the new governess to the drawing room. He hoped Iris was on good behavior. Like her mother, she could be charming when she wanted to be, but also like her mother, she could be petulant and sulky. Although his wife had plenty of reasons to be wretched, he made sure Iris didn't.

He opened the door and reached back for Miss Campbell. She skirted his outstretched hand. He hadn't quite puzzled her out. The seductress she was rumored to be wasn't obvious, although she was striking with her copper hair and mossy green eyes rimmed in gold. Past the first blush of youth, her features had matured to a sharpness just short of severe. She was too pale, but he could certainly appreciate how she could bewitch men . . . and boys.

Or perhaps it was that she held his gaze just a fraction too long. Long enough that his blood began to sing and he wanted to dive in and drown in her eyes.

Iris sat kicking her heels against the sofa. Lucian sighed.

Just inside the room, he drew up rather than walk into Miss Campbell executing a curtsy.

"How do you do, Miss Pendar? I have so been looking forward to meeting you." Her tone was dulcet without being the patently false voice adults often used with children.

Iris looked to him for guidance. He didn't think she'd ever had a governess curtsy to her or address her as Miss Pendar. Ducking his head to hide his amusement, he moved around Miss Campbell. The fire needed to be fed.

Iris continued to sit on the sofa.

Miss Campbell didn't miss a beat. "It would be proper to return the curtsy to a social equal. Or if you were the queen, you could just nod your head. But then, if you were the queen, I would have curtsied like so."

She sunk down into a deep genuflection with her arms out and her skirts circling her on the floor. Dipping her head low, she held out the moment as if Iris deserved reverence.

Miss Campbell lifted her head and smiled.

A frisson of awareness of her as a woman slid down his spine. Her smile made her come alive, and it wasn't even directed at him.

"Do you know how to pay your respects to the queen?" She rose to full height and quickly settled into a chair without a word of censure to Iris, who had behaved like the greatest hayseed.

"Iris, mind your manners," he said.

Iris ducked her head and mumbled a greeting.

He dumped the quarter log on the fire and sparks flew. For good measure he rammed the poker into the coals.

Miss Campbell turned toward him and then looked back at Iris. Twin furrows appeared between her finely arched eyebrows.

"She resembles her mother." Lucian answered her unspoken question. Iris was as fair as he was dark. With her golden curls and blue eyes, she was a perfect miniature of Lilith.

He put the screen back in place with a thud.

"Is that so?" said Miss Campbell in her gentle voice. "Then your mother must have been beautiful."

"She was," said Lucian before Iris could begin to wax eloquent about her mother.

Miss Campbell's eyes darted to his and then back

to Iris. "Of course if this were a formal occasion, then your father would have introduced us properly, but I understand you met me before."

"You ruined my mama's chair," Iris said.

Pain flickered across Miss Campbell's face. "The chaise longue was your mother's?"

Iris bounced on the sofa. "Yes."

Lucian had had enough. "Iris, behave, or you will go to bed."

Miss Campbell's hand flicked up as if to stop him. She lowered it as if his glare made her think twice.

Iris was looking at him with hurt blue eyes. He'd seen that expression one too many times on her mother's face to be swayed by it. He wished for another snifter of brandy.

"I'm very sorry about the dirt on the chaise. I never would have put my shoes on it if I were in my senses." Her forehead furrowed. "Do you normally sit there?"

"No, it's my mama's chair," said Iris petulantly. "You shouldn't have either."

Lucian rolled his eyes. He pointed to the door and said, "Go."

Miss Campbell stood.

"Not you, Miss Campbell. You stay. Iris, go to bed. If you cannot keep a civil tongue, you will not be allowed in the drawing room."

Her blue eyes filling with moisture, Iris dragged her feet to the door. She was in fine form tonight.

"Good night, Miss Pendar. I hope you will show me around tomorrow."

Iris didn't respond other than to attempt to slam the door. Miss Campbell caught it and gently clicked it closed.

"Will Mrs. Bigsby see her to bed?" she asked.

"Iris is nine. She sees herself to bed." He doubted Iris would see her bed anytime soon. The child had run wild for too long. "I apologize for her behavior."

Miss Campbell looked to the door. "Perhaps I should see her settled, then. Mrs. Bigsby informs me that is part of my duties."

"No, it is not part of your duties," Lucian bit out. Other than his valet, the Bigsbys were the only members of his house staff who had stayed on after Lilith's death.

Miss Campbell continued looking at the door and did not retake her seat.

"Do not allow Iris to manipulate you."

"Change has to be hard for her. She is used to having her papa to herself in the evening."

Lucian turned back to the fire. "Please sit down, Miss Campbell. Mrs. Bigsby will be in with the tea tray soon."

"If you would not mind, I would like to offer your daughter the opportunity to make an apology and allow her to return for tea. Then I would like to retire."

"Very well, Miss Campbell." Obviously she was not comfortable spending time alone with him, but then not many people were. Knowing with the fire backlighting him his scars were not easily seen, he slowly turned to face her. "But it must not be a half-baked apology, but a genuine one."

She smiled ever so slightly. "I shall strive for correct and mannerly. Sincerity might be asking for more than I can deliver."

He realized he'd been looking forward to adult conversation, but she wasn't here to entertain him. She was here to educate Iris. Besides, he had no interest in a woman who had the morals of a cat. He'd learned his lesson.

* * *

Velvet didn't find Iris among the myriad dolls in her bedroom or in the schoolroom. She checked the other rooms, but found them dank and disused. If the girl was hiding behind a piece of furniture, she might not respond. Velvet closed her eyes, not wanting to fail at the first task she'd set for herself.

She paused, trying to regain her breath before descending the narrow stairs. Calling softly for Iris, Velvet checked the water closet.

Opening a door, she found a masculine room with heavy dark furniture and a burgundy brocade dressing gown on top of a forest green coverlet. Her heart kicked up a notch and she hurriedly shut the door. Spinning around, she assessed the empty corridor. The last thing she needed was someone seeing her intruding in Mr. Pendar's bedroom.

Surprised no one had witnessed her faux pas, she breathed a sigh of relief. Enlisting the aid of the Bigsbys to find Iris might serve better.

After descending the stairs to the bowels of the house, she found her way by following the warmth more than anything else.

Sitting around the bare wood kitchen table were the three Bigsbys, a pale effeminate man, who must be Mr. Pendar's man, and Iris.

"There you are. I have been looking for you." As she spoke, Velvet realized that Iris had been chatting away and the sour look on Nellie's face had disappeared.

Iris slumped. Mrs. Bigsby pressed her lips together, and Mr. Bigsby pushed back his chair and stood.

"Oh please don't disturb your meal. I just have a proposition for Miss Pendar." Velvet slid onto the bench next to Iris. In most households, showing she wasn't above dining with the rest of the staff usually smoothed the path. In this one she felt like an intruder.

"You're going to tell Papa where you found me, aren't you?" demanded Iris.

"I shall have to tell him if he asks, but I see no reason for him to ask. I certainly have no intention of volunteering the information."

None of the staff resumed eating. Instead they watched her like crows waiting to pick her apart.

"If you would like to come back to the drawing room and spend time with your papa, you may—"

Iris popped up.

"But you must make a proper apology to me and to him."

Iris sat down hard. "I didn't do anything wrong."

Velvet sighed. "Yes, you did. You were rude. And while it is not so great an offense, your papa is ashamed that you would dishonor him with your behavior."

Iris stuck out her lower lip.

In a low voice Velvet whispered, "It is just words, even if you do not like me being here. Showing your papa that you are willing to try will go a long way with me. I should hate to have to be a stern taskmaster, but I can be, you know."

"Will you rap me with a ruler?"

"Only if you are rude," answered Velvet. She couldn't risk the child thinking she would never be disciplined or she would never have any control over her. "Young ladies should never forget their manners."

"What if I don't learn my lessons?"

"I only ask that you make every effort to learn, but if you do not try, we will not be able to do the amusing things like practicing curtsying to the queen, learning to dance, or playing the pianoforte."

"I want to play the harp like my mama."

"One must learn the pianoforte first." Velvet hadn't a clue how to play the harp or if any kind of instructor was available locally. "But once you do well with that, I will speak to your father about the harp."

Mrs. Bigsby shook her head, and Nellie was once again looking sour. Velvet tried to shut out their dour disapproval. She needed to show that she could get Iris to behave.

"So will you make a neat apology and rejoin your father?"

Iris didn't answer.

Velvet stood. "Ah me. Well I suppose I shall have to consult your papa about the proper discipline for an ill-mannered young lady."

"I'll slip a sweetmeat or two on the tea tray, love," said Mrs. Bigsby.

It was bribery of the worst sort, and Velvet was inordinately grateful.

"All right," said Iris with a distinct lack of graciousness.

Teaching this child to behave properly might take a full dozen years. Velvet sighed. No wonder her father was concerned about preparing her for marriage. "Thank you very much, Miss Pendar, Mrs. Bigsby." She gave the older woman a grateful nod over Iris's head. "We should hurry before your papa abandons all hope of you returning."

"He won't care," said Iris as she slunk toward the doorway.

"On the contrary. I think he shall be quite pleased."

Iris cast her a dark look. "He told my mama he wished I was never born."

"I'm sure you must be mistaken." Velvet bit her lip.

She was a newcomer here. What did she know about the secrets of this dark house?

The girl skipped ahead, which was a blessing because Velvet feared she might become hopelessly lost in the glooming darkness. The gas girandoles had not been lit. But there was another darkness in this house that had nothing to do with lack of light.

Lucian heard them outside the door for several minutes before they came in. The howl of the wind and the pounding rain drowned out their words. He closed his eyes and let the dulcet tones of Miss Campbell drift through his mind. She had a soothing quality to her voice. Yet, if she had managed to induce Iris to apologize, she was a miracle worker.

Iris's higher pitched tones and the chord of displeasure in her tone made him long for the evening to be finished. But she was a child who was not responsible for the sins of her parents. Although more and more she reminded him of Lilith. For that reason alone, he dreaded evenings with Iris.

The door opened and the pair walked in. He stood up from where he sat on the sofa.

Miss Campbell looked proper in her gray dress buttoned to her creamy white throat, and Iris looked like the indulged child she was in her ruffled pinafore and lacy pantaloons peeking out under her blue skirt. Blue to match her eyes, she'd insisted when the dressmaker came. Blue eyes like her mother's.

She turned to Miss Campbell and mumbled, "I apologize for my earlier behavior."

"I accept your apology." Miss Campbell smiled sweetly and turned Iris toward him. "Now your papa."

Over Iris's head he could see the fatigue etched in

Miss Campbell's face. He stepped closer, wanting to guide her to a chair.

"I ask your pardon for embarrassing you."

He'd be a heel to not accept her contrition after Miss Campbell had rewarded Iris's less than stellar performance. "Very well."

"Now that wasn't so hard, was it?" Miss Campbell stroked Iris's blond hair.

Iris jerked away and flounced past him to the sofa. Lucian wished he could just see her for herself instead of just a smaller version of Lilith.

"Thank you, Miss Campbell," he said.

"Mrs. Bigsby is bringing me sweetmeats," announced Iris.

He swiveled. Iris flashed such a guileful smile, he knew all was not as it seemed. He should have known better. Her mother had required bribes of dresses and gewgaws to be a proper hostess to his "boring" business associates. Likely the reward of sugary treats had inspired the show of contriteness from Iris.

"I'm afraid I resorted to bribery," Miss Campbell said softly. Then louder she said, "If you will excuse me, I shall retire."

"Good night, then," he said.

"Good night, Miss Pendar, Mr. Pendar," she said with a nod.

"Wait." He didn't want her to leave.

She raised inquiring eyes to his face. The moment stretched out as he searched for an indication she might want to linger longer, that she too longed for civilized conversation. For just a second he imagined he saw an answering loneliness.

Pressing her lips together, she looked down.

"You'll need a light to see by. It is getting dark." He

turned and found a candleholder on the mantel with a stubby candle on it. Using a spill, he lit it for her and carried it to where she stood near the door. He wanted to guide her to her room, make sure she made it safely, but that would be inappropriate.

She didn't look at him as he held out the night-light, but when their fingers brushed, a jolt pulsed through him. With the flickering flame up lighting her face, her expression was inscrutable. Suddenly eager to have her out of his sight, he reached for the door.

She gave the briefest of nods as she whispered through the opening.

"Tell me about the first time you saw my mama," demanded Iris.

He sighed and went to sit beside her. "It was seventeen years ago, and I went to a ball in London." A business associate of his father's had wrangled an invitation for Lilith's farewell ball. "When I walked in, I saw her right away."

Iris snuggled against him, and he put his arm around her slender shoulders. He had to remember she was just a child and untainted by the past.

"She was the most beautiful woman in the room," said Iris dreamily.

Or so he'd thought. "She had hair the color of sunshine and eyes like the summer sky," he added. "Every man wanted to dance with her, but she danced with me." Lucian the country bumpkin had probably looked like easy pickings. "I fell in love with her right that minute." Or so he'd thought, but what had he known? He'd only been eighteen.

"She glowed like an angel," added Iris.

Pregnancy did that to a woman. Of course he hadn't known the signs then. He'd since witnessed enough of

Lilith's repeated pregnancies to know the signs by heart now. The nausea provoked by the smell of food, the fainting, the fatigue. Next came the bloom of health in a woman's cheeks, the capricious humors. The changes to the figure started with the swell of her breasts and an overall softness to her form and progressed to the rounding of her belly.

"But then you didn't see her for months and months."

"Six to be exact. Imagine my surprise to find her here in Cornwall. I was so happy." Lilith had been less so. She begged him not to reveal she wasn't touring Europe as everyone thought. Instead she was visiting a distant cousin, whose name she wouldn't reveal. Years later she admitted she'd been terrified her cloak would blow against her and expose her protruding belly.

"And you found out where she was staying."

"I called on her three times, but she was indisposed. I knew she wanted to see me again, because she waved from her upstairs window." His own parents had returned from London with cholera. Lilith's lengthy illness had terrified him that she, too, might succumb to the ravages of her disease.

"And she agreed to marry me," he said. He'd been completely oblivious to her illness being a confinement to give birth, her pretended trip to Europe a cover to hide her condition, and his suit welcomed because she was damaged goods.

He'd been wrestling with the weight of his father's businesses falling on his unprepared shoulders, and he needed a wife to run his suddenly empty household. Lilith had seemed like a gift from heaven, because with his new responsibilities, he couldn't contemplate a lengthy courtship or extended trips to London to get a wife.

Now he pretended to her daughter that everything had been wonderful and magical.

"And she loved you very much." May God, if there was a God, forgive him for his lies.

"I want to be just like her," said Iris.

Yes, that was what he feared the most. "You are nearly as beautiful as she was. I think in a few more years you will be even prettier." He turned to face Iris. "I want you to be kind to Miss Campbell."

Iris scowled.

Miss Campbell had fainted, been put off by the smell of food, and was fatigued. Likely she was pregnant, but an unmarried woman would conceal her condition as long as possible.

"She has come a long way, and she is considered a very good governess."

"Better than Grimes?"

"Much nicer than Miss Grimes," he answered.

"You like her better too," said the sourpuss girl. "Do you like her better than you liked Mama?"

"No, of course not. I loved your mama." He coughed. He had loved her, once. Before he hated her.

Chapter 4

Velvet opened her eyes to look at her father's watch, only to remember she'd sold it for rent money. She feared oversleeping on her first day, but dawn grayed the room.

Her stomach hurt. For the first time in weeks she was hungry, ravenous even. Apparently the small amount she'd eaten last night had been enough to reawaken the gnawing beast of hunger.

Pushing back the covers, she shivered in the chilly room.

The door to the schoolroom stood open.

Her heart jolted in her chest. The door to the hallway still had the chair propped under the handle, but she distinctly remembered shutting the schoolroom door. Had Iris come in last night?

Velvet tiptoed into the schoolroom, pulling her door shut to avoid any more of the chill air invading her room. The windows overlooking the ocean were open wide. Averting her eyes, she reached out to pull the casements shut. Unable to entirely block the plunge to the rocky strip of ground below and the cliffs below that, her heart pounded.

In spite of the cold, moisture beaded her upper lip, and the world seemed to tilt wildly. Planting her hand on a chair, she breathed slowly until calm crept back into her screamingly tensed flesh. She knew her terror of heights was a weakness of mind she should be able to overcome, but looking down from great heights only turned her knees to jelly as horrible images of her younger brother's broken form after he'd fallen from the bell tower flashed in her mind.

After a few minutes her ragged breathing returned to normal. Were the open windows a trick to make her cold? Surely, no one here knew that she was deathly afraid of falling from a great height.

Had Iris opened the windows? Velvet would never forgive herself if another child under her watch had a horrible fall.

She opened the door on the other side. Heat floated out of the girl's room. Her watered silk drapes didn't move. Her windows hadn't been opened.

Iris was cocooned in her ornate carved bed, one of the dozens of porcelain dolls tucked under her arm. She looked like a princess surrounded by dollhouses and more toys than any child could ever use. But no one had listened to her prayers, told her a bedtime story, or tucked her in.

Velvet had intended to check on Iris, but exhausted by the long walk up the drive and the myriad trips up four flights of stairs, she had fallen into the deep sleep of the damned long before the girl had gone to bed.

Iris's blue gown was dumped unceremoniously on the thick rose carpet, her pinafore hanging on a doorknob.

Tiptoeing in, Velvet picked up the dress and straightened it. She opened the wardrobe to find it chock-full of a rainbow of dresses. Abandoning the idea of putting away the dress, she instead set it on a chair and folded the pinafore on top of it. As quietly as she could, she straightened the dolls and toys. Why did one child have all this?

Spying a shelf with a few thin books, she pulled one down. Did this child share her love of books? A child who loved to read was easy to teach.

Books had seen Velvet through her childhood. They'd been her companions when she was lonely and her comfort when the world was cruel. Reading had helped her temporarily escape the crushing guilt she felt after her brother's death. She opened the book and her optimism crashed.

A picture book.

Scanning the rest of them, she could see they were all picture books suitable to a child in leading strings, not a nine-year-old girl. Sighing, Velvet replaced the slim volume on the shelf and turned back toward the schoolroom.

By Iris's fireplace lay book bindings with their pages torn out. Blackened fragments of the printed pages littered the grate. Velvet's breath caught. Destroying books went against everything she held dear.

Kneeling, she tried to pull out one of the fragments, but it crumbled to dust. Picking up the remnants of the books, she found a spelling primer, a book on mathematics, and one on geography. But even the lettering had been scraped and scribbled over.

Why would Iris have destroyed her schoolbooks?

Her heart heavy, Velvet gathered the bindings and took them back to the schoolroom. Hard chairs and school tables were haphazardly arranged. A dusty globe with a pin skewered in Cornwall occupied a dark corner.

Nothing was inviting about the room.

Setting her load on the scratched desk, she checked the drawers. A bit of yellowed paper and a stopperless ink bottle were in the first drawer; a broken ruler, a cracked slate, and stubs of chalk in the next; and in the bottom drawer, several empty gin bottles clattered.

Removing the bottles, Velvet transferred them to the dustbin. The room needed a thorough cleaning and something bright to tempt Iris inside. Her first order of business would be to scrub it.

After she dressed.

She turned back toward her room.

The knob spun in her hand, clearly not triggering the mechanism to release the latch. She rattled the knob. No matter what she did the door wouldn't budge. It was stuck.

She pushed and pulled, slowly turning the knob, then jerking it, all to no avail.

Panting, she rested her head against the panels. She would have to go for help, in her bare feet and wearing only her nightgown. She cast a glance toward Iris's room, but it wasn't the child's fault that Velvet had propped a chair under the hallway door.

Surely she could slip down to the kitchen and find Mrs. Bigsby, who could summon her husband or locate a tool to remove the door handle.

Lucian left his room wearing the Turkish robe over his striped wool bathing suit. He swam for an hour most mornings, the biting cold of the ocean making him forget his life for a while. White flashed at the foot of the stairs and then disappeared up the narrow stairwell.

Surely, Iris wasn't already up and about. Usually she slept until Nellie woke her around half eight.

He frowned. It was too early for any of the day staff to have arrived.

Perhaps meeting her new governess made Iris sleep

badly. Iris hated schoolwork. Hated it enough to resort to pranks to drive away her governesses. If this one didn't work out, he would send the truculent girl to a school in Bath. But he'd be damned if he let her start her tricks again.

His rubber shoes silent on the carpet runner, he strode down the hall toward the foot of the staircase. "Iris?"

A stiff intake of breath and a slapping of bare feet on wooden treads of the stairs let him know it wasn't her.

Reaching the foot of the stairs, he swallowed hard. On level with his eyes was the new governess's bottom. Her long braid swished across the curve.

"Miss Campbell," he said.

She slowly turned and folded her arms across her chest. Her cheeks were bright with spots of pink. Her nearly threadbare nightgown was plain, buttoned to the neck, and her pink toes curled around the edge of the stair as she shrunk back against the wall.

For a rumored seductress, she looked innocent and cornered. The hint of flesh below the material reminded him of carnal desires he tried to ignore, but his blood stirred anyway.

For a long second they just stared at each other. He shook his head, glad of the thick robe hiding the surge in his groin. Damn, he didn't need this. "What are you doing?" Impatience sharpened his tone.

She gave a slight shake to her head and raised her chin. "I've managed to lock myself out of my room. The door to the schoolroom has latched, but the knob . . . seems to be broken." She shrugged. "I hoped to find Mr. Bigsby to let me in."

Had the rebellious child already managed a coup? "Iris?"

"She's sleeping."

"There are two doors." And neither had locks. Lucian scowled.

"I'm sorry to have disturbed you. I am the biggest ninny. But the other door is barricaded."

"What?"

"I was assessing the schoolroom to see what needed to be done, and I'm sorry, I'll just go fetch Mr. Bigsby." She took a step down, but stopped.

Lucian blocked her passage. The air seemed to crackle with energy, perhaps left over from last night's storm.

"I'll look at it."

She just blinked. "Oh no, I'm sure that if you just alert Mr. Bigsby, he'll be right up."

"Bigsby is down on the beach." She didn't know the household routines yet. Lucian put his foot on the first step.

She scurried up the stairs, like a scared rabbit. Her braid swung as she hurried down the hall to the schoolroom door. He tried the passage door but it didn't budge.

Sighing, he followed her into the schoolroom. The room hadn't changed since he'd had his early lessons in here, except it seemed more careworn perhaps, and he'd never wanted to kiss his tutor.

She stood to the side of the stuck door, pressing her lips together. The light of the schoolroom illuminated how very sheer her garment was in places. The outline of her figure, her slender waist, the flare of hips had his heart racing.

The knob spun in his hand.

His robe felt hot, the wool bathing suit that offered little protection from the sting of the ocean water made him sweat. Kiss her, hell, he had to acknowledge he wanted to go much further than that. He took a step back.

He kicked the door next to the handle. With a splintering crack, the frame gave. The door banged against the wall inside her room.

He held his palm out to stop it from closing all the way on the rebound. His foot stung from the impact.

Miss Campbell's mossy green eyes opened wide.

He pushed the door open and lifted his palm up. Her iron bedstead was just a few feet away, the covers still rumpled.

"Well that is one way to bell the cat." A hint of a smile hovered around her lips.

"I'll have a craftsman come and fix it." He stared at her.

Her smile faded into a worried look. "Thank you," she mumbled, and ducked into the room.

He followed her into the doorway before he thought. He gripped the frame as if that would stop him from pursuing her. Outrageous thoughts raced. In spite of her seeming innocence, she wasn't pure. She was a seductress of men and boys. She was exhibiting the early signs of pregnancy. She was in his house, in a nightgown, and no one was around.

Iris cried, "Papa."

His heart stopped cold. Behind him little feet pattered against the floor.

Velvet swung her cape around her shoulders, covering the copper braid he wanted to unplait. As her arms rose, his gaze dropped to her chest. He quickly lowered his eyes before she noticed his interest in her small breasts. A line of darned stitches ran down from the opening placard of her nightgown. Falling from her cape, dry mud pinged on the bare wood.

"Cold?" he inquired as he absently put an arm around Iris's shoulders. How could Velvet be cold when he was on fire?

Velvet—where did a woman get a name like that?—stared at him. "A little. I don't own a dressing gown."

She didn't own a dressing gown, and her nightgown should have been consigned to the rag bin a long time ago. On some level he'd recognized that the sheerness of her gown was due to the threadbare state of the material.

"What was that noise?" asked Iris.

"Miss Campbell's door was stuck." He had to get ahold of his desires. "You can go back to bed."

The screech of the chair she pulled out from where it was wedged under the passage door made him cringe. She kept the chair between them as if she planned to use it like a lion tamer would. Her gaze darted around the room, and she winced.

Following the line of her sight, he assessed the barren room. There wasn't a clothes press or dresser. Three dresses were draped on nails, and a tiny stack of linens was stuffed on the lower shelf of the washstand. Towels and washcloths should be on the shelf. Her corset was draped over the foot of her bed, the frayed and knotted black strings standing in sharp contrast to the pale material.

He realized that his refusal to release her wages wouldn't allow her to replace her worn garments. "I'll . . . uh . . . summon the dressmaker."

Velvet blanched. "No, that's not necessary. I wasn't suggesting I needed a dressing gown." She shifted from one foot to the other.

In his experience, women didn't turn down clothes, nor did they shove chairs under their door handles to keep others out without reason. But it was no surprise she didn't trust him. No one did. Desperately needing the biting cold of the ocean, he swiveled and nearly knocked over Iris.

He steadied her and set her away. "Go back to bed. There is no reason for you to be up so early."

He had to get out of here. But as he crossed the room, the leather bindings on the edge of the scratched desk stopped him. "What is this?"

Impatient for an answer, he closed the distance and picked up the books. The spines flopped loosely, revealing the pages had been ripped out. "These were mine."

They had been his lesson books from a happier time, when his parents were alive, when he'd been certain the world was a good place and he was a good person.

Iris had her shoulders up by her ears, but the minute he looked at her, her stance changed to one of shocked innocence. Wrapped in her cloak, Miss Campbell stood in her doorway. Her attention was on Iris.

Silence stretched out.

He slapped the leather-covered mill board against the desk. Iris jumped.

Velvet's eyes narrowed. "I found them like that. I also found empty gin bottles in the bottom desk drawer."

Iris turned surprised blue eyes on her governess.

"Don't worry, I can supply suitable instruction without the primers," Velvet said firmly.

He opened his mouth to yell at Iris. The little hellion deserved punishment. Except he never reprimanded her for fear he'd cross some invisible line and pile on punishment for her being her mother's daughter. He clamped his lips closed. Miss Campbell had chosen to protect her charge and cast aspersions on her predecessor.

Velvet had yet to give a lesson to the stubborn student. No doubt her frustration level wasn't high enough to set about destroying the tools of her trade. Yet. No, Iris had destroyed the books.

"One day, Iris, you will push me too far."

Velvet's gasp made him realize how badly his words must sound to a woman who suspected him of killing his wife. No wonder she had barred her door.

He bore the marks of his last struggle with Lilith, so he didn't know why the mistrust always shocked him. He wheeled and headed out the door. He needed to be outside where the cool sea air would fill his lungs and the icy water would purge his body of carnal longings. Where he could plunge his arms into the surf until he was too tired to think, too tired to remember. Swimming was the only peace he ever had.

Iris risked looking at Miss Campbell. She stood wrapped in her cloak as if she might go out in her nightgown and bare feet. She didn't know the new governess well enough to have a clue what she would say or if there would be punishment. The slight frown didn't look promising.

The best defense might be to forestall the punishment. "You're very pretty," she said.

Miss Campbell studied her. "Burning books is usually the action of tyrants or those afraid of new ideas." She raised a slim eyebrow. "Which are you?"

Her heart banging in her chest, Iris tried again. "My mama was a great beauty. I take after her."

"Fairness of face is a gift or curse from God. You cannot take credit for it. Your nature, intelligence, and behavior are the true measure of beauty."

Iris scowled. Not according to her mama. "How can beauty be a curse?"

Miss Campbell's lips tightened. She picked up the book covers and dropped them in the dustbin. The dustbin clinked. "You must never destroy a book again. Is that understood?"

"Are you going to punish me?"

"Do you not think you deserve to be punished?" asked Miss Campbell. Her voice was even and calm. She opened a cupboard and peered inside.

Iris felt a little bit as if she were swimming beyond her depth. Was Miss Campbell biding her time or was she too busy snooping around to care what happened? "You didn't tell Papa."

"I hoped you would inform him. As it is, you will have to tell him and apologize for destroying his property." She pulled out a bundle of squared sticks.

"He won't do anything. He never does."

Miss Campbell glanced over her shoulder at the splintered door frame. Her brows knit. "I do not think it would be wise to press him."

"What does relish mean?" asked Iris. "Like if you wouldn't relish doing something?"

"In that sense it would mean you wouldn't enjoy it." She unfolded the sticks and made them into a tripod.

"Oh." Why hadn't Meg just said she wouldn't like preparing the house for Miss Campbell? Although Iris couldn't see that any preparations were made. She suspected Meg was just putting on airs.

"Why don't you get dressed, and I will too. And then you can show me where we eat breakfast."

"There won't be any breakfast until Papa gets back from his swim." Iris ran over to the window. "Look, you can see him down there."

Miss Campbell made no move toward the window. Instead she brushed off her hands. "Then you may pick out three of your dolls to give away at church next Sunday. I'm sure there are poor village girls who would love to have a pretty doll. Since you destroyed three books I think it would be fitting—"

"No!" A wall of astonishment crashed down. "You can't take my dolls."

"Well if you do not pick the three, then I shall. I do not think you will like my picks."

Iris ran into her room and grabbed a doll, flung open her window and tossed it out. It fell and fell until it smashed on the edge of the cliff.

Miss Campbell went pale, which gave Iris a moment of gloating satisfaction.

But in her resolutely calm voice, she said, "Now you will have to pick out four dolls." She picked up Eve, the doll Papa had given her that he said Mama had chosen for her before she died.

"Or I will choose her and . . ." She pulled three more of the best dolls off the shelf and lined them up next to Eve. "I'll just take these until you've decided which ones you'd like to give away. And if you destroy another one, I will not return these to you."

"I hate you!" Iris screamed. Her chest felt like it would explode. "I'll never let you teach me anything."

"That is too bad," said Miss Campbell. "Because if you do not learn to play the piano, you will never play the harp." She quietly closed the door behind her and left with Eve.

Velvet dragged a second chair from the schoolroom into her bedroom and wedged it under the broken door handle. She was shaking as she laid the four dolls on the bed.

She replaced the other chair and wondered if she had

made a grave mistake. Obviously, Iris suffered from a lack of discipline.

Hopefully, the mild punishment would lead to Iris feeling good about giving to a few less fortunate girls. Did the child have any playmates? The isolation of the house might preclude it.

The door to the schoolroom rattled. "I want Eve," wailed Iris.

"I will return to the schoolroom when I've dressed. I suggest you do the same."

"I'm telling my papa. He'll make you leave."

Velvet sighed. She should have consulted Mr. Pendar about the limits of discipline.

Making quick work of stripping off her nightgown, she said, "Iris, please go back to your room."

"I'll get her back, you know." The door thumped as if kicked. "I'll find her. You can't stop me."

Wary of another intrusion while she wore only undergarments, Velvet stepped into her corset. "You may have Eve back when you pick out four dolls to give away." Velvet tried to sound calm. "Until then there will be no more discussion."

Tensed, she waited for the child to respond. But only quiet came from the schoolroom. Velvet was sure this wasn't the last of it, but she needed to enlist Mr. Pendar's indulgence for her plan. She finished dressing in the cleanest of her three serviceable gowns.

A rapping on the passage door startled her.

"Iris?"

"No, ma'am. Evans."

Why was Mr. Pendar's valet knocking on her door? She had yet to address her hair, but she didn't want to make him wait. Or was she already being summoned to Mr. Pendar's study to be dismissed?

The chair screeched as she pulled it out from under the door handle.

The slender man dressed in black held out a handkerchief wrapped bundle. "The master asked me to give you these, until new can be purchased."

Velvet frowned and looked up at the man's face. She could make out nothing from his pale eyes and nearly invisible eyebrows. He practically shoved the bundle in her hands as if he couldn't wait to be rid of it. His gaze transferred to the hard chair by the door.

She lifted the corner of the bundle, revealing sturdy corset cords and gray shoelaces.

Mr. Evans took an edgy step back. "As soon as Cook arrives, she will send up a pot of chocolate and hot cross buns."

The idea of an early breakfast sounded heavenly.

The kindness of hot chocolate and replacement strings for her corset brought a sting to her eyes. "Thank you, Mr. Evans."

His Adam's apple bobbed as he cleared his throat. "Would you like it brought to your room or to the schoolroom?"

"It isn't for Miss Pendar, too?" A stone dropped through her innards.

"You wish it brought to the schoolroom, then?" Mr. Evans blinked his pale lashes, his expression portraying the utmost discretion.

A valet was privy to his master's affairs. His efforts to keep his thoughts far from his face made her suspect his master's motives were less than altruistic. Had any other governess been treated so lavishly?

"That won't be necessary," she said stiffly. Her stomach protested. "Please tell the cook not to bother with a tray for us."

He gave a slight shake of his head, then bowed. "Very good, ma'am."

He turned to walk away.

"Mr. Evans?" called Velvet.

He turned, his thin features twisted.

She wondered at the pained look, but quickly dismissed it. "Is Miss Pendar allowed in her father's room?"

"No, ma'am. Of course not."

"Would you be able to store these dolls in his room until I can discuss their disposition with her father?"

He looked rather startled by the idea, but seemed to consider a moment and then returned with a smile. As she watched Mr. Evans leave with the dolls, she felt like the worst sort of kidnapper.

Hoping she'd not made a foolish blunder, she closed her eyes. She hadn't considered how she would retrieve the dolls from a room that was off limits to *her* too.

Chapter 5

Lucian clawed into the rowboat, physically exhausted but still on edge. He heaved in a deep breath, filling his lungs with briny air. His quivering muscles were on the verge of turning to mush.

"Good swim today, sir," said Bigsby.

Lucian didn't agree. He'd expected the swim to help him regain control, but it hadn't calmed him. His skin was red from the cold of the water, but a pair of mossy green eyes fueled a furnace inside him. It had been a long time since he wanted a woman—or at least wanted a woman badly enough that the physical urges intruded in his waking hours.

Bigsby held out the Turkish robe. Lucian buried his face in the thick material and rubbed off the water. Eventually he shoved down the sleeves of his soggy bathing suit and pushed his bare arms into the thick robe. Bigsby's rhythmic dipping of the oars drew them closer to the shoreline.

With luck, the tray he'd ordered would keep Iris and Velvet from the breakfast table. He'd been concerned about Velvet's potential for morning sickness, but now he just hoped she would stay away until he had his passions in check.

He splashed into the surf and helped drag the boat

onto the rocky beach. A wave broke over his feet, soaking his robe's hem.

Bigsby shook his head, but the grizzled old man didn't say anything.

"Go on up. I'll take care of the skiff," said Lucian. He needed to be alone with his foul mood.

The older man tossed him the rope and then began the slow climb to the top of the cliffs.

Lucian stared out at the ever-changing sea. The calm morning with gentle swells and lapping breakers gave no hint of last night's storm. On a morning like this, following another storm, he'd found his wife's body not far from here. The ocean hadn't taken Lilith's body. He wished it had. Then he could have pretended she'd just gone away.

After securing the boat, he shed his sodden bathing suit. The heavy saturated wool chafed on land. He wouldn't bother wearing the damn thing, except Iris often watched from her window. He flopped the wet material over his shoulder and then belted his robe.

He couldn't delay a return to the house any longer. Evans would have drawn a hot bath for him and would be waiting with clean linen.

The carved-out stone steps of the cliff defied his urge to rush. Some steps were three paces apart, some two, making finding a rhythm impossible. But Lucian knew them well enough to take them at a fast clip.

He cleared the edge of the cliff and halted. A hundred yards away was the house. Behind it, a mere ten yards from the cliffs, Miss Campbell knelt on one knee, the back of her hand pressed against her mouth.

He wanted to ignore her and go inside, but if she was ill, he couldn't just leave her.

His rubber shoes silent on the scrub grass, he closed

the gap. A steady breeze blew in from the ocean, masking the sound of his approach. Her attention was focused on the ground. She plucked chunks of white and pink porcelain from the grass. They clinked in the schoolroom dustbin beside her. What had Iris destroyed now? Wearily, he glanced up to see the rose curtains of Iris's room directly above Velvet. He supposed he should be grateful he didn't have to deal with morning sickness.

Velvet stopped and squeezed her eyes shut. Tears leaked out the edges.

His insides twisted. And he'd thought he'd grown impervious to tears.

"Miss Campbell?"

"Oh!" She twisted away and dashed the heel of her hand against her face. This was not a woman who planned to use her tears for effect. She was either hiding her illness or her distress from the household.

"Are you all right?" He closed the last ten feet that separated them.

"I'm fine," she said too hastily.

A painted blue eye stared up at him from a triangular shard on the ground. He bent and picked it up. "What did Iris do now?"

"She took exception to my proposed discipline for destroying the schoolbooks." Velvet put a hand on the dustbin and shifted it between them. "But it is of no matter."

The remains of a doll, her porcelain fingers broken and her head smashed, were inside. So Iris had taken to throwing her dolls out the window.

He added the eye. "You didn't seem to want to admit to me that she tore up the books."

"Yes, well that was before Iris assured me you never

punish her." Velvet watched him as if looking for confirmation.

Feeling guilty, he rolled his shoulders. "I've never felt comfortable taking a rod to her backside." He'd barely felt comfortable with the child at all. After Lilith's death, Iris had stared at him with solemn eyes, left with no one but him. He probably had bought her too many dolls, but he hadn't known what else to do, but try to make her life as carefree and comfortable as possible.

Velvet stood and he reached out to cup her elbow. She looked unsteady, and he wasn't sure she was entirely well.

The move brought them too close, and he was all too aware he wore nothing under his robe. His hand tingled where it was in contact with her arm. The tingles spread along his arm and down his body. With the ocean breeze putting roses in her cheeks and the blue-green of the ocean off-setting her coppery hair, she looked like a dream come true. His prurient thoughts rushed back.

He shouldn't have touched her.

"There are other punishments beyond corporal," she said softly.

"Yes, there are." His voice was rough. Having beautiful off-limits women in his household seemed to be his particular punishment. He fought the throbbing change in his body. He should go inside, but he couldn't bring himself to drop his hold on her elbow.

She turned her head toward him. "I wanted to ask you if you would allow Iris to give away four of her dolls at church this Sunday."

He watched her pale pink lips move, but the words failed to penetrate. He wanted to kiss her, but what kind of a man seduced a woman whom he was practically holding hostage with her wages? "We don't go to church."

She jerked her arm back and her eyes flashed. "You will not object if I take Iris."

Her statement was defiant. Not even a question. The corners of his mouth slid up, but he fought to suppress the smile. She was like a Valkyrie in her fearlessness. Most of his staff were afraid to cross him.

Her expression fell as if she feared she had overstepped her place. "A girl in society will be expected to have a proper Christian upbringing." Velvet ducked her head. "And she needs playmates her own age."

"Why?" He folded his arms and resisted saying he hadn't had friends his own age until he'd been sent to school.

"We females are social creatures. We rely on our friendships."

"Who do you rely on, Miss Campbell?"

Her eyes looked bruised before she turned away. He regretted the question.

"If you would like me to have her ready to interact socially with others, she will need to have contact with people outside of the household."

Lucian took a step toward her and reached for the dustbin. She reluctantly released it to him, and he returned it to the ground. She talked, and her voice curled around him like warm tendrils of a summer breeze.

"If you will not back me on this discipline, then I will have her stand with her nose to the corner. But I thought giving away the dolls would help teach her charity. She has so many. She can't possibly play with them all."

Velvet stared at him, and he was caught in her eyes.

Her words tumbled faster. "If you don't want to give away dolls you bought . . ."

He leaned toward her, catching her feminine scent, wanting to hold her, bury himself in her softness, and ensure she always treated him like a partner in her concerns, or so he deluded himself.

" . . . help her to make friends with the village girls."

"No." The rush of heat ebbed. "I don't want her mixing with the villagers."

Furrows appeared between her brows as she studied him. Her silent inquiry drew an explanation from him.

"She'll hear things she shouldn't hear."

Velvet bit the corner of her lip and seemed to consider her answer. "I understand you want to shelter her from the rumors you killed your wife, but hiding away isn't the answer."

He was used to unnatural silence when he entered a room and the gradual roar of whispers and sidelong glances. He wasn't used to people being direct about the accusations leveled at him. He waited for his anger to spurt forth, but her broaching the subject made him feel lighter. Instead of the issue hanging between them like an unspeakable horror, it was out and exposed.

But more was at issue than Lilith's manner of death. There were other secrets he wanted kept from Iris's ears. Skeletons he shared with no one. His relief tightened back into a knot.

"What is the answer?" he asked sharply. "How does one shield a child from gossip and innuendo?"

Velvet's mouth tightened and her gaze lost focus, as she seemed to turn inward. Pain flashed across her face.

"I don't know the answer," she finally said, as if she hated to admit ignorance.

He wanted to comfort her, hold her. Rumors had affected her life too. But she hadn't turned to him for comfort, and she'd put a chair under her door handle to keep him out. She wasn't here for him.

He moved past her, taking a couple of steps toward the cliff. He stared out at the ocean, but the calm it usually gave was elusive. Velvet filled his thoughts.

He turned and studied her. Her back was to him and she seemed extraordinarily interested in the gray granite of the back wall. Her neck curved in a way that invited kisses. The urge to have her resurfaced. His blood quickened and his body hummed with an awareness of her.

"If you do not . . ." The warm wash of her voice made him shudder. Her dulcet tones were the kind he wanted to hear when engaging in the flirtation that proceeded seduction. " . . . then I shall need to retrieve them from your room."

His room. All he heard was that she wanted to come to his room. An image of her copper hair spread across his green counterpane flooded his mind. Blood roared in his ears and pulsed low in him. If she came to his room, it must mean she was willing . . . to . . . he shook his head. She was talking to the wall instead of him.

Not everything added up. "You want to come to my room, Miss Campbell?" He closed the distance between them.

"Four of Iris's dolls are in there. I had Mr. Evans take them host—"

Needing to see her face, he gripped her shoulder and whipped her around to face him.

"—age. Oh, God," she whispered. Her eyes rounded, the pupils tightened to black pinpoints in a sea of green. The bloom in her cheeks drained.

She took a faltering step back.

Terror was not what he expected, not what he wanted.

She squeezed her eyes shut and took more steps backward until she ran into the wall. Her nails scrabbled on the granite.

Was his arousal so obvious and so abhorrent to her?

He whirled around to face the sea. He wanted to hide the scars that marked him. Many feared him. And obviously Miss Campbell had heard the charges leveled against him. Did she believe he'd tossed his wife over the cliff?

"You may do as you like with Iris's discipline."

"Th-Thank you," said Velvet on a shaky breath. "Pray, excuse me."

She slid along the wall and around the corner.

Velvet was fierce in her determination to do the right thing for Iris, even if it meant crossing him. He admired her at the same time he hated that she probably thought him guilty of tossing his wife over the cliffs, as everyone did. That she would confront him about the rumors surrounding his involvement in Lilith's death was incredibly brave. He shook his head.

His last argument with Lilith echoed in his head. He knew he was responsible for his wife's untimely death. He didn't deserve the comfort of a woman as beautiful and good as Velvet in his bed.

Velvet fought the bile rising in her throat as she gripped the rail. While she was pulling herself up as much as climbing the stairs, her shaking legs weren't helping her ascent.

She knew she would have difficulty with the cliffs so close to the house, and she'd wanted to face them on her own. Going out to clean up the doll's remains mere feet from the plunge to the sea had seemed like a good idea. But in her head the shattered doll kept blending with images of her brother's broken body. She swallowed hard against her emotions. A smashed human head left pools of blood; dolls didn't. She shouldn't have been so affected, but she was still shaking.

Or perhaps it was because Mr. Pendar had come upon her.

She'd tried to focus on him, not the cliffs mere feet from her. Keeping her back to the ocean, she'd been doing all right. His energy seemed to fill her. But when he spun her around, the fear of falling had gripped her by the throat and she panicked.

"Miss Campbell?" Nellie stood at the head of the stairs, her arms folded across her chest.

Hoping she didn't look as wild-eyed as she felt, Velvet answered, "Yes."

Worrying a broken nail, Velvet concentrated on slowing her breathing. All she wanted was five minutes in her room to regain her composure, but the scowling woman blocked her path.

"What can I do for you?" asked Velvet. She hoped the question would disarm Nellie.

"I understand you took Eve."

"The doll, yes." Velvet sighed.

"I'd like her back now." Nellie leveled a fishy eye gaze at her.

"I'm sorry, no." Velvet resumed her climb up the narrow stairs.

The woman looked taken aback by her refusal and lack of explanation.

"That doll is special to her." Nellie looked over her shoulder.

Velvet was weary of battles. "Perhaps you can help

her pick out four less special dolls to give away, then."

She'd reached the top step and stood waiting for Nellie to move out of her way.

"Mr. Pendar won't approve," said Nellie.

"He already has. I just spoke with him. Now if you will excuse me."

Velvet pushed past. Was she to have no allies in this household?

"You spoke with him?" said Nellie, her voice hushed.

Velvet turned. The angular woman had her hand against her chest, as if speaking to Mr. Pendar was unusual.

"Yes. Is Iris ready to go down for breakfast?"

"No."

"Will you have her ready in ten minutes, please?" Velvet felt snappish. Hungry, overwrought, and ready to bite the head off the next person who interfered with her. Instead, she concentrated on breathing slowly— A feat nearly impossible after climbing four flights of stairs.

"Don't you wish to wait until after the master has finished?"

"No." As hungry as she was, she saw no reason to delay. Away from the cliffs, she was regaining her equilibrium.

She sighed. It was almost as if she'd lived a lifetime this morning. She was eager to get to the breakfast table and fully fill her stomach for the first time in months.

An image of Lucian Pendar with his tousled wet hair ruffled by the sea breeze crowded out thoughts of food. A frisson of alarm shuddered down her spine. No matter how solicitous he'd seemed, he was not the reason she was eager to go to breakfast. He couldn't be.

Nellie continued to stare at her.

"I should like to begin Iris's lessons by nine," Velvet said firmly. She needed to begin as she meant to go on and firmly establish her position as Iris's governess. "I believe we have a great deal of catching up to do."

"Uh, ma'am, Iris is not fond of the schoolroom."

Nellie's pronouncement saved Velvet from ruminating on her fascination with her employer.

"Why is that?" she asked.

Tucking her hands under the bib of her apron, Nellie looked away. "She's not the most clever when it comes to book learning."

Nothing Velvet had seen in Iris suggested the girl was slow, but she couldn't discount the warnings. "Her instruction will include much more than basic subjects. I will be teaching her painting, music, and manners. Perhaps she will find some lessons she likes."

"Is that why the easel is out?" asked Nellie, as if it had been a great mystery.

A clattering of heels on the stairs brought a breathless young woman to join them. "He's back."

The maid pushed past them and ducked inside a room down the hall.

"Who was that?" asked Velvet.

"Meg," answered Nellie. "She knows better than to be around when the master comes in. Them that knows what's good for them, stays out of his sight." Nellie pivoted and strode toward Iris's room.

Velvet shook her head and continued on to her room.

A chilly breeze swept across her as soon as she opened the door. Her window casements were wide open and the thin strips of muslin that served as curtains flapped.

Her heart leapt to her throat and threatened to choke

her. All she needed to do was cross the room and pull the casements shut, but she couldn't force her feet to move.

She swallowed hard.

No other person would be afraid of open windows, four stories above a cliff. She couldn't let this terror control her. Instead she wheeled about and headed back down the stairs.

She'd be braver after she ate. Or at least she hoped she wouldn't be shaking so badly.

"That will be all, Evans." Lucian snatched his dressing gown from the bed.

"You don't wish me to help you dress after your bath?" asked Evans as he pressed the wet bathing suit in a towel.

"No, I'll manage."

"Very good, sir." Evans slipped into the dressing room.

Once Lucian was in the bath, his man would slip back in the room and retrieve the Turkish robe, but he didn't need Evans's company at the moment. The company he wanted didn't reciprocate his interest. He was probably the only man in the world who could repulse an indiscriminate seductress.

Not only had Miss Campbell betrayed her terror, the upstairs maid had gone scurrying when he startled her. He'd thought after three years the day staff would stop thinking he was just waiting to pitch the next woman off the cliffs.

He dropped the wet robe to the floor and turned to stuff his arms in the clean dry dressing gown, only to find Eve's painted blue eyes staring at him.

He winced, hoping he hadn't traumatized the doll

with his aroused condition. Then he shook his head at the thought.

The doll had been his attempt to erase a six-year-old's memories of her mother and replace them with an idealized version of a mother who cared enough to buy her child a doll for Christmas. He probably would have done better to bury Lilith's memories with her.

Not only Eve, but three other expensive dolls sat in his armchair. He brought one back for Iris on every trip he went. Every six to eight weeks he needed to travel to take care of his business interests. He frowned at the dolls.

Iris probably needed a new mother, a matronly woman who truly cared about children. He sighed. He'd considered remarriage a dozen times and always dismissed it. Perhaps he was old enough now that no one would think it odd if he married a widow with children. The house should have children. It was too big for him and Iris. Too bad he didn't know any widows who fit his requirements.

Lost in thought, he left his room and headed toward the bathroom at the far end of the hallway. He'd taken half a dozen steps when Velvet rounded the corner at the top of the main stairs. She was the last woman he wanted to see right now, but they would have to pass in the hall as she moved toward the stairs past his bedroom, which led to the nursery floor.

"Miss Campbell," he said.

She nodded. "Sir."

"If you want the dolls, they're in the chair by the window." He gestured back toward his room.

He could still read the fright in her eyes, but she raised her chin. "Iris has yet to pick the ones she will give away."

So Eve would be witnessing his dressing and undressing a while longer. Giving a brisk nod, he moved past Velvet. She seemed to plaster her body against the wall as if he were a leper she couldn't bear to touch.

He took a few steps toward the bathroom and the warm water that might release the growing knot from the back of his neck. His fist clenched, and the boil of anger, never far away, began anew. He pivoted and returned to Velvet.

"You have no reason to fear me."

"No?" She met his gaze squarely.

Ages had passed since a woman met his gaze without her attention straying to the scars, or had even carried on a conversation with him. He was uncertain of his read on her. "No. I am not in the habit of tossing beautiful women off cliffs."

"A habit would require a repeated behavior, wouldn't it?"

He was at a loss for words. She certainly wasn't shy about challenging him. His heartbeat quickened and he took a step closer.

"I'm sorry, I shouldn't have said that." She ducked her head. "It was impertinent and . . ." Her gaze darted left and right. " . . . and Mrs. Bigsby said breakfast won't be served until you are downstairs."

He frowned. "Didn't you get the tray? I told Evans to have Cook send up a light meal."

"About that. I do not wish to be treated differently than any other governess who has gone before me."

"But you . . ." He let his voice trail off. Her condition prompted his concern, but he'd been condemned for it. As if he'd been trying to seduce her with chocolate and buns. The misconstruing of his intentions was typical, but it cut him nonetheless.

He stared into her snapping green eyes. The challenge was there, her fear too. Her pale pink lips needed to be relaxed with kisses. Her willowy form should bend to his. His arousal and need were in danger of defeating him. He hated to lose control.

"Don't hesitate to treat me as you treated your previous employer either."

She gasped and went pale. "I'm not what you think I am," she whispered.

"No?" He leaned close. "*You* believe the rumors about *me*."

Her eyes widened but her voice was low and soothing. "Rumors are often riddled with falsehoods."

"And enough truth to make them appear valid," he returned.

A wash of pink stained her cheeks.

Were the rumors about her wrong? Had she been a seductress or had her previous employer forced himself on her? But then that would not explain the tales of her becoming her former student's mistress.

Her willingness to linger in the hall with him only made him want her more. Grimes would have ducked her head and been on her way—of course her avoidance of him might have been as much about hiding her drinking. Velvet wouldn't be hiding from him; he wouldn't allow it. He would know every move she made. He'd know if she catted around; not that she had a lot of likely prospects in the household, beyond him.

Her chest rose and fell in a rapid tempo. Too rapid. He took another step closer.

Her breath hitched but she didn't step back.

Her green eyes were like the sea, full of secrets and surprises. He couldn't tear his gaze away. Breathing deeply, he inhaled her soft feminine scent, a scent he remembered from carrying her up the stairs. Another step and their bodies would brush. His heart pounded and the air sizzled.

Only the thinnest thread of sanity kept him in check, but from his second invitation to his room before breakfast she had to know he wanted her in the way a man wants a beautiful woman.

He touched her satiny cheek.

Her breathing stopped, and like a deer caught in that moment before it bounded away, she tensed. The only way to postpone the inevitable flight was with slow easy movements.

Her lashes fluttered as if she were uncertain what to do. He trailed his finger down her pale smooth cheek to the corner of her mouth and then slowly traced along the curve of her lower lip.

Her breath came out in a rush, feathering over his palm in warm damp heat.

"Velvet," he whispered.

Her head snapped to the side, she clamped her lips together and her eyes shut. Her hand came up between them, stopping just short of pushing him away.

"Don't. Please. I'm not . . . not what you think I am," she whispered.

"Nor am I," he answered. He didn't force women dependant on him for their livelihood to his bed. His heart wasn't that black . . . yet. He backed away. "I'll have the craftsman who fixes your door install locks."

She raised a shaking hand to her mouth.

He swiveled, heading toward the bath that had probably grown tepid with his delays. "Use them."

Chapter 6

Velvet trembled as Mr. Pendar walked away, his caged energy holding her trapped. If only she didn't have to travel the length of the second floor, past his bedroom, to reach the narrow staircase to the nursery floor.

Attuned to every sound, she jumped when the bathroom door clicked shut. A double splash followed. Not twenty feet from her, he was naked, stepping into the bathtub. And she was trying to imagine what he looked like without clothes. Oh God, what was wrong with her?

She turned and darted toward the narrow stairs. By the time she reached the top, her lungs were straining and her vision was spotty and narrow.

Like an imbecile, she'd stood there waiting for his kiss. The way he'd traced her lower lip with his finger seemed far more intimate. Her heart thundered and her legs shook.

Gulping in air, she reached for her door. She still had to face closing the windows, although the prospect of shutting them seemed less frightening than waiting for Mr. Pendar to kiss her, drag her into his room and toss her onto the bed.

Would anyone come to save her if she screamed this time?

Even if she was saved from ravishment, there was no place left for her to go if she was turned out. Worse than that, for a second she'd just want to give in to the inevitable and learn the mysteries of the joining of the flesh.

"Did you see him? Has he gone down yet?" asked a housemaid peering out of a room down the corridor.

Velvet whirled. "I believe he's bathing."

The young woman rolled her eyes. "What is taking him so long today? He's usually downstairs by now."

Velvet closed her eyes and leaned against her door frame. She'd delayed Lucian, not once, but twice this morning. And delayed her breakfast in turn. Now, she didn't even know if she could eat in his presence. The gnawing in her gut told her she had to.

Meg opened the door to Iris's room.

Velvet shuddered.

"Are you cold?" Meg asked. "I thought it would be a good idea to air out your room on such a lovely day. I don't know the last time it was seen to." She cast a dark look over her shoulder at Nellie, who had emerged from Iris's room.

"I'm out of coal," said Velvet resignedly. Without a fire to burn off the chill, her room would be miserable. There was no way she could lug a bucket of coal up the stairs from the cellar.

She was weaker than she'd ever been in her life. The stairs were practically defeating her. Never would she have thought a few flights would wind her so. It had taken her nearly a quarter hour to get a half-full pail of water up one flight to scrub the schoolroom this morning. The days she could skip up all 122 steps of the bell tower in her father's church seemed eons ago.

The stiff breeze coming in the window cooled her flushed skin.

"I'll take care of it, ma'am." Meg bobbed a curtsy.

Iris followed Nellie out of her room. "I'm ready."

Velvet turned and found the girl decked out in a frothy yellow dress covered by a ruffled pinafore and her golden hair tamed into long sausage curls. A large yellow ribbon held her hair back from her face. Other than her sulky expression, she looked like an angel. "You look lovely, Iris."

"I didn't want you looking prettier than me."

Velvet sighed. She crouched, putting herself on the eye level of the child. "No one will think you pretty if you frown at them. What would you do if your face froze like that?"

Iris twisted left and right. "I want Eve back."

"Have you picked out four other dolls to give away at church this Sunday?" Velvet stood.

"Where did you hide her?"

Velvet shook her head. "You may have her back when you pick out four dolls to give away."

"I'll find her," said Iris, then darted toward the stairs.

"Iris!" Velvet caught her charge before she could run past. "Ladies walk indoors." Closing her eyes, she realized how hypocritical she sounded. "You and I will walk down to the breakfast room."

She caught Iris's arm in a tight grip and headed downstairs. *Please just don't let me run into him again.*

Iris gave up on trying to make Miss Campbell let her go. Her grip had loosened, but every time she started to move away, Miss Campbell tightened her hold again.

"Now where do we go?" asked Miss Campbell.

"You don't know?"

"I'm not certain," said Miss Campbell, looking

around. "I only saw briefly in the gloom yesterday. You know where all the rooms are, don't you?"

Miss Campbell's breathy voice made Iris want to be kind to her. Perhaps she was sick, as her papa thought. "I've lived here my whole life."

"If we have a little time after breakfast, you might show me around a bit."

"All right," answered Iris. Anything was better than the classroom. Perhaps she could make the tour stretch out for days. And she could look for Eve. For not knowing the house, Miss Campbell had hidden the dolls well.

"My favorite room was always my father's office," said Miss Campbell.

"I'm not allowed in my papa's study." She'd been lucky he hadn't yelled at her when she came in to tell him about Miss Campbell lying in the rain.

Miss Campbell looked down on her. "Yes, well it doesn't do to disturb a man at his work. But sometimes my father would let me join him, if I sat very quietly. His office always smelled of books."

Clenching her jaw, Iris jerked toward the breakfast room. She hated books. On no account would she show Miss Campbell there was a room full of books.

Miss Campbell wrinkled her forehead but she continued on, "Do you have a favorite room?"

"My mama's sitting room," blurted Iris before she could stop herself. She hadn't been allowed in there either, at least not while her mama was alive. But no one cared now. She could spend hours in there, and rarely was she missed. It was her special secret place now.

"Sorry to keep you waiting," said Papa just as they reached the door.

Miss Campbell's hand tightened.

"Ow!" Iris twisted away. Not that Miss Campbell's grip really hurt, but she wanted to break free. She rubbed her arm and watched Papa to see if he realized the new governess was mean. Papa didn't like governesses being mean to her, and maybe she could persuade him to dismiss Miss Campbell.

Miss Campbell's mouth flattened, and Papa opened the door. He reached out to put his hand on her back to guide her through.

Most of the staff were scared of him. Miss Campbell didn't look to be different to Iris, if the sudden forward pressure on her shoulders was any indication.

Iris rubbed her arm harder. Papa didn't look at her. He only watched Miss Campbell glide to the table. His hair dripped on his collar, which wasn't quite straight. Mr. Evans never let Papa go anywhere with a crooked collar. Everything had gone cockeyed.

He pulled out her chair, and Miss Campbell murmured "Thank you" as she sat. "Come sit, Iris."

At least her governess hadn't forgotten she was there. Papa rang the bell for the food as she slid into her chair.

"Shall we pray?" asked Miss Campbell.

Iris waited for her father to glare at Miss Campbell until she realized he didn't like God, but instead he bowed his head and asked for God's blessing on the food they were about to receive.

"Miss Campbell took Eve away," said Iris.

Without even lifting his eyes from her governess, he answered, "I know."

"I want her back."

"We all want things we can't have," said Papa.

His voice sounded strange, low and almost growly, and he kept watching Miss Campbell.

"Then you know what you must do," said Miss

Campbell. "Now put you napkin in your lap, please."

Iris considered throwing the napkin on the floor, but her papa would just send her away without letting her eat.

Mrs. Bigsby entered with a platter of buttered eggs and kippers and the newspaper tucked under her arm.

Instead of flapping out the paper, Papa tucked it beside his plate. Usually he grunted a good morning to her and then ignored her. Perhaps he would actually talk during breakfast.

"Mrs. Bigsby, if Miss Campbell comes down before me, please see she is served."

"But—" said Mrs. Bigsby.

"There is no reason for her to have to wait until I have returned from my swim."

Miss Campbell pressed her lips together as if she didn't like the notice. She didn't know what it was like waiting and waiting for Papa to come down.

Mrs. Bigsby sharply clicked Iris's plate with the serving spoon. Nellie came in with rolls, butter and jam, and the teapot. She poured all around but no one said anything.

"Grimes didn't eat breakfast," supplied Iris. Grimes didn't like to rise too early either. Not that Iris wanted to defend Miss Campbell, but there were some mornings she just wanted to eat. If Miss Campbell could get food earlier, perhaps she could too.

"The schoolroom is out of ink, and there is little paper. I would have written a list of needed purchases, but I needed ink or a pencil." Miss Campbell pushed her eggs around on her plate.

Ugh! She didn't even want to think about lessons.

Papa hadn't even lifted his fork. He just looked at Miss Campbell as if he'd rather spend all morning reading her instead of his newspaper. The corner of his mouth curled up. "I'll have writing supplies sent up to you."

Her chest hurt. He wouldn't talk to her. Iris scowled. He didn't pay her any mind. He never did. He certainly never smiled at her.

Now, he had Miss Campbell to smile at.

After breakfast, Velvet allowed Iris to pick the book she wanted to read aloud. She needed to make an assessment of her charge's reading level. The girl's voice was clear as she spoke. Her mistakes had been small, skipping an adjective or changing a definite article to an indefinite one, but something about her reading was off kilter.

Sitting on the hard-backed chair next to the girl, Velvet watched the words as Iris turned the page, her narrative no longer matching the print. Iris continued on, blithely unaware.

"Stop." Velvet reached for the upper left corner and turned back a page. Two pages had stuck together.

Iris hunched forward as if waiting for a blow.

Velvet slid off the chair and knelt in front of the girl, taking her hands. Iris's big blue eyes were swimming.

"Iris, do you know how to read?" Velvet asked carefully.

Iris jerked her hands away and pitched the book. "I'm stupid."

How had the girl made it to nine without learning to read? Velvet was shocked, but she was more concerned about Iris's aspersions about her intelligence.

The girl twisted away and held the back of the chair. Velvet rubbed between Iris's narrow shoulder blades. "Sweetheart, a stupid girl cannot memorize an entire book and recite it back."

Iris snorted.

"A stupid girl wouldn't ask what the word 'relish' meant, she wouldn't care."

"Miss Grimes said I was stupid."

"And did all those bottles in the desk belong to Miss Grimes?"

Iris nodded.

"I wouldn't value the opinion of one who is deep in their cups. In fact, I should quite likely think it in error. Perhaps your former governess was lazy and didn't want to teach you." Velvet calculated in her head. Even so, Iris should have been learning to read long before her last governess entered the picture.

With a scrunched face, Iris swiveled, looking at her.

"It doesn't matter where you are in your lessons, it only matters that we begin with what you know. Do you know how to write your letters?"

Iris turned her head away.

How bad was this? Velvet's stomach churned. "How about the alphabet? Can you say the alphabet?"

"Of course," said Iris with scorn.

"Well, if you would, please say the alphabet." While Velvet kept half an ear tuned for signs that Iris didn't recognize each individual letter, she mulled over how she could instill confidence in the girl. A few reassurances would likely not overcome her doubts.

"Very good," Velvet said as Iris landed on Z.

Iris rolled her eyes.

"We will start with recitation, then," said Velvet.

Iris's nose wrinkled. "What's that?"

"I will teach you a poem, and you will say it out loud."

"I won't have to read it?" Her voice betrayed doubt.

"No. The whole point of reciting is to show that you

have memorized it and are not reading. Perhaps you can recite for your papa when you learn it."

"Really?" asked Iris. "He'll listen?"

Uneasiness crept up her spine. Although she wasn't at all sure what she could guarantee, Velvet said, "Of course he will."

"I'll listen to what?" said Mr. Pendar from the doorway.

Iris sprang off the chair. Velvet swung around and tried to still the churn of her stomach. After going so long without eating, it had rebelled against breakfast. She'd grown full after just a few bites. Now her breakfast was like nails churning in her gut.

Lucian stood with a bottle of ink and a sheaf of papers in his hands.

"I don't have to read at all. I'm going to recite poetry," exclaimed Iris. She ran to him.

Wincing, Velvet picked up the book from the floor. That wasn't exactly what she meant.

His expression turned dark.

Velvet barely resisted rolling her eyes. Surely he didn't think she wouldn't teach Iris to read. She didn't know which one of them was more annoying. Except she felt on much firmer ground dealing with a truculent child than an employer who made shivers run down her spine.

"Iris, I'm sure your father will appreciate recitations when you can actually do them. Now, please return to your chair and remember young ladies walk while inside."

Lucian set the writing supplies on her desk. "Is everything going all right?"

Sure. She had a nine-year-old who threw books and didn't appear to know how to write her letters. She had an employer who made her jump when he was around. And she had treacherous cliffs for a view. Everything was lovely. Velvet considered her answer. "As well as can be expected."

Why had he brought supplies himself and not sent a servant with them?

"Bigsby and a groomsman will be up later to move an armoire into your room."

Velvet clasped her hands in front of her. "All right."

"All right, then." Lucian shifted the bottle of ink. His fingers were long and elegant. Never before had she gone breathless at the sight of a man's hands.

"I've asked Mrs. Bigsby to locate the spirit lamp that used to be in the anteroom off the nursery. I don't know why it isn't there any longer."

Was this his attempt to show that she wasn't getting *special* treatment? Just that the governesses had been neglected in recent years.

He straightened the papers.

"I'll have a list of supplies I need for the schoolroom to you by this afternoon." Velvet said.

He nodded.

Iris made a moue of disappointment.

Velvet stepped forward, put her hand on Iris's shoulder and guided her back to her chair. Iris would be difficult enough without allowing her to growing petulant. "We should get back to our lessons."

Biting her lip, Velvet hoped he hadn't taken the dismissal personally. But the schoolroom should be free of whatever was between Mr. Pendar and her.

"By all means. I have work to do."

Velvet woke with a jerk in the dark of the night. Before she opened her eyes, she knew someone was in her room. Her heart jumped. Dread and anticipation warred within her.

The carpenter was supposed to come tomorrow, but she had only wedged a chair under the passage door. She'd been unwilling to lock her door against Iris. Even though the child seemed surprised that she wanted to oversee her bedtime rituals, Velvet didn't think she was old enough to be isolated from all adults overnight.

Had Lucian come through his daughter's room to hers?

"Miss Campbell?" the girl said in a shaky high-pitched voice.

Velvet's breath came out in a relieved whoosh. "Yes, Iris."

"I can't sleep without Eve."

Velvet pushed to sit up. Her iron bedstead squeaked in protest. It must be after midnight.

"You know what you must do to get Eve returned to you," Velvet said firmly.

"I did. I picked out four dolls to give away. They're on the desk. I need Eve." Iris's words ended on a distressed wail.

Velvet tried to push sleep from her eyes. "It's very late. I'll fetch Eve in the morning."

"No! I need her now." Iris's demand was accompanied by a sob. The moonlight glistened on her tear-streaked cheeks. Her lower lip shook. "I did what you said. I did! I nee-ed Eve."

Velvet pulled the child against her. "All right, all right. Hush now."

They'd made good progress today. Iris was like a child starved for attention, and she had a quick mind. She memorized two poems, which she recited to her father's pretended appreciation after dinner. But better than that, Velvet began reading aloud a novel in the afternoon with Iris curled against her on the sofa. If she could open the girl to the world of books, perhaps she could break her resistance to leaning to read and write.

She didn't want to risk a setback, but the doll was in Lucian's room.

Holding the girl's narrow little body against hers, Velvet rubbed her back. Iris's silent sobs nearly broke her heart.

Why had this child learned to stifle the sounds of her crying? It wasn't normal, although Velvet remembered a time when she'd hid her own anguish and shame from her father in the same way.

She couldn't get out of retrieving the doll. Searching her mind for who could go into Mr. Pendar's room, she was at a loss. She didn't even know where the Bigsbys or Mr. Evans slept. Almost hoping against hope that she could refuse because Iris hadn't picked out dolls to give away, Velvet slid back the covers. "Let's see what you've done."

Iris tugged her into the schoolroom. With the moonlight streaming through the windows, four dolls lay out like human sacrifices on the desk. One had chipped off fingers and another had matted hair. But Velvet hadn't put any limitations on the dolls to be chosen.

"Please, I need Eve," said Iris.

Velvet wasn't getting out of this. She had to retrieve the doll. She sighed. "All right, I'll go get her."

Iris pushed her. "Go!"

"I need to dress first," said Velvet.

"No," wailed Iris, fresh tears coursing down her cheeks.

Velvet knelt down and wiped tears from Iris's face. "Come now, I can't go running through the house in my nightgown."

Iris sniffed, but the tears continued tracking down her cheeks.

"Now do you want to crawl back in bed while I fetch Eve?"

Iris shook her head in the negative. Like a lost soul, she followed Velvet back into her room.

Opening the freshly arrived wardrobe, Velvet pulled out the dress she'd worn earlier. Her corset lay on the top shelf, but Iris's meltdown hardly welcomed the delay to fully dress. Instead, Velvet pulled the dress over her nightgown. With her weight loss, she didn't need the corset to fit in the gown.

Her fingers shook as she closed the buttons. "Do you want to come with me?"

Iris shook her head.

Velvet bit her lip. Even if Iris knew where the Bigsbys slept, finding their rooms in the dark house might be impossible, but . . . "Do you know where Mr. Evans sleeps?"

"No!" wailed Iris.

"All right. I'll be back as soon as I can."

Velvet tried not to think further than the next step as she descended the stairs. Maybe Mr. Pendar wouldn't wake. Maybe the moon or a lit fire would provide enough illumination for her to find Iris's doll. Maybe she wouldn't have to go into his room.

Velvet's heart tripped and it seemed her breathing alone was bound to wake the entire household. Each creak of a floorboard nearly had her jumping out of her skin. The hair on the back of her neck had to be standing on end.

Whatever had possessed her to hide the dolls in Lucian's room? It had to have been one of those moments of sheer lunacy masquerading as genius.

At his door, she held her breath, listening. Perhaps she hoped to hear a reassuring snore. Silence echoed loudly.

She tapped on the door.

Her knees threatened to give out on her.

"Mr. Pendar," she whispered, her mouth close to the door.

He would misunderstand her reason for knocking on his door in the middle of the night. She could back away fast if he opened the door.

Only silence greeted her.

She tapped again and managed to squeak out, "Mr. Pendar."

In an agony of indecision, she waited for the door to open. It didn't.

Perhaps he was a heavy sleeper. Perhaps she could sneak inside and retrieve Eve. Perhaps she would come out of this unscathed. Taking a deep breath, she reached for knob and ever so slowly turned it.

The door jerked open and pulled her with it.

"If you're going to come to my bedroom, I'd think you could at least call me Lucian."

Chapter 7

Lucian wasn't about to question Velvet arriving in his room. His sleep had been fitful, and her image intruded on his rest. He needed her, and then she was at his door, like an answer to prayers he wouldn't have dared to pray.

He tugged her to the side and clicked his door shut. He caught her face in his hands.

"I'm here to—"

He cut her words off with a kiss. Her lips were as soft as he expected, her mouth warm and sweet. Her muffled response amused him.

Her cool hand landed against his bare chest. His skin jumped and a rush of sensation scorched straight to his groin. Could she feel the way his heart pounded? Deepening the kiss, he pushed closer.

Heat surged in him, lengthening and raising his manhood with each heartbeat. Her skin was velvety soft, and he splayed his fingers along her neck. He wanted to touch every inch of her, her breasts, her derriere, and explore her hidden cleft. Desire plowed through him.

Yet, other than her hand now fisted in his dressing gown lapel, her response had been nonexistent.

"Kiss me back," he growled against her mouth.

They thumped against the wall and he invaded her mouth. Her tentative response, the tip of her tongue touching his, brought a new surge of want coursing through him.

The realization that he was rushing her intruded on his driving need to have her. She didn't know that he wouldn't be selfish. He'd give as good as he got. The years of abstinence just had built his need to a tidal wave of lustful ache.

He gentled his kiss, pulling back to suck on her lower lip. Trailing kisses to her neck, he slid his hand down the curve of her throat, over her shoulder and down her spine. Cupping her bottom, he pulled her hips against his. How well her body fit with his.

"I—" she began.

"Don't worry, I'll pleasure you," he coaxed.

"Oh!"

She sounded so surprised by the idea that he smiled against her neck. Was the idea so novel to her?

"I . . . I . . . I—"

He found her mouth again, ending her stuttering.

A shudder rippled through her.

He pushed harder against her and swallowed her gasp of surprise. He wanted her here, against the wall. Now.

His mind raced ahead. His open dressing gown was no barrier, but Velvet wore a dress, and she wasn't indicating she was ready. Her response was uncertain, hesitant, as if she was trying to soothe him.

Why was she wearing a dress?

He slid his hand to her side, up over her ribs. A dress, but no corset. His doubts slid away.

He cupped her breast. Her willowy form was not generous, but to have her softness in his hand was a treat. Brushing his thumb across her nipple, he swallowed her whimper as the beading tip betrayed her body's response.

Passion clouded his mind and made him only aware of her. Her softness, her scent, swirled and cast a spell on him. He couldn't remember wanting a woman as much as he wanted her. Her mouth matched him movement for movement. He needed to thrust inside her and bury his manhood to the hilt.

Her every whimper echoed in his head. He tried to ease up and allow her passion to rise, but it was no good. His breath roared like a steam engine, his skin tingled, and his blood thrummed through him and engorged him. He needed her now.

Bunching her skirts, he pulled the material up while pushing his knee between her legs.

She pushed against his chest. With a groan of impatience he ended the kiss.

"Iris," she gasped.

A cold wash eased his urgency. His head snapped toward the door to be sure it was still shut and Iris wasn't peeking through a crack. But the door was latched.

"What about Iris?" he growled.

Her face pinched, Velvet struggled to push down her skirts. His world tilted.

"Velvet?" Uncertainty cut through the haze of passion.

"I came to get Eve. Iris can't sleep without her." Velvet's chin dipped and she averted her head. "I'm sorry. I didn't intend to . . ." Her hand wavered and her voice shook.

Her chest rose and fell, brushing against his at the peak of inhalation.

"I wanted to wait until morning, but Iris is nearly hysterical, and I told her she could have Eve back when—

Oh God." Her mouth twisted and she covered it with her shaking hand. "I have to get back to her. With Eve."

He pivoted, strode across the room and grabbed the doll. It was as if Lilith managed to intrude. Although to be fair, Lilith had nothing to do with the doll. Lilith had everything to do with Iris.

Holding out Eve, he returned to Velvet. She averted her head and held up her hand like a blinder.

He pushed the doll into her chest and stepped back to belt his dressing gown closed.

Velvet seemed fragile. In the pale orange glow of the coals, her face was blanched of all color. Her knees buckled. He caught her elbow, providing support. Her trembles ran up his arm. Had he been too rough? Was she feeling ill?

He cursed under his breath. She had responded, he'd felt her growing ardor. She'd returned his kisses, damn it.

Velvet curled the doll to her chest.

She didn't make a move toward the door.

He wanted to pull her into his arms and cradle her, but he doubted he could stifle his passion long enough to just comfort her. That he even wanted to was shocking.

Clicking the door open, he guided her toward the opening. He couldn't resist leaning in and pressing his lips to her neck. "Come back."

She took a quick step away. "Is that . . ." She swiveled to face him, her eyes wide. She swallowed hard and whispered, "Is that an order?"

Had she remembered she should be afraid of him? "I hired you to be Iris's governess, not my mistress."

Her lips tightened. "Will you dismiss me?"

Folding his arms across his chest, he leaned against the doorjamb. "Not for a refusal to lay with me."

She looked right and then left, then down, as if she

could find no good place to look. Scowling, he watched her discomfort. Had she thought she had no choice?

"Velvet."

Her gaze snapped to his.

"Was I wrong to think you wanted me too?" he asked.

She took a tiny step back, but color crept up her neck and stained her face. She took another step back. "I can't . . . I don't . . ." She rolled her eyes as if impatient with her inability to answer. Continuing backward in tiny increments, her face twisted. She bumped into the far wall. Her mouth rounded and her eyes widened. "It would be wrong."

The doll was pulled tight to her chest, and if he weren't thrumming with tension, he'd have been amused. Velvet played the innocent much better than his wife ever had, but then maybe she'd had more practice.

For a long moment they stared at each other. The dark didn't hide her heaving breaths.

"You better go, before I decide your hesitation is only your unwillingness to say what you want out loud."

Her jaw dropped. "I don't . . ."

He arched an eyebrow.

"Oh!"

He pushed away from the doorjamb.

Velvet scurried away. He suspected she'd had too long to think. She wouldn't be coming back, and all the male urges he'd suppressed for years were rising like a massive volcano.

He paced his room. The throbbing urge wouldn't go away. Every inch of control he possessed was destroyed by the feel of her lips, her tongue, her taste. Even the way she looked him in the eye without her focus straying to his scars got under his skin. He couldn't rid his mind of the feel of her breast against his palm. He needed release. He needed a woman under him.

He needed Velvet.

Velvet ran up the stairs as if the hounds of hell nipped at her heels. There was no *if* about it, she chided herself firmly. She'd wanted Lucian's kisses. Oh God, she had wanted to feel like a woman. And he'd made her feel things she'd never felt before. Even now her body thrummed with an energy she didn't understand. She'd wanted . . . more.

And he knew.

She tried to calm down before entering her room, but after a couple of shaky breaths, she worried she'd taken too long already.

Iris wasn't in the bedroom.

If she found her asleep in her bed, she might be tempted to throttle the child.

The dolls were still on the desk in the schoolroom. Velvet opened the door to Iris's bedroom.

Her nightgown tucked under her toes, Iris sat on the floor in front of the fireplace. Her eyes were big and glassy as she stared at the grate.

Velvet's exasperation left her in a whoosh. She was the one at fault here, not a child who had little human comfort in her world.

"I thought you'd forgotten about me." Iris sniffed.

"Of course I didn't forget about you." Velvet's voice sounded thin and reedy instead of reassuring. But the words were almost a lie. When Lucian said he'd pleasure her, she'd forgotten everything, even her mission to retrieve Eve. "It just took me longer than I expected."

Remembering the raspy burr of his voice made her flush all over. Never had any man considered her pleasure. They hadn't considered her comfort, her will, or her religion.

She held out Eve. "Are you ready to go back to bed?"

"I shouldn't need a doll to sleep, should I?" Iris wrapped Eve under her arm.

"It isn't unusual for a child your age," Velvet said evenly.

"I'm afraid if I don't sleep with her, my mama won't think I love her." Iris untangled the nightgown from her toes and stood.

"Would you like me to stay with you until you fall asleep?"

Iris shrugged.

Velvet didn't want to be alone. Not now. Not while Lucian's fingers were still imprinted on her bottom, on her breast. Her skin was alive, as if he were still touching her. He'd awoken something dark and hungry in her, a part of herself she'd managed to ignore for all of her thirty-two years.

She guided Iris to her bed and helped the girl settle under the covers.

"Why are you all breathless?" asked Iris.

Velvet winced. "I hurried up the stairs."

"Did you see my mama?"

Velvet frowned, uncertain how to answer. Iris knew her mother was dead. Was she confused by sleep?

"Mostly she stays on the cliffs." Iris plopped her elbows over the covers.

"Sweetheart, your mama has passed away."

"I know. It's her ghost." Iris yawned. "But sometimes she comes to me in my sleep and says she wants me to come with her."

"What?" whispered Velvet. Alarm slithered down her spine. Not that she believed in ghosts, but what had Iris been taught?

"She wants me to fall off the cliff too, so I can go to heaven with her." Iris flipped to her side, tucking her doll under her chin.

Velvet sat on Iris's bed and stroked the girl's curls. "No, she doesn't want you to go to live in heaven with her. Not until after you've lived a long, long life. She would want you to grow up, get married, have children and be happy. That's what all women want for their daughters."

Iris hummed a protest.

Chilled, Velvet watched as the child began to drop off to sleep. The dark almost seemed to laugh. Shuddering, Velvet pushed back the irrational fears. There wasn't a ghost.

Iris wrinkled her nose and closed her eyes. She slurred, "She wants . . . me . . . to die . . . now."

Lucian tapped a pen against his blotter. Velvet was avoiding him. She'd eaten breakfast the last two mornings before he came in from his swim, and she used Iris as a buffer between them at dinner and in the drawing room after dinner. He pushed against his forehead. He almost believed he'd dreamed Velvet's presence the night before last, except Eve was missing from his room.

If Velvet hid from him, how could he persuade her to come to his room again?

Restless, he pushed back from the desk and paced across the floor. Short of ordering her to submit, there was only one way he could guarantee her return to his bedroom, and it was ludicrous.

He wasn't about to marry another whore. Especially not one pregnant with another man's child. No, he'd convince her to come to him.

But to effect a seduction, he needed to get her to spend time with him.

Before he knew he'd formed the thought, he was climbing the stairs.

Long before he reached the schoolroom he heard Iris's childish voice: "Four times five is twenty. Four times six is twenty-four. Four times seven is . . . is . . ."

"Twenty-eight," said Miss Campbell in her dulcet voice. "Remember if you do not know the next answer, you can count four more on your fingers."

The softness of her tone wrapped around him and called to him.

Iris continued on with a stumbling recitation of her multiplication tables. Velvet encouraged and praised Iris's less than stellar efforts. He didn't remember his own tutor being so tolerant.

He moved to the doorway of the schoolroom. The sunlight slanting in the windows caught the copper strands in Velvet's hair. She leaned toward Iris, her graceful neck bent forward. That was a neck meant for kissing. His heart thudded.

"Papa!" Iris looked around her governess.

God, how had he nearly forgotten the child was in the room? He couldn't very well seduce her governess in front of her. That he even wanted to shamed him.

Velvet swiveled around in her chair, her face tightened.

He took a step toward her as if he would comfort her, but a cold realization stopped him. He was the reason for her distress.

Iris skipped toward him. "I am learning timeses."

"So I hear." He put his hand on Iris's golden curls but looked at Velvet.

Velvet lowered her chin and her gaze, breaking the connection between them.

"I understand Mrs. Bigsby has been unable to purchase all the items on your list." His words cut through the growing tension.

"What we have is sufficient, thank you." Velvet stood up and walked stiffly toward the large desk. Away from him.

The desk, the globe, and the chairs had all been moved toward the interior wall. The repaired door of her room was closed, and the keyhole for the new lock reminded him that she was resistant in spite of her responsiveness. He would have to use more finesse if he hoped to break her resolve.

"I will schedule a trip to Plymouth. There are more shops there," he said. More than paints could be purchased in Plymouth shops. Perhaps a new hat for Velvet. What woman didn't like a new hat?

"That isn't necessary," said Velvet.

"It is only a day's journey, and I have business there. Be ready to travel on Monday."

Velvet jerked. She planted her hand on the desk's broad surface. "I'm sure you don't need me to go."

Iris squirmed against his side.

"Iris would—"

"Miss too many lessons." Velvet's eyes flashed.

"—enjoy an outing," he persisted.

"I can go?" Iris bounced against his leg.

Including Iris hadn't been his original plan, but he couldn't take her governess on a trip without it looking odd. Having the child along as chaperone should make Velvet feel safe. Hell, it would make her safe. He couldn't seduce her with Iris hanging on his sleeve.

"Might I have a word with you, sir?" asked Velvet.

"Certainly, Miss Campbell." He pivoted and stalked toward the door. "I'll be in my office."

Iris wanted to accompany him to Plymouth, and Velvet didn't. He could use the child's enthusiasm to force Velvet to take the trip, but it would hardly put her in a charitable frame of mind toward him. And using Iris to further his agenda was dastardly.

As he descended to the ground floor, his hand fisted at his side. Velvet wasn't following him.

Why was she reluctant to sleep with him? If she'd been mistress to a fat old Member of Parliament, the undersecretary, and a former student, why would she shy away from gracing his bed?

He fingered the scars on his cheek. Most of the time he ignored the talon marks Lilith left on his face. Marks he'd received because he tried to restrain his wife from leaving the house. But he was all too aware of the way people, women, looked at those marks—as if he were a man of violence who took it out on the fairer sex. They weren't entirely wrong. Lilith had pushed him to violence. He hated that she'd forced him to acknowledge the primitive side of his being.

And now his desire for Velvet was making him aware of how weak his will was. As much as he filled his hours on managing and expanding the shipping business his wealth sprung from, a void still gaped within him. He was brought to his knees by primordial urges to conquer Velvet and possess her body and soul, as if he could suck her inherent goodness into his blackened heart. He wanted the challenge to his fought-for sanity to go away. Yet, he stared at his office door, willing her to walk through.

* * *

"Meg, would you come in here, please?" Velvet knew the maid was in Iris's room. She'd heard her shoveling out the fireplace.

Velvet took a piece of chalk and wrote the times tables up to five on the blackboard.

Iris's bedroom door opened. "Is he gone?" asked Meg.

"He's gone," confirmed Velvet. "But I need to go downstairs to speak with him. Would you be so kind as to listen to Iris say her tables through fives?"

Iris scowled. "I don't want lessons. I would *relish* going to Plymouth."

Velvet sucked in a deep breath but continued scrawling the tables on the blackboard. Her hand shook and a cold dread crept down her spine.

"He's taking you both to Plymouth?" Meg's eyes grew large and she turned back and forth between them.

"Not if I can help it."

Velvet couldn't imagine traveling for hours in a carriage with Mr. Pendar, and then there would have to be at least one overnight stay in an inn. How could she possibly resist a determined seduction?

"You may supply Iris with the answer if she doesn't remember." She set down the chalk and brushed her hands. She resisted the urge to check and make sure her severely pinned back hair was neat.

Vanity is a sin, her father's stentorian pulpit tones echoed in her head.

"You just want to be alone with Papa." Iris's lower lip jutted out.

"There there, love," Meg said, heading toward Iris.

"Stop!" said Velvet.

Both Meg and Iris jerked toward her. Her nervousness had made her speak too loudly. "I should much prefer to spend my time with you, Iris," Velvet went on, tempering her voice. "Not your father."

Lying is a sin, echoed in her brain. But at least she knew her role with Iris. When Lucian was around, Velvet didn't even know herself. Her errant mind kept returning to the feel of his mouth on hers, the feel of his hand against her breast, his whispered promise of *her* pleasure.

Tingles crept down Velvet's spine. More than anything, that promise made her breath catch.

Iris wrinkled her nose and tilted her head.

"This is lesson time, not time for indulgences. Iris, you will recite your tables for Meg, please. I shouldn't be long."

"I want to go to Plymouth with Papa," Iris wailed. Her blue eyes filled with ready tears.

Meg cast an uncertain glance in Velvet's direction. "He's never offered to take her anywhere before."

Was he taking a new interest in his daughter or planning her governess's seduction? "Perhaps a trip would be in order, when you have memorized all your times tables and can write the alphabet," Velvet relented.

Iris managed to look hurt. As if Velvet had set the benchmark impossibly high.

Velvet sighed. "I will return as soon as I'm able, and I expect to hear you working."

She turned and steeled herself.

Putting herself in the way of Lucian was probably a mistake. Persuading him to change his mind might prove impossible. Pining for what she couldn't have was sinful.

Velvet was out of breath before she made it to the ground floor. She tried to chase the feel of Lucian from her mind, but her heart thumped and her palms grew moist in spite of her efforts. She couldn't avoid him forever.

Alone in his office, would he attempt to touch her? Kiss her again? Her heart fluttered. Pausing, she tried to pull her emotions back. She couldn't let him kiss her again. He posed far more danger to her virtue than any man before him. With the other men who attempted her downfall, she felt absolutely no inclination to do anything other than fight off their attacks.

With Lucian, her feelings were more complex.

She entered the library and stopped dead. Running from the floor to the fifteen foot ceilings were mahogany shelves. Leather tomes and more recent cloth and mill-board bound books filled the shelves. The smell took her back to her father's study and simpler times in her life. Times when she always thought she'd have her brother, but to her eternal shame it was her fault she had no one.

In her haphazard tours of the house, Iris hadn't shown her this room. A fire crackled behind the grate, and brown leather chairs flanked the fireplace in a way that would allow the firelight to fall on the page of a book.

She took a step forward onto the Oriental carpet. She touched a stack of books on the table near her. A novel by Dickens was on top. She slid it to the side. A slim volume with the name Alfred Lord Tennyson appeared below. It was like opening a clam and finding a string of perfect pearls inside. Never would she have expected this up-to-date cozy library in this cold house.

"Miss Campbell."

Velvet jumped, startled out of her awestruck revelry. *David Copperfield* clunked open on the table.

Lucian stood framed in a doorway to her left.

"You read these?" she blurted.

He folded his arms. "I don't bring them from London to cast into the fire."

Her awestruck question perhaps deserved his derision. "Iris does not inherit her aversion to books from you, then?"

He snorted. "She gets nothing from me." He pushed away from the door frame. "You wished to protest a trip to Plymouth?"

Velvet's gaze shot to him. He seemed resigned, pensive even. And he had gone straight to the point.

"Iris is so far behind in her studies. You do know she does not read at all, don't you?" Velvet paced away from the table.

"I've heard she is difficult and perhaps a half-wit." Lucian's dark gaze followed her.

How could he speak of his daughter so disparagingly?

"I find her very bright."

He continued to watch her. How much of the trip was about getting supplies? Had she misread his intentions?

She rolled her shoulders, wanting to shake off the weight of his gaze. She focused on the shelves on the far side of the room. The volumes of Gibbon's *The Rise and Fall of the Roman Empire* drew her. "She is bright, but terrified of instruction. I have barely begun to establish that schooltime is to be spent in learning. I need time to get her on the right path."

"Is that really why you don't wish to go to Plymouth?" he asked casually. Too casually.

His voice was a low burr. A shudder traveled under her skin. He knew why she was afraid to be alone with him.

"I don't believe it would be a good idea."

He tilted his head and looked at her askance.

Velvet fought to be forthright and brave, but her world

had changed. Barely eating, barely existing, and every position evaporating before she could begin work had made her uncertain. She'd had to reevaluate everything in her life, and come up wanting. Perhaps virtue was not its own reward. She always tried so hard to live right and make amends for not taking better care of her brother, but it never seemed to be enough atonement. She hadn't expected to be a spinster at her age. She'd expected marriage and children of her own. She'd expected to be a social equal to a man like him, not a servant.

"I don't think Iris should have her routine disrupted so soon." She ran her finger along the thick spines. Iris would likely never progress to needing to study this much history.

"Miss Campbell, come sit down in my office so I don't have to shout across the library."

"I should prefer to stand." If she stood, she had a better chance of fleeing or evading his grasp. She kept him in her peripheral vision. To look directly at him made her heart hurt, and she couldn't fathom why. She barely knew him.

"You have put me in an untenable position with my charge," she said softly. "Going to Plymouth should be reward for her success, not an interruption to her studies. Now if we do not go, she will be angry, and I do not know how long it will take me to reestablish a routine. I wish you had approached me about this without her present."

"How could I do that, when you are avoiding me like the plague?" He moved toward her.

She turned and faced him. Her heart skipped a beat. "I cannot teach her anything if I am not granted control of her time."

"Already excuses." Stopping in the middle of the

floor, his expression closed off. "Have you given up on her so soon?"

Velvet felt her face work as she sorted through his accusation. He looked disappointed but not surprised. "I haven't given up on her at all. She's intelligent. I don't know why she resists learning to read, but I am quite determined to get past it."

The corners of his lips curled up just slightly. "Are you?"

"I am sure you do not mean to undermine my authority, but Iris uses every tool at her disposal to avoid lessons. A trip to Plymouth, even if it is just a few days, is likely to set her back at least a week. There is no reason that the remaining items we need cannot be sent for. I'm sure if I speak with a local shop owner, he would be happy to place orders . . ." Her voice trailed off at his expression.

"But I already have to take a trip . . . for business." He took a step closer.

The shelves cut in bands across her shoulders and middle back. She hadn't even realized she'd been backing toward them. Darting to the side, she paced the strip of wood flooring between the carpet and the bookcases. "I don't know if Iris is neglected or spoilt."

"A little of both perhaps." His forehead furled. "It occurs to me that as she is no longer an infant, perhaps she should accompany me on some of my travels. I have undoubtedly been neglectful. I mean to remedy that. A trip would kill two birds with one stone."

Which birds he meant to kill was the problem. She refused to be one of them. "Then I should ask to remain behind."

He scowled. "Why?"

Instead of making him appear less attractive, his

scowl only made her sorry to have disappointed him, which didn't make sense. "If you must take Iris, then I am sure Mrs. Bigsby, Nellie, or even Meg could make the trip."

"You are the one hired to supervise Iris. And while I am occupied by business, Iris could be engaged in lessons."

Velvet searched for a better reason, but what came out was, "I don't travel well."

His expression shifted. "Is that why you arrived ill?"

She turned toward the center of the room but kept the table spread with a huge map between them. She'd arrived ill because she was nearly starved to death. Even after a few days of decent food, she was still incredibly weak. Walking around shopping might tax her more than she could manage. Right now she regretted not taking his offer of a chair, because her knees were quivering. "P-Partially. I hadn't been eating well before I arrived."

"Is that the only reason you don't want to go, Miss Campbell?" His dark gaze cut through her, holding her hostage.

"I don't want a repeat of the other night's mistake," she whispered. But as she stared at his dark hair, his long slender hands, all she could think was a repeat of the other night was exactly what she wanted, his hands on her, that mouth on her, and all the rest that went along with it. Echoing in her head was her father's fist on the pulpit as he shouted, *Lust is a grievous sin.*

Chapter 8

Lucian stared at Velvet. *The other night's mistake.* She had come to his bedroom after midnight. Any man would have assumed she was there for a tryst, especially after his invitations. Then she had arched into him and participated. He hadn't misunderstood.

"I would only consider it a mistake if you hadn't kissed back," said Lucian.

"You ordered me to," Velvet snapped. She wobbled as if about to fall, then leaned against the library table as if it offered sanctuary.

She had a point. He had demanded she return his kisses. "I understand the word no, Miss Campbell. Never once did you utter it."

Her gaze shot to his. She looked horrified. By her behavior or his? "You are my employer, and 'no' is often an unacceptable response in a servant."

"Your *required* duties have limits." Talking across fifteen feet of space was insane. "Besides, you have no problem speaking your mind about Iris's instruction. Or the appropriateness of a trip." Bloody hell, she'd brought up the manner of his wife's death. She hadn't seemed frightened of him before his first intimation that he wanted to be her lover, but he hadn't demanded submission.

He paced the center of the room. He knew he didn't have the right to insist she join him in his bed, but he had certainly suggested he'd welcome her stepping into the role of his mistress. Had she taken his suggestion as an order? Her position as his employee clouded the issue.

She watched him walk. Her green eyes flashed with a kind of hunger that mirrored his. Her lips parted and her breaths deepened. The sparks between them were not one-sided. She had kissed him back, and found her voice to protest only when he started to lift her skirts.

He took a step toward her. She instantly stepped back. She'd been backing away from him ever since the moment he let her leave his room. Perhaps she wanted to be coy and not give in so easily. Perhaps she wanted gifts to sweeten her mood. Perhaps in the dark she hadn't noticed his scars. He grimaced.

Her color rose and she looked to the door. "I should return to the schoolroom. Meg will not be firm with Iris about her multiplication tables."

He moved between her and the door. "We haven't resolved anything."

She hesitated. He wouldn't stop her from leaving, but they would have to finish the discussion sooner or later. He refused to let a few kisses become a monstrous black unspoken barrier between them. And damn it, he knew how to exercise restraint. He reached for the bellpull as if that had been his destination. "I'll ring for tea."

She bit her lip. A longing to kiss her swept over him.

"If you will sit down"—he gestured toward the wing chairs flanking the fire—"I will promise to not ravish you."

She stared at him as if he had grown devil's horns. He lifted his foot. Swinging around the table, she scurried toward the fireplace and took a seat.

The door clicked open and he asked Mrs. Bigsby to bring tea. She looked past him and her lips turned down. Disregarding his housekeeper's disapproval, he shut the door.

"Mrs. Bigsby will return soon with the tray. Now we should discuss Iris and her lessons." That should reassure Velvet he didn't intend to shove the maps off the library table and toss her over it. Although the idea had appeal.

He crossed the room and sank into the other chair. Velvet gripped the armrests as if she were in a rocking skiff and needed to hang on for dear life. At least the high chair back would prevent her from backing away.

"I am dismayed at how far behind she is." Velvet didn't quite meet his eyes.

Iris had never been a good student. He'd gone through governess after governess who'd told him she was intractable. It was probably only a matter of time before Miss Campbell gave up on teaching her. Like her mother, Iris couldn't be made to see the value of learning anything difficult. "Yes, well you do realize she has been four months without a governess."

Velvet nodded. Her back was ramrod straight. He missed the way she'd arched, and whimpered in the back of her throat.

"Now if including Iris on a trip to Plymouth is a bad idea and will be disruptive to her lessons, what would you suggest be done?" he said conversationally.

"It is not that it is a bad idea, just that it should come as reward for accomplishing several tasks," said Velvet cautiously. "I told Iris she needed to learn to write the alphabet before she is rewarded with a trip of that magnitude."

Exhaling heavily, he studied her. She confounded

him. "Am I to assume you would refuse to chaperone Iris on a future trip too?"

Velvet looked down at her hands and pulled them into her lap. Color stole across her cheekbones. "If I felt that our inclusion was purely a reward for her achievements, I could hardly refuse. I as much as promised her that such a trip could be taken at some point."

"So it is only my timing that is ill," said Lucian.

"Iris is so hungry for your approval, I often use it as a carrot."

Lucian winced. He wished the girl cared less what he thought. Her recitation of poetry to him the last two evenings and promise to play the pianoforte for him within a fortnight had him patting her on the head like a good lapdog. He'd asked her what else she'd worked on during her lessons. She frowned, before telling him she'd learned to do her scales on the pianoforte, which Miss Campbell assured her had to be mastered before a song could be played.

"If you could be more gracious with your praise and allow me to bring her up to the mark, it would go a fair way to making my job easier."

He felt slightly chastised and annoyed. Velvet hadn't yet realized how Iris was like her mother, in that praise went straight to her head. But perhaps he had been too stingy with his encouragement and recognition of progress. "Very well, Miss Campbell. I will endeavor to do better."

Her lips twitched as if she restrained a smile. What would it take to get her to smile all the way?

Mrs. Bigsby entered with the tea trolley. The cups and saucers rattled, as she tipped it up to push across the rug.

"Thank you, Mrs. Bigsby," said Velvet.

"Meg has duties to finish before she leaves for the day, miss."

Velvet glanced toward the mantel clock. At half past four the day was nearly gone.

"I will require Miss Campbell's presence a bit longer," Lucian said. "Tell Meg she may complete her duties."

Velvet's lips tightened.

He was under no illusion about who had gone running to Mrs. Bigsby the minute Velvet left the schoolroom. "And inform Iris I am looking forward to hearing her recite her multiplication tables after dinner."

He really should try to find a real housekeeper, one that knew better than to be manipulated by a pair of big blue eyes. But then that was how Mrs. Bigsby had been elevated to her position in the first place. She was always at Lilith's beck and call. Iris showed every indication of being able to twist Mrs. Bigsby around her finger too.

"Shall I have Cook push back dinner?" Mrs. Bigsby's scowl spoke volumes.

"No. That won't be necessary. That will be all."

Mrs. Bigsby sniffed, but headed toward the library door. He reached to pour himself a cup of tea, but Velvet's hand was already on the pot. He leaned back. He had grown used to not having a woman around to do things like pour tea.

"That should serve to keep Iris on task. Thank you," said Velvet.

"If a trip to Plymouth is out of the question for the time being, perhaps a trip to King Arthur's birthplace tomorrow would be a good substitute." Lucian offered.

"Tintagel Castle?" Velvet's russet eyebrows pushed together.

He wanted to smooth out the lines with his thumb. "You know of it?"

Pink swept across her cheeks. "When I learned of the position, I read a bit about Cornwall."

Why had she blushed? Her head dipped as she offered him a teacup.

"It's not far, two to three hours in the carriage. Would that be too long for you?" He almost held his breath. He could take Iris alone, but he wanted Velvet's company. "Cook could pack a picnic for the three of us."

Velvet took a sip of her tea.

Feeling slightly desperate, he said, "It would perhaps be a good opportunity to instruct Iris on history."

Velvet pursed her mouth. "Or at least the local lore."

"Shouldn't she know both?"

"I suppose." Her face relaxed.

"You would be giving up your afternoon off, but I could give you the entire day next Saturday."

Velvet met his gaze. He could read her uncertainty.

"Iris would be with us. I will not be alone with you." He took a sip of his tea. Everything would be proper and aboveboard, and he'd be spending every second attempting to charm her into his bed upon their return.

"Very well," she said. "I suppose it will save me from appearing too stern with my charge."

"We can't have that." Did he even remember how to be charming? He'd known how once, before Lilith took his heart and shredded it. He stole a glance at the clock. They needed to go into dinner soon. It was time to contend with the more important subject. "Now, about the other matter between us."

Velvet choked on her tea.

Her gasp as she sipped had been ill timed. Hot liquid burned where it didn't belong. A cough erupted. She set the rattling teacup and saucer down on the tea trolley and fought to breathe. It was no use. Coughs burst from her burning throat while her eyes watered.

Lucian waved a snowy handkerchief in front of her face. She was mortified, but she took the square and swiped away the tears. Wanting to escape, she stood.

"Sit down, Velvet."

"There isn't anything to discuss," she protested.

"Yes, there is. Quit acting as if I'm going to attack you." He stood too and stepped toward her.

With the tea trolley blocking the path to the center of the room, he was too close. The back of her legs rested against the chair. She could sit or hold her ground.

The heat coming off his body encircled her. His scent, bay rum and something more male, intoxicated her. The warm and liquid way she'd felt when he kissed her came rushing back. She made the mistake of looking him in the eye. His eyelids lowered slightly and his dark gaze was mesmerizing. She tilted toward him.

He stepped closer, but there was still a modicum of space between them. Her skin came alive, tingling as if he touched her, but he didn't. She raised her hand, but she couldn't have said it was to draw him nearer or push him away.

His gaze dropped to her mouth. His breath feathered across her lips. Her heart caught, waiting for him to close the gap, waiting for his kiss. The slow ticking of the mantel clock echoed as time stretched.

He touched her hand, and her skin jumped. His thumb circled her wrist and brushed across the inside and down along her palm. The gentle touch was the last thing she expected and had her melting.

"I want to kiss you. I want to touch you," he whispered. She shuddered at his every word.

"I want you in my bed." He lifted her wrist to his mouth and pressed his mouth to the sensitive flesh.

Her heart fluttered and every fiber of her being quivered at his touch. Heat swept toward her woman's core, and her inner muscles tightened.

"Especially after the other night. But I can wait until you . . ." He dropped her hand, and rubbed his thumb across her lower lip. " . . . are ready."

Velvet sat down hard. Her mouth opened, and she closed it without saying anything. She wanted to say she'd never be ready, but when he moved close, her brain turned to mush and her body hummed with an energy that was ferocious for being so long suppressed. Oh, she'd found men attractive before, but she never allowed herself to even think of more than a chaste kiss.

Lucian made all that seem like child's play. He called to a raw and primitive side of her that wanted to lay skin to skin with him, to explore his physique. Her mind kept replaying that interlude in his room. His dressing gown had gaped open. In the dark of his room, she'd glimpsed the hard muscles of his chest, the ridged lines of his stomach, and lower, the stiff length of his manhood. Wanting to touch him had melded together with a need to be held, kissed, and loved.

He leaned over the chair, imprisoning her with his hands on the armrests. "I will not use your position as my employee to coerce you into my bed. But we are two mature adults here."

Her mouth went dry.

"When you are ready to pursue this pull between us, you can cast yourself into my arms." He straightened and twisted away.

Disappointment curdled her blood. Her voice low and tight, she said, "In spite of what you believe about me,

I am not a loose woman. I will not compromise my morals."

"Then you would deny us both immeasurable pleasure," he growled.

A wash of heat settled low in her, and Velvet licked her lips.

He pushed the tea trolley out of the way and stalked toward the door. Pulling his cuffs down with a studied disinterest, he said, "You had best fetch Iris. It is past time for dinner."

With that he left the library. Her rapture snapped. Lucian wasn't talking about anything more than physical pleasure. He wasn't offering to hold her or love her.

She had to remember that, even when she felt as if she was coming undone. Even when she felt she would die if he didn't kiss her. She couldn't allow him to think she'd welcome his touch, even if she did.

Lucian watched Velvet for any signs of traveling sickness. So far she seemed fine, albeit cool toward him. In the morning, he'd called for the traveling coach instead of just a gig and sent a four-horse team ahead with a post boy to make their travel quicker.

He worried that Iris's constant bouncing might disturb Velvet. Right now she was engaged in drumming her heels against the wooden underside of the seat.

"Iris, stop kicking," he said.

"Perhaps if we might stop and stretch our limbs soon," suggested Velvet.

He looked out the window for landmarks. "We'll be changing the horses in another mile or two. Will that be soon enough?"

Velvet looked down at Iris and smiled softly. "I think that will do."

His stomach twisted. What would it take to get Velvet to smile at him? She'd barely looked at him today. All he could do was look at her. Her skin was like porcelain, her hair a molten copper, and he couldn't remember wanting a woman as much as he wanted her.

Iris scowled. "Are we almost there?"

"We are only half the way," said Velvet. "Do you know of King Arthur and the knights of the round table?"

She slipped into a rendition of the age-old legends. Her voice lulled and soothed him as they swayed along in the carriage.

He added in details from Cornish legends and was pleased when her questing green eyes landed on him. For a second their gazes locked. Warmth flared low in him. He could only think of tasting her mouth again, but now was not an appropriate time. He had no intention of making overtures today. In spite of his best intentions, he'd very nearly failed to remain circumspect in the library.

Dragging his eyes away, he looked at Iris.

Her mouth agape, Iris looked back and forth between the two of them. The last thing he needed was Iris speculating about what went on between a man and a woman.

"You were saying about Lancelot," he prompted Velvet.

Velvet's throat worked, and then she turned to where Iris sat beside her and started again. "Lancelot was a knight from France. He—"

"How do you know all this?" interrupted Iris.

"From books," answered Velvet.

Iris's eyebrows and mouth flattened.

Velvet ignored the chit's petulant expression and continued her storytelling. Artfully she mentioned Guinevere's lovely blond hair was just like Iris's. The child leaned against her governess and settled in to listen.

The stop to change horses arrived almost too soon.

Lucian descended the stairs, turned and swung Iris down. Extending his hand to help Velvet, he watched that Iris did not stray. Velvet slid her bare hand into his. Her skin was soft and her long fingers brushed his. He fought the surge of desire. He should be able to assist her out of the carriage without becoming aroused.

He led her down the steps and released her. Ashamed by his lack of control, he clasped his hands behind his back. Velvet kept her eyes down. If she was aware of his pulsing desire, she gave no signal.

Although it was not so cool as to be uncomfortable, her lack of gloves puzzled him. Did she mean to torment him by the skin-to-skin contact?

Instead she leaned forward and cupped Iris's shoulders, directing her toward the inn, where they could make use of the facilities.

The sway of her hips and her smooth glide as she walked into the building mesmerized him. All the rest of the world fell away as he saw only her.

"Right handsome family, guv."

The rebuttal on his lips, Lucian swiveled to face an ostler holding the reins on the lead horses. From the deliberately blank looks on his coachman and groom and the smirk on the ostler's face, Lucian surmised they'd all noticed his fascination with Velvet.

His coachman and groom got very busy with releasing straps and buckles.

Leveling a steely look in the ostler's direction, Lucian asked, "Did you say something?"

"I asked if you wanted your spare team hooked on

straight away or you mean to have a meal," the ostler said.

As much to regain his composure as anything, Lucian pulled his pocket watch out and flipped open the cover. "Have the carriage ready in a half hour. Thank you."

That would give his men time enough to have a beer and stretch their legs.

The ostler nodded and moved to help the groom with releasing the first team from their traces.

Lucian snapped the watch closed and tucked it back into his pocket. He strode toward the inn.

He went inside and found the proprietor, ordered drinks and found a table in the common room. Velvet returned with Iris and noted the glasses on the table. Her forehead crinkled for just a second. If he hadn't been watching her so intently, he would have missed the tiny hint of displeasure.

"You don't like lemonade?" he asked.

She looked at him blankly. "I enjoy lemonade." Gingerly she untied the frayed ribbons of her bonnet. "Miss Pendar, won't you sit, please?"

The crinkle appeared between Velvet's brows again as she watched Iris slide onto the bench. Iris slumped, and Velvet lightly touched her between her shoulder blades. Iris straightened.

He wanted to reach out, touch Velvet's hand and ask her what was bothering her, but instead he clenched his glass tighter. Touching her was not a good idea. He'd want more.

Iris picked up her lemonade and downed the liquid in a long series of gulps. She thunked her empty glass on the table. "Can I go outside?"

"May I? And no, you may sit and wait until everyone is finished," answered Velvet.

"A busy inn yard is no place for you alone," echoed Lucian. A few months ago he would have just let Iris go, rather than battle with her. But then a few months ago he never would have bothered to take her on an outing. He had to try harder to connect with her as she matured into a young lady.

Iris folded her arms and hunched over. "Didn't look busy to me."

Like her mother, she didn't handle not getting her way with grace.

Lucian opened his mouth to suggest Iris close hers, but Velvet was already speaking in her dulcet tones.

"Sit up straight, please," she said. "Or do we need to practice the proper way to sit the whole time we're here?"

Iris sighed loudly and improved her posture. Velvet rewarded her with a smile and a quick back rub. She seemed to have found the appropriate mix of carrots and sticks with Iris. But then he'd probably do handstands if she rewarded him with smiles and loving touches. He stared into his glass of lemonade and wished he'd ordered gin.

"Will we have time for a stroll?" asked Velvet.

"We have time," said Lucian. He finished his glass and remained decidedly unquenched.

Velvet picked up her glass and sipped.

Iris's blue eyes followed her every movement. She shifted forward and back on the bench. "Hurry up."

"That's enough, Iris," said Lucian. "Speak only when you're spoken to."

Iris's lower lip jutted out.

Velvet sighed, but did not rush. The silence stretched over the table. She finished and reached for her hat.

"Shall we walk through town?" Lucian stood.

"That would be lovely. Don't you think, Iris?"

"Yes, ma'am."

Iris was undoubtedly trying to make him feel like a heel for silencing her. Silencing them all. But he didn't know when she'd become such an ill-mannered child. Then again he'd never taken her out in public or put her much in the way of others. He should shoulder the blame for wanting to keep her away from those who might harm her, and indulging her so much she believed her whims should be fulfilled straight away. Although how much was due to his neglect and how much was because she'd inherited a great deal of Lilith's faults, he didn't know.

Velvet managed to maneuver Iris between them as they strolled down the dirt lane that marked the center of the village. But Iris bounced instead of walked, making their progress jerky.

"Would you like to skip ahead to the end of the street?" asked Velvet.

"Can I?"

"May I," corrected Velvet. "If your father says you may."

Iris turned her big blue eyes in his direction. Lucian nodded.

"Do not go past the last building," said Velvet.

They walked a few steps while Iris bounded ahead. The smells of fresh baked bread wafted out of the bakery, while a few of the locals scurried about their business.

"She was very eager for this trip," said Velvet.

"I overestimated her ability to travel," said Lucian dryly.

The corners of Velvet's mouth curled. "Most children her age have a hard time being cooped up for hours, but I'm sure the walk will help."

"When the train tracks are laid, the journey might only take an hour at most."

"Are there plans to bring trains through here?"

"My plan is to build new railroads and depots covering the west of England. I have been working on the best routes for years, surveying the land, contracting to buy property, entering into the partnerships I need."

She studied him. "Railroads will bring a great deal of progress to the area."

"And I will have a controlling interest in most of it." If things went as planned, he would attain a great deal of power. "Soon I will be bringing together my partners and finalizing everything. We will getting the final backing of Parliament this coming session and break ground in the spring."

"Sounds ambitious," she murmured.

"Yes, but I have benefited from watching the foolhardy mistakes of others. I have even been to the Americas to see how they are handling the rapid building of rail lines."

They walked along and she asked questions his investors hadn't even asked, and he found himself sharing his methods and plans with her. Just to have someone who understood the concerns and able to share intelligent discourse about it made him feel light on his feet. She even had insights into the tricky political maze he would need to navigate.

"You certainly have thought this through." Her thoughtful expression contained perhaps a little admiration. "You are very thorough. Success seems certain."

Warmth slid down his spine. Yet, he could not monopolize the conversation with his business. "I am sorry. This day should be about pleasure and I have been boring you with my plans."

"I was not bored. I find it fascinating." Her brows drew together. "But I suspect Iris is not old enough to appreciate the subject."

Surprisingly, Iris waited for them at the end of the street. He couldn't have imagined her following Miss Grimes's directions so well. "You have worked wonders to get in Iris's good graces. She is usually too head-strong to mind her governesses."

Velvet's chin dipped and the edge of her hat shielded her expression. "She has told me that you will send her away if I fail."

He rubbed his hand down his side. He no longer trusted anyone to do the right thing without prodding. "I knew of no other way to compel her to behave."

Did she dislike his manipulations? Suddenly her good opinion meant more than he liked. He pulled out his watch and checked the time.

Two young boys scampered by, one rolling a metal hoop with a stick.

Iris ran toward him. "Papa, I want one of those. There is a store that sells them down there." She pointed and yanked on his arm.

His watch dropped and swung on its chain.

"Do we need to return to the inn?" asked Velvet.

"We have time yet." Lucian retrieved his watch and put it back in his pocket. The carriage, though ready by now, wouldn't leave without them. "Show me," he said to Iris.

Iris pulled him toward the dry goods shop, which sure enough displayed a metal hoop along with tin sol-diers and porcelain dolls in the front window. He paused at the door, Iris trying to tug him through the opening.

Velvet's lips were pressed together as she crossed the threshold. The proprietor greeted them with a happy smile. He looked over Velvet, quickly dismissed her and turned to Iris. "And what can I do for you, little miss? Would you like a peppermint?"

The man moved to a jar on the long counter and opened it. Iris happily trotted toward him. "My papa is going to buy me the big ring in the window."

Wondering why the man so quickly wrote off Velvet, Lucian looked toward her as she fingered a length of cloth and then meandered between the bolts of material.

Velvet's hat ribbons were tattered, her hems were frayed, and her boots were scuffed. Her mended nightgown and lack of a dressing gown crossed his mind. Without wages for a year, she wouldn't be able to purchase new material for clothes.

He took a step toward her. He wanted to tell her he'd been hasty in his assumption that he had to manipulate her into staying, and that he could release her wages sooner. Or better yet, he could just buy her material and have the dressmaker come make up new clothes for her.

She stared down at a table that held a silver rattle and a tiny embroidered cap. He watched as she ran her finger over the carving on a cradle. His heart stopped cold.

Chapter 9

Velvet stared at the layette and wondered if she would have had a half-dozen children by now if she'd accepted one of the three offers she had before she was twenty. Two of the men were her father's parishioners, and one was a farmer a county over. Any one of them would have been acceptable to her, but she told them all she could not desert her father while he was ill.

Not one of her suitors remained a bachelor when her father died. They probably hadn't understood how bad his condition was because he'd always managed to deliver his rousing fire and brimstone service every Sunday. Only she knew he would return to the vicarage, collapse, and not rise out of bed until Tuesday. Until the time he didn't rise on Tuesday or even Wednesday, then slipped from life on Thursday morning without the thundering hellfire or singing angels he told everyone to expect.

"Is there anything you need, Miss Campbell?" asked Lucian at her side. His voice was low and rough, as if aware he'd caught her in the midst of musing about her past.

"No, of course not."

He stared at her hand on the cradle.

Embarrassed that he caught her in a moment of regret

at not having children of her own, she drew her hand back. "I was just admiring the carving."

"Lilith ordered a cradle from London when Iris was born." He looked over to where the shop clerk retrieved the hoop from the window. "Iris was too big for it by the time it arrived." The flash of pain in his face surprised her. "The cradle is still in the nursery."

His gaze was intense, and she wasn't at all sure what he was trying to convey.

"Will this be all for you, sir?"

Lucian looked down at the cradle and then back at her. He quirked an eyebrow at her.

"I—I'm fine," she said ineptly.

Was he trying to tell her he wanted more children? With her? Her stomach fluttered, and suddenly she was out of breath.

He turned and pulled out his purse to pay for Iris's hoop.

Uncertain what to do with herself, Velvet ducked her head and turned toward the door. Her mind spun and fired like a Catherine wheel at a fair. Lucian was inept with his daughter, alternatively ignoring her and over-indulging her. He wasn't the type of man she should want to have a child with, and damn it to hell and back, she'd thought she was resolved to being a spinster and childless.

But she was breathless. As he walked toward the counter, she could almost picture a little dark-haired boy trailing behind him. His child . . . and hers.

Lucian knew Velvet was embarrassed and uncertain. Until she confided in him or her condition became obvious, he couldn't do more than drop the broadest of hints that he'd be compassionate.

When they arrived at the promontory where Tintagel Castle was located, Iris exploded out of the carriage. She hopped up and down and urged the coachman to hand her down the hoop and stick.

Velvet looked toward the round jut of land surrounded by ocean and gasped.

"Almost impregnable, eh?" Lucian handed her down. Prepared for the jolt of awareness, he dropped his hand as soon as he could. He intended to act like a gentleman.

Velvet stepped down gingerly and nodded. But she looked pale.

"It is no wonder Uther Pendragon needed a ruse to get inside a fortress here," observed Lucian.

Velvet's cheeks fired and she looked down.

He hadn't expected his oblique reference to the seduction of Arthur's mother to embarrass Velvet, but her blush suggested otherwise. That her mind strayed along the same forbidden paths as his heated him. He tucked his hands behind his back and forced his feet to step away. "Shall we go down to the ruins?"

"I should like to rest here a bit." She turned aside, so he couldn't see her face.

Why did she need to rest after sitting in a coach for the better part of three hours? With her face averted, he couldn't search her expression for clues. She must want distance from him.

"I'll go, Papa," said Iris. Her hoop, which had proved harder to control than she expected, lay in the grass beside the carriage.

He extended his hand, and Iris put her sticky fingers in his. Now his hand would be sticky too. He suspected the store owner had given her more than one peppermint, but then Iris, like her mother, could have that effect on people. Grimacing, he curled his fingers around hers.

"Have a good time," said Velvet.

"It really is not a difficult walk," he said, "and there are stairs. No need to do any climbing."

Velvet shook her head. Her lips were pressed tightly together. "Perhaps later."

"Are you feeling all right?" he asked.

"I'll be all right in a little bit. Please go on ahead."

She turned to walk back toward the lane that had brought them to the grassy area above Tintagel Head.

Iris pulled on his hand and looked up at him, her big blue eyes beseeching.

"Shall we go explore, then?" he said to her.

His parents had brought him here when he was young. He'd pretended to be King Arthur fighting on the walls with a stick sword. Perhaps Iris would want to pretend she was Guinevere. Although, he had his reservations about her taking on the role of an adulteress. He wanted to sever the connections to her mother instead of reinforce them.

Iris skipped, bouncing his arm up and down. He held on anyway. Moving to the coachman, who was releasing the horses from their traces, Lucian whispered, "Keep an eye on Miss Campbell. If she is ill, come get me."

"Very good, sir," the coachman responded.

"Can we have our picnic over there, Papa?" Iris pointed to the far headland.

"Certainly." He picked up the basket and the blanket.

Iris looked back at Velvet and smiled smugly. "I don't think Miss Campbell will want to eat."

He turned and studied Velvet. She walked away, her shoulders stiff. What had Iris done?

Damn, just when he thought she was behaving like

an ordinary child, she showed how prone to scheming she was. Although he couldn't blame it all on her mother. He too had schemed to get Velvet in his company. And his plan seemed to be going awry.

Iris climbed the piled rocks. As a castle, it wasn't very exciting, just a bunch of jagged walls without roofs or floors. But it was almost like being on an island, and one thing was certain, Miss Campbell didn't like looking down on the water. Every time she neared the window in the schoolroom, she would gasp and avert her head. The few walks they had taken outside were always away from the ocean, even though she had told Miss Campbell where they could easily go down to the shore. She'd even moved everything in the schoolroom so she didn't have to get close to the windows.

Now she had her papa all to herself. If only he wouldn't keep checking the path to see if Miss Campbell was coming.

"Be careful, Iris," he said.

"I am." She could climb a stupid wall. The stones bit into her palms. Maybe if she fell off the wall he'd rush to pick her up and forget about Miss Campbell.

She pushed away and leaped to the ground. She tumbled to the side. Waiting, she lay on the ground.

"I told you to be careful," he said in an even tone.

Twisting to look over her shoulder, she watched him sit back down on a shelf of stones. He just didn't care about her. "I could have hurt myself."

"You did jump, not fall." He sounded bored. He'd probably be all over Miss Campbell if she stumbled.

Iris let loose a puff of air. Miss Campbell hated pretend injuries and fell for them even less than Papa. She rolled to her feet. "Can we eat now?"

"We should wait for Miss Campbell." He pulled his watch from his pocket and flipped it open. "Or perhaps we should go get her."

Iris folded her arms. "I'm hungry."

Her father pinned her with a dark look. "Don't you want to wait for Miss Campbell?"

She knew the right answer, the polite answer, but instead she said, "I am all the time with her."

She couldn't run down and have cook give her an apple pastry or tease Meg into playing a game of hide and seek. It wasn't that she disliked Miss Campbell, but she was used to doing what she wanted. So far it didn't work to stomp her foot or pretend to cry. Getting out of the classroom during school hours was impossible now. Miss Campbell would just say to work or suffer the consequences. "She always tells me if I don't do my lessons, I can't go to the drawing room after dinner."

"Well if I don't see to my work during the day, then I must return to it after dinner. That is the way of the world, Iris."

"Ladies don't have work," she objected.

"Sure they do. They must see to the household, the staff, plan the menus . . . and—"

"Mama didn't."

"She should have." Papa winced and looked away. "She did when she was feeling well."

Iris could tell he was lying. Her mama mostly laid on her chaise longue and complained she was imprisoned in the house in the middle of nowhere. She said Papa only invited dreary business people and there were never any parties or decent company.

"When I grow up I want to live in London."

Papa scowled. "Perhaps you should see the city before you decide such things."

"Miss Campbell likes London."

His expression turned darker. "Does she?" he muttered.

She described the sights there as things to be seen. She also went on and on about the benefits of books, when Iris couldn't see any reason to think books were wonderful. They just made her head hurt. But it seemed to upset her papa that Miss Campbell liked London. Speculating on how to best use that information, Iris hopped on the low wall and ran along it.

The picnic basket stopped her progress. Papa was again searching the rise leading to the stairs.

Her teeth clamped together and she suddenly felt hot. He was looking for Miss Campbell again.

"She's always talking about how wonderful it is there. Buckingham Palace, The White Tower, the museums, the galleries." That was an exaggeration. Biting her lip, Iris paused. "I am sure she misses it dreadfully."

Papa turned toward her. His eyebrows flattened and his lips thinned.

Just then Miss Campbell came over the hilltop.

Papa's face transformed. His lips parted and his eyes crinkled around the edges. He looked . . . happy, and it was Miss Campbell he was happy to see.

Velvet headed down the slight incline toward Iris and Lucian. She hoped her panic didn't show. Iris scowled, while Lucian stood and watched her. Fearing she'd stumble or her rubbery legs would give out on her, Velvet took slow steps and tried to not wave her arms wildly.

The ocean breeze fluttered her hat's repaired ribbons and wafted across her skin. The ground leveled out to a smooth grassy patch. She contemplated making herself as unobtrusive as possible.

"Finally," said Iris with a grand flourish.

"Yes, she's here." Lucian picked up the folded blanket. He flapped it out and laid it on the grass in what must have once been a great hall.

Velvet went straight to the basket and carried it to the blanket.

The day would be pleasant if she hadn't been confronted with the steep descent to the sea on either side of the isthmus connecting this round peninsula to the mainland. She'd barely been able to override her fear of falling to make it across. Attempting the crossing without witnesses allowed her to focus on the ground in front of her feet and take tiny baby steps. She'd made it, but the accomplishment felt hollow. Already she dreaded the return.

She gamely stretched out the corners of the blanket, then opened the basket. The scent of roasted chicken curdled her stomach. She pressed against her abdomen, curbing the sudden rise of nausea. Concentrating on setting out the plates and food helped keep her vision narrowly focused down on the blanket.

A person with an extreme fear of falling shouldn't be on the coast of Cornwall. She absolutely had to learn to contain her phobia or she'd never survive here. But when a loved one had died from a fall, ignoring the steep precipices was hard.

"Are you feeling better, Miss Campbell?" Lucian stood at the far edge of the blanket with his hands clasped behind his back.

Embarrassed by her helpless lack of control, her

face heated. Her gaze traveled up his legs, and her thoughts flashed on the night she'd retrieved the dolls and glimpsed his powerful thighs covered with dark hairs. Her skin flamed hotter. "C-Certainly, I am fine."

His brows drew together and he dropped to his knees. He'd loosened his neck cloth and unbuttoned his collar. As if she had no control, her eyes were drawn to the dark shadow at the base of his throat.

She twisted to pull a jug from the basket. She didn't need to know if the hairs on his chest would be silky or bristly. Certainly she would never feel his bare chest against hers, but her nipples tightened as if her body wanted to.

She tried to dismiss her rampant thoughts, but her will was weakened by her terror at crossing the steep-sided land bridge.

Her fear overtook her sensibilities the day she turned twelve, and she'd spent hours in the bell tower afraid to move for fear of falling. She couldn't bring herself to climb down the stairs. A farmer of the village, putting his mules away, had seen her up there clinging to the rail and rescued her, carrying her down the long flight of stairs. She'd never again been able to stand heights.

"Iris, arc you ready to eat?" she asked more sharply than she intended.

"I've been ready forever," said Iris. She plunked down on the edge of the blanket. "What took you so long?"

"I am sorry." Velvet concentrated on the child. "I thought you might enjoy exploring with your father. I fear I am a poor adventurer."

She hadn't always been. She had often talked her younger brother into climbing to the top of the bell tower. Velvet pushed those thoughts away.

Iris blinked and suddenly looked extremely young and vulnerable. She squirmed and then announced, "I fell off the wall."

"You jumped," corrected Lucian.

Iris rolled her eyes, and Velvet suppressed a smile. Thank goodness Iris was present to break the tension and steer her thoughts away from the lascivious path they too often strayed upon. Lucian wasn't the first nearly naked and aroused man she'd glimpsed, but for some reason the images of him in his open dressing gown continued to taunt her.

Velvet set out glasses and a bottle of wine. Lucian reached for the wine and put his thumbs on the cork, prying it out. She had to tear her gaze away from his long-fingered hands. She didn't even have to guess how his hands on her would feel. She knew.

"Can I have some?" said Iris, her eyes on the bottle.

"No, you're not old enough. You can have water," answered Lucian without hesitation.

"I'm not a baby," pouted Iris.

Lucian picked up his daughter's glass, splashed a thimbleful of wine into the bottom and added water to nearly the rim. The mixture was barely pink.

Iris breathed in deeply and her eyebrows had flattened.

"I'd like water with my wine too, please," said Velvet, hoping to stave off a disagreeable snit.

Lucian gave in to his daughter far too easily and too often. The girl needed a steady dose of discipline, not the careless disregard that her father used with her. But an outing was not the time to be stern. Velvet held out the platter of sectioned chicken to Iris.

"Can I eat with my fingers?" asked Iris.

"Of course you may," answered Velvet. "It is a picnic,

and Mrs. Bigsby has packed plenty of napkins."

Iris took a drumstick, while Lucian poured a finger of wine in her glass then raised his eyebrow. Velvet gave a quick nod. She probably should have had him fill it to the rim. Drinking heavily might ease her terror when she had to cross the isthmus again.

A salad and sliced bread rounded out their simple meal. Although she probably shouldn't risk the sun, Velvet removed her hat to eat. Lucian's gaze on her hair made her regret calling attention to herself.

She jerked her head in Iris's direction, and the faintest of smiles crossed his face before he turned toward the girl. "After we eat, would you like to walk down to the shore?" he asked.

Iris nodded happily.

"You might want to look inside Merlin's cave." For once he seemed relaxed instead of tense, but he still managed to turn his body so the unscarred side of his face was toward them.

That such a virulent man would be so disconcerted by his scars surprised Velvet. But she didn't know what it would be like to face a disfigurement in the mirror every day. The only marring she had was a café au lait stain in the shape of a half-moon on her hip. The mark had been with her from birth. The midwife was pleased to find a unique feature, although it hadn't proved to be the least bit necessary.

"Do you like it here, Papa?"

"The scenery is beautiful." His eyelids lowered slightly. He glanced Velvet's way for just a second before returning his attention to his daughter.

Heat washed through Velvet. She tried to distract herself from his presence by looking at the ocean. "Lovely."

Iris wiped her greasy hand on her skirt. Velvet

winced but refrained from offering censure. She pulled one of the spare napkins from the basket and put it on Iris's lap. "Here, lamb."

"You would do well to follow Miss Campbell's example. Her manners are exemplary." Lucian wiped his mouth with his napkin. "A lady in London must have good manners or no one will invite her anywhere."

Velvet looked from father to daughter. Was he so eager to be rid of her that he was already planning her debut on the marriage mart?

Iris's face scrunched and she turned to Velvet. "Is that true?"

"Yes, much is expected of young ladies there." She tilted her head slightly and risked a glance at Lucian. "Good manners are not the least of it."

He shrugged and nodded toward Iris. "I'm told you pine for London, Miss Campbell."

"No," she blurted before she could think. She didn't miss the knowing looks, the insults, or any of the things that had come of her life in London. She didn't like fearing that strangers knew her reputation and made assumptions about what she would do. And not just strangers. She pressed her lips tightly together.

Lucian watched her.

Even he had made assumptions about her willingness to behave as a fallen woman would. She stirred her salad on her plate. He was wrong. Virtue might be a slim comfort, but it was all she had left.

Lucian stretched out his legs and leaned back on his elbows.

His casual pose made her long to stretch out beside him in a carefree manner. But such allowances led to inappropriate behaviors. She should have guarded her boundaries better in her last position. She was not a part of the family, and to forget her place created problems.

She'd allowed loneliness and isolation to provide an excuse for forging a friendship. While she hadn't thought a friendship based on mutual exchange of ideas a problem, it had led her down a path of destruction.

Lucian didn't have a wife to object. Nor had he left her in any doubt of what the nature of a relationship with him might be, but she couldn't allow herself to be tempted. Her curiosity about his ventures couldn't be indulged. Encouraging him to discuss his business with her would be too much like the way she had given her former employer the wrong impression. She was here as a governess. She'd find friendships outside the family or do without.

So when he suggested they go down to the shoreline, she insisted she would stay behind, finish eating, and explore the ruins. Iris's gay chatter drifted back as the father and daughter moved down the grassy bank, skirting the hulking slabs of granite pushing through the land.

Velvet wiped the plates with a napkin and repacked the basket, taking care to position everything so nothing would spill. While Lucian and Iris threw rocks in the water and attempted to float boats made of leaves, she walked the crumbling stone walls.

While her strength had improved in the days since she arrived, she didn't want to test it too much and sat down to wait until Lucian and Iris tired of exploring the sandy shoal. For once Iris seemed carefree, skipping and smiling at her father. Lucian stooped to dig a shell out of the sand with the girl.

They finally returned, coming up from the shore. Iris's cheeks were pink. She chirped like a magpie about the special caves. Her pinafore pockets bulged with treasure.

"We should head back soon or we'll have to travel after dark." Lucian scooped up the basket.

"No," wailed Iris. "I don't want to go."

"We can't stay here forever." Lucian started up the rise to the top of the promontory.

Velvet stood, pulled up the blanket and began folding it. She bent over and whispered in the girl's ear. "If you would like your papa to take you anywhere again, you should thank him for the day. If all he remembers is that you didn't want to go home, he won't want to take you on other outings."

Iris's stared at her, her big blue eyes filling with moisture.

"Go on," urged Velvet. "And I will do my best to persuade him to take another trip."

"He only wanted to go because of you."

Had he been more interested in spending the day with her? If so, he must be disappointed. But if he wanted her to be his mistress, he couldn't accomplish that on a picnic with his daughter along. Velvet shook off her thoughts.

"But did he not spend most of the day with you? Did he not enjoy skimming rocks and crawling through caves?" Velvet shuddered. "He would not have enjoyed those things with me, because I wouldn't have enjoyed them."

Iris just stared at her.

"I have tried to stay out of the way of you and your papa, so that you may have the time together. He seemed to enjoy the day almost as much as you have. What would you have wanted different?"

Iris's eyes grew very wide. Her mouth pursed. Then

she darted forward and threw her arms around Velvet's waist.

Startled by the sudden pressure of the girl's embrace, Velvet slowly wrapped her arms around the girl. It was the first time Iris had initiated a hug. Velvet's throat felt thick with humbling joy. She was getting through to her.

"I've had so much fun," Iris said into her waist. "Most of the time everyone forgets about me."

A bittersweet ache settled into Velvet's chest. "I think you have had about as much fun as can be had in one day. Now run on and thank your papa for bringing you here, and it wouldn't hurt to tell him how much you enjoyed this trip."

Iris nodded and ran after Lucian.

The day had been good for all of them. Too often both she and Iris grew frustrated in the schoolroom. Even the austereness in Lucian's face seemed to have eased. She set out after the pair.

Steeling for crossing the steep narrow passage to the mainland, Velvet sucked in a deep breath. She followed them up the rise, all the while telling herself she could do it. With luck they would not turn around and see her terror.

After the rise in the land, the narrow path yawned before her. Iris ran without a care to catch up to her father.

Velvet's heart squeezed as a thousand images of the girl falling ran through her head. Her carefully controlled emotions erupted. "Iris, be careful!"

The world seemed to tilt and rock madly.

Lucian turned and looked back. Iris blithely continued across.

Velvet took a step forward. The ocean churned on either side of the plummet. Her stomach somersaulted.

She tried to tell herself it wasn't a long fall, but her feet refused to take another step. How could she cross when she felt woozy?

She pressed her hand to her mouth, trying to hold back her horror. Twisting away, she looked toward the solid land, trying to regain her composure. She could cross the narrow strip. She had to. If she just kept her eyes on the ground in front of her feet. She'd crossed earlier. She could do it again.

Hands closed on her shoulders. "Velvet, are you all right?"

"I'm sorry."

"What is wrong? You're trembling."

"I'm sorry. I just . . ."

Lucian's hands left her shoulders, and then his coat was around her, enveloping her in his scent.

"Iris said you're afraid of the ocean."

"No." She was afraid of falling, smashing apart on rocks. Velvet turned toward him.

His concerned dark eyes searched hers. "Are you feeling ill? You look pale."

"I was just a little dizzy. I'm sure I'll be fine now." She stared into his eyes. Anything was better than looking at the long drop.

"I'll carry you across."

"No, that would be improper."

"You can limp and feign a twisted ankle." His mouth twisted to the side. "Or whatever you feel is necessary to preserve your reputation."

"I don't lie." Oh damn, but she should have.

"Everyone lies, especially those of your sex." He wrapped one arm around her back.

His cynicism cut through her irrational terror.

"Hang on," he commanded as he bent and placed

his arm across the back of her legs and lifted her.

"I can walk," she protested.

Lucian grunted as he took a sliding step.

Oh God, they would both fall now. Her heart beat so fast she thought it might burst. She wrapped her arms around his shoulders and buried her face in his neck. Squeezing her eyes shut, she tried to pretend she wasn't such a weakling.

"I have you," he huffed out.

His steady stride reverberated through her body, and she just tried to breathe and not strangle him.

His breathing grew ragged as he climbed the slope. Once they reached the flat ground, he set her down. "Can you walk from here?"

Velvet tried to step away from him. Her cheeks burned. Her heart was still tripping. "Yes, yes of course."

Iris ran along the lane with her hoop and stick. The coachman and groom were putting the horses in their traces.

She pushed a shaking hand to her forehead. The menservants were probably pretending to not notice that their master had just carried the governess across from the peninsula.

"Come along." Lucian kept his arm around her back and guided her.

He was strong and protective, and she just wanted to lean into him and absorb his calm. She supposed she should explain. "I'm so sorry. It's just that I'm—"

"I know," he cut her off. "John, would you fetch the blanket from the other side. Miss Campbell is not feeling well."

He knew she was terrified of falling? Of course her fear had been obvious. She felt like such a ninny. How could she have allowed her panic to get the better of her?

He probably thought her ridiculous—or worse, pretending an ailment to get him to carry her.

Allowing him to hold her and carry her was the worst thing she could have done. Because now she just wanted to give in and remain in his arms. More than his arms around her and the warmth of his strong body tempted her. His kindness and concern, even his daylong attendance on his daughter, made her see him differently.

He was a good man, a kind man, not just a man preying on a penniless governess in his employ. He was a better man than the undersecretary, who hadn't allowed her the right of a choice. The distance she'd kept between them all day was for naught. If he kissed her, she would fall into his bed. She could resist the pull today or tomorrow, but not for the weeks or months ahead.

Chapter 10

Lucian handed Velvet into the carriage. She'd nearly confessed her condition within earshot of the groom and coachman. Starting the servants gossiping about her pregnancy before she was showing would only make life miserable for her.

"I am sorry for being so silly," she said. "I thought I would fall."

"If I had known you were feeling so poorly, I would have delayed the outing." But he was almost glad of her dizzy spell. Carrying Velvet with her head tucked into his shoulder had made him want to cherish her and shelter her from harm.

Lilith had been prone to nausea and dizzy spells in the early months of her pregnancies. After she passed the midpoint, she settled into a glowing period of good health. Velvet must not be very far along yet.

"No, I would have insisted." Her face earnest, she leaned toward him and put her fingers on his sleeve. "You don't know how much your attention to Iris means to her."

The day spent with Iris had gone well enough. He'd even enjoyed it once she settled into just enjoying the adventure. She had been full of curiosity and laughter, and not grasping for his notice every second. But his motives were less chivalrous. Even now Velvet's light touched burned through his sleeve, and he'd wanted her notice.

But more than that, he'd enjoyed talking to her. Her mind was quick. Hell, he'd enjoyed looking up from the shoreline, and just knowing she was close had him feeling lighter, less burdened. He'd wanted to seduce her, but found himself just enjoying her company. He didn't want to like her. He'd seen her press her hand to her belly. The worst thing he could do was fall for another woman like Lilith, who was carrying another man's baby.

Velvet bit her lip as she removed her hand and settled on the seat. "I fear she desperately needs your affection right now."

Lucian narrowed his eyes. "Do not be fooled by her deceitful tactics. She would cajole and whine until she gets what she wants."

Velvet's eyes narrowed. "She has to do little of that to convince you to buy her things, but—"

"I have no patience for the gamesmanship." He knew he gave in too easily, but like her mother, Iris could make life miserable if she fell into a pet. Restraining his irritation, he turned away. Cupping his hands around his mouth, he called, "Iris, come now or we shall have to leave you here."

"If I may be so bold, more gifts are not what she needs," said Velvet. "She—"

"You may not. I appreciate that her manners and conduct have improved, but I do not welcome your assessment of my behavior."

"I see." Velvet dipped her head. "Forgive me for overstepping my role."

Lucian sighed. She didn't understand, and he had

probably destroyed any trust he'd gained. Rubbing his forehead, he leaned his head into the carriage. "I have no reason to deny her gifts, but I cannot spend all hours of the day with her. I have affairs to see to."

"She thinks her mother wants her to die to be with her." Velvet plucked a piece of grass from her skirt. "I was not sure I should tell you."

Lucian's throat tightened. "It is another of her wiles."

Velvet shook her head. "I do not think so. I am not so easily persuaded by her fractious behavior. This was different."

He was sure Iris didn't remember her mother in any real way. Lilith had pushed her daughter away at every opportunity. He'd spent more time with her today than Lilith probably spent with Iris in the last year of her life. But perhaps she had some memories. "Her mother doesn't want her . . . with her."

"Yes, I told her no mother wants her child to die young." Velvet leaned toward him, her hand out-stretched. "Her mother would want her to live a long and happy life, marry, have children, grandchildren."

Any mother but Lilith would want that for her child. Lilith hadn't liked it when people noticed Iris instead of her. The door handle cut into his hand. Velvet had all the mothering instincts his wife had lacked. She couldn't possibly understand. A dull ache crept into his chest.

"Velvet . . ." He hesitated. What could he tell her about Lilith? She hadn't possessed a single giving bone in her body. She'd soaked up affection until everyone around her was drained dry. Iris was so like her in many ways.

Skinny arms banded around his waist, "Papa, I love you."

His throat tightening, he swiveled, pulling out of the

child's embrace. Or was she different? Lilith only declared her love when she wanted something. God help him, but he always tensed waiting for the demand that followed the words.

"I have had the best day ever," gushed Iris.

"Here, up in the carriage." Lucian lifted her inside.

Iris giggled and settled in beside her governess. "Did Papa call you Velvet? Is that your name? What kind of a name is Velvet?"

Lucian nodded to the coachman then swung into the carriage. Velvet's green eyes turned distant. Why *did* she have a whore's name?

"It's the only thing my mother said of me," Velvet said softly. "I guess my father decided she'd meant it to be my name."

He watched her face. Her soft smile didn't reach her eyes.

"Didn't he ask her?" asked Iris.

The carriage lurched forward. Velvet's hand shot out to keep Iris on her seat.

Velvet's brow wrinkled. "She didn't survive long after my birth."

"You grew up without a mother too?" Iris looked up at Velvet, her eyes wide.

"Yes." Velvet's lips tightened.

"I'm sorry to hear that." Lucian held back from leaning toward her. His desire to offer comfort was almost foreign to him. Yet, his spine knotted. He'd thought of her pregnancy as protection for him. After all, if she was already with child, he didn't have to worry about impregnating her with a flawed seed. But he'd never considered the dangers of childbirth. A cold hand gripped his nape.

Her head turned in his direction, and for a second

their eyes met and a connection sparked between them.

"It is hard to miss what you've never known." Velvet spoke in a quiet voice while she tightened her ribbons under her chin.

"Do you have any brothers or sisters?" asked Iris.

He turned to look out the window at the passing countryside. If his children had lived, Iris would have had two brothers and a sister.

"I did," said Velvet. "I had a brother."

Releasing his fisted hand, Lucian let out the pensive breath he held and turned back to catch Velvet's gaze.

She dipped her head but not before he caught the mist in her green eyes.

"What happened to him?"

"Iris, you are being impertinent." Lucian watched Velvet.

She held up a hand. "It is all right. He died when we were twelve."

"A twin?" he asked. Dismay carved out a hole in his gut. Twins were doubly dangerous to a mother. Did twins run in her family?

"Papa, you are being pertinent," objected Iris.

"Yes, a twin. I was the elder by about two hours." Velvet looked down at Iris. "And you mean impertinent, and it is doubly bad manners to correct your father."

"Even if he is *im*pertinent?"

"Especially then," Velvet responded in her melodic voice. "Children should not correct their elders."

"If we are making you uncomfortable, you will say so," he said. But he wanted to know everything about her. What her childhood had been like, what had led her to being a governess and then a mistress to her employer?

He started to ask a question, but the carriage swayed

and Iris and Velvet leaned in tandem. With Iris present he could not probe too deeply into Velvet's life.

"Where did you grow up?" asked Iris.

"In Dorset, in a village called Brixvale. My father was the vicar of the church there." Her voice curled under his skin, pleasant and warm like a puff of apple wood smoke as she described the orchard and rolling hills near her childhood home.

He tried not to appear engrossed, but he was. How had a vicar's daughter managed to fall so far from grace?

"What made you become a governess?" he asked.

"When my father died, I could not stay in the vicarage. The new vicar and his wife were coming. I was fortunate in that Lady Durnham offered me a temporary position as governess to her niece."

"Her niece?" echoed Lucian. "I thought you taught her two sons."

"Yes, Master James and Master Steven." Her voice quivered on the name Steven. She rushed her words as she explained she'd supervised the niece for a few months before the young woman's marriage and had also taught the boys.

"It was decided I had a better command of Latin and mathematics than their tutor, so I was kept on to instruct the boys."

"You were fond of Master Steven?" he asked.

"I was . . ." Velvet twisted her hands together. "Of course, I'm f-fond of him. I'm fond of all my former . . . pupils."

Her uncertainty betrayed her. A white-hot pain knifed through him. Was she as "fond" of the undersecretary? He leaned back against the squabs and crossed his arms. His hands fisted.

He shouldn't care anyway. Staring out the window,

he saw nothing of the passing scenery. What he needed was a wife, not a mistress.

He certainly didn't need to repeat the mistakes he had made with Lilith. He needed a moral woman, not a discarded temptress in the family way. On his next trip to London he would let it be known he was ready to remarry. With his fortune, finding a good decent woman shouldn't be impossible.

But damn it all to hell. All he'd thought about during the day was the sun glinting off Velvet's hair. He wanted to let it down and thread his fingers through the copper strands. He wanted to twine it around them as they lay naked in his bed, but she continued to use Iris as a buffer between them.

When they arrived home after dark, Iris's slack weight pressed against Velvet's side as the carriage rumbled along the rutted drive.

"She's asleep, isn't she?" Lucian's voice cut through the darkness.

Awareness of how close he was sent a shock through her. "Yes."

He'd silently stared out the window most of the trip. At times he seemed broody and lost in his musings, but she didn't dare offer a penny for his thoughts. She didn't have a penny, for one thing, and she wasn't sure she wanted to know his thoughts.

The carriage rattled to a halt, and the coachman opened the door. The small circle of the coach light illuminated the base of the stairs.

"Iris, sweetheart, wake up." Velvet jiggled the girl's shoulder.

"Don't. I'll carry her in." Lucian leaned forward and put a hand on Velvet's arm.

Her heart skittered.

Rolling Iris toward him, he lifted her limp body and held her against his shoulder. Velvet tried to ignore the brush of his hands as he gathered up his daughter. But tingles rippled away from places of contact. Without raising her eyelids, Iris curled into him.

His tenderness with his daughter made Velvet forgive his indulgences. Would that her father had ever thought she deserved anything she asked for. But she stuffed down the uncharitable thought. Her father had done the best he could for her, and there was a time when he had been indulgent. When he withdrew his affection, she knew she deserved his cool disdain for leading her brother to his death.

Lucian climbed out of the carriage and waited while she descended. The chill night air cut through her.

She followed him and the groom holding the lantern up the broad stone staircase and into the dark entry hall.

As if he didn't need a light, Lucian headed up the stairs to the nursery floor. Carrying Iris didn't slow his ascent. Velvet more carefully picked her way through the dark house.

When she entered Iris's room, the soft glow of the fire illuminated Iris's golden hair and Lucian's dark head as he bent over and unbuttoned his daughter's shoes. Her pelisse was draped over the chair where her clothes often landed. Velvet picked it up and hung it in the wardrobe. She gathered the nightgown laid out on the foot of the bed.

The shoes softly thumped on the floor. Lucian urged Iris under the covers.

"If you hold her up, I can put on her nightgown," whispered Velvet.

Lucian stood and gently tugged the nightgown from

her fingers. With his hand on Velvet's shoulder, he guided her out of the room. He gently clicked the door shut behind him.

"It won't hurt her to sleep in her clothes for one night." His voice was a low burr near her ear.

He slid his hands across her shoulders and removed her cloak. The skim of his touch down her arms left behind trails of heat. Her heart hammered.

Only the moon coming in the uncovered windows lit the dark schoolroom. The black hole of her bedroom door gaped in front of her. He nudged her toward it.

She froze.

He bumped her from behind, and the shock of feeling the full length of his hard body against hers made a shudder ripple through her.

He cupped her shoulders as if to steady her. "Blast, it is dark. Why isn't your fire lit?"

Because she was only the governess, not the pampered and indulged daughter of the house. "No point in burning a fire when I'm not here."

His hands ran up and down her arms, warming her. "Yes, but you are cold. I'll light it." But he made no move away from her.

She wanted to lean back into him and soak up his warmth. The rhythm of his breathing changed, and his fingers tightened on her shoulders. Her skirts shifted as he moved infinitesimally closer. Her heart thudded in her throat.

His fingers slid along her shoulders, then up her neck. Finding the ribbons of her hat, he gently tugged them free.

First her cloak and then her hat. He was undressing her. Still, she did nothing. She didn't turn to face him. She stood wooden and mute.

He pressed his lips against her bared neck. His mouth was warm and tempting. Liquid fire raced through her body. She could turn into his arms and let this inferno of want and need consume her.

Her knees buckled. A sound too like a moan passed through her lips.

He pressed closer, supporting her. Her shoulder blades brushed his chest, sending sparks along her skin.

"Velvet," he whispered just behind her ear. "Nothing has changed in what I want."

An icy chill stopped the melt. Nothing had changed. All he wanted was to share her bed. He wasn't offering promises of marriage or babies or a life together. She wasn't foolish enough anymore to think a man equated the act of physical love with real love or commitment.

She tore away. "I can't do this."

No matter how much she wanted to.

He'd lit her fire before leaving. Velvet had paced in the schoolroom, protesting. Lucian ignored her, draping her cloak over the iron railing of her bed and then kneeling down on the bare hearth in her room.

Never had the master of the house lit a fire for her or shown concern about her health and welfare. He'd asked if she wanted anything to eat before retiring. Her heart melted at his care. He would probably be a tender and generous lover.

Even now, hours later as she stared into the orange glow behind the grate, her body tensed with an energy she didn't understand and didn't know how to dissipate. She tried to shove the thoughts away, but all through the day their eyes had connected. Often over Iris's head. When he spoke, his voice rumbled through her like the heat of a generous fire.

Her breasts tingled as she remembered his open mouth against her throat. The slide of his fingers over her shoulders provoked a clenching of her thighs. Her woman's core had grown slick with moisture. She couldn't erase the thoughts of Lucian from her mind. What would his mouth against her breast feel like? What would the slide of his fingers along her bare skin do to her? Would his manhood inside her ease the ache in her loins and in her heart?

She groaned and flipped to her other side. Pulling her pillow over her head, she tried to will herself to sleep. But it was no use. In the dark, with nothing to distract her, she thought of Lucian. He might present her last opportunity to experience the connection between a man and a woman.

No, at church tomorrow she might catch the eye of a man in the village interested in a genteel wife. But fishermen and farmers were intimidated by the breadth of her knowledge, and her cooking and laundry skills were subpar.

She flipped back to stare at the fire.

Before she knew her mind, she was out of bed and reaching for her dress.

Thumping down on her knees, she prayed for the strength to ignore temptation. Then she slowly dressed. She would walk past his room and go downstairs to the library. If she could find a book that engrossed her, surely the wicked thoughts of lying with Lucian would go away. With a spill, she lit the stubby night-light and held it out in front of her.

She kept her head down as she scurried past his room. No light peeked under the door. He had probably gone to bed a long time ago. Unlike her last employer, Lucian rose before dawn to swim. The undersecretary had snared her into many late night conversations she never should have allowed. Harold Langtree would have her read a treatise or a bill and then ask her opinion. She ended up helping him edit his papers, offering suggestions he often incorporated into his work. She should have noticed when he began to think of her as more than an intellectual sounding board.

Harold was married to a beautiful woman. That he might feel the need to have a mistress had never occurred to her. She hadn't even thought of him as a man in that way. At least with Lucian there wasn't a wife, nor had he made any bones about what he wanted.

But just because he wasn't married didn't mean he entertained the slightest inclination to offer for a fallen woman. She just couldn't act on these urges.

Velvet heaved a sigh of relief as she slipped through the library door and was greeted with the calming musty scent of books.

"Couldn't sleep?" Lucian asked.

She blinked past the black spots burned in her eyes by holding the candle in front of her. Lucian sat in one of the leather chairs by the fire. He had a book on his lap, and he wore his dressing gown over a snowy white shirt open at the collar.

Oh God, surely her mind had conjured his apparition and he wasn't really there. He couldn't be there, but as her eyes adjusted, they didn't lie.

"I'm sorry. I didn't mean to intrude. I thought you'd be abed." Velvet closed her eyes. If he kissed her now, she'd fall into his bed with no resistance. How could God allow her into Lucian's proximity when she'd asked to not be lead into temptation? Yet, the word bed echoed in her head as though it were some lure she'd cast out.

Her lips parted as if she couldn't get enough air to breathe. She could cross the room and stand before him, and he would know the wild yearnings hammering in her body. He would see it in her face, in the rapid crest and fall of her breathing. She lowered the candle so its orb of light wouldn't betray her.

The corner of his mouth tipped. He stood and closed the book around his index finger.

She whirled and grabbed for the doorknob. The candleholder tipped and hot wax splashed on her knuckles. The burst of pain was a welcome distraction.

She plucked at the quickly drying wax revealing reddened skin.

"Don't go. Much as it disappoints me, I assume you were looking for reading material, not me." He took a step toward her. "I can leave you to it."

If he came too close to her, he'd know her turmoil. She darted to the side. "I didn't mean to disturb you."

"You're not disturbing me. If I am not disturbing you, I shall continue reading."

"Please ignore me." Her heart hammering, Velvet tried not to look at him as he sank back into his chair, opened his book, and reached for the glass beside him on the table.

"You're welcome to stay here and read." Lucian's voice was low and inviting.

A shiver tumbled down her spine. Velvet pulled out a book and opened it to realize she'd found a book on mining. Any other night, it would have probably bored her right to sleep, but tonight it wouldn't hold her attention long enough to distract her from Lucian.

"Most of those are my business books. If you are looking for a novel, they are over here by the fireplace." His book was closed around his finger again.

"Business books?" she echoed weakly. To pick out a novel she'd have to go closer to him.

"Are you interested in mining?" He raised the glass to his lips.

"I don't know." She tried to read the preface but all she could think about was Lucian. The way the firelight glinted off his dark hair made pulling her gaze away from him impossible. The shadow at the base of his throat made her mouth water. The words blurred on the edge of her vision. Her heart was beating so hard she thought it might jump out of her chest. She tucked her chin down tighter.

"That book is a bit on the dry side. I could probably answer any questions you have." He set his glass down. His voice dipped lower. "About mining, that is."

He wasn't really talking about mining. And she wasn't sure she could ask a sensible question about it at the moment. She gave up on the book and pushed it back in the slot. Shipping, railroads, and fishing books were included in the titles, as well as books on newer technologies. How many different business books did one man need? She tilted a look toward Lucian.

"I have several business interests, beyond the railroad ventures you know about," he said. "After my parents passed, I expanded my family's shipping business to include overland freight as well as a fishing fleet. The railroads will be a further expansion."

"And mining?" she asked, giving in to the inevitable discussion.

"Locally I own a copper and a tin mine and have a partial interest in a quarry."

He was undoubtedly a wealthy man. Although the trappings of the household wouldn't give him away. He could have almost any woman he wanted as wife, perhaps even a daughter of an aristocrat. He had no need to align with an impoverished governess. The harsh reality of her situation penetrated the frenzy of want she'd been in for the last few hours.

"Would you like some brandy or sherry?"

The disjointed memories of the last time she'd been handed a glass of brandy in a library assaulted her. Her hand shook and the candlelight wavered. She set the light down on a library table. "N-No. Thank you."

He'd stood and closed the distance between them. "These are my plans." He gestured toward the map her candle illuminated. "All my holdings and the routes are penciled in."

The way she had allowed herself to get drawn into conversations with her former employer hung heavy on her mind. "I really just came down to get a book."

To her shame, her voice quivered.

"Are you all right, Velvet?"

She pressed back into the shelves. He had only to touch her and she'd shatter.

His hair dipped onto his forehead. And as when she first saw him, she thought he had the beauty of an angel. Only his cheeks were shadowed and he almost looked menacing. She was lost.

If prayers couldn't save her, God must suspect her lack of sincerity in her entreaties.

Chapter 11

Velvet's eyes were luminous and wide, her lips parted and her skin flushed. Lucian didn't think she'd ever looked more beautiful. He'd certainly never wanted a woman more.

Not even Lilith in the days leading up to their wedding. And Lilith had employed plenty of tricks to entice. She could put any man into a frenzy if she thought she had something to gain.

Velvet stirred feelings of protectiveness in him. She managed to project a lack of worldliness and uncertainty, in contrast to her reputation. But to not bend and press a kiss to her enchanting lips strained his control.

He'd meant to stay in his chair and coax her into coming to sit with him, but he couldn't stand the distance. As if a gravitational force pulled him into her orbit, he stood in front of her with his hand outstretched.

He didn't know if she would take it. Perhaps it was her reluctance that wound him in knots.

"If I might offer a suggestion. I have a book by Currer Bell that might appeal to you. Or have you already read it?"

"*Jane Eyre*? I have only read the beginning chapters." She slipped her cool hand into his.

His heart thudded heavily in his chest. He wanted

to draw her to him, wrap his arms around her, but continually forcing his attentions on her was a bad tactic. She might eventually submit but would never be easy about it. He needed her to come to him. She would, if he could manage patience. "Did you not like it well enough to finish?"

She smiled wryly. "The bookstore owner did not look kindly at my reading the books without purchasing them."

"You were too frugal to purchase novels? Or does reading purely for pleasure offend your sensibilities?"

Her brows drew together for a second. "No, I had neither the space nor the funds to purchase books willy-nilly."

He frowned. Surely, a good protector would have indulged her. "Did the undersecretary not pay you well?"

Her chin dipped and her eyes darted side to side. "I was paid well enough."

The stilted quiet of her voice suggested this was not a subject she wanted to discuss. Perhaps her affair with the man had not lasted long enough for her to exact gifts.

Lucian was starting to wonder if the adultery had happened at all. Velvet just didn't seem that jaded. If her affairs were exaggerated or cut of whole cloth, he did her a grave injustice in asking her to share his bed. Guilt pricked at him and stopped him from simply pulling her into his arms.

"These are foreign language books. Italian, French…" He pointed to the shelves, then tugged her toward those that were filled with novels. "You may make use of any of the books here."

She fingered the spine of a book. "I may read them all."

Lilith had never read a book or the newspapers. He didn't know if they'd made it a half year into their marriage before their conversations bored each other. He couldn't imagine ever being bored by Velvet. Her mind was quick, as well as stocked with a great deal of knowledge. "I would enjoy discussing them with you," he answered.

A shadow crossed her face. "Do you mean to discuss literature with me or s-seduce me with other men's words?"

He supposed he had the gibe coming. He'd said he wouldn't accost her. Then, when he bumped into her in the dark schoolroom, he'd gone and nuzzled her neck. Hardly the move of a man who did not intend a coerced seduction. "Would it serve?"

She hesitated. "I would hope I am not so foolish."

"What would serve?" he asked.

She shook her head and folded her lips around her teeth.

He found the book and pressed it into her hands.

"Does it end well?" she asked.

Lucian paused. Unwittingly he'd offered her a story of a governess who in the end married her master. How could he have been that stupid? "I've read it."

"You will give nothing away, I see." Her eyes crinkled as if she might smile with the right prompting.

He'd made a horrible blunder. Turning, he dropped her hand and returned to his chair. Would she take the story line as offering her a message of hope? He didn't mean it that way. He would not marry another loose woman. He should not even want to have her. If he had thought her a woman of good moral fiber, he never would have allowed thoughts of seducing her to enter his brain. He clenched his fist.

"Is it at least happy? Because I do not think I am in the frame of mind to read a tragic or dreary ending." She took a step toward him.

He groped for his book as if it would provide a lifeline. "For the said Jane, a young woman of good character, it ends well enough. Better than it would in real life, I imagine."

Velvet's eyes widened and she reared back.

"I suppose it is a homily on how remaining pure allows for reward in the end," he added.

"But do you not think that is true? People must get their just deserts." She pressed the book to her chest.

"I do not think life is so just."

She bit her lip and managed to look worried. "If not in this life, then in the next."

"Platitudes to keep the masses in line, Miss Campbell."

"I certainly hope it is more."

Was she counting on redemption through repentance? A surge of want broke through him. If she would sit down and continue the discussion. . .

The long case clock chose that moment to chime midnight.

"Oh it is so late. I will bid you good-night." She picked up her night-light.

"You will not stay and read by the fire?"

She shook her head. "No, thank you."

"Another evening, then." Lucian picked up his glass and drained it dry.

As she scurried toward the door, it occurred to him that he didn't need to correct any misunderstanding that might arise from the story. After all, he'd made no promises or offers. In fact he'd been quite clear about what he wanted. And Velvet was not a virginal young woman who should harbor high expectations.

* * *

Iris knew it was Sunday because Nellie hadn't laid out her clothes for the day and Miss Campbell was helping her dress.

"Hurry, Iris, or the Bigsbys will leave without us."

"I don't care," Iris mumbled through the petticoat over her face. "I don't want to go."

"You don't have a choice," said Miss Campbell. "As long as I am here, you will go to church every Sunday."

"I never had to go before." Iris poked her arms in the sleeves of the pink dress over her head. Part of her was excited, though. Just to travel out of the house two days in a row made her life seem exotic. She just didn't want Miss Campbell to know she might enjoy the trip to the village.

"If you don't go to church, people will think you a heathen." Miss Campbell buttoned up the back of the dress.

"Do they think my papa is a heathen? Because he hates to go." Iris watched her governess's reflection in the dressing table mirror.

Miss Campbell frowned, "I suppose some do. But more latitude will be granted a man."

Iris crinkled her nose. "Latitude?"

"Freedom," said Miss Campbell.

"Why?"

"Because men rule the world and can do as they please, but women's job is to civilize the world and make it orderly and good." Miss Campbell pulled a brush through tangles. Her stroke was much gentler than Nellie's yanks. "Besides, someday you will wish to marry, and you would not like it if his family will not have you because you never go to church. And wouldn't you like to meet other girls your own age?"

"They would be just poor village girls. No one like me will be there."

The corners of Miss Campbell's mouth pulled back. "All the more reason you should be kind and gracious to everyone. They have less than you do, but that does not mean they are any less worthy of respect than you."

"Mama said there was no one of any consequence in the neighborhood." Iris wasn't exactly sure what she meant, just that there was no point in wasting time on the locals.

"One day you will be presented to your betters. I would suggest you think carefully about how you would like them to treat you and remember to follow the Golden Rule."

"What is that?" Iris scowled.

"Oh, my child." Miss Campbell shook her head. "Do unto others as you would them unto you." Reaching for a ribbon to tie around Iris's head, she added, "That means you must treat other people as you would like to be treated."

"Then I shall tell everyone how pretty they are," Iris said. She skipped toward the door.

"Pretty is as pretty does," muttered Miss Campbell.

Iris turned at the door. "But you look very pretty today with your hair like that."

Instead of scraping her hair back tightly into a bun as Miss Campbell usually did, soft copper wings fell back from a center part. Instead of a single coil of her shiny hair, several lumps and bumps made a pretty confection on the back of her head, like a special bakery bread made with braided loops. Iris was content for Miss Campbell to look her best, since Papa would remain at home while they traipsed to the village.

"Why thank you, Miss Pendar. And you look quite

lovely too." Miss Campbell actually smiled. "I will be down directly, I just need to fetch my cloak and hat."

Iris was in good charity with her as she clattered down the bare stairs to Papa's floor. She skipped down the hall to the main staircase. As soon as she turned the corner of the main staircase, she saw her papa pacing with his hands held behind his back.

His top hat and gloves rested on the cabinet by the door, and he wore his outdoor coat.

Her excitement curled up and died. He would ruin the day. He turned silent and sad anytime they even passed the churchyard. Not to mention he would be more interested in Miss Campbell than anything else. Any*one* else.

"Papa?"

"Good, you are down. The gig is ready. Where is your governess?" He turned and watched the staircase as if he was only interested in Miss Campbell's descent.

"She's not going. You are to take me." Iris ran down the last of the steps and picked up his hat and gloves. "Come, let us hurry. I should like to be very near when they ring the bells."

Her papa frowned at her. "Is she too tired—ah, Miss Campbell."

Iris swiveled to see Miss Campbell descending with her valise that held the four dolls.

The tilted straw hat with its straggly green ribbons made her eyes show too pretty. Now Papa would be staring at her the whole time.

The monotone of the vicar washed over Velvet as he gave a windy sermon on lost sheep returning to the fold. Lucian's face was stony. She couldn't tell if the vicar's sermon was directed at Lucian or if it was just one in his usual repertoire.

The locals whispered behind her. An occasional word drifted to her burning ears. *"Evil."* *"Wife-killer."* *"Devil's spawn."* She looked over her shoulder, trying to identify the offenders. The murmurs and whispers just seemed to intensify. Her father would never have tolerated this kind of behavior in his church.

"Lucifer," was hissed just after Velvet turned back to the front.

Velvet stiffened her shoulders and tried to concentrate on the sermon. But it was no use. She'd heard so many sermons over the years, she could anticipate the points before the vicar delivered them. She knew what a church should be like. The parishioners should be concerned for the soul of a young girl, not casting aspersions on her father. Perhaps she could suggest a lesson about casting the first stone to the vicar.

The cold of the slate tile floor seeped through her thin soles. The small church had none of the ornate carving or plasterwork of her father's church. The colored glass in the windows only made the interior dark, with red and blue splotches falling across the worshippers' faces as if they had turned mottled in grotesque caricatures of death.

Iris wiggled on the seat, kicking the portmanteau holding the dolls. Velvet reached to put her arm around the girl's shoulders, only to encounter Lucian doing the same. Their eyes met over Iris's head.

For a second she couldn't pull her gaze away or settle her arm hanging awkwardly above his. His dark eyes held hers until his fingers nudged her arm down around Iris's shoulders. He'd settled his elbow on the back of the plain pew. He turned back to face the pulpit.

They sat through the rest of the service like an intimate family group. Her arm was around Iris, and his was seemingly around the both of them. His sleeve brushed her arm every time Iris shifted. Moving it away would only cause more attention to land on them. Velvet's ears buzzed. Her heart thumped. She knew when he breathed, and as if she were a shadow moving in concert with him, her breathing matched his.

The service droned to a close, and Velvet wasted no time in approaching the vicar. Lucian introduced them and stood back. The man of God had the beefy paws of a laborer. Was his parish so poor he must work throughout the week?

"We are so pleased to have you in our humble church." His hands manacled hers.

Velvet wanted out of his sweaty grip but forged ahead with her plan.

"Miss Pendar would like to find new homes for a few of her dolls. Are there any girls who would enjoy a doll in the church today?"

Disdain flashed across the man's face before a big smile stretched his lips. His pale blue eyes appeared watery. "Are you getting too big for playthings, Miss Pendar?"

Iris ducked behind Velvet.

Velvet pulled her hands free and resisted wiping them on her skirts. She leaned down to prod an answer from Iris.

"Yes, sir," Iris managed.

"I do not know if it would be appropriate for you to give your discards to others," said the vicar slowly. "Or that they would receive them."

Velvet was shocked. The dolls, while not perfect, were certainly better than most of the villagers could afford.

"Arrogant nobs," said one woman in the back of the church.

Velvet spun to look, but could not tell which woman had spoken. The locals were dressed in drab black and gray dresses, and she should have fit right in with them, except her cloak was a dark forest green, a remnant of better times.

"Perhaps you could introduce Miss Pendar and her governess to the local families," said Lucian smoothly. He lifted the portmanteau he'd carried to the aisle over Velvet's protestations. "Iris, take out the dolls to show what you have to offer."

Iris reached in, pulled out a doll and cradled it close to her. She approached a tiny girl with braids no thicker than twine and said, "If I give her to you, would you take care of her and give her a good home?"

The girl nodded, and Iris pushed the doll into the tiny girl's outstretched arms. As the little girl's face lit up, Iris trounced back to the open portmanteau and drew out a second doll. Four girls almost en masse wiggled their way in front of the group of village women. They watched Iris with hungry eyes.

All the adults had gone silent as they watched Iris approach the next smallest girl. "Will you love her and take good care of her?"

The second child answered with a tremulous, "Yes."

Velvet's chest tightened as she realized there would be one less doll than girls.

One of the older girls shoved forward, "I would very much like a doll."

Iris gave her the doll with chipped fingers. Now there were two girls left and only one doll. Iris pulled out the last doll and looked between the two girls. Both appeared near her age, and both were dressed in very simple gowns with homespun aprons. They both glued their eyes to Iris's every move.

She stepped toward one and held out the doll. The girl grabbed it and cast a smug look toward the other child.

The doll-less girl ducked her head and started toward the door. Iris caught up to her. "I shall be friends with you, and I hope I do not have to bribe you with a doll."

The other child looked up with dew-filled eyes.

"Besides, we are too old for dolls, aren't we?" Iris laced her arm in the other girl's and headed for the doorway.

With relief and pride in Iris's skillful handling of the situation, Velvet turned toward Lucian. His gaze was cold.

He inclined his head slightly. "I'll be outside."

He strode for the door, and the people shied away, opening a path for him. Several of them all but crossed themselves.

Velvet searched for a friendly face in the crowd. In one of the back pews, Mrs. Bigsby was engrossed in tying her bonnet strings and Nellie glared. But not one of the others would meet her eyes.

"Surprised he didn't burst into flames," muttered one older woman. "Coming into the church as if he was innocent as a lamb."

"Hush, Mother," said a younger woman with a baby on her hip.

Velvet looked behind her for the vicar. He shouldn't allow his parishioners to speak so. But he was gone.

She walked past the rows of rough, blackened wooden pews.

"Left her mark on him, she did," muttered the older

woman. She turned her gaze in Velvet's direction. "You watch your step, missy. Or you'll be next."

"Excuse me?" Icy fingers ran down Velvet's spine.

"Mother!" The woman with a baby on her hip hauled the older woman toward the door.

Velvet greeted a woman about her age, only to have the woman turn her shoulder as if she hadn't heard.

"Lucifer's whore," muttered someone in the back.

A cold chill tightened Velvet's spine. They couldn't know her reputation here in this tiny little fishing hamlet, could they? But why else would they include her in the aspersions against Lucian if they didn't know the slurs cast against her?

Lucian stalked toward the gig and threw the empty valise on the floor. All the village girls chased after Iris and the child she'd decided to grace with her smiles and wiles. Iris had inherited her mother's endless reserve of charm, but it would all be for naught. She would only be hurt by their perfidy. None of the village girls would be allowed to be a true friend to her. They might take the dolls, but once their parents got them home, the girls would be told they could have nothing to do with the devil's spawn. The irony wasn't lost on him.

His reputation was far worse than Velvet's. He hadn't wanted her to hear the rumors, but it was hardly better when the attacks against him spilled over to include Iris and her governess. But he could do nothing or he would only confirm the belief that he was a violent man.

As the churchgoers spilled out into the yard, he caught the looks of fear, anger, and repulsion. His fists clenched in his pockets, he stalked toward the empty churchyard. The gate squeaked as he opened it. He didn't know why he tormented himself, but his feet knew the path to the six graves.

Dry leaves crunched underfoot. The air smelled of decay. The trees were spindly, and their denuded branches reached out like a witch's talons, catching his coat as he passed.

His parents' graves were side by side, and then came the three stones marking his two sons' and a daughter's resting place. None had survived an hour. They were all born fully formed, but blue and lifeless. Then there was Lilith's grave. He remembered the day after Iris was born, when Lilith repeated again and again, "I'm sorry."

But he'd seen the gleam of amusement in her eyes that she tried to hide by keeping her head down. He hadn't believed her words of contrition. She hadn't been the least bit sorry.

Cold seeped through him and settled in his bones. Not that it was anything other than a typical brisk day in late fall. But he always felt hollow here. He glanced to the knot of parishioners and saw Velvet standing apart.

She took a few steps toward the vicar. The man turned his shoulder and guided a woman toward the village. Velvet drew to a halt and her head dipped. Inside his pockets his hands curled. He should have warned her. Or he should have stayed home. She might have found a grudging tolerance if he hadn't staked his claim on her.

The village girls were peeled away from Iris, their parents yanking the children away one by one.

Iris moved toward her governess and slipped her hand into Velvet's. He was too far away to hear their conversation, but he didn't miss the way Velvet stroked Iris's golden curls.

After a few minutes the vicar reentered the church

and closed the door with a thump. Velvet led Iris toward the gig.

A few seconds later the leaves rustled along the pathway. He supposed it was rude of him to make them wait.

"Still think it is a good idea to attend church?" he asked as Velvet neared him.

She drew to a halt behind him. Silence stretched between them. He turned to face her, and Miss Campbell ducked her head.

"I believe Iris's spiritual education is necessary," Velvet said in a reedy voice. Then more sharply she asked, "Do they know of me here?"

"I am afraid you are tarred by your employment in my household." He turned back toward the graves. "Any woman who would work, live, and eat with evil incarnate must be damned to hell."

She didn't answer.

"They might have thought your soul could be saved if you sat far away from me."

"But . . ."

Yet, he had all but sat with his arm around her. "I do not think they have read any of the scandal sheets in which you were featured," he said.

He heard her stiff intake of breath. "But you have."

"I have seen what was written in the newspapers, but probably not the more scurrilous attacks. That is the trouble when one is connected to up-and-coming political figures with rivals."

She made a sound between a laugh and a sob. "But you hired me anyway."

"I cared about your abilities to teach. Iris needed a governess dedicated to instruction, not drink. The vice of which you are deemed guilty would hardly interfere in the schoolroom."

"You knew her previous governess drank?"

"That and her stealing was why she was dismissed." There had been many more tried and failed attempts to hire another governess. His choice had been carefully considered. "I have an agent in London who questioned why you were denied a reference by the first family who hired you when you were kept on nearly a decade. By all the professors' accounts, the boys you taught were more learned when they arrived at Oxford than most are when they leave."

He turned, and she watched him with her hands carefully folded in front of her. "Your second family, while it was clear you had too close a relationship with the master of the house, kept you nigh on three years. And in spite of your being a female, they hired you to teach their sons."

Pink crept up from her high neckline to infuse her pale cheeks. She lifted her chin as if trying to negate her shame. "I see you did make inquiries."

He waited for her to elaborate on her relationship with her previous employer, but she remained mum.

"I have too many times paid for a governess to travel here only to have her quit when she learned of my reputation or had to deal with one of Iris's tantrums."

"I see," she whispered.

He stared at the white stone marking Lilith's grave. It was bigger than the markers on his children's graves. He'd had more money when he purchased it than when he commissioned the granite stones for his parents and babies, but it seemed monstrous to him. As if he could pretend a love for his wife by an ostentatious display. "I understand what it is to be alone and to have moments of weakness."

In stepping toward her, he must have moved out of

her line of sight, because she gasped. Her gaze was on the small granite stones.

He waved to the graves. "My children."

"Oh, I am sorry." Her green eyes turned toward him, horrified and full of pity.

Funny, he didn't doubt her sincerity. She stepped closer to the graves and markers. And him.

Her eyes flicked to the dates and the names on the markers. His parents', the babies', Lilith's. The questions were in her eyes, but she pressed her lips together.

"My parents died of cholera after they took me to London." His voice was steady. Time had eased the pain of their passing, but he never spoke of his children or of bringing them here wrapped in blankets. Laying them in their fresh little caskets. Waiting while they were put in the ground without ceremony. Tipping the grave digger. Biting his tongue when the vicar told him that God worked in mysterious ways.

The sunlight caught on the smooth cream and peach curve of Velvet's cheek. She had been pale as skimmed milk when she first arrived. Already she'd begun to glow. She was achingly beautiful and full of life, carrying life. She didn't belong in the cemetery. She didn't belong with him. And he sure as hell didn't want her pity. "We should go."

Her fingertips settled on his arm. "Iris—"

"Is waiting," he finished for her. He pushed his hat down on his head and strode down the path to the gig.

There were days when he didn't know if he hated Lilith because of Iris or in spite of her. Lilith had taken his love and twisted it until he didn't know if he was capable of being a good man again. Iris deserved better. Velvet deserved more than he could offer her. And he wanted so much more.

Chapter 12

Velvet mumbled a quick prayer over each of the small graves before following Lucian. Children died, but there were single dates listed on the tombstones. Only the first two had names, a boy and a girl. The last was simply listed as Baby Boy Pendar. No wonder Iris's survival surprised Lucian and his wife.

The deaths had followed year after year, beginning with his parents and ending with the last baby, then a gap to his wife. The tragedies surely explained the dark withdrawal in Lucian. No doubt so many losses had strained his bond with his daughter.

He and Iris needed the serenity found in worship. She understood how accepting God's plan could lead to healing. She could guide Iris to a better existence, and perhaps help Lucian find redemption. He wasn't a bad man, even if he had sinned—not that she believed the accusations of the villagers. In a gruff way, he was kind; not the sort of man who could cold-bloodedly murder the mother of his children.

She turned and ducked under the overgrown tree barring the path. Other graves were better tended, their grass shorn and the freshly fallen leaves swept away. Did they hate Lucian so much here?

If they had seen him as she had, standing by the

graves of his family with a stark yearning on his face, they could not think so badly of him. It was the first time she'd seen Lucian vulnerable. She'd wanted to wrap him in her arms and hold him the way she would have held Steven or James when they fell or were taunted by other boys. If only she'd realized that Steven had taken those embraces in a way she didn't intend.

"Psst." Behind the church a woman stood pressed against the wall, as if she didn't want to be seen by Lucian out front.

Her shawl was over her head, preventing Velvet from seeing her face.

Velvet veered toward her. "Yes?"

The woman pressed a finger to her lips, then beckoned her closer.

Warily, Velvet moved to the wrought-iron fence separating the graveyard from the garden behind the stone structure.

The woman looked over her shoulder and moved closer. "That's the grave you'd be wanting to know about," she whispered.

Velvet followed the line of the woman's finger. Tucked in the far back corner of the graveyard a single grave lay set away from the tended graves, almost unnoticed. A metal plate with the raised letters MYRA GOWAN marked the spot.

"I seen how you looked at him," hissed the woman. "She looked at him that way too. Got herself with child."

Fighting the rising heat in her face, Velvet moved closer and looked at the date. Calculating in her head, she concluded that Myra would have died a few months after Iris's birth. "Who was she?"

But only the sough of the wind answered her. Velvet turned, and the woman was gone. Shaking her head, she moved to the gate and the gig where Lucian and Iris waited.

He stared ahead stonily, and she didn't dare ask him who Myra Gowan was or how she had died. He didn't hand her into the gig, but then she was only the governess.

She ducked her head, looking anywhere but at Lucian.

They drove along, passing the Bigsbys on the rutted lane. The moors stretched out in a desolate sweep of land, but the day was mild. London this time of year would have been damp and dreary with dirty streaking rain.

Here the clear sunlight sparkled off mica specks in the granite boulders. The carpet of grass remained largely green in spite of the lateness of the year. Velvet couldn't decide if she liked the open expanses or missed the trees and manicured parks of London. Nature was wilder here, not tame and ordered as in the city.

For the first time in a long time she felt she had a purpose. Lucian, angry at life's injustices, had turned from God and neglected Iris's spiritual well-being. Iris needed to be shown the path to, if not holiness, at least goodness. With her own upbringing in the church, Velvet was confident she could bring Iris into the fold.

Iris chattered about her new friend as Lucian let the horse walk home. He left them at the front steps and drove the gig toward the stables. Velvet tried not to watch like a loony bird as she led Iris inside the still house. Was her attraction to Lucian obvious to everyone?

She sighed as she climbed the stairs. With only the few remaining hours of her day off, she needed to find the laundry room and do her washing. After piling her linens in a basket, she headed down the servants' stairs to the kitchen.

Mrs. Bigsby pulled an apron around her ample frame, while Nellie backed out of the larder with a covered platter.

"Luncheon will be on the table soon, miss," said Mrs. Bigsby. "If you'll go wait in the morning room."

"Where is the laundry room?"

"You can't do washing now. It's the Sabbath," said Mrs. Bigsby. "Leave your things, the washerwoman comes on Wednesdays."

Velvet resisted rolling her eyes. Her things were so threadbare she didn't dare risk a rigorous scrubbing and boiling. Without her wages, she needed her underthings to last another year. She walked across to one of the half-dozen doors and opened it to find a stillroom. "I still need to know where the laundry is."

Nellie nodded toward a far door.

Velvet headed toward it. As she backed toward the hinged door, she said, "Mrs. Bigsby, who was Myra Gowan?"

Nellie dropped the covered platter and it thudded on the floor.

Mrs. Bigsby's face turned red and her eyes became slits. "Nellie, what is wrong with you?"

Velvet set down her basket and went to help gather up the spilled roast beef. Nellie dropped to her knees and hung her head down as she picked slivers of meat from the floor.

"I noticed Myra was rather young and buried alone." She had been nineteen when she died.

Mrs. Bigsby thumped a heavy pan on the stove with a resounding clang. "We don't speak of her here."

Nellie's mouth was pressed so tightly closed, Velvet

doubted she'd get an answer from her. Velvet shivered. Who was Myra, and why had a villager thought to warn her about a long-dead girl?

Lucian stared at the letter on his desk. It was written on watermarked paper, the creases perfect thirds. He hadn't expected anything like this when he decided to spend the remainder of the afternoon catching up on correspondence before he left tomorrow. Of course he hadn't know what to expect when he saw the precise script on the envelope and the return address for Mrs. Langtree in London.

He didn't expect a reference at this late date.

Instead it read:

Dear Mr. Pendar,

    It has come to my attention that you have recently hired a person to instruct your daughter. I feel it would be remiss of me to not warn you of the viper you have taken to your bosom. I hesitated to write, but felt it was my Christian duty.

    Rather than pass judgment, I shall simply lay out the facts. A certain Miss C— was a member of our household. She developed a peculiar interest in my husband and his acquaintances. I may be a fool, but I took him at his word when he said Miss C— helped him with his political endeavors. I was even grateful for her interest, because I do not have the constitution to follow the discourses on governance. Little did I know I was being played for a fool.

    On the fifth of January my youngest son suffered an injury. My husband had a guest, a rather

prominent older MP, and had engaged the ser-
vices of Miss C— to take some notes for them
during their meeting. I will not give you the name
of this man, although it has been suggested in the
papers, but I should not like to cause him further
harm. But I digress. My husband was called away
to help. Sometime later, my son was begging for
his governess, and in an effort to soothe my dis-
traught child I sought her out.

I was mortified to catch her closeted with the
MP in the library. She was in a wicked state. Her
skirts and petticoats were about her waist, and
her pantalets were about her ankles. She was
sprawled upon the sofa. The MP was standing
still fully clothed. So I know she was playing the
wanton, displaying her private parts with such
abandon.

I fear she had indulged too much in the drink
my husband kept in the room. I was so shocked
I could not speak. I had never had any reason to
suspect she was immoral. If you doubt this, I will
tell you Miss C— has a crescent moon birthmark
on her hip. You might have one of your female
servants confirm this. The MP quickly fastened
his clothing and left.

I was swayed by her tearful entreaties and
clearly intoxicated state that she had not known
what she was doing and thus allowed her to stay
on. In truth I believe I was so shocked I could
hardly think straight.

I warned her that such wickedness would not
be allowed in our household.

Barely a month later I went alone to the the-
atre. My husband begged off from attendance

with excuses of urgent work. I returned early to find Miss C— in my bedroom in an open to the waist nightgown. My husband was in a frenzy, tearing off his clothes. She was making the most shocking noises. Of course he stopped when he realized I had returned. Miss C— continued to screech like a cat in heat.

You can understand why I insisted the footmen throw her out on the street right that moment. My husband tried to defend her, but I would have none of it. I told him I understand men have certain needs outside of marriage, but I would not condone that kind of woman in my household or in my bed. I believe he was tempted beyond rational thought.

I was not willing to be made a fool again.

I fear her wickedness does not end there. Lady D—, who recommended this viper to me, has informed me that Miss C— tried to ensnare her younger son. He made several visits to her apartments and gave her money. They had to threaten to cut off his funds so he would stay away from Miss C—. While he is a young man now, this is a boy she helped raise. Preying on a former pupil is certainly the most disgusting of acts.

Lady D— was profuse in her apologies, but she too had been fooled by the character of Miss C—. While I do not know all the details of this liaison with Lady D—'s son, I am convinced it was quite sordid.

Miss C— will certainly destroy the character of your child. Please do not be deceived by her modest behavior. She could hold butter in her mouth without it melting. This woman is a Jeze-

*bel whore who corrupts those who would treat
her with goodness. At some future date should
you wish to have your child accepted in society,
having her name linked in any way with V— C—
will only put her beyond the pale. I hope you will
heed my warning.*

The letter was signed with only an initial and a dash,
as if it were an epistle to a lover. Lucian rubbed his
face. He pushed back from his desk and went in search
of Velvet. He had half begun to believe that Velvet's
reputation was undeserved, since she didn't have the
knowing way about her that Lilith had.

Velvet wasn't in her room or the schoolroom. Iris
was playing with her dolls in her bedroom. Upon seeing
him, she popped up and ran to him.

"Where is Miss Campbell?" he asked.

Iris shrugged. "She took a basket of clothes
downstairs."

He nodded and pivoted out of her room.

If she was so indiscriminate in her lovers—an old
politician, a married man, and a wet behind the ears
boy—why was she refusing to join him in his bed? A
white hot anger boiled in his chest. He fisted his hands.

"Papa," called Iris. "Why do you want Miss
Campbell?"

"Go back in your room. This doesn't concern you."

A few minutes later he stopped in the kitchen, a rare
enough event that Nellie's mouth dropped open. Bigsby
stood so fast the chair he was sitting in toppled over. But
it was Sunday. All the day servants had the day off, so
the Bigsbys were the only household staff present. They
had the minimal duties of heating and serving the meals
Cook had already prepared.

"Mrs. Bigsby, I will be leaving at five in the morning. Be so good as to inform the rest of the household."

"Mr. Evans—"

"Has already packed for me and will be accompanying me. The coach and coachman will stay in Plymouth until my return. Miss Campbell is in the laundry?" His words were clipped.

Nellie ducked her head and wiped her hands on her apron.

"Yes, sir," Mrs. Bigsby said. "Would you like Nellie to fetch her?"

"No, need." He crossed the room.

"Do you need me to show you the way?" Nellie lurched toward him, seemingly recovering her composure.

"No." He'd lived in the house all his life. He knew its rooms, even the ones he didn't inspect on a regular basis.

When he entered the room, Velvet was bent over a washtub, her sleeves pushed back above her elbows. A strand of hair had slipped loose and caressed her flushed face.

"The washerwoman comes on Wednesdays," he said.

Velvet looked up, her eyes wide and her lips parted. She straightened and pulled her dripping forearms from the washtub. "I've been told. I'm in the habit of seeing to my own washing."

Behind her, two nightgowns, three petticoats, and a chemise dripped on the flagstone floor.

"I've received a letter from a Mrs. Langtree."

The color drained from Velvet's face.

He'd hoped she would look surprised or confused, but she looked . . . guilty, as if she knew exactly what the letter contained.

His gaze shifted to her wet nightgowns. They were

plain, without sheer lace panels or plunging necklines. The button plackets weren't even set particularly low.

Who the hell was she? Everything he saw pointed to a modest, moral woman. Everything except the passion he'd tasted on her lips the night she'd come to his bedroom.

"I wish to discuss the contents of that letter."

She pushed back the strand of loose hair. Her shoulders slumped. "Very well."

"In my office . . ." He was about to say immediately but hesitated. " . . . when you are through here."

"Thank you," she said.

He had to decide what to do with her, and she was thanking him? Clenching his fists, he walked back to his office. Lilith had fooled him, but he'd been eighteen and hungry for all the joys of marriage, companionship, family . . . sexual relations. If his parents had been alive, he might not have been so alone or so impulsive. He might have waited to marry.

Had he allowed Velvet to fool him too? The letter could be full of lies and exaggerations. Or he was just an idiot.

Velvet finished wringing out her pantalets then hung them on the drying racks.

Whatever Mrs. Langtree had written, it wouldn't be good. She would have little defense against the facts. A sick feeling crept into the back of her throat. She swallowed repeatedly, to no avail.

She carefully poured out the rinse water and tried to straighten her clothes to appear presentable. But the truth was, once her reputation was shattered, no man ever looked at her in the same way. She thought she'd gotten away from the horrible innuendoes and treatment. But perhaps as her punishment in life she could never truly get away. She had to pay for letting her brother die.

Her heart thundered in her chest and her hands shook. Lucian's seeking her out in the laundry room couldn't bode well.

She made her way through the gallery along the back of the house. Long shadows alternated with the orange glow of the setting sun. The colors moved over her as if she were passing through the darkness and flames of hell. She paused outside the library. Drawing in a deep breath, she tried to steel her nerves. But her breath caught and her heart quivered in her chest.

The door clicking open sounded like a gunshot. Velvet tried to close it without jumping out of her skin. Each step toward Lucian's open office door was like a march to face a firing squad.

He knew of her reputation. She didn't expect him to dismiss her, but to require compliance in a way she couldn't agree to.

She moved into his office trying to maintain her dignity, but each step felt jerky.

Behind a cluttered mahogany desk, Lucian scratched a pen across a page.

He plunked his pen down and three drops spewed off the point onto the blotter. He flung a letter across the desk. "Read this."

The end sections stood up where the sheets had been folded. She took the pages and flattened them with shaking hands. Lucian leaned back and scowled at her.

The words swam in front of her. Forcing her eyes to focus, she read with growing horror. Each statement shredded her dignity. How could anyone reading this ever think her worthy of respect?

All along, Lucian's scrutiny made her want to curl into a tiny ball and hide away. Her hand fisted until half-moons indented her palm.

When she reached the end and the threat to Iris, the demon claws of despair gripped. Oh, God, she could not allow her tattered reputation to interfere with Iris's future.

With painstaking precision she realigned the sheets and folded them back along their original lines. The silence roared in her ears.

"Well?" said Lucian.

"What would you have me say?"

"Is that what happened?"

If her chest grew any tighter her heart wouldn't fit inside. Her mouth felt tight too. "Yes. Her rendition of the events is for the most part factual."

His nostrils flared and his stare turned hard. He folded his arms. "Really?"

Velvet held her shoulders square and met his narrowed gaze. "That is what she saw." She had admitted to the bare bones truth of what Mrs. Langtree relayed. How much more indignity did she need to suffer? Her face burned. "And you do not need to have Mrs. Bigsby examine me. I have a stain in the shape of a crescent moon on my hip."

His upper lip curled and he stared at her until she looked away.

"Explain, Miss Campbell, how you came to be found with your skirts around your waist?" He thrust his chin toward her.

In the past, people who should have known her character had scoffed at and then dismissed her explanations. Knowing her for such a short period, Lucian would have even less reason to believe her. She didn't waste her breath defending herself. Instead she focused on the last part of the letter. "If you intend to dismiss me for the danger I present to Iris securing a decent future, then I ask you give me wages enough that I can exist until I can find work."

He glared at her. His gaze dropped down, insolently raking over her. Against her will, her body responded with coiling heat and tightening nipples.

A sick feeling caught at the back of her throat. Just as Mr. Langtree had before him, Lucian would demand she submit. Once she refused him again, her days of being a governess were undoubtedly over. Perhaps she could find work in a hostelry. Her ears burned as her father's voice echoed in her head. *Pride goeth before destruction, and a haughty spirit before a fall.*

Where did virtue rank? Deep inside her a rift opened, and a black despair boiled forth. She was in hell. Wanting to tear the condemning letter to shreds, she twisted it in her hands.

"If you choose your lovers so indiscriminately, what exactly is your objection to me?" he demanded.

She knew he wouldn't believe her, but she said, "I do not take lovers."

"All the evidence is to the contrary." His words were tight. "You manage to look so affronted, Miss Campbell, but I have had a brief experience of your weakness."

Her face felt like it might crack. Mrs. Langtree had even prepared him for false innocence. She had nowhere to turn. Allowing him the liberties she had fought against went against everything she'd been raised to hold dear. She had never deliberately chosen sin. Resisting the temptation to give in was paramount now. "Wh-What about Iris?"

Lucian chopped the air. "Iris's prospects aren't at issue."

"But—"

"No man concerns himself with his wife's governess. This is about you."

Why would Mrs. Langtree care what became of her? Why would that woman force her to choose to become the loose woman everyone thought she was or to starve on the streets? In clipped words she said, "No, nothing has changed. You knew the accusations leveled against me. You just have more details of the so-called proof."

He stood and leaned toward her. The lamp on his desk splayed fiendish shadows on his face. She recoiled, but his obsidian eyes pinned her in place as he circled the desk to tower over her. She didn't dare retreat.

"Does my scar offend you? Or is it the blackness of my character?"

She stared at him. Her heart pounded, and more than fear tensed her muscles. In truth she objected least of all to him. She wanted to feel his touch. Late in the night, the memory of his mouth on hers kept her awake. He only had to lean in a little farther and their mouths would meet. Her lips tingled in anticipation.

"Well?" he demanded.

"You said you wouldn't force me." Her chin lifted and she fought the instinct to cower. He wouldn't force her, and she couldn't choose to risk her soul.

"Am I that hideous to you?" He pushed closer until she could feel his harsh breathing on her skin and see the pulse of a muscle under the pink crescent scar.

Sensations wild and out of control raced through her body, threading jolts of fear, desire, and anger into a tightening riot in her core. "No, of course not."

"Then what would it take to get you in my bed? Gifts? Money?"

"Marriage." The word shot out and shocked her.

His face contorted. He jerked back. The air eddied around her face in his wake.

"I will not marry another whore." His low voice retreated to the shadows in the corner of his study.

Whore? He'd called her a whore. She hurtled the folded letter on his desk, scattering papers. In a strained quivering voice she said, "I would never marry a man who thinks so little of me."

"You have a worse problem than your reputation."

"Yes." Marriages for women her age were rare, even rarer for women of no means. At best she might find a poor vicar or a yeoman farmer willing to marry her. She was more likely doomed to spinsterhood. "But I refuse to believe I am beyond hope, and I will not consent to being your plaything."

"Don't hold out too long, Velvet. I will never marry you. But I could make your life very easy." His voice grew silky.

Her heart beat so hard each thrum echoed in her ears. Her whole body shook. God forgive her, the idea of allowing him to protect her held attraction.

"You could use new dresses, gloves, perhaps you'd like a pair of emerald ear bobs to match your eyes." Blocking her escape, he drew nearer until she could feel his breath on her nape.

It had been years since she had a new dress or gloves, but it was the way her skin tingled as he approached her that lured her toward temptation. Whatever was between them woke a hunger in her. He might be her last opportunity to experience what happened between a man and a woman. If he touched her, she might shatter or transform into a wanton creature she didn't know.

A jumble of silent prayers left her lips, for strength to resist, pleas for him to touch her and take the decision out of her hands. God never answered her prayers in the way she expected. Each second stretched to a razor-thin blade of indecision.

"Why are you trembling? Are you that afraid?" His hands closed around her shoulders.

Her knees buckled and she thrust her palm against the desk to keep from falling. "I don't know. I've never felt like this."

"Velvet—"

"Who was Myra Gowan?" The question seemed to spring from nowhere, or perhaps divine intervention put the image of the forlorn grave marker in her head.

He shoved her away. "You are dismissed."

Dismissed? Just like that? Her heart dropped through her throat and sank like a stone. Would she be cast out into the dark of night?

Chapter 13

Velvet fisted her hands in her skirts, and her face drained of color. Tiny lines appeared in her forehead. "Sh-Should I pack my things tonight?"

Lucian stared at her. It took him a minute to realize her anxiety was because she thought he'd ended her employment.

He waited to see if she would reconsider her options and consent to being his mistress. He despised himself for the weakness, but it had been so long since he'd felt the softness of a woman's hands on his skin or the drape of her hair over his chest. And damn, Velvet's hands were slender and feminine, her hair a riot of fire, and her mouth an invitation to sin.

A long time ago he'd sworn off women, but Velvet walked across the floor, and he grew hard and urgent.

He'd sworn off women after Myra's death, actually. The mention of Myra had been like a plunge into the ocean in the coldest part of the winter. The heat of his anger drained from him. The memories of Myra were raw, and he wouldn't discuss her. But who the hell had told Velvet? And how much did she know?

Velvet stared at him, her eyes wide and glittering in the darkening gloom. Her trembling chin lifted in defiance. He didn't understand her resistance to him, but then she wasn't the first woman to find him objectionable. Another woman in her position would have caved under the pressure and consented to become his mistress, but Velvet was like no other woman.

He finally took pity on her. "Dismissed from the room, Miss Campbell. You may retain your position as governess to Iris."

"Oh," she expelled on a puff of air.

"It is probably past time for dinner. You should go fetch her."

"Certainly." She tripped toward the door as if afraid he'd change his mind.

His wanting her started all over again. As he watched her reach for the door and cast an uncertain glance over her shoulder at him, he knew he could have her with the promise of marriage.

Marriage.

Lucian sank down in his chair and rubbed his face. The thought had crossed his desperate mind before she mentioned matrimony, before the letter, before she conceded the letter was factual. When she had, he felt as if he'd been punched.

He'd thought the rumors must have been overblown. He'd thought her a victim of circumstance. He'd thought he could claim her child as his or perhaps take her on an extended trip so the birth date wouldn't raise eyebrows.

He'd expected anything but her admitting to being found naked to the waist, sprawled on a sofa. Yet, her concern had been about Iris. He admired her courage and strength and compassion. Even as he hated her convictions, her firm resolve to resist temptation only made him want her more.

His mind conjured a picture of her, all long legs and

milky white skin. He swallowed hard. He still wanted her, but clearly she didn't want him.

His heart thumped with violence in his chest. The dips in the ocean each morning weren't going to be enough for him to control his urges. He grabbed a glass paperweight from the desk and hurtled it across the room, where it shattered against the wall.

He'd spent years honing his control to fine art, but around her he was in danger of losing the firm grip he kept on his passions . . . again.

Velvet made it around the corner before she collapsed against the wall. Her emotions were as gnarled and knotted as an old fishing net.

She'd expected Lucian to be disgusted or appalled, the usual reaction to hearing reports of her exploits. Instead he'd been furious at her refusal to allow him the same liberties she'd supposedly allowed the other men.

Sucking in deep breaths, she pushed against her rebelling stomach. She should be giving thanks he hadn't dismissed her or demanded her compliance, but mystified better described her emotional state.

He could have forced her to submit, but he didn't. For that a gushing gratitude swept through her. How could the villagers not see he was a good man? How could they call him Lucifer?

Perhaps she had done him an injustice by assuming he wouldn't listen or give credence to her explanations. He, more than any other, could probably understand how false accusations might distort the truth. Although the truth sounded fantastical even to her.

Knowing she couldn't allow Iris to see her in turmoil, Velvet closed her eyes and searched for calm.

The last thing she wanted to do was sit down to dinner with him, but she had to pretend everything was normal for Iris's sake.

Pushing away from the wall, Velvet made her way to the stairs. She could have used a candle, but she was familiar enough with the way now to climb to the nursery floor.

"Iris?"

The girl shot out of her room, "I thought everyone forgot about me."

"No, of course not." Iris's future was her main concern. Velvet wrapped an arm around her shoulders.

Iris dug her toe into the carpet. "Well it is your day off, and Papa said I must not bother you."

If only *he* had remembered that. "How could I forget about you? Especially when you handled a difficult situation with grace today."

"I did?" asked Iris.

"Most certainly. I do not know that I would have handled the problem of two girls and one doll so well." Velvet frowned. Lucian had not been pleased. "We do need to go down to dinner."

But Velvet pondered Lucian's dismissal of the threat against Iris. Granted, a governess's misdeeds would pale alongside the accusations of murder against her father, but he didn't understand how a powerful political family could influence London society.

Or perhaps as his sole heir, Iris's drawbacks would be overlooked. Velvet took the girl's hand and led her downstairs to the dining room.

The crackling fire and stubby dripping tapers in the candelabra waged a futile fight to rid the room of darkness. Lucian stood with his back to them, shoulders squared, one arm held in the other behind his back and his feet equidistance apart. His rigid stance radiated restrained energy.

Velvet's heart caught in her throat. She wanted to touch him and see if he relaxed or remained furious with her. In spite of the scar, he was an attractive man. He certainly could find another woman to satisfy those needs. But the thought of him turning to another woman scraped and clawed at her. The trembles she'd managed to still returned full force. Oh God, she didn't want him turning to another woman. She wanted him for herself.

He swiveled. "Well don't just stand there."

Velvet jumped.

Iris tugged her hand free and skipped to her chair.

Almost running, Velvet made it to her chair before he could assist her. Her breathing grew rapid. With great deliberation she pulled her napkin into her lap.

She could feel his gaze burning through her as she smiled at Iris.

"I will make all the village girls my court as if I were queen," announced Iris.

Lucian's attention snapped to his daughter. "You can't make them into your pets, Iris."

Iris leveled a glare at him and jutted out her lower lip. "But I am their better, am I not?"

"Do you not think they may prefer a more even friendship? I think you would too." Velvet's fist clenched in her lap. "It is never pleasant to be reminded one is inferior."

"You will hardly have time to be friends with the village children." Lucian rang the bell imperiously. "You have studies."

Velvet sighed.

"You disagree, Miss Campbell?"

"Every young lady needs companions her own age in order to learn good social skills. If she had siblings—"

Lucian's quick wince flooded her with remorse.

"—or regular companions, she won't be overwhelmed in society. She won't be desperate for the attention of others and be less at risk for faux pas."

The Bigsbys carried in a beef roast, bread, and a sad dish of shriveled green beans. Mrs. Bigsby set the platter down with a decided thump. Her mouth was stretched in a thin line.

Lucian's gaze raked over his daughter. "I don't think we're in danger of Iris becoming a wallflower. She has a great deal of her mother in her."

He didn't sound pleased. He had implied his first wife was a whore, but that didn't comport with the glowing portrait he normally painted for Iris.

Confused, Velvet turned to Mrs. Bigsby. "I'm sorry we are so late."

"The food is overdone," she muttered.

"That will be all," said Lucian with finality. "Did you suffer a lack of companionship, Miss Campbell? Is that what happened?"

"No, I had my brother and developed friendships with members of my father's church."

"As an adult were you not so lucky?" His voice was low, but with an edge.

He surely didn't mean to discuss this in front of Iris.

"I was far from my friends," she said softly. Velvet turned to the child. "Do you need help with the meat?"

Lucian turned the platter and sawed off a hunk of the dried edge of the roast, then sliced a juicer slice and plunked it on Iris's plate. He repeated the process and placed a generous serving on Velvet's plate. He frowned and added an additional piece. "Have some green beans, Iris."

"They're icky."

He pointed with the knife. "I said have some and pass the dish."

"Vegetables are good for the complexion, Iris." Velvet said softly. "Girls who don't eat their vegetables don't stay pretty for long." It probably wasn't the complete truth, but she wasn't above using a little manipulation to avoid a confrontation. A girl left to her own devices for years couldn't be expected to buckle under just because her father had finally decided to take an interest in her eating habits.

Lucian frowned at her.

"Did Mama eat her vegetables?" Iris asked.

Lucian sighed. "Certainly she did. She did everything she could to retain her beauty." He rolled his eyes toward Velvet. "If you are insistent on Iris having companions her own age, perhaps she should be at school." He turned toward his daughter. "What do you say, Iris? Do you feel you are learning under Miss Campbell's tutelage? Or would you be better served by a school in Bath?"

Iris slumped in her seat.

Velvet's throat tightened. A girl in school would have no need of a governess. Was her position going to be dependant on becoming his mistress, after all? Disappointment darkened and curled her insides like papers tossed in a fire. She slid her napkin from her lap and folded it beside her beef-laden plate. She had no appetite anyway. "For a child starved for friends, school would be a blessing. But a child too far behind in her studies would be ostracized."

Iris looked between them. "What does ostracized mean?"

"You'll have to ask me tomorrow. I am off duty, and if I may be excused, I should like to enjoy the rest of my evening."

"Don't move," barked Lucian.

Velvet glared at him. She did not enjoy being the mouse in his cat and mouse game.

"Am I too far behind?" asked Iris.

"You are behind. You have gone too long with inadequate or no instruction," said Velvet softly. "But you will catch up, if I have any say at all."

"Are you campaigning for your job, Miss Campbell?"

"I do not like my prospects for employment elsewhere."

"Stay. You need to eat. I would hardly take a nine-year-old's advice on her education."

"Why would you ask me then, Papa?" Iris's eyes grew big.

"Yes, why? Do you mean to toy with us all through the meal?" asked Velvet in a low voice.

He blanched, then threw his napkin on the table and pushed back his chair. "You may be excused or you may stay. I will be in my office." He stood and bowed. "The choice is yours, Miss Campbell."

She stared at his retreating back and felt more uncertain than ever. Did he mean the choice of employment was hers or only the meal? Her heart fluttered in her chest. Velvet bit down hard on the inside of her lip.

"Is he cross at me for making friends with the girls?" asked Iris.

"No, no, of course not. He . . . he just read an unpleasant letter." Velvet tried to smile at Iris.

"No. He is upset because you made him go to the church. He hates the church." Iris threw her napkin across the table. "It is all your fault." She ran toward the door.

*   *   *

"Why isn't Papa swimming?" Iris's shrill cry cut through Velvet's sleep.

She had to stop tossing and turning at night and get more rest. Pushing back the covers, she winced at the coldness of her room. Her window was unlatched and cracked. The low sound of Nellie's voice drifted through the schoolroom, followed by Iris's increasingly panicked tone.

The girl ran into Velvet's room and launched onto the bed. The iron bedstead swung and creaked.

"You have to stop him," Iris said. "He has to say good-bye. He never says good-bye." She threw her arms around Velvet's neck and sobbed.

The schoolroom doorway framed a frowning Nellie. "He's already gone."

"No-o," wailed Iris.

Velvet stroked the girl's tangled curls. "What is all this tragedy?"

"He's gone."

"Your papa?" Velvet looked over Iris's head to Nellie for explanation.

"He left for Plymouth first thing this morning," said Nellie.

He had said he needed to take a business trip with or without them. But he'd left already? Without saying good-bye to either of them? Velvet's shoulders dropped.

Iris shifted off the bed and pulled her by the hand. "We have to go after him. If we run across the moors we might catch his carriage on the road."

For one insane second Velvet considered the idea. "No, Iris, you're not dressed. I'm not dressed. He will be back."

"He'll be gone forever," wailed Iris.

Less than charitable thoughts tumbled through Velvet's head. Was Iris trying to avoid the classroom? She pushed the girl's slender frame back so she could see her face.

Real tears streamed down her cheeks.

Using the edge of her sleeve, Velvet wiped them away. She pulled the girl against her and rubbed her narrow shoulders.

"How long is he usually gone?" she asked Nellie.

Nellie shrugged. "As long as it takes. A week . . . two."

"Forever," stressed Iris.

"So do go with Nellie and get dressed. After breakfast, we can start our lessons. If you show much improvement, perhaps he will take you with him next time."

"No, he won't! He hates me." Iris shoved away and ran from the room. "He wants me dead!" The door to her room slammed with a resounding bang.

Velvet sighed. "Is she always so full of drama this early in the morning?"

Nellie stared at a point past Velvet.

"He didn't want her to live," she said flatly.

"What?" whispered Velvet.

"Her casket is down in the cellar. He'd already ordered it."

Velvet's ears reverberated as if she were hearing everything through a long tunnel. "I think there is a difference between expecting her to not live like her siblings and *wanting* her to die."

Nellie's eyes moved slowly through the room. A shudder rolled down Velvet's spine. She needed to shut the window, but she didn't dare allow Nellie to see her terror.

"No, he wanted her to die. Just like he wanted his wife to die and he wanted Myra to die."

Velvet's throat closed. "Who was Myra?" she asked.

"She's the reason none of the staff will sleep here anymore." Nellie turned slowly and lumbered across the schoolroom floor, her footsteps like punctuation marks to a sentence she'd delivered with no more passion than she'd relay the state of the weather. Why would no one talk of Myra Gowan? Why had Lucian cut off the conversation when asked about her?

"Nellie, how did she—"

"I will speak no more of her."

The days passed in a tedium of lessons. Iris resisted, Velvet persisted, until the girl's head was spent every morning bent over her slate, painstakingly constructing each letter of the alphabet.

"That is a *d,* not a *b*," said Velvet, leaning over the schoolwork.

Iris slammed the slate down on the table and crossed her arms. "I don't know the difference."

"A small *d*'s hump faces the beginning of the sentence, or the left, and a *b*'s hump faces the end of the sentence or the right. Show me your right hand."

Iris rolled her eyes.

"If you can show me your right hand, we will finish with the alphabet for the day. We'll work on deportment instead."

Her face scrunched tight, Iris held out her left hand and quickly withdrew it and stuck out her right hand.

Velvet sighed. "Is it hard for you to tell the difference? You know, you do write with your right hand."

"Is that why it is called the right hand?"

"They're different words that sound the same. We

could tie a ribbon around your right wrist until you can remember which is which."

"I could wear one of Mama's bracelets," said Iris.

"I think that would be a perfect solution," said Velvet, standing.

"We'll have to go get one." Iris shot to the door. "Come on."

Velvet followed Iris down the stairs and past Lucian's bedroom. Iris looked furtively around and then opened the next door and darted inside. Waving her hand frantically, she said, "Hurry."

Velvet balked. "Are you supposed to go in there?"

"I come here all the time." Iris's eyes darted wildly about. "It is just Mama's sitting room."

Relenting, Velvet entered the room. With an airy lightness, gold brocade covered the chairs and a settee. The walls were creamy, and tiny pink rosebuds on the pillows added a splash of color. Green piping married the room to Lucian's, without the dark masculinity of his room.

Iris clicked the door shut. Drawn by the portrait of Lucian, a woman, and a baby above the pale marble fireplace, Velvet crossed the floor. The carpet was so plush it was like walking on peat moss. Unlike the rest of the house, there were no signs of wear in the furniture.

"That's my mama and me," said Iris.

Velvet took in the artist's rendition of the family. Lucian was well-captured but seemed disconnected from the golden-haired woman seated in front of him. His unscarred face was stoic, stony even, although not without life. Shifting her scrutiny to the woman, Velvet recoiled. Iris's mother was portrayed with a coy smile and a come-hither look in her eyes in an almost unflattering way. She had been beautiful, not in the cold way the undersecretary's wife was, but in a way that was almost too warm, too . . . knowing.

The baby in her lap seemed almost an afterthought. As family portraits went, it was more like three individuals posed together, but without any affinity for each other.

Velvet frowned. She was seeing things that weren't there. She was predisposed to dislike any woman who had held Lucian's affection. She shook off her prejudices. After all, it was just a portrait. Emotions weren't frozen for all posterity in an artist's brushstrokes.

"She's very pretty, isn't she?" said Iris.

"You're prettier," said Velvet sharply. Iris was still fresh and innocent in a way her mother hadn't appeared to be. "Why isn't it hung in the gallery with the rest of the family portraits?"

Iris shrugged. "Papa said I may take it to my married home if I want to. He said I shall have my mama's things when I am older."

As if no longer interested, Iris ducked into an inner sanctum. Separated by a large archway was the bedroom. Iris opened a wooden case on a bedside table. Inside was a tangle of gold, silver, and beaded necklaces. Rings and ear bobs were mingled without regard for whether they appeared to be made of pot metal or gold.

Iris pawed through the mess. "Miss Grimes stole a bunch of Mama's rings and broaches. But the joke was on her because Papa keeps all the precious bits and pieces locked up in his office."

Bangles and beads clinked on the bureau top as Iris fished out wads of the jewelry.

Velvet's fingers itched to untangle and sort, but after hearing that her predecessor had stolen some of the items, she backed away. Perhaps Lucian withheld Miss Grimes's wages too. Iris wouldn't know how a shilling or two fetched from a trinket could turn into a meal or fuel for a fire.

"I like this." From the very bottom, Iris pulled out a silver charm bracelet with love tokens and lockets. "Which wrist?"

Velvet lifted Iris's right hand and pulled the thick chain around her forearm. She would of course pick the jingliest one possible. One of the coins was etched R & L, another bore, *To my love, Lil, yours always, R.H.* Iris triggered the catch of a round locket. "Look, it's an eye. Why would anyone paint just an eye?"

It was common practice to have only a small portion of a lover painted so as to conceal the identity. Velvet winced. A man's blue eye with a sandy brown eyebrow gazed up at her. That certainly wasn't her husband's eye. A frisson of unease passed through her.

"It would be very hard to paint the whole face in such a small picture." She closed the locket. "This might have been a very personal treasure of your mother's. Perhaps you should choose another."

"I want this one." Iris's expression was mulish.

To be fair, the girl had been trying hard to please with her schoolwork, which seemed extraordinarily difficult for her. Velvet wished she'd insisted on a ribbon. She fastened the clasp. "What will your papa say?"

Flipping her hand back and forth, Iris skipped across the room, making the charms rattle.

Perhaps the eye was of her uncle. Her mother had been fair-haired. "What do you know of your mother's family?"

Iris stopped cold. "My grandmama and grandpapa used to visit before Mama died." She folded her arms behind her back. "After Mama was buried, they had a terrible row, and Papa made them leave."

The girl backed away then, her pleasure at the bracelet gone. A tear dribbled out of her rapidly filling eyes. She ducked away.

"Iris," muttered Velvet. "What's wrong?"

She wrapped the girl in her arms. Her slender shoulders shook. Her quiet sobs were like the ones in the middle of the night and reminded Velvet of the way she had grieved for her brother, afraid to make a sound for fear of her father hearing.

"Th-They didn't say good-bye," choked out Iris.

Velvet backed onto the bed and held Iris as she wished she'd been held when she suffered the greatest loss in her life. She stroked the child's narrow back. "There there. Everything will be all right."

But would it?

Chapter 14

I ris skipped ahead on the lane to the village. Velvet hoped the child could continue friendships with the village girls. She needed the opportunity to just giggle and be silly with another girl her own age. Her life was filled with adults.

Since it was her day off, Velvet could linger a while after the church service. Iris had worked hard at her lessons all week, she deserved to have a little fun.

Iris waited for her to catch up. "Who decided how letters would look?"

"I don't know. I suppose some ancient Roman." Velvet considered. "Or perhaps an ancient Phoenician." Her steps were steady. Unlike when she first arrived, she wasn't all out of breath, even though they'd been walking long enough that the house was out of sight behind them.

"They just look like a jumble of lines and curves without any sense, and they always jump around on the page."

Velvet's step faltered. The letters *jumped* on the page for Iris. Perhaps she should ask Lucian to get his daughter's eyes checked, but there was no need to alarm Iris. "The letters the ancient Egyptians used were more like little pictures."

"That would be better." Iris reached out for her hand.

Feeling honored, Velvet took the girl's hand. "No, because they have many, many more symbols you would have to learn and draw. Our alphabet, which captures sounds instead of trying to make a picture for each word, is better."

Iris scrunched her face. "Am I stupider than your other students?"

Velvet drew to a complete stop. A raw pain settled under her breastbone. "No, of course not. You must not think such a thing."

Iris twisted her foot in the dirt. Velvet had to work harder at hiding her impatience at Iris's failure to learn to read and write. After all, if she couldn't see well, then the fault was not with Iris.

"The other governesses said I was dimwitted."

Velvet knelt down and gripped her by the shoulders. "No, sweetheart. I have never had another student ask who designed our alphabet. That is the kind of question only a person with a curious mind just bursting to learn would ask. We should try to find out the answer." Good Lord, what had Iris's other governesses said to her?

Iris looked back along the track. "I am only good at deportment. I bet all your other students knew their letters at my age."

"Iris, it is true that you are behind in schoolwork, but not all lessons come easy for everyone. You *will* learn." She vowed to make sure Iris succeeded. "And somewhere there is a girl who tries and tries to walk gracefully and cannot manage to keep a book on her head, or a boy who cannot recite a poem to save his life. Everyone has unique skills, including you."

Iris twisted out of her grasp. "In the spring, the grass is covered with heather. It's very pretty."

"I shall look forward to seeing it." Sighing, Velvet rose to her feet. She had to undo the damage of the past, but she knew to pile on compliments about Iris's intelligence would only make the girl think it was coming on too thick to be true.

A few more yards and the little houses of the village came into view. One of the girls stood by the church.

Iris waved, but the girl ducked behind a woman and turned her back toward the path.

Frowning, Velvet wondered if the girl hadn't seen Iris. She put a hand on Iris's shoulder.

It only got worse. During the service, Iris looked over the back of the bench at the girl she'd made friends with. Only the other girls all looked at anything but her.

In a low murmur, Velvet urged Iris to face forward. The vicar droned on and on. What was wrong with these people? Even if Iris's father had killed her mother, why would they take it out on a small girl? Iris folded her arms across her chest. Velvet grew hot and her ears began to buzz.

After it was over, all the villagers seemed in a great hurry to get outside. By the time Velvet and Iris made it to the stoop, all of the families with children were scurrying away.

Determined to get to the bottom of the distinctly unchristian behavior, Velvet strode toward the vicar. Iris hitched her step beside her. Velvet tried to slow her steps to a more ladylike glide.

"Mr. Thackery, would you be so good as to explain why all the girls have been pulled away?"

He looked at her chest, which infuriated her. Her breathing grew rapid.

Slowly, he said, "I'm sure I don't know, ma'am."

Velvet realized the futility of pointing out that he

was a poor shepherd to his flock. She softened her voice. "Then perhaps you would explain why one of your parishioners thought I would be interested in Myra Gowan's grave."

Mr. Thackery shook his head. "She was a poor misfortunate soul. May she rest in peace." He turned away.

Velvet said sternly, "Sir." She hadn't been a governess for a dozen years without learning how to compel answers with a firm tone.

He stopped and glared. "She was a servant at the Pendar household."

Iris ducked behind Velvet's skirts.

"And?" prompted Velvet.

"I shouldn't like to speak ill of the dead." He opened his eyes wide and bobbed his head toward Iris.

Iris tugged on Velvet's arm, but she wasn't done yet.

"Why should she be of importance to me?"

"She was a fallen woman."

"I see." An icy coldness dripped through Velvet. Could she never be thought honorable? She would have thought that in Cornwall, at least, her reputation would have been too far distant.

"Can we go home now?" asked Iris.

Velvet closed her eyes. Nothing would be gained by staying in a place where she was judged and condemned.

"Have a good day." The vicar returned to his church, then shut the door.

"*May* we go home," corrected Velvet. "And yes, I believe we should."

They hadn't gone far when Velvet spied the broken fingers of Iris's old doll sticking out of a rubbish heap. She moved to the other side of Iris, hoping to block the child's view, but it was too late.

"I'm never coming back here!"

"Iris." Velvet bit her lip. Letting the locals chase them away from church wasn't the answer, but were the villagers so ignorant as to throw away an expensive doll just because it had come from the Pendar household?

Iris yanked free and ran.

What kind of a topsy-turvy world was it, where going to church made one feel like an outcast?

During the second week of Lucian's absence, his carriage and a wagon filled with servants hired from Plymouth rattled up the drive with the news that there would be guests returning with Lucian in two days. The house was to be made ready.

Their normal quiet was interrupted by a flurry of activity. Rooms were aired, carpets beaten, and fresh linens placed on the beds in the unused rooms.

Iris could hardly sit still for lessons.

The schoolroom door opened and Nellie leaned in. "Miss Campbell, there's a courier come with a letter for you."

Velvet frowned. Why would a letter be specially sent for her?

"You have to go down. He says he must put it in your hand." Nellie frowned.

Iris popped out of her seat and shot out of the door. More sedately, Velvet followed down the stairs, with Nellie lumbering behind.

"How did you get here?" Iris's childish voice bubbled up from below.

"Rode me 'orse," answered an unfamiliar male voice.

Mrs. Bigsby stood stiffly at the foot of the stairs. A man with mud-spattered trousers and a long wool coat stood with his cap in his hand. As Velvet descended, he displayed a gap-toothed grin.

"You must be Miss Campbell." He reached inside his coat and pulled out an envelope. "Gov said give it only to the one with red 'air, 'e did."

The cockney accent of the courier gave Velvet pause. Who would have sent her a letter from London? She hesitated to take it from his outstretched hand. The last letter from London hadn't been good.

"You could have give it to me. I would have seen she got it," grumbled Mrs. Bigsby.

"Right," said the courier. "Can I 'ave a spot to eat 'fore I 'ead back?"

"Nellie, show him to the kitchen," Mrs. Bigsby instructed. She flashed a glare in Velvet's direction, spun on her heel and then opened the library door. The smell of lemon oil drifted out.

Velvet peeked down at the address. Lucian's jagged scrawl jumped out at her. Had he thought better of allowing her to keep her position? The back of her throat went dry.

She turned toward the stairs.

"Aren't you going to open it? Is it from Papa?" Iris circled around Velvet in an excited skip. "Mrs. Bigsby got a letter too, but it made her cross."

"Let us return upstairs," Velvet answered. She wanted to delay the moment, but her heart fluttered in anticipation.

They passed rooms with doors and windows open wide and fires burning in the grates. Servants passed laden with draperies to be beaten. Almost unable to stop herself, Velvet slipped a finger under the seal.

"How can you stand to wait?" asked Iris on an exaggerated sigh. "Papa never writes when he is gone."

That didn't ease Velvet's worries. "Well, perhaps he would if you could read his letters."

"No, he will not. He did not write to Mama either. She never knew when he was coming back." Iris skipped ahead, her charm bracelet jingling as she bounced. "But she got a picture card from her friend."

The letter was almost burning in Velvet's hand. Feeling faint, she folded back the flap, then pulled out the single folded sheet.

My Dear Miss Campbell,

I wish to apologize to you for my reaction to your former employer's letter. I treated you harshly when I had no right. Forgive me.

I have invited several guests—or rather the idea of hosting a house party was thrust upon me after a chance remark, and I could not refuse. I beg you to undertake overseeing the kitchen and menus for the two weeks the guests will stay. There are accounts at the shops in Trerice. Have Bigsby purchase anything needed to feed a dozen or more guests and their retainers. Spare no expense.

I have informed Mrs. Bigsby of this arrangement. She will have enough to see to with the additional help. I was fortunate enough to persuade the owner of an inn in Plymouth to close down for a fortnight and allow me to hire his staff.

Velvet, I have thought of you often. I miss being near you. I beg you will not think ill of me regardless of any tales you hear.

Yours truly,
Lucian Pendar

With a shaking hand Velvet refolded the letter. Her heart pounded as if he were here, touching her. He tied her in knots.

"Did he ask about me?" Iris asked eagerly.

Velvet started. Just when she was prepared to adore him, she hated him for the pain his casual disregard of Iris did to the child. She was his daughter, not an afterthought.

"He didn't say anything about me." Iris looked at the floor.

"Oh, sweetheart, the letter is just instructions for me to help prepare for the guests. See, it is only one sheet." Velvet waved the page. For perhaps the only time, she was glad Iris did not read.

"What does it say?" asked Iris.

"He says we must help Cook with the menus." Velvet put the letter back in the envelope and tucked it into the pages of *Jane Eyre*. "Come along, you must learn to run a household staff for when you have your own home."

"That's all he wants, me to grow up and marry so he never has to see me again," wailed Iris.

"Iris, stop being so dramatic."

"No, it's true. He only wants to be around you."

"Most fathers don't spend much time with their children, but he spends at least an hour with you every evening when he is home." But the time was treated as if it were his duty, not as time he looked forward to spending with his daughter, and Iris knew it. Velvet winced. "He brings you gifts when he goes away."

"The girls in the village hate me. He hates me. Mama is the only one who loved me, and he killed her."

"Iris!" Icy claws clamped down on Velvet's spine. How could a girl who adored her father think such a thing? Who had tormented her with such suppositions?

"It's true. I heard it. She was yelling at him about he never made her happy, and he never let her go to London. She made him bleed, and he told her, 'Get out of my sight or I'm going to kill you.' Then I heard a thump, and I never heard Mama again."

Velvet nearly choked, her throat was so tight. A chill slithered down her spine. Was there any truth in the allegations? "Iris, you must never say such a thing or even think it."

But Iris ran to her bedroom and slammed the door.

"It was a nasty row," intoned Nellie from the schoolroom doorway.

Velvet spun around. How long had Nellie been standing there? "What happened to Iris's mother?"

Nellie shrugged. "Fell off the cliff. Shouldn't have been out in the storm. But then, it don't do to cross the master."

Nellie's reply didn't comfort Velvet at all.

Two days hence, in late afternoon, the arrivals began trickling. Struggling to contain her building excitement, Iris bounced in her seat.

"Papa will call me down to meet his guests, won't he?"

"I don't know," said Miss Campbell.

Iris popped to her feet. "I'm going to change to my best dress so I'll be ready."

"Iris, we are not done with lessons for the day."

A knock on the schoolroom door prompted Miss Campbell to turn. Meg peeked around the door. "Begging your pardon, miss. You are needed in the kitchen posthaste."

"You may change," Miss Campbell said before leaving, "but you must return here and practice your letters."

Iris rolled her eyes. She was too excited to practice dreary letters. Her papa was home!

After changing, Iris returned to the schoolroom and sat back on her stool. She waited and waited.

Finally, Nellie came and said, "I'm to bring you down to your papa before bringing you a tray for dinner."

Iris hopped off the stool. "Where is Miss Campbell?"

Nellie sniffed. "Never you mind. Your papa is in the library."

Iris sighed. Finally, Papa sent for her. Her heart danced merrily in her chest. She would make him proud, curtsying the way Miss Campbell taught her. Her heart might dance, but she would glide across the floor like a lady.

Nellie held out her hand, but Iris ignored it. She wasn't a baby to be left in the nursery all night. She was turning into a young lady.

She darted toward the stairs and then recalled it wouldn't do to be seen running through the house like a child. "Will Miss Campbell be there?"

"She's in the kitchen." Nellie's voice was stiff, like she disapproved. Or perhaps she was mad because of her hand being ignored.

Iris sucked in a deep breath. She desperately wanted to make Papa proud, but she wished Miss Campbell would be there. Her governess had a way of looking at her that allowed a course correction. Papa's hopes seemed to have risen too. Miss Campbell made him believe she could succeed where everyone else failed, but that worried Iris more than anything. She hadn't been here long enough to learn of the inevitable failures to come.

"Are they very grand ladies?" she asked.

"The *guests* are very grand." Nellie clunked on the

wooden stairs. "Hurry along, I shouldn't like your father to be kept waiting."

Iris followed after Nellie, skipping to keep up with the tall woman. Nellie ate miles with each of her steps. Following her, Iris couldn't glide like a lady. "Are their dresses pretty? Are any of them as pretty as my mama?"

Nellie grunted. Iris kept asking questions, hoping she might get an answer, but Nellie was in one of her grouchy moods.

Nellie opened the library door and pushed a breathless Iris forward. The door clicked shut.

Papa turned in front of the blazing fire. "Iris."

Forgetting all her plans to be a perfectly mannered miss, Iris hopped forward, her bracelet jangling on her wrist.

His eyes narrowed.

Too late, she pulled her hands behind her back. "Did you have a good trip?"

His mouth stretched thin. "What do you have?"

"Nellie says I am to meet the guests." Iris tried to smile but her face refused to comply. Instead her tummy felt filled with rocks.

"Show me your wrist," Papa commanded.

Iris could see no way out of showing him she wore her mother's jingly bracelet. She thrust out her hand.

He grabbed her hand and yanked her into the light. He lifted up a charm and scanned it.

"Miss Campbell said I could wear it so I could tell my right hand—"

"How dare you wear this?" he growled.

Iris tried to snatch her hand back before he snapped it off like a rabid dog. "You said I would have my mama's things."

He yanked. The locket scraped her wrist as the bracelet wrenched free of her hand. "I said when you are grown and gone you'll have your mama's things. Not now."

"Ow!" Iris circled her wounded wrist with her other hand.

He flipped the catch on the locket. His face turned white and then red. As if he could smash it like paper, he squeezed the locket in his hand. Then he hurtled the thick chain with its charms into the fire.

"Go," he thundered.

"Papa," she pleaded.

"I don't want to see you." He spun and leaned against the fireplace shelf. "Go."

A sob caught in her throat and she backed away. He hated her. She twisted the doorknob and fled through the house. Her shoes clicked on the hall floor, echoing. Even with a house full of guests, she was more alone then ever.

Chapter 15

Wiping moisture from her brow, Velvet hurried through the gallery. The drawing room doors were thrown wide. The fire blazed and several lamps burned on the tables. She'd never seen the room so well lit. As she hovered in the dark hall, Lucian paced into view. Her breath caught.

He tugged at his snowy white shirt cuffs. She paused, taking in his sartorial elegance. He pulled back his black frock coat, exposing a burgundy and black satin vest with a shawl collar instead of his usual plain black vest. After removing his watch, he flipped it open and frowned at the face.

With the scarred side of his face turned away, he appeared every inch a wealthy handsome gentleman. She suited the role of impoverished upper servant. Never had their differences in station been so clear.

She must have made a sound because he tilted his head toward the hallway.

"Vel— Miss Campbell?"

She stepped forward into the circle of light spilling from the room.

"My guests will be down soon." He strode forward and pulled her into the room. "I will need you to serve as hostess. I have business I must conclude, so I will be occupied with the gentlemen most of the evening."

From the amount of food being prepared, a score of guests were here. She'd never presided over so large a gathering. And she hadn't acted as a hostess since her father died. She sucked in a deep breath. He'd warned her, but she'd expected a small gathering of his business associates, not a huge fashionable party.

"When I asked them to bring their families, I had hoped . . ." His voice trailed off. "Most of my guests brought their wives and oldest daughters." His eyes dropped down her front, and his nose flared. His fingers tightened on her arm.

His gaze lingered so long on her chest, she looked to see if a bit of food was clinging to her bodice.

His upper lip curled before he twisted away. He probably found her simple gown distasteful in contrast to his dressing for dinner. What did he expect? She was a governess. Her lace fichu she could have used to dress up her plain gown had been sold to the secondhand man.

After the second it took him to compose his features, his gaze returned to her face. "You're flushed."

"I've been helping in the kitchen. I promised Cook and anyone who stayed a ride home in the carriage."

"Fine, fine." He hardly seemed to listen as his eyes searched her face.

Voices and footfalls descending the stairs drifted to her ears. He started as if he'd heard too.

His voice lowered to a caress. "You will need to bring the ladies back here for tea after dinner. I will signal you when it is time to leave the table."

"Iris is looking—"

"We need to discuss Iris later." His whisper turned cold.

"Ah, Lady John and Sir John, come in." Lucian

dropped her arm and stepped forward. "This is Miss Campbell, she'll serve as my hostess tonight."

A woman of a certain age entered, and her husband followed behind her. Gold taffeta rustled as she moved forward. Her nod of acknowledgment barely moved her dangling ear bobs.

Next to enter the room were the Ridleys. Velvet was summarily introduced.

Mrs. Ridley sparkled with jewels. "May I present my daughters, Mr. Pendar? This is my eldest, Evangeline, and next, Amelia."

Two sable-haired girls of an age to make their debut stepped forward. Both were dressed in white, with elaborate ruching and ruffles betraying the deceptive simplicity of their gowns. Evangeline gasped and Amelia went stiff. For a long second they stared at Lucian's scar.

His eyes narrowed as he bowed. Without acknowledging their stares, he said, "Miss Ridley, Miss Amelia."

He turned ever so slightly, presenting the unscarred side of his face to them as he introduced Velvet.

The process was repeated as the Bowmans and their adult daughter entered. Miss Bowman gave Lucian a simpering smile and then lowered her doelike eyes. The sausage curls around her face bobbed.

A dapper little man named Mr. Anderson followed with his wife, who stooped as if trying to hide the six inches she had on her husband. A young woman who had inherited her mother's height was with them.

Shortly after, a stout man with thick muttonchop whiskers was introduced as Captain Darling. His familial contribution included a pleasantly plump daughter with an engaging smile that faltered at the sight of Lucian's scar.

"Perhaps you would like to take a seat by the fire?"

Velvet held out her arm toward the far side of the room. "Although, Mr. Pendar would warn you, it is too warm there."

"Yes, thank you," answered Miss Darling on a gush of air, as if moving as far away from Lucian offered her a welcome relief.

Lucian's lips tightened wryly.

Obviously, the fear of the female guests bothered him. Velvet leaned toward him, wanting . . . wanting to ease the turbulence. He just didn't seem the kind of man who could have murdered his wife. Unless it had been some kind of horrible accident. Velvet shook off the thought.

"Good evening, Pendar," said the next man to enter the room.

"May I introduce Miss Campbell? Mr. Hale."

Mr. Hale jerked. Then he took her hand, a gesture none of the others had felt necessary. His sandy moustache twitched as he looked her over.

Feeling inspected and found inferior, Velvet tugged to remove her hand. "Pleased to meet you."

"And you are?" he asked.

"Miss Pendar's governess," Velvet answered at the same time Lucian said, "My hostess."

Mr. Hale's blue eyes flickered. For a second there was something familiar about the arch of his eyebrow, but Velvet was sure she'd never met him before.

"Robert, how are you?" said Sir John heartily. He stepped forward to clap Hale on the shoulder. Finally freed, Velvet melted back.

The company segregated, with the women gathering in front of the fireplace and the men standing near the door.

Velvet stepped back, allowing the men their boisterous interchange. She took a step toward the fire, but two of the women shifted so their backs were toward her. The ladies were bedecked with glittering necklaces on their bared necks. She was clearly out of place.

She touched the button of her high-necked gown and thought of the gold cross she'd had to sell. As a servant, she had no reason to expect to be included. Besides, they all knew each other, while the names of the different people clashed in her mind.

Velvet sought a dark corner of the room where she could fade into the background and observe. Slipping behind the curtain of the farthest window seat, she sat down. She wished she could leave and take a tray in the schoolroom, but as Lucian's hostess, she needed to be available to the guests.

The Miss Ridleys and their mother strolled the perimeter of the room arm in arm. Their exercise brought them near Velvet's hidey-hole.

Evangeline said in a low undertone, "I wouldn't have him if he offered. You can have a go at him if you wish, Amelia."

"Stop. He's a perfectly acceptable man, and wealthier than any other possible suitor for you," sternly whispered Mrs. Ridley.

Velvet shrunk back. Was Lucian's bachelor status the reason they came?

They stopped their stroll mere feet from her. They were perhaps as interested in the privacy as she, and they might not have realized she was tucked in the dark recess.

"I couldn't possibly consider him, Mama," said Amelia. "He is so old and . . . and . . . that scar."

"They say he killed his wife," said Evangeline.

Resisting the urge to protest, Velvet pressed her lips

together. How dare they accept Lucian's hospitality and speak so disparagingly of him?

"Hush." Mrs. Ridley yanked her daughters closer. "There was an inquest. The servants reported he did not leave the house. Your father has done business with him these many years, and he would not have suggested you two come if he did not find Mr. Pendar suitable in every regard."

"Servants lie," Evangeline said in an undertone.

Lucian moved around the room doing a fair imitation of a congenial host. Velvet couldn't help but notice his every move. He smiled at Miss Bowman, who managed to make her blond curls clustered on either side of her face bob. The young woman was stylish, pretty, and obviously of the proper class to make him a wife.

Why were so many ladies of a marriageable age present? They were of his station and young, with rich fathers. Her eyes stung. Swallowing hard, Velvet lowered her head. She was solidly on the shelf and dressed like the servant she was. The comparison could only show her lack of worthiness.

"If he asked us to attend en famille, then why did Papa insist all the younger ones stay home?" asked Amelia.

"There was no need to have all the little children underfoot. If Mr. Pendar had not intimated he was considering marriage, I would not have come, and we certainly should not have brought you two."

Velvet's heart knocked hard in her chest, as if it had been stilled with the plunge of a knife. Clearly a slew of young women of marriageable age were present, and only two bachelors beside Lucian. She couldn't catch her breath and the room spun. Grasping the curtain, she tried to regain her equilibrium.

Resuming her stroll, Mrs. Ridley continued, "Now doesn't he have a lovely home, and the scenery is spectacular. Any wife of his is sure to be indulged."

"The furniture is old," muttered Evangeline.

"And ratty," added Amelia. "The only modern piece is that chaise longue, and it is stained."

Velvet winced, knowing she had made the stain. From across the room Lucian watched her with narrowed eyes.

"Is your given name Satin or Chenille or some such?" asked Mr. Hale, seating himself next to her on the narrow window seat. He surely didn't know of her. Campbell was not such an original name, and Lucian had not given her forename.

God forgive her, but she lied. "Jane."

Feeling sick at her stomach, Velvet stood. Mr. Hale followed suit and stood so close her elbow brushed his midsection.

"Not Velvet?" asked Mr. Hale. His blue eyes were bold as his gaze raked over her.

"What kind of a name is Velvet?" she asked. *The only thing she had from the mother she'd never known,* screamed the answer in her head.

Understanding her only possible role was as his whore and hostess until he married, Velvet turned her back on Lucian. She couldn't let him see how much his flaunting of her demand for marriage hurt.

Lucian dove into the waves and swam. The icy water stung his skin like a thousand needles, but did little to settle the turmoil within him.

Last night Velvet had been gracious and modest playing the role of hostess to perfection in spite of his guests' inclination to ignore her. Everything had gone smoother than he had a right to expect. Except for Iris. He'd overreacted, and he needed to make amends.

The dinner had gone off with several courses and removes, and Velvet kept everything moving forward. He hadn't known his staff was capable of producing such a well-orchestrated meal.

This morning just before dawn he went to Velvet's room and found her bed empty. Disappointment and jealousy fermented within him, until he knew of no cure but the biting cold of an ocean swim. But the rhythm of his strokes was doing little to soothe his passions. Damn her! She was like a cancer in his mind.

Hale had paid her particular attention at dinner. Had she already chosen him to be her lover? Or was she sneaking off to meet the vicar? Nellie had informed him that Velvet made a point of speaking to the man every Sunday.

He wanted to believe Velvet was the moral woman she seemed, that she wasn't breeding. Except several things pointed to the contrary.

He'd almost begun to believe he'd been mistaken about her condition, but in the short time he'd been away, her bosom had filled out. Another of the early symptoms of pregnancy. Feeling faint, fatigue, nausea, and displaying swelling breasts and luminosity, she was exhibiting all the signs.

He'd witnessed all the changes in Velvet just as he'd witnessed them four times in Lilith. It had been almost a decade, but he hadn't forgotten.

Lucian stopped swimming and checked the shore-line. The riptides could be deadly, which was why he usually had Bigsby follow him in the boat. But he'd told Bigsby he wouldn't be swimming while his guests were here. He should have realized he couldn't be around Velvet without being twisted in knots.

Reluctantly, he turned his strokes back toward the shore. He wouldn't risk getting pulled out to sea over another loose woman.

Velvet woke in the early dawn. Blinking at her surroundings, she was momentarily confused. The carpeted and papered room was much more lavishly furnished than her stark room. She slid off of the covers, careful not to disturb her sleeping bed partner. She took a minute to rearrange the blankets over Iris's curled form.

When Velvet had finally returned upstairs near midnight, she'd found Iris sobbing in the darkened schoolroom. The girl was dressed in one of her best dresses, with a big ribbon in her hair. The bow was skewed, indicating she'd tied it herself.

Velvet tried to reassure Iris that her father had not banished the girl from his sight forever. But Iris had been past consoling. Instead, Velvet put the girl to bed and stayed with her until they both fell asleep.

Now she needed to confront him. Furious with Lucian's reaction to Iris, she headed downstairs intent on catching him before he left for his swim. No matter how important his business was, he had to take time for his daughter. She was the only family he had left.

When she knocked on his door, Mr. Evans opened it and told her Lucian was gone and so was his bathing suit and robe.

Not to be deterred, Velvet stormed outside. He'd gone too far this time, and she meant to let him know in no uncertain terms.

Her gown was wrinkled and the strong ocean winds

whipped her hair, yanking it from its moorings. She should have taken the time to change and made herself presentable, but she was determined to have it out with Lucian now.

She avoided looking at the cliffs or the drop to the ocean, but her heart pounded nonetheless. The land jutted out as if pointing a finger toward the cove where Lucian regularly swam. Across the thin expanse of land were steps carved into the rocky cliffs. Velvet froze, dreading the descent.

She fisted her cold hands. She could do this. The path was safe. Lucian traversed it daily. But the plummet to the sea and the roar of the crashing surf chilled her heart. If she were meant to fall to her death, surely she would have done it years ago from the bell tower. But her heart didn't believe she was safe. She could no longer determine if the mad pounding was anger or terror.

Tucking her chin down to avoid seeing anything but the grass in front of her feet, she wobbled forward. As the ground dropped toward the rocky decline, the wind swirled above her, but ceased to molest her.

Once the sandy shoreline came into view her feet froze. It was too far down, the steps too steep. A sob caught in her throat.

Then Lucian came into view, traveling up the uneven ledges carved into the cliff face. His face darkened as he caught sight of her.

Velvet questioned her resolution to confront him. His hair was tousled and wet, his bathing suit dripping from where it was slung over his Turkish robe.

"Where were you?" he demanded.

"I would ask the same of you. Could you not spare Iris five minutes of civility?"

Lucian approached like a dark storm. His gaze scoured her disheveled appearance. His nostrils flared. "Where did you sleep last night? Why weren't you in your bed this morning?"

His question surprised her. How did he know she hadn't slept in her bed?

"Good God, have you no decency?" His lip curled in a sneer. His hand clamped over her wrist. "Must you appear before me with the signs of lechery in your dishevelment?"

He shook her.

More of her hair slithered free of its mooring. Damn, must he always assume the worst? Anger gathered steam within her.

"Who were you with?" he shouted.

"Your daughter." Mindful of the bruises on Iris's wrist, Velvet twisted her hand away. "She is heartbroken."

His eyes flickered. "She is a sly thing who has twisted your sentiments to suit her whims."

Velvet wanted to shake him. Didn't he understand how much power he had to wound Iris? "She sobbed most of the night. That is more than a scheming child can manage. Did you have to berate her for wearing her mother's bracelet?"

Lucian's mouth tightened. "Why would you allow her to wear a marker of her mother's infidelity?" he growled. "What were you thinking?" He pushed closer.

A bolt raced through Velvet, she took a step back. Was he past caring what he revealed? "I had no idea there was such a piece in her mother's jewelry box. How should I tell her that one piece should not be worn? What excuse should I have given her?"

"Damn it to hell, you had only to see it once to know she should not wear it. Or did you think I possessed a blue eye?" He stepped menacingly closer. His eyelashes were damp and his eyebrows had flattened over his dark eyes. White lines bracketed his mouth.

"I thought the miniature could have been a brother or some relic from before your marriage. I have no knowledge of your wife's family or her behaviors." Velvet tried to speak calmly. "In any case Iris can barely decipher letters. She certainly could not have read the inscriptions."

Lucian growled. "You push me to distraction. You knew. You approved."

"I *suspected*," corrected Velvet. She swiped a strand of hair away from her face. "I did not *know*."

He raked a hand through his damp hair.

"Had I dressed her, I would have discouraged her from wearing it, but I was occupied seeing after your bride buffet."

He shook his head ever so slightly, as if startled by her vehemence.

Velvet hated to think what she'd revealed. She'd come to tell him he must see to soothing Iris. Her own hurt was irrelevant. "You left without telling her good-bye. You return and berate her for wearing a bracelet she could not have known would wound you."

He shook her off. "Iris has too great a champion in you."

"She needs someone!" Velvet took a deep breath and decided to try a different tack. "She loves you desperately. She just needs to know she is secure in your love, not patted on the head like a good hunting dog and sent back to her kennel when you have no need for her."

"Do not censure my behavior, Miss Campbell. I have done well by her, indulged her. She wants for nothing."

"She doesn't need more things, she needs her father's

love! Iris is in agony, and you must make amends for your behavior last night."

"I must? I must, Miss Campbell?" His jaw pulsed and he leaned toward her.

Velvet grabbed his arm. "Please, I beg of you. She is a child who is desperately alone." When a daughter doubted her father's love, life was hardly worth living. A fact she knew all too well. "If you care about your daughter at all, you will reassure her that you love her."

"You don't understand."

"What don't I understand? Iris thinks you hate her." That wasn't all that Iris thought about him. "How can a father treat his own daughter so callously?"

"She is not my daughter," he spat.

As if she had been slapped, Velvet recoiled. "What?"

Lucian winced and shook his head. "Bloody hell!" He fisted both his hands in his hair and bent forward. His wet bathing suit slid from his shoulder unnoticed.

Velvet stepped back. Her thoughts reeled. She tried to sort out what she knew of Iris's birth. Iris was his wife's babe. "You can't know she isn't yours."

Straightening, he shook his head, his mouth twisted wryly. "I know. I forsook my wife's bed after the death of our third child. The specialist we consulted in London suggested we abstain lest we have another stillbirth."

Her mouth rounded. Her mind blanked, as she could think of no response.

"I don't speak of it. *Ever.*" His narrowed eyes cut through her. "No one knows."

"You cannot tell Iris. You would destroy her."

"I don't intend to tell Iris." Lucian growled, "I didn't intend to tell you."

He glared at her as if she drew out the secret by witchcraft.

Why had he told her? Velvet wanted to shake off the confidence.

"Some may suspect, but they don't know. The only ones who ever knew were Lilith and Myra." His voice vibrated with a deep emotion.

"And they're dead." Velvet bit on her tongue. A chill slithered down her spine. She still didn't know who the woman was, how she died, or why no one would speak of her.

"You can't ever tell anyone." He sounded manically detached.

Velvet backed away from him. "I don't know who Myra was." She wished she'd never come outside, never confronted him.

"She was Lilith's maid. She was in London with us." His face twisted but he stepped toward her. Emotions rioted across his face, his voice vibrating in stark contrast to the way he'd said she couldn't tell anyone the secret of Iris's parentage.

"She was more," whispered Velvet.

"She was my mistress before she was murdered."

Velvet backed farther away. She didn't want to be within ten feet of him. How could it be that two women who shared his bed experienced violent deaths? Had he played a role in ending their lives? Had she totally misjudged him? Fear clawed at her, and she put her hand to her throat.

"Don't look at me that way," he said. Shock cast so chill a feeling in her it was as if cold damp air blew up her skirts.

"Velvet," he said low and calm, although his eyes widened in horror and his head tilted back. His gaze cast down to her feet. He stood still as a statue.

Loath to take her eyes off of him, she remembered

with a jolt they were near the cliffs. She twisted to see how close she was to the edge.

She could see down and down. For a second her mind couldn't comprehend. The surf crashed loud against the rocks, and the stiff breeze buffeted her where she tottered on the rim. Panic knifed through her. Her throat closed. Her knees turned to water. Oh God, she was about to fall to her death.

Chapter 16

Far down below her the rocks waited like teeth in a hungry maw. Velvet's heart jolted to a stop. She would be torn to shreds on them. Sprays of saltwater stretched to reach her as if to pull her down into the salivating sea. She couldn't tear her gaze away from the death fall.

"Look at me," Lucian lulled in a soothing voice. "Take my hand." Reaching out, he stepped toward her.

She jerked. Her arms windmilled as if to keep her on the edge. But she was no bird who could fly away from danger.

"Velvet, you can't die. My life wouldn't be worth living."

His curious words cut through the howling wind. She had to try to step away. The ground tore under her foot. As her leg slid over the edge, her knee caught on the lip.

Lucian gasped and pitched forward.

Scrambling and clawing, she thrashed away from the edge then stumbled to her feet to run. She crashed into his arms. Like a madwoman, she continued to run, away from the fall, away from death, away to him.

His arms enfolded her. "I have you."

Still she wanted farther from the cliff. Her churning feet tangled with his legs. Her throat too tight to allow out a scream, she tried to climb over him as if he were a barrier between the fall and safety. They stumbled backward and went down with a grunt.

Yet, his arms never left her. "You're safe. I have you," he repeated.

Sprawling on top of him, she straddled him.

With the awareness of one who has just looked death squarely in the face, her senses magnified. The grass underneath them crunched. Solid ground. Behind and below, the waves surged on the shore with their ceaseless rhythm. She hadn't fallen.

A lock of Lucian's dark hair damply clung to his corded neck where his pulse raced quicksilver. His heart beat while hers stood still. His reassuring murmurs flowed over her, and she went limp. The way he cradled her made her feel safe. She hadn't died.

"You scared the hell out of me. I didn't think I'd reach you in time." His lips brushed her skin as he spoke.

He hadn't wanted her to fall.

Her hands fisted in the thick pile of his robe. He smelled of saltwater, and his mouth against her temple undid her.

Awareness rose in her. Her breasts pressed against his solid chest as it rose and fell in fast bursts. She wanted closer. His every breath ricocheted through her as if he breathed for her. Against her abdomen his manhood hardened, yet his hold was comforting, not sexual.

His hands slid across her back and entwined in her hair. "You're all right. I have you."

Rearing up, she stared down at him.

His dark eyes tenderly searched her face. Nothing of his earlier anger darkened his visage. His gaze held hers. He was such a beautiful man.

She hardly noticed his scars anymore. But they were

part and parcel of the evidence held against him. Reconciling the suspicions of murder with the kind man she knew was impossible. In spite of everything, she couldn't believe he'd deliberately harm women he cared about. Would a man capable of such evil shower his wife's misbegotten child with expensive dolls and insist on spending an hour with her every evening?

He shuttered his expression as if he knew she was thinking of the accusations leveled against him. She knew what it was like to hide the pain of being judged guilty when innocent. They were alike in so many ways. She understood and shared his ostracism from the rest of the world. She too knew what it was like to be shunned. The responses of his young guests had hurt him. Velvet wanted to take that from him.

Reluctantly he loosened his grip.

She was bereft. A keening pain passed through her. She never wanted him to let go. She wanted more than the thick tufts of his robe in her hands. She wanted to know what it was to be alive. She hadn't died, but she hadn't been living either.

Never breaking their gaze, he pushed up to his elbows. Releasing her grip on his robe, she pushed the material aside and planted her hands on his chest. He gasped. His chest was warm where her hands were cold, as if she had risen from a watery grave.

Feeling the springy hairs under her fingertips, she pushed him back down. His eyes darkened as he complied.

Her life began again. Her heart beat. Her breaths came in gasps, forcing her lips to part. A strange energy filled her flesh. Alive to every sensation, tingling and desperate for touch, she leaned into him. He made her feel alive in a way she never had before, and she wanted more.

"Velvet," he breathed. He slid his hands up her arms, cupping her shoulders.

His mouth was just below hers, close enough she could feel his breath on her lips. Their lips met. Her sigh mingled with his growl.

She belonged here in his arms. Her lips tingled. His kiss fired her skin. Pushing his robe open farther, she flattened her palms against his firm chest. He slid his arms across her back, anchoring her to him. But there was no need. She was where she wanted to be.

Their mouths locked together, and with every touch of their tongues, her heart gushed.

He strained up against her. Exploring the corded fibers of his muscles, Velvet marveled in the difference between them. He was hard where she was soft. Strong where she was weak. He was her perfect complement, the man she was meant to become one with.

He fisted his fingers in the hair at the nape of her neck and pulled her head back. For a second his gasps caressed her lips.

"Do you know what you're doing?" His dark eyes searched hers.

She was past hesitation, beyond thinking of virtue as anything more than a cold cage keeping her nearer to death than life. She just wanted to feel, and by Poseidon's trident, Lucian made her come alive. She had been sleepwalking through life, but he made her awake. And even with her obvious participation in the kisses, he still gave her a choice. Her heart softened and filled. "Yes," she whispered, straining back toward him.

Her answer unleashed the energy she always sensed

pent in him. His kiss was deeper, more insistent, and his hips strained up against her. He caught her thigh, pulled it higher and then rolled so she ended up underneath him. From hip to breast he skimmed his hand over her curves, leaving molten heat in his wake.

She arched into him. Lucian made an animal sound deep in his throat. He cradled her to him as he unfastened the button at her neck. He shoved back the edges of material. Stroking with his long fingers, he wrapped his hand around the base of her throat.

He seemed fascinated with her neck, running his fingers along the length of it. "I've wanted you for so long."

She tried to listen, but her flesh was waking.

He searched her face while he undid another button. "I want you more than life itself."

"Yes," she answered, because her brain could produce no other word. In this moment she wanted to live life completely.

Then he unbuttoned the next button and the next. He yanked down her shift. Her heart pounded and her skin heated as his exploration continued. He was not gentle but impatient, as if he could hardly stand the delay to touch her skin. She had no such barrier to him. Her caresses of the rounded muscles of his upper arms seemed to please him. She wanted to please him.

She stretched to bring their mouths together. His passionate groan was everything she could have hoped, and it touched her deep inside.

He tugged at her corset as if he could get the unyielding material to move out of his way. As he succeeded in cupping his hand around her bared breast, his growl of triumph reverberated through her. His lips left hers and he trailed his open mouth down her neck across her exposed bosom. Taking her tightening nipple in his mouth, he provoked a wantonness she hadn't known she possessed.

Sensations wild and deep broke through her. As he nipped and tugged, currents flowed to her woman's core. Seeking this novel and unfamiliar pleasure, she arched against him. A moan broke free in her throat as his thumb teased the other pebbled tip. He seemed intent on allowing the sensations to ebb and flow as he withdrew to circle outside the sensitive peak.

Her fingers sank into his damp hair as she tried to reguide his mouth to repeat the wildness. He instead trailed nips down the slope of one breast to the valley between and then gave the other his licks and sucking tugs. The cool air caused her unattended nipple to tighten even more. Her hips rolled and she wanted more of him.

He yanked his belt untied and pushed at her skirts. While the attention to her breast made her hips twist, his hand on pantalets ties caused alarm to flood down her spine. Her wet flesh embarrassed her.

He slid his fingers into her woman's cleft. Not sure she was ready for this new familiarity, she pushed at him. The hurried rush of his touches seemed too fast. She wanted to ask him to slow, but he found what he was seeking, and a jolt of pure sensation made her legs twitch.

He lifted his head as if to measure her response. She couldn't look at him as he provoked these fathomless excitements. He seemed to know her better than she knew herself. She hadn't known such pleasures were possible.

"Please," she whispered, not understanding the force overtaking her. She wanted to try and match him and meet his urgency. "Kiss me."

He shifted again and engaged her in a deep kiss. So many things were happening in her, she hardly knew how to concentrate. With one finger rubbing the nubbin in between her legs, he brushed his thumb over her sensitive nipple, and his soul deep kiss joined them in a tidal swell of ardor. She wanted to tell him to do one thing, but how could she forgo any of those?

A new pressure was added at her core. She dug in with her heels, trying to move away from it. She rocked from side to side and pushed at his shoulders, but the pressure continued.

She reached down between them and encountered the hard thick length of his shaft.

"Guide me." He spoke through clenched teeth.

A flood of new wanting poured through her, but she was ignorant. Instead she lightly ran her index finger over the throbbing length.

He moaned and yanked her hand away and increased the pressure.

He stilled her twisting hips and pushed forward. His manhood was too thick or big. Her body refused entrance. She whimpered at the growing discomfort.

Shoving his hand under her back, he clamped one hand on her shoulders, mooring her. His damp hair brushed her neck as he tucked his head down.

Then a pang ripped through her as he penetrated her. A sound between a sob and a yelp broke from her throat.

The thickness of his member stretched and filled her. He jerked back and stared down into her face.

Expressions flashed in quick succession: doubt, confusion, concern, and passion. Followed by a tender look. He stroked her cheek.

Heat flared in her face. The intimacy of his invasion was too strange. She bit her lip, unable to hold back her vulnerability. He would see all she felt about him, and she had no way to hide the truth.

"You are so beautiful," he whispered. Pressing tender kisses to the corners of her lips, her nose, and her eyelids, he gently embraced her.

She was hopelessly lost. His rapid switch to gentleness transformed their encounter from a tumultuous physical thing to a caring act. Her emotions surfaced. Her heart filled, and she could not stop it. She'd never felt this way about any other man. She suspected she never would. He was the one.

Lucian stared down at Velvet. Her lids lowered as if she were unable to bear his scrutiny, yet their bodies were locked in the most intimate of acts. He strained to stay still and allow her to adjust to him.

Yet his thoughts shouted, *Mine.* She was *his.* He was the *first.* Her only lover.

The growing tentativeness of her touches had frustrated him. Then the resistance he encountered made him think he was too out of practice, but she wasn't that good an actress. The way he entered her as if crashing through a barrier was unique to her and confirmed her inexperience.

His body thrummed with want. He had a thousand questions for her, but for whatever reason, she'd given herself to him. Desire rocketed through him and created a fresh surge of need.

Slowly he rocked his hips back, watching her face for signs of discomfort. Her passage was so narrow, thrills shuddered down his spine and his shaft throbbed. Although he wanted to slow, he was lost to the powerful pull of release. He thrust forward.

Her eyes popped open, the green glittering and soft, and her mouth rounded in an "Oh."

She curled her legs around his hips, and his thin cord of control snapped.

He should have taken hours to seduce her and wake her to the pleasures to be had, but he could do no more than rock into her until he climaxed with a powerful ecstasy that started at the back of his neck, then moved down his body, gathering force like a towering wave until he could do no more than ride the crest and fall into her.

In the aftermath, he panted, trying to sort out everything. Velvet squirmed under him, but he didn't want to separate from her while she was still unfulfilled. He slid his hand between their bodies. Her flat stomach quivered. Flat stomach. He managed to find the passion-slicked bud and rubbed.

"Don't," she whispered, and jerked her head away from his kiss.

In his selfishness, he'd allowed her passion to cool. "Velvet."

"I have to go back inside."

He found the tender spot behind her ear and teased it. "Don't deny me your pleasure."

For just a second it seemed she would allow him to complete the act for her, but then she twisted underneath him. "Don't. I can't." An edge of panic tightened her voice.

He pushed up to his elbows, stroking her hair. The last thing he wanted was to withdraw and roll away from her. "Velvet—"

"Please, I don't want to be missed."

"It is early still," he protested. She didn't want to be discovered copulating on the cliffs like a wild animal. He glanced toward the house. Only the very upper windows in the nursery wing were in his line of sight. Velvet's room, the schoolroom, and Iris's room. "Iris won't be awake yet."

Velvet twisted to look at the house.

"Her room is the only place we could be seen from." When he understood their encounter would escalate to making love, he should have led her inside to his room and bed, and damn the chance of being found out.

Velvet blanched and bit her lip. Her glance toward him was so fast he almost missed it, but then her gaze fastened on his Adam's apple.

Her unwillingness to look him in the eye hurt. "Are you all right?"

She gave a quick short nod.

A nearby herring gull screeched. Velvet flinched with every muscle in her body, including those of her woman's part. His flaccid member throbbed as though called back to duty. The white and gray bird landed on the pile of his wet bathing suit and pecked at it as if to discover hidden treats.

The gull made sure the passion was past, and Lucian reluctantly accepted that this encounter had ended in spite of his desire to continue for her. He pressed a chaste kiss on her cheek, which seemed to surprise her.

Lucian slowly withdrew and pushed to his knees, pulling down her skirt. Velvet struggled to tug up the corset he'd managed to shove down an inch to free the breasts he was sure had increased in size since the first time he'd cupped the rounded flesh in his hand.

Bloody hell, he'd been treating her like a woman awake to every passion, and she was a neophyte unaware of the potential of her response. She was passionate, he'd gotten enough of a taste of that to know. But he'd misjudged her horribly.

"Why?" he asked.

She jerked her head up and her green eyes glittered in the early morning light, but they looked bruised. She dropped her gaze and buttoned her dress. Her hair had completely fallen down and curtained her face. "I thought I was going to die."

He winced. He supposed he could ask for no better reason for her submitting to an act she'd resisted. Pushing her hair back, he examined her pinched and pale face. "You should have told me."

"You wouldn't have believed me." She chewed her lip and looked away.

Her regret twisted his gut. He didn't know what to do to change her mind. His lust had gained the upper hand over his tender feelings toward her, and he'd handled her badly. "Velvet—"

She twisted to her feet. "I have to get back inside."

Belting his robe, he winced at the smear of blood on his penis. As if he needed more confirmation. He still couldn't fully comprehend everything that had passed and changed between them.

She walked quickly across the expanse of moors. For a second he just watched her glide over the grass. She was his. Completely and wholly his. She just didn't know it yet. Hurried and rushed as it was, he didn't think he'd ever had a more fulfilling experience. He felt like he could soar with the gulls. And he was staring at her like a lovesick fool and letting her get away.

Then he grabbed his wet bathing suit and the couple of hairpins he'd popped from her hair and ran after her.

He caught up to her at the side door.

"I don't think we should go in together." She stared at the door, as stiff as if a metal rod had been inserted in her spine.

"We would if we had just had a discussion." He

wanted to hold her but settled for holding out the two hairpins. "I'm sorry, I probably lost some in the grass."

Never once looking at him, she took them, twisted the mass of her hair into a chignon and did her best to anchor it.

He brushed a broken blade of grass from her shoulders. "We need to discuss what just happened."

She jerked away from his touch, and her mouth flattened as she reached for the doorknob. In a prim schoolmarm voice she said, "There is no need."

He leaned close to her. "Then will you come to me tonight after the guests retire?"

"No. I don't want to repeat . . . what happened. I was not in my right mind."

He jerked back, sharp pain piercing his breastbone.

Before he could think how to respond, she sucked in a deep breath and opened the gallery door.

Stunned, he watched her dart through a nearby servants' door. It was as if she'd ripped out his heart and taken it with her.

"Sir, your bath is waiting."

Lucian spun toward the open hall door.

With his head cocked to the side, Evans stood there.

Evans would have been watching from Lucian's room to know when to run the bath water. Had he seen anything? Whatever he had seen, he could probably surmise the rest.

"Can I count on your discretion, Evans?" Lucian held out his bathing suit as he approached.

"Certainly, sir," said Evans, taking the wet striped wool with an expression of disdain.

Evans had been with him a long time, but he was generally so unobtrusive, Lucian never gave the man a thought. And he couldn't now. Not when his thoughts circled and worried over Velvet's reaction. What had been going through her head? Was it nothing more than having had too close a brush with death, and that he was there to experience her affirmation of life?

In the end she'd acted as though she couldn't be away from him fast enough; as if she'd made a terrible mistake. Nothing Lilith had done wounded him as much as Velvet's dismissal.

What had she done? The thought pounded in Velvet as she raced up the narrow back stairs. Oh, God, what had she done?

She'd resisted all advances for the last year, and then *she* had thrown herself at Lucian. *After* she'd begun to suspect him of murdering his wife and possibly his former mistress. Her heart told her that he couldn't have, but her heart had told her Mr. Langtree was her friend. Yet, Lucian was the one who gave her every opportunity to say no.

She rounded the corner and pushed open her door. All she wanted was five minutes to regain her composure and remove all traces of the illicit tryst. But she couldn't wash off the stain of sin. That would remain in her heart and soul. She couldn't believe she'd chosen to lie with Lucian.

Nellie turned, looked her up and down and said, "Where have you been?"

Velvet winced but squared her shoulders. "Outside."

Her window was open again.

"Cook wants you down in the kitchen."

"I will be down as soon as I freshen up."

Nellie nodded and backed toward the schoolroom. Her eyes darted to the made bed and back to Velvet.

"Would you please not open my window every day? It is too cold out."

"I don't open it," said Nellie.

Meg burst through the door, her arms full. A dozen brown paper and string packages fell to the floor. A few thumped and rolled. Others landed with a plop and didn't move.

"Oh, I'm sorry, miss," said Meg. "These came yesterday, and Mrs. Bigsby told me to bring them up straight away, but I got busy."

Nellie stepped back to the doorway and folded her arms.

Velvet's heart thudded against her chest. "What is in them?"

"Things for the schoolroom." Meg shrugged. She bent, picked them up, and began piling packages on the chair. "I hope nothing were breakable."

There was more here than could possibly be the few additional items she'd requested.

Meg glanced at Velvet and did a double take. "What have you been doing?"

Nellie looked interested too.

"I went outside to talk to Mr. Pendar." That much was true anyway. "I slipped and fell." Almost true.

"Lord above, you look a fright," said Meg.

"Yes, I'd like to clean up. Would you please bring me a pitcher of water?"

"Open the packages," said Nellie.

"Later." Velvet dreaded the contents. If the packages contained anything personal, Nellie and Meg would guess at the relationship between her and Lucian.

A sob caught at the back of her throat. She turned to the armoire to gather fresh underclothing and hide her emotions. She felt on the verge of cracking. She'd half expected Lucian to follow her upstairs, but he hadn't. Why would he? He'd gotten what he wanted.

Maybe in her secret heart she'd hoped for him to say he loved her or would marry her. Instead he'd said she was beautiful. In a few minutes she would go downstairs and help the house run smoothly to impress a potential bride for him.

For a second Velvet toyed with the idea of demanding her wages and leaving, but she couldn't hurt Iris, deserted by so many in her short life. Velvet was nothing more than what everyone accused her of being: a past-her-youth, fallen woman. She bit her lip, holding back tears. Destiny had decreed she would be alone. Any chance she'd had for a decent marriage she'd tossed away in a romp on the edge of a cliff.

For a few moments she'd been soaring, seeming floating on the air like the seabirds, but then she fell, and fell hard.

Paper crinkled behind her.

"Oh look, miss. It is a lovely dressing gown," Meg exclaimed.

Nellie and Meg had fallen on the packages like gulls on crumbs. Strings and brown paper littered the floor, fluttering from the breeze.

"This one is paints," said Nellie in a dull monotone.

Meg swirled while holding the chocolate brown dressing gown to her shoulders. Nellie was staring at Velvet with a look of astonishment mixed with disgust.

"Stop!"

Meg quit spinning, and the plush material swayed at her feet.

"Please, wrap it back up." Lucian probably thought she was showing her gratitude for his present. "There must be a mistake. And for heaven's sake, shut the window."

Meg glanced over at the window. "Why do you open it every night if you don't want it open?"

"I don't," whispered Velvet.

Nellie made the sign of the cross, as if she thought an evil spirit was responsible.

Who was opening the window? Velvet shivered uncontrollably. Nothing was right in this mad household. Not even her. She'd behaved like a woman possessed and thrown away the only thing she had of value.

Chapter 17

Dried and dressed after his bath—a bath he should have offered to Velvet—Lucian ascended to the nursery floor. Velvet was right. He needed to make amends with Iris.

He fingered the peace offering weighing down his pocket. How Iris would respond to it he didn't know.

The girl couldn't know that her resemblance to her mother pained him to look at her. He couldn't count how many times he bit back bitter words about Lilith. And he had to acknowledge there would never be a good reason to let her learn of her true parentage. If he meant to denounce her, he should have done so before her birth. The truth now could only wound her.

Velvet's door stood open. The maidservant inside darted out as soon as she saw him. But Velvet was nowhere to be seen. Not in her room or in the schoolroom. Air rushed out of him as if he were collapsing like a spent balloon. He hadn't realized how anxious he'd been to see her again.

He retreated to Iris's room, where his knock on the door elicited no response.

Gently pushing the door open, he peeked inside. Iris lay in her bed, her blond curls haloing her face.

"Iris?" he queried softly.

She blinked.

He waited while the sleep lifted from her. He had no idea how to reassure the child. If Velvet was right, Iris needed more than he gave her. Less things and more of him. He'd known for longer than he cared to admit he could be a better father to her. But like most men, he preferred the much simpler route of giving presents.

"Papa?"

"Would you like to eat breakfast with me?" he asked. Before Velvet came, they'd eaten together in the morning. Even though he'd thought her incessant chatter drove him to distraction, he now believed she'd actually been putting him in a better frame of mind.

"Yes." Eagerly, she shoved back the covers and scrambled out of bed, but then paused. She tossed him an uncertain look. "Is Miss Campbell going too?"

"I don't know where she is right now." He cleared his throat. "I will wait for you in the schoolroom, then."

Where was Velvet? He closed the door and rushed into Velvet's room. The unwrapped packages were laid out on her bed. Her portmanteau was tucked in the armoire with her other clothes. He heaved a sigh of relief. For half a second he'd feared she'd left. Turning to the windows, he looked out, scanning the cliffs in every direction.

He closed his eyes, willing his heartbeat to slow. Velvet was not melodramatic like Lilith had been. Surely she wouldn't fling herself from the cliffs. Especially not when she was so terrified of falling.

He realized her weakness at King Arthur's castle must have been her fear of falling. He'd thought she'd been feeling faint, but her symptoms just as easily fit freezing in panic. It certainly hadn't been pregnancy.

He shook his head and retreated to the schoolroom.

Soon Iris opened her door and walked sedately across the room. Her slightly puffy eyes and reddened nose along with her failure to skip or bounce as she usually did stabbed at his heart. Had he wounded her as severely as Velvet claimed? Guilt swamped him.

"I am sorry for yelling at you last night." He sank down into one of the schoolroom chairs. "There are times when it is painful for me to be reminded of your mother, and I punished you for it."

Iris hesitated in front of him, carefully watching him. She bit her lip.

He half expected her to ask if he still missed her mother. When she didn't, he was relieved he didn't have to lie. Iris's uncharacteristic silence concerned him. "Miss Campbell tells me it upset you that I did not say good-bye before leaving."

Iris's eyes widened. She slowly nodded, not used to him discussing her upsets.

"Did you not know I was leaving?"

Iris shook her head.

"Miss Campbell did not tell you?"

Iris finally spoke in a soft voice he had to strain to hear. "She didn't know."

He frowned. Mrs. Bigsby should have informed both of them, but then maybe the housekeeper assumed he had informed Velvet. "In the future, I will endeavor to make sure you know when I am leaving."

"And say good-bye?" asked Iris.

"And say good-bye," affirmed Lucian. "I left very early. I didn't want to disturb your rest."

Iris's eyebrows lowered.

He squirmed a bit under her scrutiny. He reached into his pocket.

She brightened. "Did you buy me a gift in London?"

His hand stilled. How much had his ceaseless gifts encouraged Iris to be greedy and grasping like her mother?

He shook his head. "No. I did not know what to get a girl who is too big for dolls." Resolving to pay more attention to the effect his actions had in the future, he pulled the heavy gold bracelet out of his pocket and laid it across his knee. "This is a family piece, and you must promise to pass it on one day to your child."

Iris gaped at the ornate Spanish band inset with pearls and topazes. Her voice awed, she asked, "Is that the bracelet in the paintings?"

"Yes. The set has been in the family a long time." Lilith had refused to wear it in the family portrait because she thought it too old-fashioned. "My ancestors were privateers in service to Queen Elizabeth."

"Privateers?" She glanced at him, but then as if drawn, she stared back at the bracelet.

"Kind of like pirates with a royal license to plunder from enemy ships." He lifted the piece. "Would you like to wear it?"

"Isn't it supposed to be for your wife?" Iris pulled her hands back as if afraid she might snatch it.

"I don't have a wife, and I want you to wear it."

She rolled her shoulders and stared at him with wide blue eyes.

"Will you make me give it back when you get a new wife?"

"No."

Slowly she raised her arm.

He winced at the reddish marks on her wrist—marks he had caused. He fastened the clasp around her slender wrist, hoping the weight wouldn't be too much. "I trust you to take care of it."

"Nellie says you're going to get a new wife."

"Possibly." He glanced toward Velvet's room. Everything had changed now, and he didn't know what would happen.

"Do you want a new wife?" asked Iris.

Lucian strove to switch the conversation. "Every Pendar eventually passes on the set to his oldest son, but I don't have a son."

Iris looked up at him. Her eyes were so blue and clear, without a hint of guile. She probably didn't understand what he was saying.

"I have you," he finished with a rough voice.

"I'm sorry I wasn't a boy," she whispered.

"No, don't think that. I wouldn't trade you for all the riches in the world. You are perfect the way you are. Come what may, you will have the rest of the set on your wedding day to pass to your children."

Iris shifted from one foot to the other and turned the bracelet on her wrist. Her nature was still compliant enough she might have agreed to wear the bracelet because he asked her to. "What if your new wife wants me to give it back?"

"I will not take it away from you."

"A new wife could give you a son, couldn't she?"

The images of his three dark-haired babies, too still and too blue lying in their bassinets, chilled his heart. He couldn't risk getting another woman with child with his defective seed. He knew that and had been very careful—since Myra anyway. Velvet wasn't the only one who lost her head on the cliff this morning. "I don't need a son."

Iris frowned at his vehemence. Then she tilted her head to the side. "Can—*may* we go eat now?"

"Certainly." Standing, he held out his hand to Iris.

Iris slipped her little fingers into his and smiled up at him. He heaved a sigh of relief. He hadn't realized how much he counted on her unstinting affection. He didn't have a right to it, but he needed her ungrudging acceptance.

Velvet was exhausted by the time all the guests began to make their good-nights. She'd avoided Lucian all day, but found almost every time she looked in his direction his dark eyes were on her. Her heart would lurch a little, and he would look away to one of his guests, most often Miss Bowman or Miss Darling. He too seemed intent on keeping his distance.

His aloof demeanor drained her almost as much as Cook's constant demands and her own striving to keep the guests happy without them being aware that she was doing anything.

She was headed for the door leading to a servants' stair when a hand on her shoulder stopped her. Without turning she knew the hand belonged to Lucian. A shudder traveled from the top of her head to her toes.

"Wait in the library. I will be there as soon as I am free." He leaned close, his breath brushing her ear.

What was wrong with her that she went weak in the knees when he was close? "I should like to retire."

His fingers tightened. "Then make ready for bed and meet me in my room," he whispered.

She spun away. Despair choked her. In one rash act she had become everything she'd fought against. Just like every other man before him who thought her a whore, he thought he had the right to her.

The corner of his mouth lifted. "The library it will be."

Velvet closed her eyes. "I should check on Iris."

"Be in the library in fifteen minutes or I will come

for you." He ran his thumb along her shoulder.

A shudder tumbled down her spine.

After wishing for him to acknowledge her for most of the day, now she wished he hadn't. What would happen when they were alone? Would they discuss terms of her becoming his mistress? Terms she would find demeaning, no matter how gently broached.

He hovered, waiting for her reply, but his scent flooded her nostrils and his heat made her want to collapse against him.

She should just use the locks he'd had installed, or plead a headache, but she couldn't force out the words. It took every ounce of her willpower not to cling to him and relive every sensation from this morning.

"I will not be deterred by a locked door, so do not think to avoid me."

Her first morning here he'd kicked her stuck door with enough force a lock couldn't stop him.

"Very well," she said with what dignity she could muster when she had no real choice.

As she hurried away, excitement and dread stewed in a cauldron of emotions. What would happen when they were alone again?

Would he pull her into his arms and kiss her until her judgment evaporated and she became the wild unfamiliar creature she had been on the cliff?

The one thing she was sure wouldn't happen: he wouldn't declare his love for her. Even though her heart beat awkwardly with the hope that he cared for her just a little.

She headed up the servants' stairs and entered the dark nursery floor. In her cold room she found the single candle she'd been allotted and carried it to Iris's room to light.

Iris wore a heavy gold bracelet. Velvet hadn't had time to question the girl where she'd found it. The piece, although faintly familiar, didn't look like any of the jewelry found in her mother's trinket box. Iris's heavy breathing indicated her sleep was deep. By now she'd been in bed for hours.

Velvet had missed tucking her in and overseeing her prayers. Instead she pulled the covers around Iris's shoulders and leaned down to press a kiss to her forehead.

With her lit candle, Velvet returned to her room. She wanted nothing more than to crawl in bed and hope that when she woke, she'd discover today was just a bad dream. Instead she knelt to ignite the coal in the fireplace.

After she had the blaze going, she carefully folded the dressing gown and rewrapped it in the paper and twine. She couldn't accept the gift because it made her feel cheap. A dressing gown was too intimate and implied too much.

Pulling her door shut to keep in what meager heat her lump of coal might generate, she headed back downstairs with the package.

The library was dark except for the fire crackling behind the grate. Light spilled from Lucian's office. For a second she thought she might be alone, and she heaved a deep sigh. The smell of leather-bound books fortified her.

Then the shadows moved, and Lucian appeared in his office doorway.

With the backlighting, she couldn't see his expression. But he carried the letter from Mrs. Langtree in his hand.

Her throat caught.

"Are you all right?" he asked.

Velvet didn't know how to answer. She was tied in knots and so ashamed she wanted to crawl in a hole. A slight tenderness in her private parts strangled any affirmative response.

"I wasn't exactly gentle."

Heat flooded her face. Tightening the package containing the dressing gown against her chest, she choked out, "I'm fine."

"I didn't know there was a reason to be," he continued. "I was not expecting a novice."

Her knees went weak. "I didn't know you'd be able to tell."

"I've been trying to understand why you would tell me this letter is factual when clearly this reputation you have is undeserved."

"Was undeserved," muttered Velvet. She couldn't claim innocence any longer, not after she had thrown herself at Lucian.

Lucian crossed his arms and leaned against the mantel. His body was long and lean, and she knew his flesh was firm under his clothes. His brow furrowed as he watched her.

His dark eyes seemed to drink in her every move, and without warning she was trembling all over. She wanted to throw herself in his arms. This morning he had been inside her. A fresh burst of desire spiraled through her.

"And I thought you were pregnant."

She shook off her fascination with him as she realized what he'd said. "Pregnant?"

"You've fainted. You've been sick and had a hard time tolerating fish and other pungent foods. You insisted there was nothing wrong with you that time wouldn't cure. Pretty much a definition of pregnancy. Your figure has grown more rounded. And you definitely are glowing. You said the letter was factual. The only question I had was which one of the men was the father."

"I'm not pregnant." His opinion of her was worse than she anticipated.

His mouth twisted. "You might be now."

Oh God, she hadn't even thought of that possibility. Her knees buckled and she caught herself.

"Sit down before you fall down."

She moved to one of the Moroccan leather chairs flanking the fireplace. Staring into the lively flames, she considered that Lucian might have gotten her in the family way. Turn it as she might, the thought didn't fill her with the alarm it was due.

"So explain to me how you could be found with your skirts around your waist and remain untouched?"

The memory of how they had coupled on the cliffs that morning made her face burn hotter.

She lowered her head. "Lord . . . the MP attacked me. He insisted I drink with him. I only remember taking a few sips, but I was insensible. Mrs. Langtree came upon us in the nick of time."

She hadn't even realized she was half naked until Mrs. Langtree hissed, *Cover yourself.*

"I think he put something in my drink, it was very bitter."

"And Mr. Langtree?" Lucian's voice hardened.

She put her palms out. The package fell to her thighs. "I thought we were friends." She had to acknowledge her role in the fiasco. "I allowed too much familiarity between us, and when he thought we should . . . I should." She shook her head. "He assaulted me in my room when all the rest of the household was away. I tried to run away, which is how we ended in his wife's bed." Her voice quivered and she couldn't stop it. "He said if I spread my legs for a fat old man, then I could bloody well spread them for him."

But Lucian had been different. Even in that moment on the cliff he had given her a choice.

Lucian's eyes narrowed.

Velvet swallowed. He didn't believe her. Beyond her mortification at having to explain everything again, a deep rending pain seared through her chest. Lucian, who had more proof than any other of her purity, didn't believe her. Former purity, she reminded herself.

He thumbed through the letter and then tossed it in her lap. "And the noises you were making?"

Velvet looked at the missive. *She was making the most shocking noises . . . Miss C— continued to screech like a cat in heat.* "When I ran, he caught me and threw me up against the wall."

Her nightgown had been ripped open, and her struggles had been nothing against a determined man.

She'd tried to run down to the housekeeper's room, but he'd caught her on the family floor. Her head had slammed into the wall with a sickening thud. "I hit my head and was dazed, and I might have been whimpering. My screams hadn't been heard. I learned later he'd dismissed the servants for the evening."

"And Mrs. Langtree rescued you again."

"Yes, I thought she was my angel." Until Mrs. Langtree threw her on the streets. "I know it sounds preposterous that two man tried to ra—" She couldn't force the word out. Her voice dropped to a hushed whisper, and she cradled the package back to her chest. "—have their way with me in so short a space of time, but I had been a dozen years in employment and had never had a problem. I was unprepared and naive. I allowed Mr.

Langtree to think I might be open to a deeper relationship. I did enjoy the intellectual stimulation of talking to an adult, and I let him know I had much pleasure in his company."

A sob caught at the back of her throat, but she forced it down.

Lucian's expression flickered, and he turned to kick a log in the fire. Sparks flared. Velvet jumped at each snap.

"Did you encourage him to think you would enjoy a physical affair?"

Velvet shook her head. "I never thought of him in that manner. He was married."

"I have seen most of the cast of your little drama in London. Mr. and Mrs. Langtree—she is a remarkable beauty, is she not?—then there was your Steven," Lucian's voice turned softer.

How had he known it was Steven?

Velvet frowned and fished out the letter from where it was trapped against her chest. She turned to the last sheet. Mrs. Langtree hadn't mentioned Steven by name or initial.

Before she framed the question, Lucian sneered. "Your face changes when you speak of him."

Her shoulders dropped. Her expressions must reveal her betrayal by a young man she loved like a mother, and Lucian had cast it in a completely wrong light. Could she never rid herself of the slurs?

Her nose tingled and she fought to keep composed. She couldn't look at Lucian.

"How old is this boy?"

"Did you not see him? He is nineteen."

"A man, then. Certainly old enough to make his own decisions."

"I applied to him for money. I had nothing to live on." She curled her shoulders. "He mistook the request. I should have looked for humble work in an inn or shop. I had no intention of selling my . . . my . . ." She searched for a word. Body sounded too crass, virtue sounded too mealy-mouthed.

"Favors," he supplied.

"He accepted my refusal. Although I suppose he thought I would eventually succumb to his charm or my pecuniary distress."

"I'm sure you would have raised him better than to be so unmannerly as to force a woman."

Her face burning, Velvet wanted out of the room. Her humiliation was complete. Any hope of kindness or caring was completely destroyed. Thrusting out the package, she stood. "I cannot accept this dressing gown. The cotton I will use to teach Iris to stitch samplers, but I cannot take so personal a gift."

She hadn't been certain if the yards of material was meant for her to fashion new undergarments, but she wouldn't take anything for herself. It smacked too much of prostitution. She pushed the dressing robe at him.

Scowling, he took the package and tossed it onto the other chair. "I may have given you a bigger gift. Even now you could be carrying my child."

"The chances are small. I am not young and . . ." Velvet stroked her arms, feeling cold. If she was reading the signs in her body right, she was due to begin her courses in the next day or two.

The fire's heat didn't seem to reach her. If Lucian took her in his arms, she would feel warmer, but he backed away.

"I hope to high heaven you are not carrying my child," he said vehemently, and strode across the room.

Her chest felt as though a horse had kicked it. She gasped for breath.

The clink of the decanter against the rim was like a death knell.

"Would you like a brandy?" he asked.

Maintaining her composure in the face of his detached interrogation was growing harder. The back of her eyes burned, and she blinked rapidly. "I would like to retire."

"We're not done. Sit down."

His voice brooked no disobedience. Velvet sank back into the chair. He regretted this morning on the cliff too. In all the ways she envisioned this talk going, this was the last thing she was prepared for. This coldhearted examination of her past and his rejection hurt.

He took a long drink and returned to stand in front of her. Bending down, he picked up the letter that had fallen to the floor and tossed it in the fireplace. The sheets curled and blackened like her hopes. Her past was not so easily shed by burning the letter.

"I think we should take precautions against your conceiving in the future."

"I . . . I . . ." She gaped. Her eyes darted up trying to read his expression on his shadowed face, but she quickly lowered them. He was so beautiful it hurt. "I won't continue to . . ." None of the usual euphemisms made sense, and she tried to collect herself to continue. "I was not myself, and I don't think I could live with myself."

He took another long drink. "My children have all been born dead or dying, and I shouldn't like to put you through that."

Had he not heard her? "I won't continue as your mistress."

"Was it so horrible?" he asked. The glass plunked on the mantel before he leaned over her.

Velvet looked right and left and settled for staring at his chest. Not horrible, but she'd been aware of a lingering disappointment all day long, as if she'd missed something, but she didn't intend to explore it further. And barring another near death miss, she didn't think she'd lose her sanity so completely.

"I can do better, you know." He stroked a finger down the side of her face. "If I hadn't been sure you were experienced, I would have spent more time waking your passions."

Air seemed in short supply, and her body seemed to have a mind not connected to hers. A rush of warmth plowed through her. Tingles and shivers built to a rising crescendo within her. He could make it better? Her thoughts turned wicked.

But she was unprepared for his shift in tactics. She pushed at his chest. "Please don't."

But even that was a mistake. Her palms remembered the feel of his heated skin and the springy hair on his breast.

He pulled away and picked up his glass again. "You were a virgin. You could be with child. Of course I have to marry you."

"No," she whispered. His grudging declaration of obligation cut her deeper than she could imagine. He didn't care about her, didn't act as if he really wanted to lie with her again. He could pull back and walk away, drink his drink with nonchalance, while she was a quivering mess, incapable of a coherent thought.

"What?" he asked sharply.

"You don't have to marry me," she whispered. "It was one time. No one need ever know." *Foolish, fool-*

ish, girl. She wanted to be married, but not to a man who wouldn't give her children. A marriage without affection should at least be entered to create a family. She searched for a way to keep him apart from her. "I want children."

His hiss was low, and she wanted to draw the words back.

He spun and hurtled his glass into the fire. The flames reared in a bluish glow. And for the second time today she had made one of the most stupid mistakes of her life.

Chapter 18

Lucian couldn't breathe. Velvet's refusal to marry him sliced him to the core. The room turned red. "Bloody hell!"

He gripped the mantel, fearing if he let go he'd wrap his hands around Velvet's throat. Her beautiful, swan-like neck. She wanted children. With three words she'd emasculated him. Not the three words he wanted to hear. Not the three words he had planned to utter next as a requisite part of a proposal, before her "No" cut him. He couldn't do anything about his cursed seed.

Silence roared by.

He'd been trying to be calm and discuss things, not just sweep her into his arms and insist upon marriage. He'd wanted her to know he had thought about it and although it pretty quickly occurred to him that he had to marry her, he wanted to. He couldn't believe she'd said no.

Who was she to demand anything? She'd been destitute before he hired her. He held onto the anger because to let it go would leave him in despair. He stared toward the decanter, wanting to dive into the oblivion of drink.

"You can't be thinking," he spat out when she didn't make a sound. "I can give you anything you want."

Except children. "More than you'll ever have as a governess."

She winced. "I've only ever wanted a family." Her voice was breathy and low.

"Velvet." Saying her name hurt. On the cliff's edge she'd for a brief moment made him feel whole, made him feel he had a purpose for living, made him feel as if he had a chance of finding happiness with her. "If I could give you healthy children, I would."

An image of her holding a babe sliced through him. Velvet would undoubtedly cherish babies, not pawn them off on nursemaids. By God, he wanted children too, but it wasn't to be. He sucked in a deep breath. How could she make him hope for such a cruel thing as another baby who would die?

"You don't know what it is like." The tightness in his chest threatened to cut off his words. She didn't have the faintest inkling of what it was like. To watch as the life drained from little faces bearing his stamp. To wrap them and carry them to the churchyard. To stand by as cold dirt was shoveled on top of a tiny box containing a still infant. The thud, thud, thud of dirt on the baby's coffin. He couldn't bear to do it again. But he might have to. He might have impregnated her, and he had to make her see there was only one option. "You could be with child now."

"You're right. I'm tired. If I am with child, I'll marry you. It would be the right thing to do." Her voice sounded tinny and barely penetrated through the rush in his ears.

"I'll announce our pending nuptials tomorrow at dinner."

"I didn't agree." She sounded as calm as she ever did.

Although his stomach churned, he tried to sound as rational as she did. "An announcement isn't final, but

would allow us to marry with speed if it proves necessary." Or she could break it off. Would she have the will
to end a publicly declared engagement? He wished for
his glass back. He could pour another brandy, but he
suspected he would be tempted to throw it again.

"No announcement. You'll upset your guests."

"I imagine it will relieve a few of them."

He turned, and she was curled into a ball in the chair
with her arms around her legs. Her posture was so
unlike her normal ladylike reserve, it stopped him cold.

Her eyes glittered as she stared steadfastly into the
flames. Had her refusal been about more than his inability to father children?

"Just so you know. I wasn't looking for potential
brides." He brushed at a wet spot where the brandy had
splattered on his leg. "I asked my associates if they had
young girls they could bring for a visit." He may have
mentioned he should get married again, but more than a
day or two had separated the comments. "I meant girls
Iris's age."

"Oh," Velvet whispered. Her lower lip quivered until
she sunk her teeth into it.

"I should have made myself clearer."

Not that he could stand to marry one of the insipid
girls in his "bride buffet." He couldn't picture any of
them as a life partner, nor did he find their inability to
look at him without seeing his scars tolerable. "In case
you are with child, we shouldn't wait."

"It is not as if my reputation will suffer," she mumbled.

His hands fisted. "No. Mine will."

Velvet had always confronted him when she thought
it necessary, but that didn't mean she didn't fear him.
She'd nearly backed off a cliff to get away from him
after he told her Myra had been murdered. Then she had

thrown herself at him. Nothing made sense.

He touched his scar.

Her eyes tracked his hand and filmed with moisture before she shuttered them. She was not as unaffected as she would have him believe.

His thoughts spun and landed on a hard truth. This morning she believed Iris was his. Velvet hadn't known he couldn't father viable children. His stomach burned.

She dropped her feet to the floor as if she had reached a new resolve. "I should like to wait to discuss this further until we know it is a necessity."

Her words were like knives slicing him to ribbons.

"You'd make a good mother for Iris." He winced. Using her affection for Iris was pathetic. But he would do anything to cement the deal. He could get her with child, but the thought shamed him. He couldn't put another woman through that, let alone one he loved.

He stared at Velvet as the realization solidified in his mind. He loved her. When had that happened?

He wanted to hold her and kiss her, and all he had was a halfhearted conditional agreement to marry. He wanted to wake up with her beside him. He wanted her to be his wife. Her intelligence, her calm, her fortitude all drew him. He couldn't think of one thing he didn't admire about her. Except, she didn't seem to return his feelings. How could he bare his heart to her when she could so easily dismiss his offer?

He'd thought he was content alone, but he loved Velvet. What could he use to convince her before she slipped away?

He bent and ran a finger down the side of her face. Her skin was so soft, and her lips parted. "Spend the rest of the night with me. Let me show you what you missed."

Her head jerked up. Her eyes were glassy and she seemed to stare through him. "Iris has nightmares. I don't want her to not be able to find me."

Her ready excuse ripped at him. To look at her strained face made him bleed inside. "Go then."

But when she reached the door, he wanted to call her back. She was taking his heart with her and leaving behind only the package containing the dressing gown. He almost pitched it in the fire too, but instead carried it to his office and tucked the present in a desk drawer.

He rubbed his face. How could he woo a woman who refused his gifts? She wanted the one thing he could not give any woman. And he feared she suspected him of murdering Myra and Lilith, but he couldn't bear to ask if she trusted him. Even after her death, Lilith was still destroying his life.

In spite of her exhaustion, Velvet had a hard time getting to sleep. Several times she resisted the urge to go to Lucian's room and at least apologize for hurting him, but there was no good reason to go in the middle of the night. The dark angst in his face when she'd mentioned children wouldn't leave her. But nothing she could do would change her mind or his.

She tossed and turned. All her life her father had made one message clear. Congress between a man and a woman was designed for procreation. To debase the act by making it only about pleasure was a sin. Marrying and avoiding conception seemed like the greatest sin of all. She loved children. She'd never given up on the idea of having her own.

When she finally dropped off to sleep, a cry rent the night.

"No! No! No!"

Her heart pounding, Velvet threw back the covers and ran across the cold floor. She jerked open the schoolroom door. "I'm coming, Iris!" she called.

Another door clicked. Had Iris woken someone else with her cries?

With her arms outstretched to avoid bumping into anything, Velvet scuttled across the schoolroom.

Once inside Iris's room the glow of the ever-burning fire in the child's room lit the way.

Iris knelt on the foot of her bed and tears tracked down her face.

Velvet heaved a deep sigh seeing the girl safe and unharmed.

"My mama came and said it was time for me to go, because Papa is getting a new wife."

"Hush," soothed Velvet. Sitting on the bed, she smoothed Iris's hair away from her face. "It was just a bad dream."

Velvet concentrated on slowing her racing heart.

Iris plowed into Velvet's arms, holding tight.

Cradling the small form, Velvet soothed the child. Iris was unsettled. Her routines had been interrupted, and like any child uncertain of her place, she found the break in routines distressing. She'd probably heard the servants speculating on the number of eligible young ladies present and feared even more disruption to her life.

"She was here. St-Standing in my door. She s-said I had to go with her." Iris sobbed.

"No, sweetheart. It was just a dream. She wasn't here." Velvet stroked the young girl's back. "Let me tuck you back into bed."

"Don't go. I'm scared."

Velvet disengaged from the girl. "I'm right here. I'm

just getting you a handkerchief to blow your nose." She crossed the room and opened a dresser drawer.

"Sh-Sh-She'll come back," Iris continued. "Please don't leave me."

"Iris, you are too big for me to stay every night with you. You must remember to pray and say, 'Satan get behind me.' An apparition will not linger when you pray to God to protect you."

"I tried to pray! She just laughed at me and said prayers couldn't help me."

As Velvet turned back, she noticed the door to the corridor was ever so slightly cracked. A chill shuddered down her spine.

"Oh, sweetheart, I'm so sorry." She held the handkerchief to Iris's nose and urged her to calm down. "I am here, and I won't let anything bad happen to you. I'll stay until morning."

A bad dream didn't have the power to open doors. And couldn't ghosts walk through walls? Was this an apparition or something worse?

"Are you ever going to wake up?" asked Iris.

Velvet's shoulder was pushed back. Refracted light danced across the plaster ceiling. The sun had risen high enough to be shining on the water.

Alarm jolting her all the way awake, she jerked up.

"Papa told Nellie you were to be allowed to sleep in, but you've never slept this late."

Velvet pushed her braid behind her back. She was refreshed in the way only a good sleep could do. "How did he know I was still asleep?"

"He came up to take me down to breakfast with him." Iris turned the bracelet on her wrist. "He gave me this yesterday. He says it is a family heirloom, but

I don't know what an heirloom is. I think it must mean jewelry someone stole a long time ago. Papa said our family used to be like pirates."

"No. An heirloom is possession that has been in the family for a long time. It looks very old and valuable."

"Pretty too," said Iris.

With a smile, Velvet pushed back the covers on Iris's bed. "I must get dressed."

"Papa showed me all the old paintings it's in." Iris folded her arms behind her back and looked down at the carpet.

Velvet hesitated. "I'm glad."

When she least expected it, he surprised her. Beyond giving Iris a gift that meant something, he was spending more time with her. Plus he had heard her concerns about Iris's need for friends her own age and made an effort to address the issue.

"He's being very nice to me because he doesn't want me to be upset he threw Mama's bracelet in the fire."

"That and he loves you," said Velvet. For an inexplicable reason she felt in great charity with the world. Perhaps it was the excessive rest she'd received. Or in the bright morning light, she just couldn't see Lucian as a sinister figure capable of intentionally harming anyone.

"No. He just doesn't want me mad."

"Iris, if he doesn't love you, why would he care if you're angry with him? He doesn't have to spend time with you if he doesn't want to. Some papas only see their children once a week." She ruffled Iris's hair.

The girl ducked away from her. "You are not usually so happy."

Velvet didn't understand it. She should be worried or angry, but instead she felt alive.

Hurrying through the schoolroom, Velvet knew she

shouldn't relish being indulged and allowed to sleep late. She turned and looked at Iris. "Did you tell your papa about last night?"

Iris tucked her hands behind her back and shook her head. "He looked at me funny and asked if I had a bad dream. I didn't want him to think I was a baby." She rocked back and forth.

Great. Velvet smiled wryly. Now Lucian would think she was avoiding him by sleeping in his daughter's bedroom. "You shouldn't lie, Iris."

"I didn't. I didn't have a bad dream," she insisted.

Velvet reached for her door. The blast of cold air was hardly a surprise, but the shreds of material and paper swirling through her room were. For a second she couldn't comprehend the raveling strips of green, black, and white. But her thoughts slowly congealed on a hard truth. Her clothes had been shredded. The flurry of shifting material revealed upended books on the floor. "Oh no."

Her father's books were destroyed. Her last link to her papa. The books were the only thing she had resembling an heirloom. Dazed, she entered the room and found even her undergarments in rags. Everything she owned was ruined. Torn to bits.

"Papa, Miss Campbell said she'd like her package now." Iris tugged on Lucian's sleeve. He pushed away from the billiard table.

"This is your daughter?" asked Sir John.

Lucian leaned his cue stick against the wall. "Yes." He hesitated briefly before he added, "This is my daughter, Iris." The words came out rusty. He couldn't remember a time he'd ever spoken them, but he didn't think the men noticed. Lucian put his hand on her shoulder as he introduced her around.

Iris dipped curtsies and piped, "Pleased to meet you," to each of the men. But a tiny quiver in her voice alerted Lucian that all was not well.

"You'll have to excuse me, gentlemen." He guided Iris to the hall.

Once they were out of the gentleman's room, he asked, "What is wrong?"

Iris's blue eyes pooled and she sniffed. "Miss Campbell thought I did it."

"Did what?" What had happened? A tiny spark of hope that Velvet had changed her mind was extinguished by Iris's strange announcement.

Iris took a step back, her eyes taking on a glassy look. "I am to ask you for the package and for you to come upstairs to see her room. She said not to speak of what happened until she had discussed it with you."

"Very well." Lucian moved to the library.

Iris waited at the foot of the stairs.

Dressing gown in one hand and Iris's hand in his other, they ascended to the nursery floor.

Velvet waited in the corridor. Her eyes appeared huge in her pale face. The counterpane from Iris's room was wrapped around her hunched shoulders. "I'm sorry to disturb you."

Something was very wrong. Velvet wouldn't have called him up before she was dressed. Dread snaked down his spine. He shook his head and handed her the dressing gown. "Good thing I didn't throw it in the fire."

Her lips pulled back, but if she was attempting a smile, her failure was spectacular. She dropped her gaze to the floor.

More confused then ever, he followed her gaze. Bare toes peeked out from under the nightgown's frayed hem.

"So what changed your mind about accepting?"

"I have nothing else to wear, except stockings." She opened her bedroom door. With a flat tone she said, "My stockings were spared."

Pieces of material scattered, as the breeze from her wide-open windows blew through the room. Long strips slithered like snakes over the chair and bed as if they'd been thrown in a frenzy. Torn book leaves fluttered. The well-crafted sewing shears he'd purchased in London lay open on the wooden floor.

As if he'd dove into the icy cold ocean, his breath was knocked from him. The amount of destruction was shocking. Who would do such a thing?

He strode across the space and pulled the casements shut. "Why are your windows open?"

"I don't ever open them." Velvet bit on her lip and looked right and left. "I don't know who does."

She unwrapped the dressing gown with shaking hands. He had to find the culprit.

Iris was the only one to destroy books, and the tricks she had played on previous governesses had been cruel. "Iris!"

Her hesitant look reminded him of her mother's wide-eyed lies. "Papa?"

Velvet took a step between them with her hand out.

He struggled to remember Iris was not Lilith. Her hurt when she thought Miss Campbell blamed her confounded him. He didn't believe she was sophisticated enough to fake that. "Do you know anything about what happened in here?" he demanded.

"I didn't do anything. Mama did it!"

He reared back. "Iris, your mother is dead."

Velvet put her hands on Iris's shoulders while beseeching him with her eyes. "Iris didn't do it."

"She's destroyed books before. And—"

Velvet shook her head.

He let her silent plea ease his fury. Making his voice gentle, he asked, "Did you hear anything? Did you see who came in here?"

Iris shook her head.

"I should have used the locks," Velvet said. "I shall from now on."

Lucian winced. The locks he'd assured her wouldn't keep him out. He wasn't the one she needed to keep out.

Holding out the counterpane to Iris, Velvet said, "Would you take this back to your room, please?"

The girl's blue eyes were big and round as she stepped away from where she cowered by the door.

Velvet smiled at her as she handed over her burden. As soon as Iris turned away, Velvet's expression fell.

Unable to stand back, he closed the distance between them. She stepped away as she pulled the dressing gown around her shoulders.

"Velvet."

She held up her hand. "Don't. There are practical problems that must be addressed, such as I cannot play hostess to your guests without clothes."

Had she found hostess duties so distressing she destroyed her own wardrobe? He dismissed the thought as soon as it flashed through his mind. She never would have destroyed the books. Velvet had too much reverence for the written word.

She picked up the spines of books and stacked them on the chair. Turning her back to him, she swiped her fingers under her eye.

He pulled her against his body in spite of her reluctance. She sagged against him. Lucian let out a breath; he hadn't been sure she would allow him to comfort her.

"It's all right. I have you."

She gasped and started to step away.

He remembered his words were a repeat of the words he'd murmured to her yesterday. He'd meant them for comfort then. He meant them for comfort now. But comfort flitted from his thoughts.

Her body fit against his so well, and her scent filled his nostrils. Desire stabbed him with an intensity that stole his breath.

He fought to keep sane. "I will replace everything."

"You cannot replace Papa's books." Her hushed voice was almost inaudible.

"If I have to search the breadth of England to find copies, I will."

"They were precious to me because they were my father's. They were the only things I had left of him. I had to sell all the others." Her normally modulated voice crested to a squeak. She swiped at her face again.

Her tears left him devastated. He couldn't take the pain from her, and the only solution that kept popping into his mind was to make love to her until she couldn't think or remember.

Velvet twisted away and resumed cleaning the shambles of her room. "I'm sorry. Your book was destroyed too." She held up the copy of *Jane Eyre* and flipped through the shorn pages.

"It doesn't matter."

Her brow furrowed and she turned it upside down and shook it.

Iris peered around the door from the schoolroom.

"Iris, go downstairs and tell Mrs. Bigsby to send for

the coach. Bigsby will have to go straightaway to Trerice and bring back the dressmaker."

Once he heard the clatter of her steps on the stairs, he
said, "Only a guilty child would try to blame a ghost."

Velvet pressed her lips together and shook her head.
"Whoever did this took the letter you sent me. Iris
wouldn't take a letter she wouldn't be able to read. She
would have destroyed it with all the rest of my things."

He'd meant that letter for only Velvet's eyes. With a
sickening dread he began to suspect the attack was not
directed at her, but at him. What would have happened
if Velvet had been in the room? Was she only spared
because she was sleeping in Iris's bed? It was Myra all
over again.

She picked up strips of material, gathering them into
a pile.

He could hardly stand to look at her picking up the
remnants of her possessions. Now she truly had nothing,
and she still wasn't turning to him. No. She was sleeping in Iris's bed to prevent him from finding her alone.

"Come with me."

"I cannot go anywhere, I'm not dressed," she
protested.

"Now." How could he protect her when she wanted
nothing to do with him? For her own safety, he should
send her away, but the idea of it stabbed his heart.

Velvet balked when Lucian opened his bedroom
door. She turned to go back up the stairs.

"Velvet, there are clothes in my wife's dressing
room."

"I can't—"

"It is the best I can do until the dressmaker arrives.
Even then I doubt she can complete a dress in a day."

His obsidian eyes held hers. "I'm trying to clothe you, not undress you."

His blunt retort didn't reassure her. In her own room his gasp as she leaned into him had electrified her. She'd wanted to reach up and pull his head down to kiss her. Just his being close made her forget common sense.

She couldn't stand in the hallway in a dressing gown. Down the passageway a door clicked. She darted into his room.

His tight smile didn't reassure her. The room was as she remembered it, dark wood and green hangings. With his hand at the small of her back, she shivered.

He guided her through a series of doors, through his room, through the connected sitting room, through the archway to the bedroom, and through a door to a room with shelves, trunks, and armoires bursting with clothing. Satins and silks, lace and fringe, and more shades of red and purple than Velvet could imagine left her slightly nauseated.

She took a step back into Lucian.

He caressed her shoulders. "Lilith was shorter than you, but if you wore fewer petticoats it shouldn't matter."

Her senses rioted. Lilith was obvious much fuller figured too. "Why would one woman need so many dresses?"

"She didn't." Lucian pulled a dressmaker's box off a shelf. "She never wore half of these." He pulled back tissue and exposed a rose silk. Tossing it aside, he reached for another box.

Velvet had thought Iris possessed too many clothes. "I can't wear your wife's clothes."

"They aren't being used. The dressmaker will be able to alter a dress faster than she can make new ones."

He was right. Not only would it be faster, it would be more economical.

He pitched aside another box. Then found one he liked. "Here, I know she never wore this."

Folding back the sheets of tissue, he revealed a black bombazine dress. Velvet heaved a sigh of relief. Most of the dresses would clash with her red hair. He pulled it out, and she saw the tiny jet buttons down the back. She would never be able to get it fastened without help.

"Try this on. I need to go downstairs to write instructions to the dressmaker."

"Tell her to bring only sober materials suitable for a governess. I only need a dress or two."

Lucian's face tightened and his dark eyes went flat. She'd hurt him again.

"Don't be stubborn, Velvet. You need clothes. Lilith's things are not needed or used by anyone. Choose gowns you want or I will insist the dressmaker bring material for dozens of gowns in the latest fashion."

"I don't want—"

"You've made it clear you don't want to be burdened with a sense of gratitude toward me." He folded his arms. "But I have an obligation to redress wrongs committed in my own house. If I find out who destroyed your things, I'll wring her neck."

Velvet's stomach lurched. "Don't say such things. Violence is never the answer."

His eyes narrowed. "Don't preach to me. You haven't assumed the right."

She lowered her eyes. He had to be referring to his offer of marriage and her delay to full acceptance.

It was foolish. She could have more clothes than she could ever wear and be mistress of a large house. She could have things and more things, but what she yearned for more than anything was a loving family. What chance was there for love with Lucian?

Before their encounter on the cliff he'd said more than once he wouldn't marry her. He didn't love her. And she'd feel shortchanged. What kind of happiness would she have if he wouldn't give her babies? Without love or hope of children, her life would be drearier than it was now. Or would it?

But she could be carrying his child. "I'm sorry."

"You will sleep in this bedroom tonight."

His demand came at her out of the blue.

"No." Her heart raced, and for a second her hopes soared.

"Yes. Until I find out who did this, I want you close where I can hear you."

"Iris—"

"Can sleep in here too." His dark eyes pinned her. "If you feel you must have her protection." He pivoted and left as if he could no longer stand to be closeted in the dressing room with her.

But then he came back. "I had the furniture replaced shortly before Lilith died, but if you want, I can have another bed brought down."

The offer confused her. "No, don't be silly."

What was he doing? Was he trying to get her used to the pampered life she could lead as his wife? Or did he truly fear for her safety? She opened her mouth to ask, but he had turned on his heel and left.

Chapter 19

Miss Campbell tried to conduct lessons, but even she was distracted. Iris couldn't concentrate either. She was too sleepy, and the house was full of interesting people. Besides, for once Mama was angry with someone else. Miss Campbell might get the slaps and pinches Mama inflicted when she was angry.

Tucking her head down, Iris pretended she was working on her letters. Miss Campbell would peek at the slate soon and realize progress wasn't happening. But just as Miss Campbell leaned over to look, the door opened.

Iris's pounding heart slowly resumed a normal pace. Meg brought in the seamstress, saving her from being caught. After a quick conversation the three women shoved back tables and chairs, opening the center of the room.

"Iris, you can sit over there and work on your slate," said Miss Campbell.

"I best get back downstairs." Meg bobbed a curtsy and left.

The seamstress opened her black case. Inside were a bunch of scissors, thimbles, needles, pincushions stuffed full, and spool after spool of thread perched on pegs. She wasted no time in getting to work on measuring Miss Campbell. Then she told her to take off her dress.

Working with a mouthful of pins, the seamstress said, "'If 'or arm," and "'Urn."

Standing on the stool in the middle of the schoolroom, Miss Campbell seemed to understand, as she lifted her arms and turned on command.

"Your corset is very plain," Iris said. Mama had worn scarlet corsets with ruffles and lace.

Miss Campbell frowned and pushed the material against her chest.

"'Op 'ooing," said the seamstress.

Iris stopped pretending she was working on her letters and moved into her governess's room, where two dresses lay on the bed. One was the yellow and green striped gown that Miss Campbell had worn until the dressmaker arrived. Another was a shimmery peacock blue dress with purplish fringe hanging from the hem and arrow point neckline. None of them looked like Miss Campbell's former dresses.

"Where did those dresses come from?" she asked.

Miss Campbell watched her carefully. "Your mother's dressing room."

Iris frowned. Her mother had always worn clothing that made looking anywhere else impossible. She sparkled with beads or rustled as she walked. The dresses Miss Campbell had almost seemed too quiet to have been mama's. "I don't remember them."

"They were still in the boxes from the dressmaker's. I don't think your mama ever wore them." Velvet turned to the dressmaker. "Can you inset material in the neckline?"

The dressmaker took the pins out of her mouth. "Why would I do that? You've a nice bosom, even if you are not as chesty as the woman it was made for."

Miss Campbell's face colored.

Iris wondered if borrowing Mama's dresses would make her madder. Maybe the gowns in heaven were sparklier than the ones here on earth, and she wouldn't be angry about the gowns she'd left behind. Iris swallowed hard. She'd rather Mama was mad at her than with Miss Campbell.

Maybe Mama was mad because Papa threw her bracelet into the fire. Or maybe she didn't like the idea of Papa finding a new wife. Iris suspected she didn't like the way Papa listened to Miss Campbell.

"I won't be able to reset the waist. It is too high for you."

Miss Campbell shook her head. "It doesn't matter."

"Take it off now," said the dressmaker. "I'll have it ready for dinner tonight."

Miss Campbell glanced toward the window with the afternoon sun. She stepped off the stool and turned her back to the dressmaker. "If you would be so kind."

The woman unfastened buttons quickly and slid the crinkly black dress off Miss Campbell.

"I thought if the fringe could be removed from the blue . . ."

The schoolroom door opened. Mrs. Bigsby entered. "The room across the hall is prepared for you," she said to the dressmaker. "Someone will be up with your bolts and bags shortly."

She left the door open, even though Miss Campbell was shivering in her shift and petticoats. The petticoats were far lacier and beribboned than she normally wore. Had they been Mama's too? Miss Campbell reached for the dressing gown. Mrs. Bigsby narrowed her eyes. "Best get that on, Mr. Pendar is on his way up."

But Papa already stood in the doorway behind Mrs. Bigsby.

Velvet gasped and tried to stuff her arms in her sleeves quickly.

Papa's eyes tracked Miss Campbell's every move. It didn't seem to matter that Miss Campbell dressed in plain dresses, Papa always watched her. Even with Mama's look-at-me clothes, Papa had hardly ever looked at her. He'd probably seen Mama's face all stretched ugly when she was angry too many times.

"Show Mrs. Whitson to her room, Mrs. Bigsby."

Mrs. Bigsby's mouth dropped open, but she summoned the dressmaker.

Papa shut the door after two women left. Miss Campbell stood with her hand fisted around the edges of the dressing gown at her throat.

He beckoned, and Iris trotted toward him. "You and Miss Campbell will be sleeping in the room adjacent to mine."

Iris stumbled to a halt. She suddenly was as cold as Miss Campbell in her undergarments. "Mama's room?"

"In what used to be your mother's room. It isn't hers anymore."

"No. She doesn't like me in there." Iris shook her head and backed up. Her throat closed in. Her mother never allowed her in her room. She had suffered more than one slap for being in there when Mama didn't want her there. It was one thing to sneak in there when no one noticed. But the last place she wanted to sleep was in her mother's room. She ran and threw her arms around Miss Campbell's waist. "I won't."

Papa hunkered down. "Iris, I want you and Miss Campbell safe near me."

Miss Campbell held on, but Mama didn't like her in

her room and wouldn't like her sleeping there. "I won't! I won't! I won't!"

"Iris—" Papa began, but Miss Campbell shifted, and he stopped. "Convince her."

Papa just didn't understand.

"It will be all right, Iris," said Miss Campbell. "Your papa and I will keep you safe."

It wouldn't be all right. Iris trembled. Neither Papa nor Miss Campbell would be able to keep her mother away.

Papa watched her with his eyes full of accusations. Iris turned her face into the plush material of Miss Campbell's dressing gown.

"Your mama will never think to look for you there," whispered Miss Campbell.

Being dead, Mama seemed a bit like God who could see everything all the time. She would find her and get her to do as she was bid. Mama always did. Since Mama finally wanted to be with her, no one would be able to keep her safe.

"All right?" asked Miss Campbell in her soft persuasive voice.

Both Papa and Miss Campbell were against her. They were the two people in the world she wanted to make happy. So she nodded, because there was no way she could resist them both. But she knew it was a mistake to agree.

Lucian followed Velvet's every move throughout dinner, while she did everything she could to avoid his gaze. He had to protect her better than to put her in the room next to his. The few times their eyes met, her gaze darted down and pink crept up her bared cleavage and over her face. He wanted nothing more than to swoop her up and carry her far, far away, where he could keep her safe.

He could send her and Iris away to Bath and set up apartments for them. That way she'd be safe, away from him, away from whomever had destroyed her things, away from the curse hanging over his household. He could hire her new servants so if the attacker was among his staff here, he or she wouldn't have access to Velvet.

Velvet reached for the saltcellar, and her neckline gaped, exposing the valley between her breasts. His breath whooshed out as desire pounded in him. His napkin and the table barely covered his response.

He wanted her more than he had before their moment on the cliff, and he hadn't realized that was possible. To be near her and not touch her was torture. He feared if he touched her and she responded in the way he dreamed, his control would shatter. His restraint stretched thinner and thinner as the hours passed, but she had refused him, leaving him beyond frustrated.

If they could have had time alone, he'd have plied his hand at changing her mind. But his guests required his attention.

Velvet led the ladies to the drawing room after dinner. Signaling for the port, Lucian wished his guests to perdition. They interfered with his ability to work during the day and enjoy Velvet's company in the evening. But he managed to inquire after Anderson's steamship investments, and talk quickly turned to their latest joint business venture.

Lucian waited until the two men who had lit cigars stubbed them out, then he rose to his feet. "I believe we should join the ladies."

He politely remained at his place while Hale took his time retrieving his jacket from where he'd discarded it on the back of his chair. The others filed out still engaged in talk of business.

"That governess you have, she's quite striking, isn't she?" said Hale. "Does she hail from London?"

A fission of alarm shuddered down Lucian's spine. "She was born and bred in Dorset."

Hale smiled with one side of his mouth. "She was with the Langtrees, wasn't she? She told me her name was Jane, but one of the maids gave her away." His eyelids flicked low. "I always wanted to lay on velvet."

Before he realized his intention, Lucian's fist connected with teeth and tearing flesh.

Hale staggered away, his hand to his mouth. "Damn, man."

"Touch her and I'll kill you." Lucian's blood was coursing through his veins with a shocking heat.

Hale spit blood. His eyes wide, he took a step back and reached for his handkerchief.

Searching for sanity, Lucian sucked in a deep breath. "My apologies."

Hale held up a trembling hand. "No, no, my mistake. I'll—I'll just take my leave."

"I overreacted," said Lucian. He needed Hale's assistance in Parliament. "The situation is complicated, and Miss Campbell suffered an act of violence this morning. I am overprotective. Please accept my sincerest regrets."

Hale's eyes were wide and moisture beaded his forehead. His bloodied lip began to swell. "Of course. Of course, but I'll just be leaving."

His fists clenching by his side, Lucian muttered, "I beg you will reconsider."

"I shouldn't like to stay in the house of a man prone to fits of violence." Hale's mouth pulled back in a toothy grimace. Then he winced.

Punching Hale had been uncivilized, even if the man had made a crass comment. And Velvet would be the first to condemn him for his violence. He needed her to soothe the raging beast within him. She always made him calmer, when she wasn't twisting him in knots.

"We both know you have had that coming for a long time," said Lucian. But until today he had never felt the urge.

The brute hostility had come over him without warning, and his actions had been inexcusable. He couldn't blame it on the restraint of his passions. He couldn't even blame it on past transgressions by Hale. Closing his eyes, he wondered if the violent streak he always tried so hard to control was what kept Velvet from accepting his offer.

Oh, God what had he done?

Velvet kept Iris in her sights as she poured tea. She'd kept the girl with her, other than when she brought her down to eat her dinner at the crowded servants' table. Mrs. Bigsby had protested that a tray was to be prepared for the child, but Velvet insisted she be allowed to stay and brought to the drawing room immediately following her meal.

Apparently Iris had been in the drawing room quite some time before the ladies arrived. She'd been slumped on the sofa, her face a picture of petulance. Without her toys, and unable to read, play a musical instrument, or sew, she had no way to occupy herself. What a lonely sort of existence the girl must lead. Velvet was almost tempted to give up on the letters and pursue teaching Iris simpler occupations. But her boredom disappeared as she was introduced to the ladies, especially the younger women. With her inclination to compliment, Iris quickly had the favor of several of them.

But Velvet could see her sharply assessing all the ladies present. Was she trying to determine which one she would choose for a stepmother? Velvet wished Nellie had not told Iris her father was looking for a bride. Even if it had been true—and Lucian said it wasn't—worrying Iris only made her more insecure.

The gentlemen arrived shortly after Velvet had distributed teacups to all the ladies. As she searched for Lucian, anxiety slithered down her spine. Working to maintain proper posture, she nodded to the men and poured tea for those who approached. She had to talk to him, and she didn't know when she might have the opportunity.

Iris moved to a footstool at the foot of the chair where Velvet sat. Before long her weight pressed against Velvet's leg. It was well past Iris's bedtime, but Velvet was unwilling for the girl to be alone. Leaving Iris vulnerable to whatever or whoever was frightening her in the night was unthinkable.

As Velvet surveyed the room, she noticed that not only was Lucian missing, but also Mr. Hale, the one man who seemed to know of her reputation. But he could do her no worse damage than she had done to herself.

She knew the minute Lucian entered. The air became charged, and in spite of everything, her stomach fluttered. How could he affect her so?

Her heart thumped in her chest. Like a caress, the air brushed her skin as he moved near her. With shaking hands she poured tea for him.

"Won't you make up a fourth for a game of whist,

Mr. Pendar?" Miss Bowman slid her hand onto Lucian's arm. "Captain Darling and his daughter have agreed to play."

Velvet lowered her gaze so she could only see Miss Bowman's hand on Lucian's sleeve.

"Would you give me leave to take my daughter upstairs first? It seems she has lingered past her bedtime." But he took a slow sip of tea as if he intended to hover over Velvet all evening.

"If I might be excused," Velvet said, "I'll take her upstairs." Eager to be out of the room, she set her teacup and saucer on the tea cart.

"Your daughter is quite charming," Miss Bowman said. "She was telling me all about your visit to King Arthur's castle. Is the place near enough we could go see?"

"If you so desire, a visit will be arranged." Lucian's delivery was clipped.

Velvet jerked her head toward him. Was his impatience obvious to Miss Bowman?

"How kind," she purred, and leaned her breast into Lucian's arm.

Swallowing a stab of jealousy, Velvet stroked Iris's hair. Iris didn't stir. Leaning down, Velvet saw that the child had fallen fast asleep.

"I do believe I need to carry her," said Lucian. "Mr. Anderson, would you be so good as to fill in for me at whist until I can return?"

Miss Bowman's full lower lip jutted out, but Lucian didn't seem to notice as he disengaged his arm and bent to scoop up Iris.

"If you would be so good as to get the door, Miss Campbell."

As she held the drawing room door while Lucian

passed through carrying Iris, she heard the murmurs begin behind her.

"I don't know what her governess is thinking, allowing such a young child to stay up so late," said Miss Bowman in a not so discreet undertone to her mother.

The words burned through Velvet.

"It seems he allows the governess a great deal of latitude," said one of the Miss Ridleys.

Velvet didn't turn to see which one.

"If you ask me, he pays far too much attention to her," said Miss Bowman. "I don't think it prudent to have a governess of uncommon looks."

Miss Anderson spoke in her hesitant voice. "I'm sure he is just making sure all is going well. My mother says it has been an age since he made any attempt to entertain."

Her ears burning, Velvet slid out of the room and shut the door behind her. She trailed up the stairs behind the pair.

Iris cradled against his chest, Lucian waited for Velvet in front of the door to the lady of the house's room. "As soon as I lay her down, I will go with you to fetch her nightclothes and whatever you need. I have not informed any of the servants of the plan."

Keeping the information from the servants would be impossible. Once the servants knew, the guests would learn, and the whispers would become even worse. And she wasn't sure it was at all necessary. She leaned around him to open the door. "You should stay with her. She is frightened of her mother, but I am convinced it is not her mother who is tormenting her."

"I am concerned about your safety as well. Iris will be safe enough with the doors locked, but it was not a ghost who destroyed your things this morning. I fear your liaison with me has made you a target."

"What?" Her voice was shriller then she intended.

Iris moaned.

He grimaced and shook his head at Velvet as he carried Iris across the sitting room to lay her on the settee.

Velvet bit her lip, unwilling to wake Iris with an argument with her father. Iris was at risk, not her.

A fire blazed in the fireplace and a stack of linens sat on a chair. All the personal effects in the room had been cleared away. If none of the servants had been informed, he must have cleared the room and started the fire.

Lucian bent down. Slowly lifting and lowering each of Iris's legs, he gently removed her shoes, carefully placing them on the floor without noise. He tossed an afghan over her. Then he strode across the floor and locked the passage door. He beckoned Velvet toward the connecting door to his room.

She hesitated.

"Come. If I am away for more than a hand or two, Miss Bowman will send out a search party."

Velvet ducked her head and followed him. Miss Bowman would marry Lucian in a heartbeat and dismiss her the next.

Lucian stepped away from the door as she passed through, then turned and closed it. He inserted a key and locked the door.

He reached out a hand for her.

Velvet folded her arms and stepped back. Her heart began to pound. She couldn't delay sharing the news he would likely welcome. "I'm not p-pregnant."

In spite of her best intentions to sound calm and rational, her voice quivered. Her heart leaped to her throat, making her chest feel hollow.

Emotions flashed rapidly across his face. Had his dark eyes revealed pain? Her hopes spun dizzily.

But his expression settled into a glower. She was aware of every nuance of his face, from the muscle ticking under the puckered pink scar to the dark lashes rimming his narrowed eyes.

Her heart thudded painfully. She hadn't expected anger.

"You are certain?" he asked on a low growl. "You are not using a ruse to keep me from you?"

Her face burning, she lowered her head. "This afternoon my courses started." To discuss such personal details with him made her cringe.

Silence ticked between them.

He slowly let out a long sigh.

Her nose stung and she blinked rapidly. She hoped he'd ask her to marry him anyway, and she could convince him to attempt children again. She turned. It was done. Her foolishness had to end now.

"You must be relieved." Velvet headed for the passage door and opened it. She had only to go abovestairs and fetch her things and then she could be alone.

"Yes." His voice was tight and harsh. "Are you?"

"Of course," she answered, and if her voice was a little higher than normal as she moved down the hall and Lucian followed, at least it did not quiver. She told herself it was for the best.

"When my guests have left, I will see about setting up apartments in Bath for you and—"

An involuntary sob burst from deep inside her. Her heart burned as if it had been cast into a fire. He meant to set her up as his mistress. There was no need to make her his wife, no need at all.

"Velvet?" His voice was hesitant.

She stopped her hurried stride toward the stairs but didn't turn around.

He slid his hand across her shoulders, and her knees went weak.

"Are you disappointed?" His low vibrant voice curled around her, gentle, compassionate, concerned.

Shrugging she struggled to hold her tears at bay. The moment she'd realized her courses had begun to flow had been as if her every hope had been snatched away. She was crushed. He had no reason to marry her, and she had never had a reason to expect his love. Apartments in Bath smacked of a cold business arrangement.

Yet his hand on her shoulder made her want to abandon all dignity and throw herself into his arms and accept him on any terms. She'd already thrown herself at him once and destroyed her virtue. Now he knew he could have her as his mistress. She pulled away. "Don't. You must get back to your guests."

"You're right. We'll speak later."

She shivered, dreading a continuation of what had gone before. She wanted everything, children, marriage, Lucian's love, and for a brief moment she'd thought it might be possible. She'd thought she had seen that kind of adoration in his eyes, but no doubt it was just the foolish hopes of a ruined old maid. But her punishment for the sin of daring her brother to climb onto the ledge of the bell tower opening wouldn't be complete unless she got an occasional glimpse of heaven before being cast down into the pits of hell to burn again.

Chapter 20

Unable to concentrate on the game, Lucian struggled with the hands of whist. His thoughts kept churning over Velvet's news. He should be relieved she hadn't conceived, but he wasn't. He feared he had lost his advantage. He should have pressed her while she was uncertain of their future.

He discarded a suited high card on a trick that had already been trumped. Miss Bowman looked at him incredulously. His play was so poor, she probably thought him a complete dolt.

He was also worried about Velvet's safety. The more he mulled over the attack on her possessions, the more it seemed she was in danger. If he planned a day away from the house to Tintagel Head, as he promised Miss Bowman, he left Velvet vulnerable. The idea made his stomach roil. As soon as the clock struck half past eleven and he could reasonably retire, he stood and claimed fatigue.

Edgar Bowman caught his arm before he left the room. "If I might have a word in private with you."

Hating the delay, Lucian nodded, led the man to the library and poured them both a brandy.

"It seems Hale has withdrawn from our agreement." Bowman wasted no time in getting to the point. "You won't have enough influence in Parliament to get the legislative support we need without him."

The railroad deal that Lucian had been trying to broker for nigh on five years was in danger of falling through because of one rash moment. His life, his plans, were once again spinning out of his control. Tugging on his cuffs, he tried to affect a manner of disinterest. "He insulted a woman under my protection." Lucian winced. "In my employ."

Bowman took a stiff belt of his drink. "Yes, well, my daughter rather fancies marriage to a rich, understanding man. I believe she's taken a liking to you."

"She's a lovely young woman." Lucian's stomach churned. He had a sick feeling he knew how these two unrelated bits of information tied together.

"Of course she's rather fond of the theatre and ballrooms. Not so fond of the sea. I expect she'd like to spend a great deal of the year in London."

Lilith had always wanted to spend more time in London, but Lucian hated the city. Tension crept up the back of his neck. "You need not sell her so cheaply."

Bowman laughed. "Cheaply, I think not. I can persuade Hale to return to the deal, and we all will profit."

Lucian rubbed his forehead. Marriage to Miss Bowman to complete his shipping empire. A year ago he would have leaped at the opportunity. But his heart pounded and a cold sweat trickled down his spine. "I should have to think about it."

Bowman narrowed his eyes as he watched Lucian. He took a sip from his brandy. "As for your employees, I can safely guarantee you might do as you like as long as you don't attempt to keep a mistress in a house where my daughter lives. Although, I think we can say she won't stay here unless her family is here too."

Did he need to get Miss Bowman married in a hurry? Was she sullied like Lilith? Or had his reputation for ignoring Lilith's peccadilloes tainted him? Lucian could no longer withhold his shock at the way Bowman bartered his own flesh and blood child. "What is wrong with your daughter?"

Bowman narrowed his eyes and then watched Lucian as he finished his drink. "Aren't too many men in England she considers rich enough for her. With ten daughters and three sons to see settled, I can't have her holding up things. Two of her sisters are already engaged, but they await the marriage of the eldest. If a wealthy husband is what my girl wants, I hope to comply." He lifted his glass in a mock toast.

Lucian bowed.

"You need my support too," said Bowman with sly look.

Swallowing hard against the rage building in his breast, Lucian needed to escape the room. He needed to throw something. He very carefully set his brandy on a table and moved away from anything he could launch. Throwing things was a less than desirable behavior he'd acquired from too many years with Lilith.

"You do know whom you are dealing with?" asked Lucian through clenched teeth. If the deal went through, he would become one of the most powerful men in England.

"A man with murder allegations hanging over him," said Bowman mildly. "Not many people are willing to ally their family and business with the devil. You need us worse than we need you."

Lucian's head felt like it might explode. He could no longer breathe. If only Velvet had allowed him to announce an engagement, he would not be in this position. "I will think about your offer."

What kind of man married his daughter to a suspected murderer? He would never allow Iris to enter into such a crass bargain, but then he'd just been informed that his wife would not live alone with him. The marriage would be a business deal and a sham for which he'd pay dearly. "I bid you good-night."

Lucian didn't wait for Bowman to respond, but took the stairs to his room two at a time.

Evans was waiting for him.

"You can go. I plan to read awhile." Lucian moved to the fire. The key to the connecting door burned in his pocket. Velvet was on the other side of the door. He could not go in angry or he would throttle her.

Evans nodded. His expressionless pale eyes flicked toward the locked interior door. "Would you like your dressing gown, sir?"

His man would have expected to remove his jacket and waistcoat before reading. Lucian stripped off his necktie. His nightshirt and dressing gown were laid out on the bed. "I can manage by myself."

"Very good, sir," said Evans with a bow.

As soon as his man left, Lucian locked the door behind him. No doubt Evans had his own ideas about what the clicking lock meant.

What he needed was a physical expenditure of energy until he was too exhausted to think. A swim at this late hour was out of the question, but his mind turned to the only other solace he had ever found. He needed Velvet to soothe him.

The knock on the door made Velvet jerk her head toward the bed to be sure Iris hadn't woken.

"Velvet, open the door."

She set aside the sewing and crossed the room.

She heard the scrape of a key in the lock just before she reached it. "I'm coming," she said as she cracked the door.

Lucian pushed the door open all the way. His brow was furrowed and his look dark. "Are you all right?"

"Yes, of course, we're fine. Iris is sleeping," Velvet stepped to the side of the opening.

His stride was tightly leashed, as if he restrained a black energy. He walked all the way through the archway to the bed and gazed down at Iris. His hands fisted at his sides, then he stretched his fingers out as if willing away his anger.

Clearly he was upset. What had happened to rattle him so?

Hesitating to move, she remained by the door. Pivoting sharply, his gaze took in the pantalets she'd been stitching, the coverlet thrown around her shoulders, and the pile of books untouched on the side table. "Were you waiting on me?"

Unease slid down her neck and tightened her throat. She had been waiting for him. She couldn't unbutton the tiny buttons in the center of her back, but with the energy radiating off him, she hesitated to ask for his help. "I was sewing."

He paced to the corridor door and turned the handle. The locked door didn't budge. "I expected to find you in bed."

Velvet glanced toward the bed, fearing his harsh tones would wake Iris. Heat stole into her cheeks. "I was trying to finish, before retiring."

"Are you done?" he asked.

She shook her head.

"Then finish." He turned toward the fireplace and picked up a poker.

The idea of unfolding the half-stitched undergarment in front of him made heat rise in her face. She really needed the new pantalets she'd reluctantly cut from the plain white cotton he'd sent. "What is wrong?" she asked.

A shower of sparks flew up from the wood, as he prodded the fire and added a new log.

Done with the fire, he brushed off his hands and paced across the room. "You should have agreed to marry me when you had the chance."

Her breath snagged on the back of her throat and her insides fell. She had known what she risked when she told him she wasn't with child, and she'd desperately wished God had allowed her to get pregnant. Then Lucian wouldn't have a choice but to marry her.

But what did she offer compared to the young and wealthy daughters of tradesmen? How could she even have thought he might willingly choose a life with her? Her eyes burned with tears that threatened to spill. Desperately, she sought to hide her anguish.

He made a triangular circuit of the room. His long legs chewed off the space so quickly, the room shrunk.

"The sooner I can get you to Bath, the better."

She pressed her lips together and looked away. His words and the implication that she would accept being his mistress cut through her, and a sharp pain seared through her heart. Her nose burned. She wasn't going to Bath. At least not under his protection. Moving to open the door connecting to his room, she said, "Please leave before you wake Iris."

He caught her shoulder and spun her toward him. "Don't you dare cry. Don't act like you wanted to marry me."

Velvet's thoughts spun. She did want to marry him.

She wanted to love him and be loved by him, but what came out was, "I wanted to be a mother."

He flinched. His hands tightened painfully on her shoulders. Her heart thudded hard, each jolt coursing a new ache through her. She wanted to call the words back. Hurting him gained her nothing.

Even so, she was aware of the flicker of a muscle under his scar, the rise and fall of his chest. Flashes of his kisses and touches on the edge of the cliff pounded in her brain. Her gaze dropped to his mouth.

Then he was kissing her. Her reason left with a whimper.

His mouth ignited her. Molten fire rushed through her veins and burned in her core. There was nothing gentle in his kiss. Instead the raw energy he battled to restrain poured into her. She wanted it all. His anguish, his desperation, and his love. He touched a place deep inside her and made her feel alive, made her believe she could heal him.

They thumped into the wall and he pushed against her. His member throbbed against her belly. Reaching up, she pulled his head down to her. Brushing her fingers over his face, she relished the beginnings of roughness of his beard. Her fingers encountered the ridges of his scar, and she traced over it.

Jerking his head back, he recoiled. He stared at her and his dark gaze searched hers. Her breasts rose and fell, pressing into his hard chest. Her nipples tightened, wanting his attention. Her body was a riot of want. Yet, he stared down into her eyes, and she was lost in their dark depths. She couldn't have looked away if her life depended on it.

He lowered his head and pressed his lips to hers. The shift to gentleness weakened her knees and gave her a glimpse of sanity. Iris was sleeping just a few feet from them, and she was incapacitated by her monthly. She put her hand to his chest and pushed. "We can't do this now."

"We could," he said simply.

Her face flooded with heat. The idea sickened her and drew her at the same time. She shook her head and twisted to struggle free.

He chuckled. "You needn't be so shocked."

"It's wrong," she hissed. She pushed her shoulder into his chest. A multitude of sins followed fornication for pleasure alone. Her father had preached again and again that the lure of gratification led to one's demise. Congress between a man and a woman was for procreation, and Lucian would know that if he attended church on a regular basis.

And he must have forgotten she was in the midst of her courses. "I . . . I am—"

"Shhhh. Just let me hold you," he whispered.

His breath brushed across her ear, and his hold was firm. He was far stronger than she. If he refused to release her, she could do little short of screaming and waking Iris. But she didn't feel in any danger from him. His hold was different than Harold Langtree's had been. As her heart and breathing slowed to a normal rhythm, he relaxed his grip.

He tucked her head against his shoulder and rested his head over hers.

Kissing him was wrong, but her resistance evaporated the minute he'd looked deep into her eyes. Why was she so weak around him? Why was the path of sin so tempting? She'd never felt a strong urge to become intimate with any man but him.

The threat didn't lie in him, but in her own treacherous response to him. But whether it was to just be his lover or be his wife, he would not give her children. Not because he couldn't, but because he didn't believe God would grant them children who would live.

As she searched for answers, she knew it was just a matter of time before she succumbed to the feelings and desires only he managed to stir. But she wanted marriage and children, not just stolen passion and sin. "Please leave," she whispered.

Lucian went to his own room cursing himself. She wanted children. He dreaded burying another baby. He knew no solution that would satisfy them both.

He could get her with child. He could go through the months of waiting with the fears, the hopes, and the inevitable death of an innocent child because of his cursed seed. He knew how to make it through each day when there was no reason to go on living, but he couldn't imagine how he could live with himself allowing Velvet to go through the horror of watching a baby die. Velvet had no idea what she was asking for.

He sank down on his bed and ran his hands through his hair. He could choose the pain of losing her, rather than see her destroyed by watching either her dreams or her children die.

He needed Velvet. Like no one else, she calmed him. She made him feel whole. But she wanted the one thing in life he could not give her. It wasn't that he didn't want family, he did. The row of graves at the cemetery told him he couldn't. If he got her with child, he would bury another baby.

Shedding his jacket, he contemplated marriage to Miss Bowman. She was pretty and young and would no doubt do her duty as a wife, and he could complete his plans to have an all-encompassing shipping empire. Maybe she wouldn't mind not having children. Hell, maybe she would prefer he didn't touch her.

Maybe if he married Miss Bowman, he would free Velvet to pursue her dream of a family of her own. He could give Velvet a competence, not so much that it would raise suspicions, but enough that she could live in whatever way would make her happy.

He unbuttoned his waistcoat. The door cracked. Hope surged in his breast.

"Would you help me with my buttons?" said Velvet in a small voice. Her cheeks were stained red and her eyes were on the floor. "I cannot reach."

Obviously, the last thing she was attempting was seduction. He stood and crossed to the door. She presented her back to him. Lilith's clothes were designed for a woman who used a maid to dress and undress. And since the dressmaker had tightened the bodice to fit Velvet's narrower frame, she could not shift it to where she could reach the buttons, although undoubtedly she'd tried. Three tiny buttons in the center of her back remained buttoned, while the rest were open. While he wanted to undress her and show her how much he wanted her, he had to restrain his impulses.

He reached to unfasten her gown. Her proximity was torture. But for his cursed seed, he could pull her into his arms, promise to marry her, and make love to her until dawn. Instead he steeled himself for what he had to do. "Tomorrow I will arrange for the carriage to take you and Iris to Bath. I will give you funds to book lodgings."

She spun to face him. Her jaw had dropped and her eyebrows were raised, showing her surprise. "Iris?"

He turned her back around to finish. "Yes, you have

made it clear you do not wish to continue with me, but I hope you will remain Iris's governess. I will of course release your full wages if you do not. Or since you would have the responsibility of maintaining a household and hiring servants, I will increase your wages accordingly."

Her head dipped forward. The curve of her neck begged for kisses. Rather than caress her and reach for the laces on her corset, he curled his fingers until he had enough control to continue.

After releasing the last button, he pushed open the gown's back. She twisted away from him and reached for the door. "Thank you."

"Could you both be ready with the school supplies by the day after tomorrow?"

Holding the loosened dress to her chest, she said, "Shouldn't we wait until after your guests leave?"

"You have done a marvelous job of preparing the household. The meals have been better than I ever expected, but I cannot think you are safe here. Not after someone destroyed your things." Didn't she understand she wasn't safe from him either? He couldn't have her so near and not desire her.

"I think I thwarted someone's plan to do some mischief with Iris. I see no reason to go to Bath now."

Lucian rubbed his aching forehead. If he had to propose to Miss Bowman, he didn't want Velvet here. He'd tried to marry for love once, and it had been a dismal failure. Perhaps if he married for business . . . "Velvet, you have to leave my house. A man can only take so much." He revealed far more than he meant to in that statement.

Her eyes narrowed and she searched his face.

He tried to retrieve the situation. "I have buried far

too many of those I care about. Do not ask me to risk it again."

"Are you talking about children or women?" she asked on a low note.

"Both." If he only cared about his businesses, he would never again risk the wrenching pain of losing a loved one. If he just accepted he would never have family in any traditional sense, his heart wouldn't be shredding to tiny bits in his chest.

He could swim in the cold ocean and destroy the physical needs of his body, but the swims never helped him understand why God had decided to deprive him of loving parents, a wife, a mistress, and children.

Business associates he understood. They didn't love him or hate him, and they only stayed connected to him because they had something to gain.

"Perhaps you should take an assumed name in Bath. You could start over as a respectable woman with a new name and improvised history." Perhaps there was a chance she could meet a man and marry and have the family she wanted.

The idea of her in another man's arms burned in his stomach as if he had drunk poison.

Her face changed to a scowl and she stepped back. "I will not go to live in Bath. Not now, not ever."

She shut the door. He wanted to beg her to protect herself, but she wouldn't allow him to protect her. He knew if she didn't leave, he would end up destroying her too.

The days passed uneventfully. Lucian escorted Miss Bowman to dinner and tried not to notice Velvet. His nights were spent tossing and turning, knowing she was just beyond a single door. But to open the door was to lose to temptation.

His mind was mildly relieved by the dressmaker's presence. If she found his instructions to remain in Velvet's and Iris's presence at all times strange, she didn't say so.

All too often Miss Bowman hovered at his elbow. Even his office was no longer a sanctuary. As the mid-morning sun streamed across his desk, she wandered in from the library with an open book in her hands.

"I understand you bathe in the ocean every morning," she said.

His gaze flicked over her. "Most mornings."

He returned to writing out bank drafts to settle accounts for several of his businesses. He'd hoped to get some necessary work done before the rest of his guests descended.

"How does one get down to the shore? There seem to be nothing but cliffs around here." Miss Bowman smiled most pleasantly while closing the book without marking her spot.

"There is a path with steps."

"Would you show me? It seems to be a particularly fine day." She dropped the book on his desk.

"Perhaps you should ask your parents permi—"

"Oh pish, they shall not object if we take a stroll. We will be outside, what could happen?"

"Anything that could happen inside could happen outside, Miss Bowman." He knew.

She tossed her head, making the sausage curls framing her face shake. Her eyes sparkled. "I don't know if that is a threat or a promise."

He wanted to say a threat and tell her to go away.

Instead he stoppered his ink, wiped the nub of his pen, and then stood. "Perhaps you should fetch a wrap."

She skipped into the library and pulled a shawl and bonnet from a table.

"I see you've come prepared," he said dryly.

If he were to marry her, he should spend time with her. He opened the door and then led her through the gallery and out the side door. The wind whipped her skirts as she giggled. She seemed a pleasant girl, but her girlish laugh reminded him she was only a few years older than Iris.

"Do you like to read, Miss Bowman?"

"Only if there is nothing else to do. Although I do like the ladies' magazines."

He extended his arm and put her on his scarred side. Her eyes narrowed as she looked at the red marks. If she were to marry him, she'd have to get used to it. Perhaps in time she could look at him the way Velvet did, as if she saw him, not just the scar.

Miss Bowman chatted about the weather and the breeze, and he contented himself with letting her ramble on about nothing.

When she ran out of breath, he asked, "Do you like it here, or do you prefer London?"

"Doesn't everyone prefer London?" she asked without guile.

"No, not everyone."

Her eyes narrowed speculatively for just a second. She tilted her head and said, "London is amusing, but it is always nice to get away during the summer. I imagine it is quite lovely here in the summer months."

Clearly, she expected to spend the social season in London. Her skirts brushed his legs as they walked across the dead grass.

He wondered if he would be content with a wife living in London. He could go to town more often, every couple of weeks, but he wouldn't live there. Although there would be less chance of impregnating her.

"Do you like children, Miss Bowman?"

Her mouth pursed and then she turned away. "I like them well enough. I have a lot of siblings still in the nursery."

She couldn't know that her distaste was more of a blessing to him. Except he only felt hollow as he contemplated a life that was not so different from what he lived now.

As they neared the steps in the cliff, he searched the grass where he and Velvet had experienced their encounter. His breath caught and his pulse raced. The spot bore no evidence of a tryst, but how he looked at it had changed.

"Is that where your wife fell?" asked Miss Bowman.

Lucian jerked his attention back to her as cold slithered down his spine. "No."

Her gaze was speculative, and she dipped her head. "Was she the one who clawed your face?"

"I should rather not discuss it," said Lucian.

"My papa spoke with you, did he not?" She cast a look at him under her eyelashes.

"He did." Lucian wondered if the rocky beach below was the sort of romantic spot where he should propose. "Here are the steps to the beach."

They began the descent. Instead of his usual quick pace, he restrained himself to assist Miss Bowman down the uneven path.

"Papa says you are one of the most astute businessmen he knows. He says you are building an empire."

Lucian stared out at the slate blue sea. He didn't

know that he was so astute or that he just had little else to occupy his time. While on the verge of expanding his shipping enterprise, the accomplishment felt hollow. He wasn't even all that fond of spending the money he earned now. "Surely you don't wish to speak of business."

"You are a very hard man to get to know, but I shan't be deterred. I feel it would be in my best interest to understand everything I can about you. I am a very practical sort of woman."

He barely restrained a snort. She was a cold woman inspired to passion only by money. He said what he assumed she wanted to hear. "My wife and I fought over her indiscretions. She was prone to fits of rage and she did claw my face, but I did not kill her. If that is what you wish to know, Miss Bowman." He gave a slight bow. "I should prefer never to speak of it again."

"Mama said she deserved what she got."

Shocked, he yanked away from Miss Bowman's grip. "No one deserves what she got."

"Oh, I am sorry. That was thoughtless of me." She pressed her lips together and her eyebrows flattened.

Her expression reminded him more of anger than contrition. Cold and grasping were definitely the right attributions for her.

"I should very much like my daughter's memories not to be tainted by events surrounding her mother's death." No matter how many words he used, he could never explain the complicated emotions he had about his marriage. "I once loved my wife very much."

Miss Bowman blinked and seemed confused by his declaration. She took a few steps on the beach. "You bathe here?"

"Yes."

"If I might inquire, what does one wear when bathing?"

"A bathing suit, Miss Bowman."

"Oh, then might I watch you some morning? The water seems so very violent."

"It calms me," said Lucian.

She turned and came to stand in front of him. Turning her face up to his, he noted the tightness around her eyes. "You might kiss me if you like, Mr. Pendar."

She pursed her lips and lowered her lashes.

Strangely reluctant to take her offer, he asked, "Have you kissed many men, Miss Bowman?"

Her jaw dropped. "Of course not."

"So your desire to live in London is not to conduct extramarital affairs?"

Her mouth still open, she shook her head. The horror in her expression would have been hard to fake. "You do not wish to live in London? Everything is there, Parliament, banks, newspapers, playhouses, operas, and the shops. Everyone who is anyone is there for the season."

"This is my home." He put his arms behind his back. He was mildly relieved that she apparently had every expectation he would live with her. Lilith had begged to have her own residence in London. "I admit it needs refurbishing and more modernizing, but I have no inclination to spend time on such things."

Her eyes sparkled. "Those are things a wife should see to."

Was spending his money the only thing that excited her? Would she find any pleasure in a kiss or did she only see it as means to tempt him? He stepped closer and lifted her chin. Her lips were dry and tightly pursed.

Reluctantly he pressed his lips to hers. He felt nothing more than a mild male willingness to mate with anything in a skirt. She was young and pretty, and he should have felt more attraction.

"Do you mean to ask me something, Mr. Pendar? I believe we have come to an understanding, have we not?"

He should propose, but instead he said, "You are very young, Miss Bowman, and you have only spent a week in my company."

"I have known of you nearly all my life," she sputtered. "I would not have allowed you such liberties if I did not think . . . that you . . . oh bother."

"No one will doubt that you remain chaste, Miss Bowman," he told her. Looking at her lips, he had the distinct impression it wouldn't be worth the trouble of teaching her to kiss correctly.

"What?" she asked. "Have I done something wrong? Why are you looking at me like that?"

He shook his head.

She pressed the back of her hand to her lips. "I hope you are not d-disappointed."

He turned to look at the sea. Even now his thoughts had turned to Velvet. He had disappointed her, but he was certainly not. Their encounter had been awful, it was no wonder she had no desire to repeat it. But she made his blood heat, and for a brief moment he'd tasted her passion.

"I am a social pariah. I do not know if you have considered how that will hamper your hopes to mix in society."

"Money buys entry into almost every level of polite company," she insisted.

"Then perhaps you should allow me to escort you to the opera in London. If it is not my scar terrifying people, it is the rumors swirling around my wife's death."

"You sound like my father." Tears sparkled in her eyes. She folded her arms across her chest. "He says if another female of your household or close acquaintance meets a bad end, you will be hanged."

Even though the sun shone, a dark pall cast a shadow over his world. "I think, Miss Bowman, we should get you back to the house before you are missed."

She spun and took the steps fast enough that he worried her skirts would trip her. He followed behind ready to catch her if she took a misstep.

As she said, he couldn't afford to have another woman's violent death associated with him.

Chapter 21

Velvet found the days torturous. The guests were all abuzz with Lucian's attentions to Miss Bowman. They had even walked alone several times, and Lucian was distant in his dealings with her. The schoolroom was not even much of a sanctuary, with the constant battles with the dressmaker to keep her dresses plain.

"R-Rick of limb-b," said Iris.

"Rack of lamb," corrected Velvet.

"Why is there a *b* if you aren't supposed to say it?" asked Iris.

"I don't know. English had silly rules." She rubbed the girl's shoulders.

Watching the meal planning with the kitchen staff had piqued Iris's interest. Yesterday, even though it had taken three times as long, she had written out today's menu one painstaking letter at a time. Velvet was grateful for anything that made Iris want to learn.

"Are you ready to take the menu down to the kitchen?"

Iris hopped up and snatched the paper from the desk. "Will Cook be able to read it?"

"Of course she shall," reassured Velvet. Even if she couldn't, they would go over what it said. Besides, the remaining contents of the larder and pantry had determined the menu.

They descended to the lower level and opened the green baize door leading to the bowels of the house.

"Miss Campbell," called Mrs. Bigsby in stentorian tones. "I'd like a word with you?"

Velvet paused. She steeled herself to turn around. Mrs. Bigsby's displeasure was apparent in the grooves from the corners of her lips to her chin. She'd been avoiding the housekeeper, who didn't like having her place usurped by a governess.

Iris paused and looked between the two adult women. Her eyes grew big and round.

"What can I do for you, Mrs. Bigsby?" asked Velvet warily.

"Where are you taking Miss Iris at night? Nellie tells me she has not slept in her own bed in well over a week."

"We are sleeping where Mr. Pendar instructed us to sleep."

Mrs. Bigsby's upper lip pulled up, and then her mouth flattened into a thin line. "I hardly think that it is appropriate that you have Iris with you when you . . . entertain the master."

"I don't 'entertain him,'" protested Velvet, but her cheeks burned. "Perhaps you should voice your concerns to Mr. Pendar."

"We're sleeping in my mama's room," said Iris. "Miss Campbell locks the doors every night, although Papa comes in and kisses us good-night."

Out of the mouths of babes.

Velvet's ears burned and she wished she could crawl away. "He kisses Iris good-night and sleeps in his own room, and I do not enter it." It wasn't strictly the truth, but close enough. She'd never been in his bed, which actually might be more respectable than their encounter on the ground. "We are both concerned about Iris having *nightmares*."

Fortunately, Mrs. Bigsby seemed too shocked to respond, but the gasps of two maids going through with breakfast trays no doubt meant all the servants would soon know. It was amazing they had managed to keep it quiet for a full week.

Iris opened her mouth to say more, but Velvet interrupted. "Cook needs that menu now."

Velvet's furious blush probably condemned her. Pushing Iris forward, she practically ran to the kitchen. Had Iris been awake that first night when Lucian came in the room? Just outside the door she whispered, "Your papa does not kiss me good-night. It was only once—"

"Yes, he does. He waits until almost morning, and he comes in our room and kisses me and tells me to go back to sleep. Then he looks at you a long time and kisses your forehead." Iris bit her lip. "He always looks sad. Why don't you want my papa kissing you?"

But she did want him kissing her. Her hands shook as she led Iris into the kitchen. The shaking took over Velvet's entire body as Iris handed over the menu.

"What is wrong with you, Miss Campbell?" asked the cook. Her little mouth pursed between her puffy cheeks. "You aren't sick, are you? You've been looking mighty pale these last few days."

"I'm not ill," she answered. She was heartsick, and no matter how she denied it, she was in love with Lucian. And maybe there was a chance he cared about her. "I just need some fresh air. Iris, please wait for me here."

Velvet rushed through the kitchen and out the cellar door. Tears burned her eyes, and her sobs threatened to choke her. She had been so certain Lucian did not see her as more than a moment's indiscretion. After all, on the cliff she had thrown herself at him. But if all he ever wanted from her was a physical encounter, why would he watch her sleep?

She strode forward as fears assaulted her. What if Iris *dreamed* her papa's presence? Velvet swiped at the tears. She couldn't fall apart now.

As she paced the length of the kitchen garden, she realized a couple was talking on the other side of the fence. Wanting to be alone with her thoughts, she slowed her steps and began to tiptoe away from the voices.

"Are you certain our daughter would be safe married to him?" a female voice asked. "That scar . . . and what happened to his first wife. I know our Eliza would never be so unmannerly as to conduct an affair under her husband's nose, but I cannot be easy about this scheme."

"Eliza wants to be rich. Pendar will certainly make her that. He will make all of us rich. I have explained she will always have family around her."

Velvet searched her limited knowledge of the young ladies for which one was Eliza, but of course it had to be Miss Bowman.

"Are you sure he will propose, because Eliza reports he says he must give her time to know her own mind, and he wants to escort her to the opera in London before tendering a proper offer."

"He will see the sense in marrying our daughter if he wants this railroad deal."

Velvet gasped. Was Lucian being coerced into marrying Miss Bowman? She clapped a hand over her mouth. She knew she should quit eavesdropping, but she couldn't tear herself away.

"What was that?" said the female.

Velvet ducked and looked for a place to hide.

"Just the sea, love. It is so restless. Eliza will be safe

with us in London for most of the time. Beyond that, should Pendar ever step out of line, why the disappearance of a female from his household would be enough to see him hanged. No, I imagine he'll be controllable."

"My God, you are not suggesting . . ."

"Not to worry, my dear. At least one serving wench could be bribed to disappear and start a new life in America or some such."

"But no one would be able to prove—"

"Yes, well with his mistress found with her head bashed in and his wife thrown over a cliff, he will surely not be offered the benefit of the doubt."

Velvet's heart raced.

"And someone would need to run his affairs," said Mr. Bowman in a speculative tone.

"I see," said Mrs. Bowman. "But I shall never forgive you if our daughter is harmed."

"She's a tough one. Reminds me of myself, if I do say so. Come what may, she'll land on her feet."

The voices moved away, and Velvet tried to still the wild beating of her heart. She had to warn Lucian of the hellish pit he was about to fall into.

Miss Campbell raced by as if she'd seen a ghost. Iris popped off the stool where Cook made her sit in the corner of the kitchen.

"You'll get trampled, miss. There's too many going to and fro with knives and all that. Now how do you think I'd feel if you accidentally got tossed in the soup?" Cook said.

Taking a page from Miss Campbell's book, Iris said, "The meals have been so good, Papa is eating too much."

"I 'spect he works up a good appetite swimming like

he's fleeing demons," said Cook. "Go on, now. I'm sure your governess is going to look around and wonder why you're not right behind her."

One of the day girls looked like she was about to burst with wanting to talk to Cook. Iris suspected they wanted to talk about grown-up things. She sighed and left the kitchen. If the girls in the village weren't so stupid, maybe she could have girl secrets with someone her own age.

She trailed after Miss Campbell and saw her cross the hall and open the library door. Iris swallowed hard and walked across the cold echoing marble. She only hoped Papa would not be too mad that she had revealed his secret visits. But she wasn't stupid. If Papa had to marry, she much preferred Miss Campbell to Miss Bowman.

Miss Bowman looked at her as if she were tempted to sweep her out with the dust.

Iris opened the heavy door and slipped inside. Her footsteps turned silent as she stepped onto the heavy Indian rug. Miss Campbell stood in the doorway to Papa's office, but she had gone very still.

"Yes, did you need to speak to me, Miss Campbell?" asked Papa.

Miss Campbell stepped back into Iris and twisted around, steadying her. Her eyes were wild. Her expression was scary, because Miss Campbell was so good at staying calm. She hadn't even looked this upset when she discovered all her clothes destroyed.

"It will wait." Miss Campbell caught her hand and squeezed hard.

"Iris, take Miss Bowman and show her the pictures in the gallery. Count how many times your bracelet appears."

Miss Bowman leaned forward in the chair where she was lounging in Papa's office. She slowly stood and plastered a fake smile on her face. "Shall we sally forth, Miss Iris? I have been wanting an opportunity to get to know you better."

"No," Miss Campbell said. "It is quite all right. I can wait until later." She backed toward the door and dragged Iris.

Miss Bowman smiled like a cat lapping cream and started to sit back down.

Papa arose from his chair.

Much as she hated the idea of spending a minute alone with Miss Bowman, Iris yanked her hand loose and displayed the band circling her wrist. "My bracelet is in six paintings. I will show you, Miss Bowman. I can point out the other jewelry Papa still has in his strongbox."

Miss Bowman looked torn.

Papa walked past Miss Campbell and opened the library door. "We'll only be a minute."

Miss Bowman put her hand on his sleeve as she passed. "Don't worry about us. I'm sure Iris and I will have a lovely time getting to know one another."

Her smile fell away as soon as the door closed behind them. Pinpoints of red grew in her cheeks and her mouth tightened. She didn't look very pretty when she was angry.

Iris muttered a quick prayer that Miss Bowman's face would fix like that, but she supposed Miss Campbell would chastise her. It didn't matter, because God was a loving parent, who knew when to say no to prayer. At least according to Miss Campbell, God often said no, and one must trust He had a plan.

All the same, Iris didn't like Miss Bowman's anger

directed at Miss Campbell. Maybe she had been the one to rip up the clothes. Maybe she didn't like the way Papa looked at Miss Campbell. Maybe Miss Bowman wanted Papa all to herself.

Miss Bowman stared at the door. "What does she want with your father?"

Her words were so mean, like a dog ready to bite, Iris feared she just might attack Miss Campbell. Scrambling, she sorted through reasons Miss Campbell might want to talk to Papa, reasons that would not alarm Miss Bowman.

"I'm in for it now," said Iris.

"Why? What did you do?" Miss Bowman swiveled and bent down in front of her. "Have you been naughty?"

Unprepared to answer, Iris stuttered and finally blurted, "I tore up my lesson books."

Miss Bowman laughed. "Oh, you have been very naughty indeed. Do you not like your lessons?"

Iris shrugged. She felt disloyal to Miss Campbell. Even though the letters always seemed to swim on the page, Miss Campbell was helping her to make sense of them. The struggle seemed unbearable at times, but she finally had begun to feel she might succeed. "I like playing the piano. One day I shall play the harp like my mama."

"How old are you?" asked Miss Bowman.

Iris opened her mouth to say she was nine, but Miss Bowman didn't wait.

"My sister Evelyn is eight, and my sister Margaret is twelve. I should imagine when you visit you could get up to all sorts of pranks with them." She walked toward the gallery. "George is in between them, but like all boys, he is awful."

She walked ahead of Iris and stared at a painting. "Is

that necklace part of the family collection?"

Iris shrugged. She had no idea which pieces were in Papa's possession.

Miss Bowman walked down the gallery studying the portraits. "You are very fair to come from so many dark-haired people."

"I favor my mama. She was very pretty," said Iris.

Miss Bowman cast her a sour look.

"I would like to have a brother, even if he were awful," said Iris.

"Don't count on having one," muttered Miss Bowman.

"Papa wants a son, even if he does say he would never trade me for the world."

Miss Bowman flattened her mouth and said, "It is not good for a father to be too fond of his daughter . . . or her governess."

Velvet hesitated. It was embarrassing enough to tell Lucian she had been eavesdropping, and worse in that she might appear to be trying to rid herself of her romantic rival.

"You had something you wished to tell me?" asked Lucian. He moved to lean over a table where the map of England was displayed.

"I was in the garden, and I accidentally overheard Mr. and Mrs. Bowman discussing . . ." Velvet couldn't finish. She wanted to run away, but how could she allow Lucian to go into an arrangement where he was in peril?

Lucian straightened and folded his arms across his chest. "My possible marriage to their daughter?"

He watched her with his dark eyes intense.

A flush crept up her cheeks. "Yes, or their plans to keep you in line after your n-nuptials."

He raised an eyebrow.

She had to just spit it out. "Mr. Bowman spoke of bribing a young woman of your household to disappear, and you would be held accountable and possibly hanged, and he would gain control of your finances."

Lucian's brows drew together.

It sounded almost too fantastic as she said it. "I just thought you should know."

"A polite fiction for his wife perhaps." Lucian planted his hands on the table and leaned over the map. Lines of potential rail routes covered the map. The culmination of the plans he had been striving toward for years. His forehead furled. "I suppose I must not step out of line, then."

Was he to marry Miss Bowman? Had she lost any chance for a future with him? Her mouth quivered and she fought the sting in her nose. She'd known that men didn't regard intimacy with the same depth of feeling women did, but she'd hoped his proposal meant more than that he felt guilty. If she'd said yes to his offer and allowed him to announce their plans, she could have had marriage to him. And even if he didn't want children, he'd risked it on the cliff's edge. Couldn't she have hoped for more incidents of his getting carried away with passion?

Feeling beyond foolish, she looked down. "I'm sure I don't mean to interfere in your decisions, but I thought you should know."

Mr. Bowman's tone had struck her as evil.

Lucian looked through her. "It would take more than a woman's disappearance for me to be hanged for murder."

Chills rolled down Velvet's spine.

His dark gaze swept down her new dress as if it revealed her body rather than modestly concealing it. "It would have to be a woman with whom I'd had intimate relations, and there would need to be a corpus delicti. Which is why I suggested you reside in Bath."

Stunned and confused by her quickening pulse, Velvet took a step back. Even knowing he had little interest, she wanted to feel his body against hers. "What?"

"There would need to be a corpse, Miss Campbell. One cannot be hanged for murder without a corpse."

The hairs on the back of her neck raised. How could he discuss murder and hanging so calmly? How could she think of intimacy with him, when everything was so wrong?

"If I want this, I must marry Miss Bowman." He pushed the map so it floated to the floor. "My hands are tied."

For a second the only sound was the flap of the paper and the soft crumple as it landed. His jaw pulsed and his cold anger scared her.

Velvet took another step back. How could he cut deals with men who threatened to kill an innocent woman just to keep Lucian in line? "What kind of men do you do business with?"

He turned toward the window. "The kind of men who will lie down with the devil if need be. These men are willing to overlook certain things in exchange for making a profit. They don't care if I am a murderer."

"Are you?" she whispered. She swallowed hard. He'd never denied it.

The question burned Lucian like a hot poker rammed through his chest. Velvet had never given him the impression she suspected him of murder. Now that she seemed to come to the conclusion that everyone else jumped to, he could hardly breathe.

He rarely bothered to answer, because no matter how he answered, he wasn't believed. Miss Bowman seemed excited by the idea that he had murdered his wife even though he'd told her hadn't.

If Velvet believed he had murdered Lilith and Myra, whatever affection she thought she felt for him would be destroyed. She was too good to yearn for a man she believed capable of such heinous acts. And if she no longer cared about him, she could move on and have a chance to pursue her dreams.

He opened his mouth but could not force out an affirmative response. Instead he said, "If I told you I was, would you consent to go live in Bath?"

She made a mewling sound.

He couldn't turn and look at her, because then he would cross the room and hold her. Even now in the midst of one of the worst conversations in his life, he wanted her. He wanted her in the worst possible way. He wanted her goodness and her pushing for him to be the best man he could be, and he wanted to show her how wicked she could be in his bed.

All of it was tangled up in his mind, and he could find no way that he could take what he wanted and make her happy. He was more than willing to marry her, but that would mean no children.

"I don't know what you're asking," she said softly.

"I'm asking you to remove yourself from my household. I don't want you at risk. You'd never have to see me again. I would ensure you could live modestly and perhaps meet a man who would marry you, give you children, and love you as you deserve to be loved."

In a feathery voice, she asked. "Is that what you want?"

No! He leaned his heated forehead against the cool glass window but found no relief. "I want what is best for you."

He sounded rational and calm, but inside he was frothing and churning like a storm-whipped sea. He couldn't turn around and look at her for fear of what he would do.

"I don't know that Bath is the solution," she said softly.

Oh God, please let her understand. "There will be no good outcome if you stay here."

The paper crinkled as she picked up the map. She smoothed it on table.

Ten years of dreams and hard work were represented on that map. If Myra then Lilith hadn't both died, his plans would have been coming to fruition long ago.

Velvet's hands rattled the paper. She drew them behind her back.

"When I complete that, no man will dare speak ill of me," he told her.

Her gaze rose from the plans. Her green eyes looked bruised. He hated the pain he must inflict so she would move on with her life and search for happiness. A happiness he wanted her to find. Marriage to him would have brought her endless misery.

"I see," she said.

What did she see?

"I must get Iris to the schoolroom." As if she could no longer stand to be in his presence, she bolted toward the door. "We have delayed lessons too long."

"Will you go to Bath?"

She paused at the door with her head dipped. He wanted so badly to close the distance between them and press kisses on her nape.

She answered so softly he had to strain to hear. "Yes."

Then before he could call her back, she had opened the door and exited the room.

His success at getting her to accept the arrangement clawed at him. It would be for the best. She would not be his mistress, a role she was ill-suited for. She would not be a childless wife. She would not be a part of his life. Undoubtedly, she would come to realize she had escaped from the hell he could offer her. He ripped the map from the table, balled it up and threw it in the fireplace.

As the paper caught and the different colored inks flared in purple and green flames, Lucian wished for Velvet to come back, because without her nothing was left of him.

Chapter 22

Velvet paced the sitting room floor. Just feet away, Iris was tucked into bed and sleeping soundly. But Velvet had spent the day in a welter of emotions. Now in the quiet of the night, she sorted through the things Lucian had said and done.

Putting together the railroad lines and expanding his shipping enterprise had been his driving ambition over the last few years. It was the only thing that made him animated. To achieve it he had to marry Miss Bowman.

The income would make him wealthier, but Velvet could see no indication he found any particular joy in money or the things it could buy. He would gain power, but he lived too isolated to reap the real benefits of his potential clout. Besides, working for the Langtrees had given Velvet plenty of exposure to people who craved power for power's sake. Lucian didn't fit their mold.

So why was this shipping empire so important to Lucian?

He'd said, *When I complete that, no man will dare speak ill of me.*

Velvet rubbed her face. She understood the absolute helplessness and fury when accusations leveled against her were false. Though this morning when Mrs. Bigsby had insinuated she was "entertaining" the master, she was embarrassed, but the undeserved pain and impotent anger she'd felt over the last year were curiously absent.

If Lucian had murdered his wife or his mistress, surely he would find the accusations annoying, but not hurtful. The way Iris reacted to being accused of destroying her school books, compared to her reaction when being questioned about the destruction in Velvet's room, was as different as night and day. The accusation pained him, not like a guilty man, but like a man who didn't know how to prove his innocence. But he thought by gaining power he could at least silence the gossip.

Velvet checked the door to the corridor. Satisfied that it was locked, she moved to the connecting door to Lucian's bedroom. Drawing a deep breath, she unlocked the door and twisted the handle.

Her heart skittered and her palms were wet. By willingly going into his room, she was turning her back on her upbringing and morals. She only prayed God understood.

"Lucian," she whispered on a shaky voice.

She searched the darkened room, expecting to find him abed. Instead he stood facing the fire, leaning against the mantel, his hand wrapped around a bronze bust.

He turned his head. For just a second his face reflected stark yearning. Anticipation shivered through her.

"What do you want?" he asked harshly. His gaze dropped over the chocolate brown dressing gown and returned to her face with a hint of confusion.

A shiver threaded through her. "Could we talk?" she asked. Her voice sounded small, hardly the persuasive tone she wanted.

He gestured toward the door to the sitting room she'd just left.

She shook her head. "In here."

"Not a good idea, Velvet," he growled.

"Why not?" she asked.

He straightened to full height and turned to face her. His dressing gown was loosely belted at the waist. The gaping lapels revealed his bare chest. He glanced toward his bed and back at her.

Heat skittered down her spine. She swallowed hard and tried to smile but failed miserably. Her nerves were stretched taut and she had no experience in these matters. But she remembered the feel of his chest and her all too short exploration of it. "I wouldn't wish to risk Iris overhearing."

Disappointment flicked across his face.

"I wish to explain—"

"Please do," he interrupted.

"I will not stand in the way of your achieving success with the expansion of your freight and shipping business." Her decision had not come lightly. She would fade quietly into the background, and he could marry Miss Bowman.

He grunted and folded his arms.

She took another step into the room. "I will go to Bath as you asked."

"Velvet," he said on an anguished note.

Her breath drew in rapidly. "I know you have tried to repulse me because you thought it best for me. You have even tried to convince me of your guilt, but I know you did not murder your wife."

He covered his face with his hands and sank down into the wing chair by the fire. "Velvet, you must leave now, or I can't be responsible for what happens."

"I'm not leaving, but I think it is time you told me the truth. I deserve that much."

He dropped his hands and watched her. For a time there was only the crackle of the fire and the sound of their breathing.

As if it required Herculean effort, he turned toward the fire. "You must understand, *I am* responsible for Lilith's death."

"No, whatever happened was beyond your control." Velvet said with complete conviction. Claiming responsibility was not the same as admitting he'd committed murder. Her brother's death was her fault, but it wasn't as though she'd pushed him from the bell tower. She could not believe Lucian had thrown his wife over the cliff. At the worst there had been some terrible accident. "Tell me the events of that night, so it no longer hangs between us. I hate feeling that I should fear you."

"You do not want to know," he protested.

He might be right, but she trusted him. Every time she turned around, he surprised her with his kindness. He was not the monster he allowed people to see him as. "I, of all people, understand what it is like to be falsely accused. Or to have the truth warped beyond all connection to reality and to just accept everyone around you will have a distorted view of you. But I know you. You are a good man. Whatever happened was not planned by you."

He just stared at her, and Velvet felt her resolve crumbling. How could she love a man who wouldn't tell her about the most significant event in his life? "I told you of incidents that I had no wish to recount."

But as the silence stretched thin, disappointment curled coldly down her spine. He would not allow her to share the burden of whatever horror occurred the night his wife died. She tried one last time. "If nothing else, you would not have wished to hurt Iris by harming her mother."

Lucian's heart pounded. He wanted to twist away, protest she had no right to know anything. She had refused to be his wife—or perhaps after learning the truth, she would change her mind about his goodness.

"All right," he said. "I will tell you, if you will stay the night."

Her cheeks pinked and she looked away.

He was ashamed of himself, but the bargain was on the table.

Seemingly gathering resolve, she met his gaze with a defiant gleam in her green eyes. But her blush had deepened to a bright red. "I had intended to."

Heat rushed through him. But if she intended to stay, he'd made a poor bargain, far below his normal standards. "I should insist you marry me, because a wife cannot bear witness against her husband."

He searched her face for a hint that would indicate she wanted to marry him.

Instead her eyes narrowed and she lifted her chin. "Quit trying to scare me."

Admiration for her audacity mingled with the desire to bed her. Although his desire was bittersweet. Nothing in her indicated she wanted marriage. But then he'd pledged he would not stand in the way of her having the kind of marriage with children she wanted. They would both be giving up too much to marry each other, but marrying Miss Bowman and letting Velvet go seemed a special kind of curse he had to bear.

She waited, her face earnest and her eyes large. She rubbed her arm, and he wished she touched him so. "Well?"

"I will tell you everything you want to know before

the sun rises." With any luck he would lull her to sleep long before he had to reveal anything.

Her mouth twisted, and she turned toward the door. "You have no intention of telling me anything," she said on a low note.

Oh God, she was leaving. His chest squeezed as if he'd been too long underwater and couldn't breathe. He crossed the room in quick strides and caught her around the waist, her unfettered waist. The lack of corset registered in his mind even as he feared he had pushed her too far. "Don't go," he whispered.

Her sweet scent swirled in his head, and her hair was loose, only tied back with a length of ribbon. He bent and pressed his lips to her exposed neck.

"Please, don't go," he pleaded. Of course she couldn't while he confined her, but to let go would be harder than anything he'd ever done.

She twisted and pushed at him. He had to release his hold, but he tugged the ribbon free, releasing her glorious fiery hair. The strands of molten copper and gold caught the fire's light as it shifted and spread over her shoulder.

Her chest rose and fell as she stared at him. Desire, thick and unrelenting, surged through him. Her lips parted. He bent and sampled them.

Her soft mew told him everything he needed to know. She had come into his room with every intention of sharing his secrets and his bed. His heart soared, while his member rose. Sliding his hands along her jaw, he tilted her up for a deeper kiss. All the while he watched her, until her eyes fluttered closed and she sighed into his mouth.

Once he tasted her surrender, he scooped her up and carried her to his bed.

"Lucian." Her palm flattened against his chest as he bent to lay her down on the green counterpane.

"Shhh. I have dreamed of seeing you lying here with your hair undone almost from the first time I saw you," he said.

She pushed up to her elbows. "I want to know what happened."

"I pledge to tell you, but first let me show you what it should have been like the first time we made love."

Her lips parted and her eyes rounded.

Reaching for the fasteners on the dressing gown she had tried so hard to refuse, he undid the top button.

Her hands closed around his, hindering his progress.

"Could we get under the covers?" she asked in a small voice. Her lips trembled.

He frowned. Wanting nothing more than to shed his dressing gown and hers, he hesitated. "What is wrong?"

"I don't know what to do. I've never . . ."

"I'll take care of you. Trust me." He caressed her silky hair. "No rushing this time, love."

She worried her bottom lip with her pearly teeth. He pushed the coverlet back, urging her between the cool sheets. He shed his dressing gown.

She gasped and looked away from his nude body. Her innocence reminded him that he needed to take care of her in all ways.

The cool night air teased his heated skin. Turning, he went to his dresser to retrieve the sheath he needed to wear and then slid into the sheets beside her.

Velvet couldn't help but peek at him. His long form was ridged and rippled with muscles, and his manhood stood at attention. An answering softness in her called to him. Yet, her mind raced. By refusing to tell her what had happened with his wife, he confirmed her worst fears.

She should leave, but there was no way she could tear herself away. As he stretched out beside her, she scooted farther under the covers. Her dressing gown twisted. Lucian followed her until the length of his body rested against her. He rolled up on an elbow and looked down on her. "Don't be frightened."

His dark gaze made her edgy, but she couldn't look away. Not even when he trailed his fingers down her cheek. He ran his finger over her lips. Anticipating his kiss, she wet her lips. He groaned as he lowered his mouth to hers and slowly kissed her and kissed her until she went soft all over.

Unlike on the cliff, he seemed in no hurry to free her breasts or pull up her shift. He skimmed her face. Running his hands down her arm, he ended the caress by entwining their fingers together. All the while his tender kisses evoked a sweet delight.

The energy she'd been alarmed by on the cliff simmered and built within her. She wanted the pressure of his weight on her. She wanted to be brave enough to bare her body as he did. She wanted him to feed the sensations instead of tormenting her heart with his gentle ministrations, which were more like an expression of love than just a drive toward physical pleasure.

A sigh of impatience left her.

Lucian smiled against her lips. Pulling back slightly, he asked, "Want more, dear heart?"

Dumbstruck, she nodded. He was so beautiful, if a man so masculine could be called so. Thick lashes rimmed his dark eyes. His skin was golden from the mornings in the ocean. His smile was so rare it melted her to see it now.

He reached for the frogged buttons of her twisted and too hot dressing gown. With exquisite care he removed her covering, until only her thin shift was between them. He ran his hands up her bare arms, making her shudder.

Wondering if she had the same power to make him feel, she imitated his movements. He sighed and his lashes brushed his cheekbones.

Testing the hard ridges of muscles, she ran her fingers over his shoulder.

"Touch me lower," he growled.

She complied, sliding her hand against his warm skin, over his back, down his ribs. Her heart pounded as she took in his deep breathing. She hesitated at his hip.

Lucian flattened his hand over hers. He guided her hand between them and pressed it to the hard male appendage. "See how much I want you," he whispered in her ear.

His kisses against her neck brought a new flood of yearning. Gingerly, she explored the velvety skin over his hardness. He moaned and then shifted her hand back to his hip. "You will make me too eager, and I want to touch you."

"I want you to touch me too," she whispered.

"Nothing I would rather do." He inched up her shift. "Sit up, love, so I might remove this."

Shivering with anticipation, she complied. Shifting behind her, he drew the material over her head and tossed it away. His lips between her shoulder blades startled a moan from her.

He slid a hand around her ribs and ran the tips of fingers over her quivering stomach and over the curve of her breast. She arched toward the sharp spike in sensation as he caught her nipple.

As he kissed down her spine, jolt after jolt of delight rippled down her back. Her heart tripped.

Lucian gently lowered her to the bed and pushed the

bedding down to pool across her hips. Naked before him, she curled her fingers around the covers.

"Trust me, Velvet. I want to look at you. You are so beautiful."

Releasing her grip, she reached for him and tried to pull him down to her, but he resisted. Looking down on her, he ran his fingers slowly over her exposed skin. "Your skin is so soft."

Her skin was so sensitized, she felt his every touch everywhere, but mostly between her legs. She brushed her hand over his chest and looked her fill at the hard lines and planes of his body. Every inch of him filled her with a delicious appreciation.

"I thought you were an angel, the first time I saw you." She flushed hearing the breathless admiration in her voice. He would think her silly.

"My thoughts were more earthly," he whispered.

He leaned and pressed kisses to her shoulder. Then with a languorous deliberation, he trailed nips and little sucking pecks under her collarbone and lower until he suckled on her increasing sensitized breasts.

Her hips twisted and her woman's flesh was swollen and begging for attention, yet he slid against her and engaged her in a deep kiss. Every inch of his skin against hers electrified her.

She moaned a protest as he trailed kisses down her chest and across her stomach. He inserted his knee between her and caressed her thighs while urging them apart. Eager for the repeat of having him inside her, she complied. Yet, his kisses traveled lower. As his destination became clear, her heart raced. She attempted to close her legs, but he was there, his shoulders preventing her.

The first press of his mouth to her brought a burst

of raw sensation. Unable to fathom where the jolts of sensation were taking her, she pushed him away.

He simply sank lower and lapped at the tender flesh of her inner thigh, then the back of her knee. Her body thrummed with a building excitement.

Regretting her resistance, she sobbed. He knew better what she wanted than she did herself. As if aware of the shift in her mood, he returned to the seat of her pleasure. Her body had a will of its own as she writhed and strained toward and away from him. The intimacy was almost more than she could bear. The sensations built and burst over her in throbbing waves of rapture.

She cried out, but Lucian coaxed her through. He kissed her quivering stomach, and every touch shook her and seemed to touch deep inside her soul. He kissed her lips, and she felt as if she'd melted on the sheets. "My turn," he whispered.

But then he rolled to the side. Velvet tried to catch her breath but was too amazed by what had happened. She hadn't known how shockingly good what he'd done felt. But the distance between them bothered her. She wanted him between her legs rocking into her. She wanted to be joined to him now, tomorrow, and for the rest of their lives.

As she reached for him, she realized he was placing a sheath on his male member. Regret that there must be anything between them made her heart hurt. He positioned himself on top of her. Then he stroked the hair away from her face as he probed her slick cleft.

He stared down at her as he pushed inside of her and made them one. Awake to every sensation, her woman's core pulsed around him as he stroked in and out. She held her breath. And it seemed as if she had been waiting her whole life for this moment with Lucian.

He felt like heaven and sin combined in a pleasure more powerful than she could understand. She stroked his perspiration-slick back and down over the hard muscles of his backside. Letting her know he liked her touches, he crooned encouragement and praise.

She explored him with the intent of learning how to make him come apart as she had. His infinite gentleness, in spite of the building urgency she sensed in him, combined to make her feel treasured, alive, and wide-awake.

"I love . . ." he whispered against her lips.

Did he love her? A rush of pleasure flooded her body.

Everything in her tightened and spiraled. She moaned out in a new climax as he showed her his love with the thrust of his body.

" . . . making love to you," he finished.

"Lucian?" she whispered. She wanted him to repeat what he'd said. Had she missed part of it, or had he stopped before declaring love? With her racing heart, she feared she had dreamed the words. She had gone ahead of him in her affection.

He shuddered and groaned as his thrusts became frenzied. She held him and stroked his back and lower still. His tension was palpable. Then he seemed to shudder all over as he tucked his head into her shoulder and groaned.

His breathing was harsh as he slid his hand down her arm and threaded her fingers with his. A few seconds later he pulled away, separating their bodies. Even though she was sated and replete, the loss was if he had ripped part of her away.

Confusion drained part of her pleasure as he slid out of the bed. He hadn't said he loved her, but his gentle handling made her believe he did. Or perhaps her hopes had blinded her to reality. Tears stung her eyes. She loved him, and after tonight she couldn't imagine how she would face a life apart from him.

Lucian tried to remain calm as he crossed the room to the pitcher of water Evans had taken to leaving in his room at night. He'd nearly poured out his heart to Velvet and had barely stopped himself. She didn't want a barren marriage, and that was all he had to offer. To declare his love would only trap her even more into a relationship she would find immoral.

As he removed the sheath that would prevent pregnancy, it seemed a huge barrier between them. But as he considered it, he didn't come up with any viable options. He washed off and returned to the bed. Now he would have to come clean to her.

Her magnificent mane lay tangled against her porcelain skin, and she had an arm over her face. Her back was to him, the smooth curves to her rounded hip beckoning to him and stirring a new interest in making love to her.

He slid in behind her. As his heated body came in contact with her cool skin, he sensed something was wrong. Sharing his warmth with her, he curled around her and brought the covers up over her shoulder after he pressed a lingering kiss to the curve of her upper arm. "Velvet, are you all right?"

"I didn't know it would be so wonderful," she choked out.

Was his stoic Velvet emotional? He stroked her skin and cradled her. Perhaps he should tell her the depth of his feelings for her.

"Will relations be like this between you and your— Miss Bowman, when you are married?"

Her words came out crowded together, as if the idea

couldn't be restrained, but they cut nonetheless.

He rolled to his back and stared at the ceiling. "No."

He contemplated the years ahead of him with a woman who loved his money, not him. Sexual relations with her would feel good, but he didn't see how he could ever feel the same way about Miss Bowman that he felt about Velvet. Truth was, it might not be long before he simply suppressed any physical needs with sea bathing to the point of exhaustion.

He wanted to share his bed, his life, his hopes and dreams, with Velvet.

"I haven't actually proposed to Miss Bowman," he pointed out.

"How can you know it won't be the same?"

"Velvet, I know. This between us is rare and special."

She made a noise that sounded suspiciously like a sniff and sat up. "I should go back to the other room. I wouldn't want Iris to wake and wonder where I am."

He didn't want her to go. Holding out the only crumb he had to offer, he said, "I thought you wanted me to tell you of the night her mother died."

She didn't answer as she reached for the dressing gown tangled at the bottom of the bed.

He risked everything and said, "It would never be the same with Miss Bowman, because her only affection is for my wealth, and I don't love her. I love you, Velvet."

Chapter 23

Velvet hesitated. Lucian loved her. The words filled her with joy. He loved her. His tenderness was not a sham. With every kiss, every caress, every moment in his arms, her conviction had grown stronger. He had been showing her, just as coming to his room and making love with him was her way of showing him the depth of her feelings.

"Lucian," she sighed.

"I love you," he repeated firmly. "You make me feel whole. No one else has ever done that."

He reached out to caress her shoulder, his hand sliding down her bare arm evoking a soul-deep yearning for him. Her bones seemed to melt when he touched her. If only they could hold the rest of the world at bay.

No matter what had happened with his wife, she would love him until the end of time. He was the man she was meant to be with. If only she could stay here in his bed forever.

Yet, a certain wariness kept her happiness from being complete. He loved her, she loved him, but he was still suspected of murdering his wife.

How could she stand in the way of Lucian silencing his accusers? His life would be better if he were not hounded by the past. He'd hinted at marriage, but a marriage to her might harm in more ways than she could count.

She could do nothing to restore his reputation. With her own past, she could do more to destroy it. And she had political enemies who might interfere with his current businesses.

Every fiber of her being screamed at her to turn around and throw herself into his arms, but instead she plucked at the bedspread. "Tell me of the night Iris's mother died."

Lucian released a deep breath. She was so aware of his every movement. But she couldn't turn to look at him or he would see the yearning in her face.

"Why was she so angry she clawed you?" Velvet prompted. If he trusted her enough to tell her what happened, perhaps she could help absolve him of the guilt he felt.

"She wanted to go to London. I forbid it."

Lucian left a great deal unsaid. Velvet suspected she might have to drag every kernel of the truth out of him. "Why?"

"She gloated about giving other men healthy children."

"Children?" squeaked Velvet. She only knew of Iris. Was one of the graves in the churchyard for a healthy child? Shock made her hands curl into the covers, and she went cold all over with gooseflesh raising her skin. She drew up the covers and brought her knees to her chest.

Lucian sat up and pulled her dressing gown around her shoulders. That he cared if she was cold, even as she interrogated him, brought a lump to her throat.

He slid out of the bed and pulled his own dressing gown on. "Iris has a half brother, born before my marriage. He is apprenticed to a master shipbuilder in Bristol. After I learned of him, it took me some time to track him down. He was not raised as a gentlemen, so apprenticing him to a tradesman seemed the best I could do for him." Lucian snorted. "I am sure there are those who must believe he is my bastard, but he is not."

Velvet was ashamed that she had questioned his goodness. And if his wife had been so unkind, how must her demands for children have seemed to him?

Lucian moved to the fireplace and tossed another log inside. The fire crackled and a shower of sparks cascaded upward. He sat in the wing chair facing her.

"After she attacked me," he said, sliding his hand along his scars and staring into the fire as if he didn't dare watch her response, "I threatened to kill her if she stayed another second in my presence. If I hadn't told her I planned to petition Parliament for a divorce, she never would have gone out in the storm. She never would have fallen off the cliff."

Velvet pushed her arms into the dressing gown sleeves and slid out of the sheets. She stepped up to the chair and stroked his hair. He caught her hand and pulled it down to kiss her palm.

"Do you think she fell accidentally?" she asked carefully.

Lucian rubbed his face. "I don't know. I've always wondered if she deliberately jumped. Until the attack in your room, I've always leaned toward her death being accident or suicide. But, I just don't know. It is possible someone pushed her over the edge."

"What was the thumping sound?" she asked. Velvet believed him, but she didn't want to leave any stone unturned. She never wanted to suppress any niggling doubts.

He twisted away from her. "What?"

"Iris heard your argument. She said there was a loud thump, and her mother never spoke again." Whatever had happened, Lucian needed to let it go.

He considered a moment and then said, "The thump must have been when Lilith threw the bust at me. She knew she'd gone too far. She fled or I might have done her harm." Lucian's expression crumpled. "I had no idea Iris overheard."

Velvet crooned softly to him, "One day you will have to explain to her what happened."

He shook his head. "I can't. I hated Lilith. I thought she'd killed Myra in a fit of jealousy, but I never meant for her to lose her life."

"It's not your fault," said Velvet. But guilt didn't always answer to reason. She knew because she had always borne the weight of responsibility for her brother's death. She'd believed God was punishing her, but everything in her life had contrived to bring her here where she could no longer hide. If all the bad things hadn't happened, she never would have found Lucian.

"Much has happened since I arrived." She was explaining badly, but stumbled on. "I will go to Bath and start a new life if that is what you wish, but I cannot conceive that I will ever feel about another as I feel about you."

His face twisted. He opened his mouth to speak.

She held out her hand, stopping him. If he insisted on marriage she would fall apart. "I love you, Lucian."

He moaned and pulled her against him, burying his face in the plush folds of her dressing gown. "Then, please, Velvet—"

She pressed her fingers to his lips. She feared her courage would desert her if he stopped her. "I am not the same person I was when I arrived. I have wrestled with everything I believed was true about me, but I didn't know who I was. I was sleepwalking through life before. You have made me come alive."

He kissed her fingers, and flutters stirred in her belly and lower.

"You will never know how thankful I am for that," she said.

The click of a door made her spring back guiltily.

"Evans, give me another hour," said Lucian. But there was no response.

Lucian frowned and headed toward the dressing room, where the servant's door was hidden.

Velvet scurried toward the connecting door. She had no wish to be discovered by Lucian's manservant. Even if all the servants were aware of how close she was sleeping to Lucian, old habits died hard.

She twisted the knob and entered the dark sitting room. The lamp she had left burning had gone out, and the fire was just a tiny orange glow amidst ash.

Her eyes took a minute to adjust to the darker room, but then she saw the black gaping hole where the door to the corridor should have been.

Her heart squeezed and she ran toward the bed. The covers were tossed back and only Eve lay on the sheets. "Iris!"

The room didn't contain any sign of the child.

"Why is that door open?" asked Lucian.

"It was locked before I entered your room. I checked it."

"She must have let herself out. Perhaps she went to the water closet," said Lucian.

Velvet ran down the hall to the bathroom. Iris was not inside. Lucian bumped into her.

The welling of panic climbed in Velvet. Oh God,

while she had been making love to Lucian, Iris had been stolen from her bed. She turned and gripped his dressing gown. "Someone has taken her."

"No, she has probably just gone looking for you." Lucian looked around. "I will check upstairs."

"She's outside," insisted Velvet. Fear clawed at her throat and filled her with cold dread.

"She wouldn't go outside in the middle of the night," protested Lucian. "She's afraid of the dark."

Velvet didn't want to waste any more time. She'd told him before that Iris believed her mother wanted her to jump from the cliffs. She pushed around Lucian. "I'm checking the cliffs."

"Wait! If she isn't upstairs, I'll wake the servants," he said as he ran toward the stairs to the nursery floor. "Nothing could be seen outside without lights. Besides, she is wont to hide in the house."

Velvet ignored the slap of her bare feet against the marble of the entryway and ran to the front door. There seemed a million steps to the drive. "Iris!" she yelled.

The wind whipped her words from her lips and plastered the dressing gown against her flesh as she ran around the house. Indigo clouds scudded across the sky, blocking the light from the moon and stars. The always hungry waves crashed on the shore.

The scrub grass tore at her feet, but Velvet ran toward the cliffs. She cupped her hands around her mouth and shouted. "Iris!"

Was she already too late? Her heart pounded so hard it was all she could hear.

Nothing interrupted the wall of black at the edge of the cliff, not a single little girl in a white nightgown.

"Iris!" Velvet screamed. Tears stung her nose. She couldn't bear it if something happened to the girl. All the desperation of when her brother had fallen from the bell tower returned to her. This couldn't be happening again.

Lucian found Iris's bedroom empty. The schoolroom was empty, and Velvet's room was empty. His banging on the dressmaker's door brought Mrs. Whitson from her bed.

"Whatever is going on?" She stood blinking in her doorway with a wrapper held closed at her throat.

"My daughter is missing. Help me look for her." A mind-numbing alarm began to infiltrate his soul. Iris couldn't be outside. She had to be hiding in the house. "Iris!"

He had to wake the servants and involve them in the search. Taking the stairs two at a time, he hurtled down to his room and yanked the bellpull viciously. Evans would respond quickly. He raced down to the main floor and burst through the baize-covered door to a part of his house he rarely visited.

He pounded on the door to the Bigsbys' suite. "Get up."

After an endless delay, Mrs. Bigsby swung open the door, a huge monstrosity of a bed cap tied under her chin. "What is going on?"

"Get all the servants up. Iris is missing. I want the house searched from top to bottom."

Her eyes widened.

Mr. Bigsby in his striped nightcap appeared behind his wife. The grizzled old man went white. "I'll fetch Nellie. She'll know all of Iris's favorite hiding spots."

"I'll fetch her," said Mrs. Bigsby.

"I don't care who the bloody hell fetches whom, just get everyone up and search."

Lucian turned on his heel and ran toward the kitchen.

Perhaps Iris had grown hungry. He crashed into the kitchen. "Iris, are you in here?"

Standing fully clothed in front of the stove, Nellie stirred the coals to life.

"She's not in here," said Nellie.

"Have you seen her?" he asked. Thank goodness she was up already.

Nellie turned slowly. "She is with Miss Campbell, is she not?"

"No. Go out to the stables and wake the groomsmen. Tell them to get lanterns and ropes." If Iris had gone over the cliff, as Velvet feared, he wanted to be prepared.

Velvet's face had been so pinched, he knew she feared the worst. But Iris was not stupid. She knew the cliffs could be dangerous. She knew her mother had died from a fall. And she had been happy lately. Iris just wouldn't have gone outside in the predawn hours.

He turned and threw open the doors off the main hall. Dark rooms echoed with his calls.

"Sir, I have your clothes," said Evans behind him, startling Lucian half to death.

"I don't need clothes. I need my daughter." Oh God, where was she? "Iris!"

Mumbling half-broken prayers and pleas, Velvet reached the cliffs. "Iris! Please, God, please, God, let her be all right."

Then faintly, ever so faintly, a sound like a kitten's mew arose from beneath the whipping wind.

"Iris, where are you?"

"Here," was the cry, faint and far away.

Velvet ran toward the sound. "Keep shouting. I'm coming."

As she homed in on the faint voice, Velvet's heart squeezed and she could barely breathe. Her legs quivered as she ran along the edge of the drop-off. Every part of her being protested, but if Iris was over the edge, she couldn't allow her panic to stop her.

Surely, when Lucian finished searching the house he would find them outside. As she neared the blackness that marked the end of land, Velvet called out, "Where are you?"

"Here. Please come get me. I'm cold."

Velvet dropped to her knees and crawled toward the edge. Her head spun and she kept recalling her brother's fall, watching him drop and drop to the cobbled stones below. The sickening thud as he hit. Her stomach lurched.

Bile rose in her throat and she fought it.

Looking over the edge, the blackness was almost complete. Then the clouds moved and she saw a patch of white thirty feet below. Velvet closed her eyes. She had to sound calm and reassuring for Iris.

"Are you hurt?" she asked.

"I don't know," the girl wailed. "Please get me up. I can't feel my fingers."

The clouds continued to move, exposing more and more moonlight. Iris clung over the edge of a rocky ledge, but her purchase looked far from secure. Below her the drop was sheer, another sixty or seventy feet to the ocean.

"Pleeeease!"

"I need you to stay calm," said Velvet. "Your papa will be here soon. Just hang on."

Where was Lucian?

"I'm slipping!" screamed Iris.

Her terror echoed in Velvet's ears. She couldn't stand

by and watch as another child fell. Her brother had cried out before he fell, but she'd hesitated too long before reaching out to save him.

Just to her left the drop-off was less severe, a slope that led to the ledge Iris dangled from. Bits of scrub and grass grew out of the uneven cliff. While the drop was still steep, it was not entirely vertical. If she could get Iris on that small ledge, they both could wait for rescue.

Her heart squeezing in her chest, Velvet slid on her stomach to the edge. With handfuls of grass, she lowered herself over the side.

Her hands shook, her legs shook, and her teeth chattered, not from cold, but from pure terror. The cold, she didn't even feel. She inched slowly down the slope, grabbing brush and rocks. Her nails tore and broke, but Iris was in worse shape.

"Hurry!" the girl cried.

The ground crumbled away and Velvet couldn't breathe. She slid, grabbing and clawing. The thud in her chest felt like she'd been hit by a cannonball. Oh God, she was going to fall all the way down to the dark ocean. Clouds obliterated the light of the moon, and only the dark, the restless rhythm of the ocean and Iris's whimpers filled her senses.

Evans pulled on his smalls and hopped around him fastening buttons, in spite of Lucian's inability to stand still.

"Sir, if you would just step in," said Evans.

"Mrs. Bigsby, where the hell is everyone?"

"They're searching, sir." Mrs. Bigsby lit lamps and passed one to a maid who put her hand on the side of her face as she went by rather than look at him in his state of undress.

Mr. Bigsby sat in one of the chairs by the door, moaning and rocking back and forth. Lucian wanted to slap him and tell him to help, but the others had answered his call.

Lucian pulled open the billiard room door. Evans danced around him. A quick glance inside confirmed that Iris was not inside.

He tripped over his dresser and then decided Evans would be less of a nuisance if he allowed him to dress him. "Where the hell are the groomsmen? You should be looking for Iris," he shouted at Evans.

"As soon as you are decent, sir. You scare the maids enough fully dressed."

Lucian growled, threw off his dressing gown and held his hands out for Evans to slip his shirt over his head.

The house servants began to gather in the hall. He could see from the wide-eyed scared expressions that Iris hadn't been found.

As he scanned the group, two faces were missing. "Where the hell is Nellie? She should be back from the stables by now." Why hadn't Velvet returned? Either way, if she'd located Iris or not, she should be back.

But then if Iris had fallen off the cliffs, Lucian doubted that Velvet would be able to find her in the predawn darkness. He didn't want to even think that his daughter could have fallen. Her mother's broken body on the rocks flashed in his thoughts.

His spine felt as if a knife were jabbing it, and a dull ache pounded in his head. No, this wasn't happening.

Heedless of Evans's efforts to tuck in his shirt, Lucian ran out the front door. Not a single light burned in the long, low stable buildings and no men were stirring. He swung through the first door and ran up the stairs to the quarters above.

Pounding on doors, he shouted for rope and lanterns. He'd thought it would save time to send Nellie, since she was already dressed. Clearly he'd been mistaken.

Without waiting, he raced outside and toward the cliffs.

"Velvet! Iris!" he shouted.

The restlessness of the ocean signified a storm moving in. The night was so black he couldn't see. Almost by instinct he headed for the place where Lilith had fallen. The drop was straight down there.

Where the hell had Velvet gone? If he'd lost her or lost Iris, he wouldn't have a reason to live.

"Iris!" He cupped his hands around his mouth. "Velvet, answer me."

"We're here," he heard the faint call below, just as the first fat raindrop splattered him.

Lucian stumbled as the tension dropped out of his muscles. Thank God, they were alive. Moving to the edge, he dropped to his belly and leaned over. Far below, the unnatural white of a nightgown stood out against the granite and dirt. His breath caught.

A flash of lightning illuminated the two figures clinging to the side of the cliff. They were so far down, he feared if he tried to get to them, he'd send them plunging to the rocky sea. "Hold on! Help is coming!" he shouted.

The skies opened and let out a torrent. Dear God, would they be able to hang on as the dirt changed to mud and the granite turned slippery?

After what seemed like forever, Evans herded men toward him. Lanterns bobbed and many of the men gasped, seeing how far down Iris and Velvet were. One man came running from the stables with a coil of rope over his shoulder.

Lucian almost knocked him over in his haste to tie one end around his waist. "Lower me over the side," he barked.

He plunged over the edge, and the mud slid underneath him.

Iris screamed.

"Hurry!" Velvet's voice was high and reedy. "I cannot hold on much longer."

The rope slid up under his arms, restricting his movements, but the men above slowly lowered him. When he was close enough, he grabbed a fistful of Iris's nightgown. The rope sawed into his sides, but he ignored the chafing. He had to get to Velvet.

A second length of rope dropped over the cliff. "Send the girl up!" shouted Captain Darling.

Velvet's face was strained and her eyes wild. She shook as she clung to a rock.

"Velvet."

"Please, get Iris safe."

"I have her." With a strength he didn't know he had, he pulled Iris to him. Straining, he reached down as Iris smothered him with her arms around his neck. "Velvet, take my hand."

"I can't let go," she wailed.

Iris sobbed and threatened to strangle him, but still he reached for Velvet.

"Lower me!" he shouted. "Iris, it is all right. I have you. I will not let you fall," he murmured into her golden curls while he watched Velvet cling to an outcropping of granite.

"Send the girl up," repeated the captain.

Velvet's fingers slipped.

He lunged as the rope lowered with a jerk.

"Papa!" screamed Iris.

Barely catching Velvet's hand, he pulled. His shoulder strained. The rope slipped and for a second he thought all three of them would plunge into the sea. When the motion stopped, he coaxed Iris to reach for the second rope. "Wrap it around you. You have to be brave, Iris. I know you can do it. I can't let Miss Campbell fall."

He talked Iris through tying a bowline knot. "That is exceptional for a first time," he told her as she completed the knot that would hold her securely. "Pull her up!"

The men above hauled Iris up quickly. Velvet's trembling was so violent they both shook. With Iris on her way to safety, he used every last bit of strength he had to pull Velvet to him. He gathered her in, and unmindful of the wavering light of lanterns and the watchers above, held her tight against him and buried his face in her hair. "I thought I lost you."

She made a sound somewhere between a sob and a laugh.

A few seconds later the looped end of the second rope landed beside them, and he helped Velvet into it. The men hauled them both to the top.

Velvet collapsed on the ground as Captain Darling pulled the rope over her head. Iris stood beside Velvet and patted her head.

Lucian knelt on the edge of the cliff and gathered them both to him.

"I lost the bracelet, Papa," sniffed Iris. "It caught on a bush and stopped my fall, but then it snapped."

"It doesn't matter," he said, kissing her forehead. "I should have died if I lost you."

Velvet continued to shiver violently. She was muddy

from head to toe. "You put on clothes." Her voice was flat and disappointed.

"Forgive me. I thought if you found her, you'd come back for help. I had no idea you'd climb down the cliff." Given Velvet's fear of falling, he never would have expected her to go over the edge. He should have known she would be brave in her quest to save Iris.

"There wasn't time." The wind stole her faint words.

"She saved me, Papa. I was about to fall, and she saved me."

"I fear I made us both fall farther," said Velvet.

Evans wrapped Lucian's Turkish robe around Velvet and a blanket around Iris. "If you like, sir, I could carry the girl inside. I've told the staff to light the fire in the library and bring tea."

Rain streamed down and the men milled around, coiling the ropes and hesitatingly watching them.

Barely able to stand separating from Iris and Velvet, Lucian stood. He needed answers, but making them suffer the rain any longer was silly.

"Miss Iris, should you like a horseyback ride?" asked Evans.

Lucian stared at his normally fastidious dresser, kneeling down in front of the girl.

Iris nodded and climbed on. Evans rose and trotted toward the house.

Lucian picked up Velvet and followed. In the bubble of silence that enveloped them, he held her close. "How will I ever repay you?"

Velvet tucked her head into his shoulder. She moaned softly, "It is all my fault. I should have been in the room with her."

"No, love, you saved her. If not for you, she might have fallen all the way down." He shuddered. Losing

Iris wouldn't have been any less painful than losing one of his newborn babies had been. Perhaps it would have been worse, since he'd had longer to love Iris. "I thought you were the one in danger, when you tried to tell me it was Iris."

Velvet's cold hand twisted in his shirt. "I still cannot believe Nellie would . . ."

Nellie? Nellie was behind this? She was a lumbering awkward clod of a woman, and while he thought her strange, he'd never thought she posed a danger to anyone.

"The kitchen door is closest, sir," Evans called back.

One of the men held open the garden gate.

They descended the steps to the kitchen and entered the warm room. Several of the kitchen staff scurried around. The smell of coffee belied the horror of the near fatal accident.

Lucian set Velvet on her feet. She was bedraggled, with her hair streaked with mud. Never had anyone looked more beautiful. Evans bent and let Iris down.

His arm around Velvet, Lucian reached to put a hand on Iris's hair.

Mr. and Mrs. Bigsby sat flanking their daughter at the kitchen table. Bigsby looked sick and couldn't meet his eyes, but Mrs. Bigsby stared back hard. Nellie watched the group with no more interest than she would watch a vegetable delivery.

Lucian beckoned to one of the grooms. "Don't let Nellie go anywhere."

Footsteps and murmurs indicated the kitchen was gathering a crowd. He heard the word pass out through the door to others that Iris was safe.

Lucian stared hard at the woman who had tried to kill his daughter. "What is wrong with you?"

Nellie turned blank eyes on him. Bigsby rocked back and forth and moaned.

Velvet put her arm around Lucian's waist and pressed her palm against his chest.

"She didn't mean nothing," said Mrs. Bigsby. "She— She were sleepwalking, she were."

"She threw my daughter off a cliff while she was sleepwalking." Surely even Mrs. Bigsby didn't believe that. No judge or jury would believe that.

"She wasn't sleepwalking." Iris pressed closer to his legs.

He dropped his hand to her shoulder, reassuring her.

Nellie's face twisted and she half stood, pointing at Evans. "You, you . . ." Her face turned red.

Lucian swiveled to look at his valet. How was Evans involved in this?

Evans stepped closer. His placid face twisted into an angry caricature. "I what, you evil witch?"

"You said you were just burning fires in the mistress's chamber to get rid of the damp before Mr. Pendar took a bride. You didn't tell me *she* was staying in there. He was supposed to marry me."

"What?" Lucian recoiled. In what world did Nellie ever think he would marry her?

Bigsby looked up, and tears streamed down his face. "She's mad. She killed the other two. I know she did. Can't stand it when you look at another woman."

"Hush your mouth," hissed Mrs. Bigsby.

"Mrs. Pendar deserved to die like she did. All she ever did was make you miserable," shouted Nellie.

Velvet clapped her hands over Iris's ears. Her protective instincts touched Lucian in a way nothing else could. But for her, he likely would have lost Iris.

The groom shoved Nellie down. "Did you take a rock

to that poor Myra girl's head? What did she ever do to you?"

"That whore was carrying another man's child. I know how much that hurt you," Nellie said to Lucian. Her expression turned pleading. "You didn't need no other woman foisting another man's baby on you again."

Myra's pregnancy had been what made it safe for him to bed her. He'd never been in any doubt about the father, nor had she.

"Send for the sheriff, so I may swear out a warrant for all three of them." Lucian picked up Iris and carried her out of the kitchen. He pulled Velvet along behind him.

The group parted, and not only were his servants hovering, but Bowman and a couple of his other guests. "Glad your girl is safe," said Bowman.

Lucian just pushed past the man. He didn't care about railroads or business dealings. He only cared that he hadn't lost Iris or Velvet.

"What is she talking about?" Iris asked.

"She's crazed," muttered Lucian. "Don't worry. She'll never come anywhere near you again."

"She killed my mama, didn't she? She said if I wasn't around, Miss Campbell would have to leave."

"Miss Campbell is never leaving."

Velvet squeaked.

As he entered the main hall, several of the female servants milled about. A few of his guests stood waiting for news. "We found her," he told them. "You may return to bed. I'm sorry to have disturbed your rest."

Evans came up behind them. He instructed two of the maids to take Iris up, get her into a warm nightgown and run bathwater for Velvet. "The library, sir. Miss Campbell, I will return when your bathwater is ready."

Lucian pulled Iris to him and held her tight for a long

minute before he let her go with the maids from the inn. "Don't ever scare me like that again."

"I did not mean to," she said.

"I know, sweetheart. I know, but I can't stand the idea that I might have lost you. I love you, Iris." His eyes burned, as the fear he hadn't allowed himself to feel earlier gripped him with icy claws.

"I love you, too, Papa." Iris patted his shoulder. She whispered in his ear, "If you have to marry, could you make it Miss Campbell?"

"I should like nothing better," he whispered back. Reluctantly he let Iris go. He curled Velvet against his side and turned to Evans. "Did you know Nellie was obsessed with me?"

"I knew she ran off the household staff by scaring them, but I had no idea she had murdered your wife and Miss Gowan. I'm sorry, sir. I shall be less remiss in the future."

"I'll hold you to that. As the butler, you will have charge of all the staff."

"Very good, sir," said Evans as he tried to mask a fist thrust in the air with a shooing wave toward the loitering staff.

Lucian led Velvet into the library. A quick glance around told him the room was empty. He closed the door and pulled her toward the blazing fire.

"Velvet, I cannot give you children, but there are plenty of foundlings and orphans in the world. I can promise we can take in as many as you want."

She didn't respond. His desperation clawed at him.

"Iris is as much a daughter to me as if she were mine. Could you live with that? We could raise them as our own."

She tilted her face up to his. Tear streaks had channeled through the mud on her face. Her hair was tangled and stringy with dirt. Her dressing gown was filthy and torn. He wanted her more than he wanted life itself. But had he lost her forever?

"It is the best I can offer, Velvet."

"Are you asking me to marry you?" she said in a tiny voice.

"Yes, please marry me. I don't think I can bear to live without you by my side."

Stretching out her hands, she turned to the fire. "You no longer need to marry Miss Bowman in order to repair your reputation, but what about your plans to expand?"

"None of it means anything if I can't have you." Lucian gripped her shoulders and turned her. "I never would have married Miss Bowman. I kept finding reasons to delay making an offer. I love you, Velvet. I love your courage, your tenacity, your goodness, and even the way you challenge me."

Her green eyes searched his. "You don't need—"

"You make me believe I can be a better man. I need you to feel whole. Please, I beg of you, marry me."

"Then yes," she whispered. "I will marry you."

He pulled her to him and held her like he'd never let her go and never intended to let her out of his sight ever again.

Epilogue

Velvet put a hand to her aching back, bent and sucked in a deep breath as the pang shot through her lower abdomen. When the pain passed, she finished her preparations of the bed. She waddled out the door and down the stairs. Opening the library door, she braced herself. "It's time."

Lucian stood so fast his chair toppled backward. He went white, the scars standing out against his skin in stark relief. His mouth pulled back in a grim expression. Ignoring papers falling to the floor, he rounded the desk. "What are you doing? Shouldn't you be in bed?"

Velvet offered him a faint smile. "The midwife is on her way. And walking won't hurt."

Lucian steered her out of the library. "It can't be time, you aren't due for five weeks."

"I am as big as a house. Perhaps I conceived before the accident." The accident when Lucian's sheath had ruptured.

He'd gone white then too. In the last few months he had lost weight and his face seemed perpetually creased with worries.

She had another suspicion about why she was so big, which she shared with the midwife, but Lucian was too on edge to further distress him.

Velvet's belly tightened. The pain, sharper and harder than before, caught her off guard. Gasping, she leaned forward and caught Lucian's shoulders.

He supported her until the pain eased. "You can't do this now," he whispered.

"I don't think there is a choice, love," she told him, and cupped his face.

"John has finally gone down for his nap," said Iris as she descended the stairs. "He was fighting it the whole time, but I read him his favorite story."

Lucian turned to his daughter and his face darkened. "You are never having children. You are never getting married."

Iris's face crumpled.

"Lucian!" Velvet protested.

Iris adored her foster brother John, even if the dozen years between them made her more of a second mother than a sister. Lately, though, her thoughts had turned to young men and marriage and children of her own.

Velvet turned to Iris and said, "What he is trying to say is he can't face the idea of losing you right now." She shook Lucian's shoulder. "She is barely fourteen. You cannot tell her she can never marry."

"But there are boys sniffing around her already," he protested darkly.

"He is trying to say you are a beautiful young woman," Velvet told Iris.

Iris scrunched her nose in response. She no longer cared so much about external beauty.

"We should never go to Bath again," muttered Lucian. "The whole point was to find a doctor to be here for this."

Lucian had wanted to hire a doctor to live with them, but Velvet was more comfortable with the local midwife.

Iris tripped down the stairs. "Are the bab——"

Velvet shot her a silencing look.

"Is it time for your lying in?" Iris asked instead.

Velvet nodded, while Lucian growled "Yes."

"What can I do?" Iris slid her hand under Velvet's elbow.

Velvet didn't want to be on the stairs when the next contraction came. Reaching for the railing, she lifted one foot. "I don't think there is anything to be done yet."

Lucian swept her up. "You can hold her door for me."

"Lucian, you cannot carry me." She weighed a ton.

His jaw set, and he proved her wrong as he took the steps at a steady clip.

She sighed and tucked her head against his shoulder. "I may need you to keep your father calm," she said to Iris.

Iris rolled her eyes but gamely said, "I shall try."

But five hours later Iris stood beside the bed and wiped Velvet's brow with a damp cloth. "Papa is going mad. I thought John would distract him, but he scared the living daylights out of him. Meg is cleaning up the glasses he broke, and Delilah has taken John out for a walk."

"I have never seen a man more upset," said the midwife. "You'd think he'd never gone through this before." She glanced pointedly at Iris.

"Yes, but he lost several babies, and my mother did not survive childbirth," explained Velvet. "Let him come in."

"Don't like men in the birthing room. They just get in the way," groused the midwife.

"He can help me sit to push," said Velvet. With her huge belly, the midwife and Iris had to pull her up with each contraction.

"I'll go get him," said Iris.

Poor girl had been running back and forth all afternoon.

When Iris returned with Lucian, he hesitated in the doorway. He'd cursed and cried and thrown things, but nothing would rid him of this crushing dread that he would never see Velvet alive again or that the child was too early to survive. Not even John could cheer him, although usually the toddler's ceaseless "whys" amused him.

Velvet looked around the midwife and said calmly, "Come sit behind me and help me sit to push."

Her green eyes were clear and her skin was flushed. Her hair was only slightly mussed, no worse than it ever was after making love. Velvet's eyes glazed then, and the midwife pulled her up to partially sit.

"Push, push, push," coaxed the older woman. "Her contractions are coming fast. It won't be much longer."

Lucian hurried to the head of the bed and took over supporting Velvet.

The gray-haired woman lifted the sheet over Velvet's knees and said. "Ah, we have a head of dark hair. Takes after Papa, looks like."

She reached under the sheet. Lucian didn't even want to know what she was doing.

Velvet gasped and breathed hard. Before he even had time to settle in behind her and try to make her comfortable, she was straining again.

He braced her shoulders and kissed her cheek and tried to hold his emotions in check. How he would be strong for Velvet when the child turned blue and ceased to live, he didn't know.

"Keep pushing," instructed the midwife.

Velvet cried out.

Lucian had never felt more helpless in his life. Then a tiny squall filled his ears.

"You did it," he whispered to Velvet.

The midwife held a skinny-legged red infant on one arm, while she wiped the baby down with a towel. With a rapid-fire efficiency, she ignored the lusty wails, tied off the cord and sawed through it. Then she tied a red ribbon around the tiny wrist. She swaddled the baby and thrust it toward him. "Hold your daughter, sir."

Velvet strained forward and moaned. Her eyes closed, and once again she held her breath. He took the squirming, mewling bundle and attempted to brace Velvet with his other arm. Everything swirled around him as he tried to comprehend what was happening.

"This one is in a hurry," muttered the midwife. Once again she reached under the sheet, which blocked his view.

A few minutes later there was a second infant, with male organs seemingly far too large for his scrawny little red body. He jerked his arms as if falling and trying to catch himself. His angry cries filled the room.

"Healthy lungs," said the midwife as she tied off the cord, then cut it and wrapped the baby.

"His father's temper," answered Velvet, reaching out for the second infant.

Lucian supposed he deserved the dig. The infant in his arms blinked open her blue eyes and stared up at him. Her little rosebud lips pursed. If they all lived, he couldn't imagine he'd ever have reason to be angry again.

A daughter and a son?

Velvet promptly unwrapped the infant boy and checked his fingers and toes. She twisted and checked her baby girl.

Lucian stared at the pink skin, waiting for the color to fade and the babies to turn blue.

"A little on the small side, but healthy as all get out," said the midwife as she washed her hands.

"I want my mama," yelled John in the corridor.

Velvet smiled. "They'll need good lungs around here."

She looked tired but not exhausted. The babies continued to mew and remained pink. His world spun. He couldn't believe this was real.

He bent and kissed the tiny forehead.

"Everything looks good," said the midwife. She carried a large bowl toward the door. "I'll be back in a few minutes to help you nurse them."

The door clicked shut behind her.

"Are you all right, Lucian?"

"Of course I'm all right. You are the one who just gave birth. Twice." Tears stung at his eyelids, and he turned to hide his weakness from Velvet.

She wasn't having it. She reached around and put her free arm around his neck. "Now that wasn't so bad, was it?"

It had been horrible, the most painful eight months of his life. Every second he'd feared losing her, feared losing the baby. Not even his daily swims could calm his battered nerves. Never once had he believed this happy moment would come. Even Velvet's serene acceptance of the situation had grated on him.

"Shall we discuss names?" asked Velvet, bringing him back to the ordinary in her soothing way.

"Lucian and . . ." He hesitated. After Nellie's trial and conviction, they'd begun their family with their foster son. When they collected him from the orphanage, Velvet had asked if they could name him John for her brother, but with this pregnancy he'd refused to discuss names when she asked. He hadn't planned on naming a son after himself. Especially not a name that could be twisted into Lucifer.

The door opened and, his chubby face streaked with tears, John ran across the room and climbed onto the bed. "Mama!"

"I'm sorry," said Iris. "I tried to keep him out. Come, John, Mama is tired."

"How about another flower?" Velvet curled an arm around John. "Rose?"

"Lucian and Rose," he murmured. He really should rethink naming a son after himself. "Or perhaps Henry and Rose."

Iris smiled softly. She was ten times as beautiful as her mother had been. "Lucian and Rose. Henry and Rose would always have me thinking of the Hundred Years War."

"John, meet your new brother and sister, Lucian and Rose," called Velvet.

"Baby," said John eagerly, while Velvet put little Lucian in Iris's outstretched arms.

"May I hold my daughter?" Velvet asked.

Lucian reluctantly placed Rose in her arms and wrapped his arm around her shoulder. The babies seemed healthy. Velvet seemed healthy. Iris cooed to the new infant, while John tried to poke out Rose's eye.

Lucian caught the boy's hand. "Gentle."

John lost interest and slid off the bed.

Seemingly sensing their need to be alone, Iris reluctantly laid baby Lucian in the basinet by the bed. "I better go catch him, and I'll ask Cook to send you up a tray."

Only then did Lucian notice there were two bassinets and two of everything needed for a baby.

"I love you," he whispered to Velvet before the door had closed on his daughter.

"And I love you," she answered. "You have given me more than I ever hoped for."

"And you have made my life worth living again," he whispered. "My cup runneth over."

Her lips pursed. "I told you to trust in God."

So perhaps he wasn't totally forgiven for the bear he'd been for the last few months, but he'd make it up to her. "I should have known to trust in you."

He kissed her as a husband kisses his treasured wife. He stopped only when Rose protested being squished between her parents, although he'd taken care not to hurt her or Velvet.

He cupped the infant's head. His living, breathing child.

"So when I am well, there will be nothing between us," Velvet whispered.

He heaved a deep breath. Four children were enough for him, but obviously Velvet wanted more. Her eyes shined so brightly he couldn't deny her anything. "If that is what you wish."

"We'll see," said Velvet with a knowing smile.

And his heart was truly so full, he didn't think it could be contained in his chest. But baby Lucian's protests made sure he could not dwell on how happy he was with Velvet as his wife. Perhaps, though, if he had a lot of sons, he should once again consider expanding his businesses.

Then again, who had time for business dealings with babies to rock, John to take digging on the beach, and fending off Iris's overeager suitors? He lifted the tiny baby from the bassinet and cradled him. No, life was perfect and bright.

Author's Note

Lucian and his first wife suffered from Rh incompatibility, a medical condition not understood or treatable until after 1940, when the Rh factor was identified in the blood of Rhesus monkeys. An Rh-negative mother such as Lilith can develop antibodies against an Rh-positive baby. While Lilith's first child was fine (presumably fathered by a man who passed the Rh-positive gene on to his son) during that pregnancy she developed antibodies to the Rh factor. All subsequent Rh-positive babies fathered by Lucian were born suffering from blue baby syndrome. Lilith's body recognized the Rh-positive component of their blood as an antigen, and the resulting antibodies crossed the placenta and attacked the infants' blood cells. In order to survive, Iris had to receive an Rh-negative gene from her sire. But knowing that Lilith had borne two healthy children to two different men left Lucian to believe his seed was flawed.

My mother's second cousin Ruth Ann, born in 1942, was one of the first "blue babies" to ever survive. One of the doctors had recently read a paper about the Rh factor and recognized that might be the reason Ruth

Ann was turning blue and failing shortly after her birth. He saved her life by giving her a complete blood transfusion. Nowadays a simple shot is given to an Rh-negative mother that prevents her from developing the antibodies.

*At Avon Books, we know your passion
for romance—once you finish one of our
novels, you find yourself wanting more.*

May we tempt you with . . .

- **Excerpts** from our upcoming releases.

- Entertaining **extras**, including authors' personal photo albums and book lists.

- Behind-the-scenes **scoop** on your favorite characters and series.

- **Sweepstakes** for the chance to win free books, romantic getaways, and other fun prizes.

- Writing **tips** from our authors and editors.

- **Blog** with our authors and find out why they love to write romance.

- **Exclusive content** that's not contained within the pages of our novels.

Join us at
www.avonbooks.com

AVON

An Imprint of HarperCollins*Publishers*
www.avonromance.com

Available wherever books are sold or please call 1-800-331-3761 to order.

FTH 0708